DAUGHTERS

OF THE

DRAGON

A COMFORT WOMAN'S STORY

BY WILLIAM ANDREWS

Praise for DAUGHTERS OF THE DRAGON

William Andrews has created a masterpiece of fiction
- Midwest Book Reviews

I finished reading "Daughters of the Dragon" and remained still in my chair with the book in my lap. I was enveloped in the characters and their stories. Imagining the horrors that these women endured and the courage to confront those who perpetrated them...

The author's descriptive passages made me sense the beauty of the country, the desperation of war, and the humanity, good and evil, of each character.
- AMiB: Amazon Power Reviewer

Very emotional story that is hard to put down. Well-developed characters and vivid descriptions bring the experience to life. Sad that it is based on historical truths, but definitely a story that needs to be told. Reading this book provides a poignant look into the Korean culture and a true sense of the strength it takes to be a survivor.
-KE Burke" Barnes and Noble reviewer

I have to admit, I was not sure about this book. A white man telling this story.... I just didn't know if he could pull it off. But he did. It was powerful, unsentimental, and not gratuitous. I am beyond impressed. The reality of this story is still VERY raw across Asia, and it is important that it be told in order to understand the current relations between Japan and its neighbors.
-Rosanne: GoodReads Reviewer

Have you ever read a book that you don't want to end because it is that good? That is how I felt about Daughters of the Dragon: A Comfort Woman's Story. The author handles this difficult subject with great care; the story is captivating and well-paced. I will look forward to reading the next book by William Andrews.

-Minty Mom: Amazon reviewer

This was an awesome book, about something that you never hear of. The devastation is impossible for anyone to comprehend, and yet the courage and strength that these women had is fantastic. I HIGHLY recommend this book. I read often, and many, and this book easily rates in my top 15. I can't wait to read more by this author.

-Ryan Ober: Amazon reviewer

This book is both a tragic and triumphant telling of the atrocities that over 200,000 Korean women had to endure at the hands of the Japanese soldiers during WWII. It is an unforgettable story that for too long has not been told. The author provides historical information that is easily read and powerful. I highly recommend this book to everyone who loves to read and shares a thirst for knowledge. I am looking forward to more from this author!

-Karen Rogers: Amazon reviewer

Also by William Andrews

The Essential Truth

An Exercise in Sacrifice

DAUGHTERS OF THE DRAGON © 2014 by William Andrews

Printed in the United States of America.

This is a work of fiction. Names, characters, places and incidents either are the product of the author's imagination or are used fictitiously, and any resemblance to any actual persons, living or dead, events, or locales is entirely coincidental.

Cover design by Suzanne Pfutzenrueter.

Library of Congress Control Number: 2014900030
ISBN: Print   978-0-9913958-5-9
                         EBook   978-0-9913958-4-2

MADhouse Press LLC
5904 Halifax Ave South
Minneapolis, MN 55414-1991
www.madhousepress.com
info@madhousepress.com

To order additional copies of this book, contact your on-line retailer or visit:

www.williamandrewsbooks.com

or

www.madhousepress.com

For all the women forced to be comfort women.

Acknowledgements

To my wife Nancy who always supported me in this and all my endeavors; to my daughter Elizabeth who inspires me; to all my family, friends, and colleagues who read the book and provided input; thank you.

"Honor does not stand alone."
Confucius

ONE

My first name is a palindrome. When Mother was alive and I was in one of my moods, she would say, "I see we have the backward Anna today. I hope the forward Anna will come back soon." I often wrote my name with the capital "A" at the end so when someone said I spelled it backward, I could say, "No I didn't. It's a palindrome."

Since my name is the same backward as forward, I used to make fun of everyone else's backward name. Mother was Nasus and Dad was Htennek, even though everyone called him Ken. My dog was Ydnas and we were the Noslrac family. I had to write the names backward so I could pronounce them, but Dad could do them in his head. It was truly amazing. You could give him any name and he'd immediately say it backward. Even long ones like Aunt Elizabeth. "Thebazile Tnua," he'd say without missing a beat.

I was born in Korea twenty years ago and adopted by Htennek and Nasus when I was five months old. All I've ever known is life with my adoptive parents. But people constantly reminded me that I wasn't their birth child. We didn't look alike of course—I didn't have Mother's wavy

auburn hair or Dad's Nordic eyes. We had different personalities, too. Mother was fiery and impulsive, Dad was a stoic Scandinavian, and I was somewhere in between. Sometimes people would look at me with my Caucasian parents and ask dumb questions or say stupid things. It would upset my mother royally. Most times, she'd just ignore them and complain later about "insensitive, stupid people." But once, when a waiter said I was "gourmet Asian take-out," she went postal on him. She actually called him insensitive and stupid to his face. I was so embarrassed. I mean, he didn't mean anything by it, although it really was a lame thing for him to say.

I didn't think much about being adopted while I was growing up, and I didn't think much about my birthmother, either. Most people think adopted kids like me have this need to connect with our biological roots so we can discover who we really are. They think being "take-out" is totally different than being "homemade." But we're not different at all. I mean, my birthparents were just my gene donors. My *real* parents were the ones who raised me, the ones who were there when I needed them, the ones who actually *wanted* me. And why should I have cared about my birthmother anyway? I had this perfect life—awesome parents, my studies at Northwestern, Chad Jenkins and his adorable smile. My Korean birthmother was a million miles away, probably raising the kids she'd decided to keep. I'm sorry, I didn't care.

But everything changed when Mother died of pancreatic cancer. Dad was devastated. I had to drop out of Northwestern and move back home. Dad said I should stay in school, but I didn't see the point. My heart wasn't in it. I was going to be a senior and I still didn't know what I wanted to major in. And Mother's death shook me. For the first time in my life, I was afraid. I was afraid of making a

mistake, heading in the wrong direction, and ending up like some other kids my age—adrift, directionless, a loser.

Back home, everything was so different. It was sad of course for Dad and me, but it was more than that. It was tragic, if you know what I mean. Every day Dad sat alone in the living room with the drapes closed and the lights off. When I got home from the grocery store or a jog, he'd ask how I was doing from inside his darkness. I'd lean against the kitchen door and we'd exchange some small talk. Then he'd make dinner wearing his grilling apron. I'd head to my room past my parents' bedroom and sometimes I'd expect to see Mother inside. It was weird, and I realized that someday I'd have to come to grips with the fact that I didn't have a mother anymore.

Except that I did—a million miles away. In Korea.

Adopted kids call our gene donors "birth parents" instead of "natural parents" or, God forbid, "real parents" so we don't imply that our adoptive parents are somehow unnatural or not real. Growing up, people told me that my birthmother made the adoption decision because she loved me. That's why we say, "adoption decision" rather than "give up for adoption." The former supports the love theory—a thoughtful decision to do what's best for the baby. Who knows? It might be true. But honestly, I don't know for sure. And that's why I decided to come to Korea and meet my birthmother.

So here I am, sitting in the lobby of this orphanage in the middle of Seoul waiting to meet her. It's the place they brought me when I was three days old. It's in a poor section of Seoul, which they somehow managed to avoid on the first ten days of our tour. The building is crumbling and sad and somewhere between gray and green. The other American families on our tour finished meeting with their birth families an hour ago and are hanging around waiting for me. They keep shooting looks at me as if it's my fault they have

to wait. Sorry people, but I don't know what's taking so long either. I want to get on with it way more than you do.

I made this photo album for my birthmother. I spent a ton of time on it. It's the story of my life—from when I arrived from Korea in front of dozens of my family and friends at gate 33 of the Red Concourse of the Minneapolis St. Paul airport, to the last photo of me and Mother together, in the hospital the day before she died. I pasted each photo into the album just so and added captions in my very best handwriting.

I must say, it's perfect. It has to be. I mean, think about it. If my birthmother really made the adoption decision out of love, then I want her to see that I turned out all right and she did the right thing. On the other hand, if she gave me up because I was just some inconvenience, well then I want her to see that she made a huge mistake. After all, I'm going to graduate from college someday and maybe even go on to grad school. I want her to believe that her little inconvenience grew up and is having an awesome life without her. Okay, so maybe I'm exaggerating, but it would be true if I could get my act together. Of course, she doesn't need to know that.

My stomach is churning sitting here waiting. I'm so nervous I can't stand it. Dad says we should ask someone why it's taking so long, but before we can, an American social worker comes and tells us to follow her. From the pinched smile on her face, I can tell this isn't going to be good. I grab my photo album and we follow her into a small meeting room with bad lighting. We sit at a rickety table. The social worker shakes her head. She isn't smiling anymore. "Anna," she says, "I'm sorry to have to tell you this. You can't meet your birthmother. You see, she died."

I stare at her for what seems like forever. I'm not sure I heard her right. In fact, I'm not entirely sure if any of this is actually happening. "She's dead?" I say.

The social worker nods. "I'm afraid so. I'm sorry."

After I take a few seconds to process this tidbit, I ask how my birthmother died. The social worker, a large woman with straight gray hair, tells me she died twenty years ago, in labor—with me. *With me*. Perfect. I ask about my birthfather. The social worker opens a manila folder. She thumbs through papers and stops at a page. She tells me my birthmother wasn't married when I was born and they don't know who my birthfather is. I ask if I have any birth brothers or sisters. She says they don't know. "Given the circumstances of your adoption," she says, "it would be impossible to find out."

Wonderful. The churning in my stomach turns into a knot. I feel like everything is crashing in on me. I want to scream at these people for not knowing about my birthmother. Instead, I look down at my photo album and run a finger along the words "My Life" written in my very best handwriting.

"How could this happen?" Dad asks, trying to help. "Why weren't we told? Before we came here?"

"Mr. Carlson, they're poorly funded here," the social worker says. "They're understaffed and they can't always check the facts."

"Anna's been looking forward to this meeting for months," Dad says.

The social worker does something between a nod and a shake of her head. "I know. We just found out. I'm so sorry."

Dad looks at me. "Maybe I should talk to the orphanage director."

I just want out of here before this train wreck gets any worse. "Let's just go," I say. I grab my photo album and leave.

I walk into the orphanage lobby and head for the exit. Everyone's staring at me. They want to know what happened, why they postponed my meeting for so long, and

why it lasted only a few minutes. I don't look at them. It's none of their business what happened to me. I clutch my photo album to my chest and realize it shows that I didn't get to meet my birthmother. I see a wastebasket in a corner and go for it. But when I get there, I can't throw it in. I spent so much time on it.

I walk out the front door. It's hot and muggy in Seoul. The bright haze hurts my eyes. Off to the side, our tour bus is idling. Diesel fumes invade my nose. I turn away and close my eyes. I can't believe this is happening to me. What a disaster. I feel so incredibly stupid for coming here. What else could possibly go wrong in my life?

After a few minutes, I turn to go to the bus. There, standing in front of me is an old woman with a thick braid of gray hair. She's pressing a package into my hand. She leans in close and whispers, "This is for you. Do not show it to anyone. It is important that you hear my story so you know what it means. There is an address inside. Come alone."

I look at the package, then back at the woman who's hurrying away. "Wait!" I shout. She doesn't stop and disappears inside the orphanage. I look again at the package in my hand. It's a little larger than a billfold, wrapped in a faded brown cloth, tied closed with twine. I start to open it, but Dad comes out of the orphanage looking for me. Behind him, the other families are heading to the bus, doing a bad job of trying not to stare at me. Dad puts a hand on my shoulder and tries to reassure me with a smile. I slip the package in my purse and we follow the other families onto the bus.

As we head back to our hotel, I can only think about my birthmother. I wanted to talk to her, make a connection, you know? I wanted to see what I'll look like in thirty years. Well, at least I got one of my questions answered. There was no adoption decision—not out of love or out of convenience

either. No. I was put up for adoption because I killed my birthmother. How nice.

I look out the window at the streets of Seoul. It's rush hour and everyone's heading home. I wonder what it would've been like if my birthmother had lived. I'd be one of them—a homemade Korean instead of gourmet Asian takeout living in America. I'd speak their language, listen to their music and think like a Korean.

Maybe I wouldn't be so cursed.

TWO

THE BUS ENTERS the Myeong-dong district where our hotel is. Dad has his head back and his eyes closed. Poor guy. My little ordeal here was probably hard on him, too. Since Mother died, he's tried to be there for me. He thinks it's his duty to be both my father and mother, even though I'm constantly telling him I'm okay. But who am I kidding? I mean, I was the one who pushed to go on this trip so I could connect with my biological roots. I was the one who was so eager to meet my birthmother. That had to hurt him, but he never said a thing. Sorry, Dad.

I remember the package the elderly woman gave me. *Don't show it to anyone*, she said. *You must hear my story*, she said. I reach inside my purse and take it out. I turn it over and open the cloth. Inside there's a piece of paper with an address in Seoul in beautiful cursive handwriting. I pull back one more fold of cloth and there is a comb with an inlay of a two-headed dragon.

The comb is the size of a woman's hand, made of dark green tortoiseshell, gently bowed with long tines. In the

handle in tiny pieces of what looks like ivory, is a two-headed dragon. Solid gold curves along the spine. Its size and shape makes it look delicate, but in my hand, it feels sturdy.

I wonder why the old woman wants me to have this. Whatever the reason, I can't cope with it now. Not after what happened today. But before I wrap it up, I take a closer look. The comb is amazing. It absolutely gleams in my hand. The two-headed dragon with its curled tongues, tiny teeth and claws seems to reach for me. I run a finger over the gold spine. It's smooth and cool, and I realize I've never held anything so valuable in my entire life. Suddenly I don't feel so wiped out. I look around to see if anyone's watching me. Everyone's looking out windows or talking quietly. I quickly wrap the comb in the cloth and slip it into my purse.

We finally get to the Sejong Hotel in the middle of Seoul's financial district. We drag ourselves from the bus to the hotel. Inside the marble and glass lobby, our tour director, Dr. Kim, comes up to Dad and me. He asks if he can have a word with me. I just want to go back to our room and crash and cry a little. But Dr. Kim, a small, energetic retired professor of Asian studies, has been just great on our trip. Maybe he knows something about my birthmother. I tell Dad I'll catch up with him and follow Dr. Kim to a corner of the lobby. He tells me he saw I was looking at something on the bus. "Something valuable," he says. He wants to know what it is.

I tell him it's nothing, but that doesn't satisfy him. "Anna, if you were given something we must know, we must know. The government requires that we record everything given to American children placed through our agency."

"It's just a comb, Dr. Kim," I say.

He stares at me as if I'm a child. "It's against the law, against the law for heirlooms to leave our country," he says

firmly. "Anyway, if it's just a comb, you should be willing to show it to me."

It's a law? I don't need an even bigger mess than I already have, so I take out the package and show him the comb. He leans in and his eyes grow wide behind his thick glasses.

"This is not 'nothing'," he whispers. "I should take it and give it to the right people."

"The right people?"

He slowly shakes his head. "You cannot have this, Anna."

"Why not?" I ask. He doesn't answer. Instead, he tells me again that I should give the comb to him. "It's important," he says. "You must do the right thing. Give it to me. I take care of it, I take care of it."

I almost give it to him. Then I remember the woman said the comb means something. I think it might actually mean something to me, and based on Dr. Kim's reaction, I suddenly want to know what it is. I fold the cloth around the comb and put it back in my purse. I tell Dr. Kim that I don't want to break any laws, but I want to show it to my dad first. I manage a polite smile.

I walk to the elevator and push the button. As the doors open, I turn to see if Dr. Kim is still there. He's looking straight at me. "Trust me, trust me, Anna," he says. "You do not want that comb."

I step into the elevator and let the doors close.

*

When I get to our room, small and modern with light-colored wood furniture, Dad's crashed out on his bed. He's folded his hands across his stomach like they do with a corpse. I toss my backpack and purse on the desk and look in the mirror. An Asian woman stares back at me. She's the

backward Anna and I don't know her. She's pretty, I suppose. Dark hair; smooth skin; slender and straight. I want to know who she is, but on this trip, I'm not getting any answers.

Dad asks what Dr. Kim wanted. The woman in the mirror tells him that Mr. Kim wanted to see something someone gave her at the orphanage.

"Someone gave you something at the orphanage?" he asks.

"Yes. Outside, after our non-meeting meeting."

Dad raises his head off the pillow. "What is it?"

I turn from the mirror and show him the comb. He climbs off the bed for a closer look.

"Good lord," he says. "It's magnificent."

"The woman said I should go to this address to hear her story." I hand him the note.

He reads it and shakes his head. "I don't know about this, Anna. Seoul's a big city and you don't know who the woman is. What did she look like?"

"She was older, but... I don't know. I didn't get a good look at her."

"What did Dr. Kim say?"

I take the note from him and wrap the comb in the cloth. "He said I shouldn't take it. He said I should give it to him so he can give it to the right people, whatever that means."

"Maybe you should."

"Yeah, I guess, but I want to find out about it first. I want to go to this address."

"When?" Dad asks. "We leave tomorrow."

"Not until 7:00 at night."

"Yeah," Dad says, "but the bus to the airport leaves at 4:30. During the day, we're supposed to go to Itaewon to shop. I have to pick up my new suit."

"And I wanted to buy that celadon pot I saw there," I say. "It doesn't matter though. I want to do this instead."

He thinks it over for a second, then says, "Maybe I should go with you."

"The woman said I should come alone," I reply.

He blows out a sigh and sits on the end of the bed. He looks defeated like he has since Mother died. I sit next to him. I promise him I'll be careful.

He nods. I give him a quick hug and go to the bathroom to get ready for dinner.

*

That night after we settle in our room for the night, Dad finally asks if I want to talk about my birthmother. Yeah, I do. I want to talk about a lot of things. I want figure everything out and get back on the right track again. But for some reason, I say I don't want to talk. Not now. He looks both hurt and relieved and drags himself to bed.

It breaks my heart to look at him. I thought this trip might help him, but it hasn't. He hasn't said more than a few dozen words since we came here. He doesn't study the tour books or ask endless questions of the guides like he always did when we traveled with Mother. I think being here reminds both of us of her. She would have loved it.

I lie on my bed staring at the ceiling and try to remember the highlights of our tour—the palaces, the museums, a disturbing trip to the demilitarized zone between North and South Korea. And today, the visit to the orphanage and the awful news that I killed my birthmother. I try to pull everything into a complete picture, but I can't. It's all too raw. So I crawl under the sheets and wonder what I'll find tomorrow at the address that came with the comb.

THREE

WEIRD DREAMS HAUNT me all night. Mother used to say that dreams are who you are when you're too tired to be yourself. When I was young, I always tried to remember my dreams. But they were totally bizarre and left me afraid of who I really was. So today when I wake up, I push my dreams away. I'm still tired and realize it's one of those days it'll be a supreme effort to cope. I pull the covers to my chin and wish I could stay in bed. Then I remember the comb and my plan to go to the address and find out what it's about. I force myself to get up.

Dr. Kim told us we'd leave for Itaewon at 9:30AM. Dad's already showered and mostly dressed. He's got his face in the mirror, shaving. I say good morning and he grunts one back at me. I hope he'll agree to help me. When he comes out of the bathroom, I tell him I want to go to the address to see about the comb. I ask him to tell Dr. Kim that I'm sick and have to skip going to Itaewon.

"Are you sure you want to do this?" he asks, pulling on his shirt. "Maybe you should give the comb to Dr. Kim, like he said, and come with me today."

"Dad, please," I say in a way to remind him that I'm not a child anymore.

He sighs and agrees to tell my fib. "Promise you'll be careful," he says.

I tell him not to worry and that I'll be here at the hotel when he gets back from Itaewon. He hands me two hundred dollars from his billfold and gives me a sad smile. He heads out the door.

*

After Dad and the rest of the families leave, I sneak out of the hotel and crawl in a tiny white taxicab. I give the driver the address that came with the comb. "You sure, lady?" he asks. From the X's and O's in his name on his cab license, I can tell he's Chinese. He's anorexic thin and stringy hair hangs over his ears. I read the address to him again. "Okay," he says. "Thirty-five dolla' American. Or thirty-five thousand Korean won."

The fare seems high, but I really don't care, so I say okay. We pull onto the main boulevard and head south toward the Han River. The sky has a brown haze and it looks like it'll be another sweltering day. We drive through Seoul's financial district and past big department stores like Kosney's and Hyundai and dozens of high-end boutiques like Bulgari, Gucci, and Jimmy Choo. There are hundreds of smaller shops with neon signs in Hangul, English, Japanese, Chinese, and a few languages I don't even recognize. Trendy cafés compete with high-end restaurants. Street vendors push their merchandise at the people walking by. People fill the sidewalks and cars cram the streets. We drive across the

Han River over the Map-o Bridge. In every direction, city skyscrapers stand like soldiers at attention.

We cross another bridge and turn a corner into yet another shopping area. I can tell the driver is taking the long way, probably to justify his bogus fare. Okay, whatever. I'm feeling better and actually enjoying his little tour. I push myself to the edge of the seat and roll down the window. Smells fill the taxi—street food, automobile exhaust and big city grit. There are neon lights, and signs in Hangul, and people dressed in all different styles, and tiny cars, and taxis with blue tops, and noisy trucks with more Hangul lettering on the side. Everywhere apartment buildings tower over the city. Car horns honk, truck engines roar, street vendors shout, and energy fills the air.

So this is Korea. Now that I'm finally free from the tour, I'm seeing what it's really all about. It isn't just the palaces, museums, and tourist traps we've seen on our trip. It's here, on these streets. This is where I was born. I share DNA with these people. Maybe my answers are here.

And now I have this comb. There must be something to it. It could be important. I haven't had a chance to study it carefully so I take the package from my purse and open it. I bring the comb close and look for something I might've missed. The almost black tortoiseshell is a perfect match to the white ivory of the two-headed dragon. The elegant tines and gentle bow of it are amazing. The gold spine gives the comb a perfect balance. I wonder how an elderly woman got a hold of such a magnificent thing. I wonder why she thinks I should have it.

"What you got there?" I snap my head up. We're at a stop light. The driver has an arm over his seat and he's pointing at the comb.

"Just a, ah… gift," I say.

"A gift?" he asks. "You kidding? It real deal! Who you give it to?"

23

"No, no. It was given to me." I quickly fold the cloth around the comb and shove it inside my pocket

The driver grins revealing bad teeth. "You lucky! Very, very lucky. It real deal. Real deal!"

I sit back and ask how much further we have to go. He tells me we're almost there and turns back to his steering wheel. The light changes and we drive on.

Soon, the neighborhoods become dirty and the colors change from bright to drab. We're in what looks like Seoul's version of a ghetto. There are only a few people on the street and something I haven't seen in Korea before, litter. I roll up my window and slouch down in my seat. We turn down a narrow street and pull to the curb. The driver tells me we're at my address.

We've stopped in front of a nasty, eight-story apartment building. Rusty air conditioners hang from half the windows. From an open window, a woman is staring vacantly at the street below. An old man shuffles along the walkway. Above a crumbling entry are letters in Hangul and the number 315. I ask the driver if he's got the right address. He assures me he does. "You want I wait?" he asks.

I scan the street and rows of slummy apartment buildings and realize that if my driver doesn't wait, I'd have to walk for blocks in this scary neighborhood to find another cab. "Yeah, that's a good idea," I say.

"I wait," he says, turning off the engine. "Fifteen dolla' American every fifteen minute. First, you pay thirty-five for here."

I take thirty-five dollars from my purse and hand it to him. I climb out of the cab and look up at the building. I tell him I don't know how long I'll be. He tells me he'll wait as long as I need. "Fifteen dolla' every fifteen minute," he repeats.

I walk to the entrance. There are rows of silver buttons on a huge intercom system. I take the note from my pocket

and read the apartment number, 627. I scan the buttons until I see it. I don't press it.

This doesn't feel right at all. It's way too intense. And Dad was right—it isn't safe. I turn to go back to the cab. The driver is watching me. *Real deal,* he said. I put my hand in my pocket and finger the comb. I remember how the dragon almost seemed real. I turn back to the intercom and take a deep breath. I push the button. Several seconds later, a woman's voice comes on the speaker and says something in Korean.

I say my name. There's an uncomfortable pause and I wonder if I got the address right. Then the voice says in perfect English, "Welcome. I am so glad you came." She tells me to go through the security door and take the elevator to the sixth floor. She says her apartment is on the left.

The security door buzzes and I walk through. It's gross inside. The lights are harsh and over-expose the stained carpeting and smeared walls. There's an ancient, broken payphone in the hall. I step inside the elevator and push the button for the sixth floor. The elevator jerks up and a few seconds later, it jerks again to a stop. I get off and when I find apartment 627, I swallow hard and knock.

The door opens and the old woman greets me.

FOUR

SHE'S WEARING DARK blue slacks frayed at the hem and a thin cotton sweater over a clean white blouse. Her thick, grey hair falls down her back. She has eyes that are kind, but intense. Her skin is amazing. The only flaws I see are a small scar on her upper lip and another one over her eye.

"Good morning, ma'am," I say with a half bow.

She examines me with an odd smile. She steps aside and says, "You may come in."

I remember to take off my shoes and step inside a small, clean apartment not much bigger than our den back home. I smell the sweet, spicy scent of *kimchi*. There's a low dresser drawer, a rust-stained sink, a ceramic, double-burner stove, and a miniature refrigerator. On a cheap low table below the apartment's only window is a purple flower blossom in a glass bowl. Next to it, in a plain wooden frame, are two photographs.

She points at the table and tells me to sit. Her posture is perfect, like I've seen in upper-class Korean women on our tour. She doesn't take her eyes off me and I feel that she's

sizing me up. I wish I'd spent more time on my hair and worn a dress instead of jeans.

"You must have been disappointed you couldn't meet your birthmother," she says. Her English is flawless. She has no accent at all.

"Yes," I nod. "How did you know about that?"

"I volunteer at the orphanage. I have for twenty years now."

Twenty years? It was a little over twenty years ago that I was brought to the orphanage. This is starting to feel creepy and I'm already regretting coming here. Maybe I can make this quick. I tell her I don't think I should have the comb and that I came to return it. She says I might change my mind when I hear her story. I ask her why but she doesn't answer and continues to stare at me. I fidget in my chair. I realize I don't know her name. I ask her what it is.

"My name is Hong, Ja-hee. And I am your maternal grandmother."

"Seriously?" I gasp. I take a long look at her. When a birth child looks into her parent's faces, she sees herself. She has her mother's eyes or her father's chin. But for twenty years, I never had that connection to anyone. Until now. Even though she's sixty years older than I am, the resemblance is clear. She's petite like me and has my high cheekbones. I'm thrilled that for the first time in my life, I see myself in someone else. Suddenly, I'm not at all anxious to leave.

I try to remember the right way to behave toward a Korean grandparent. "I'm glad to meet you, ma'am," I say with my eyes low like I remember they taught us in our tour orientation. "What would be the right way to address you?"

"Since we have just met," she says, "perhaps you will feel most comfortable calling me Mrs. Hong."

"Yes, of course, Mrs. Hong," I say.

"I understand your adoptive mother died last year."

The image of my dying mother comes rushing in and I feel guilty for the selfish joy I had just seconds earlier at meeting someone from my birth family. I look at my hands and nod.

"It is difficult to lose loved ones. Isn't it?" she says.

"She loved me," I reply. "And I loved her, too. It was an awful loss. I guess that's why I came here, to Korea, to meet my birthmother. They told me she died giving birth to me. What happened? What was she like? Do I have any brothers and sisters? Who is my birthfather?"

Mrs. Hong turns to the window. She keeps her chin high, but her eyes turn soft. She isn't smiling anymore. "You have many questions, Ja-young."

"Ja-young? Oh, that's my birth name. My parents named me Anna."

"Very well, Anna. You say you have the comb. You can give it to me now."

I get the package containing the comb from my pocket and set it on the table. She stares at the lump of cloth but doesn't reach for it. She waits a minute, then, she takes the package and slowly unfolds the cloth. When she sees the comb, she brings her other hand to her mouth and the lines around her eyes deepen. I think she might cry. "I don't take it out much anymore," she says. "It brings back too many painful memories."

I move to the front of my chair. "Excuse me for asking Mrs. Hong, but if you don't want it, why don't you just sell it? You could probably get a lot for it and move to somewhere... you know, more appropriate."

"I was tempted many times," she says without looking up. "But I could not. It is too important to sell, Ja-young... Anna. And, you must have it."

"But Dr. Kim—he's our tour director—he said I shouldn't take it. He said there's a law or something against heirlooms leaving the country."

Her eyes snap to me. "Did you show this to him?"

"I... I had to," I say. "He saw I had it."

"What did he say? Tell me exactly."

"He said I should give it to him so he could give it to the right people."

Mrs. Hong clucks. "That is a problem. He might know what it is." She quickly wraps the comb in the cloth and sets the package on the table.

"Anna," she says firmly, "I asked you to come here because I want you to do two things. First, you must hear my story and that of the comb with the two-headed dragon. You will know what the second thing is after you have heard my story."

"Of course," I say. "I want to hear your story, but I don't want to get in trouble."

"Listen to my story, and you will know what is right."

I let out a sigh. I wonder what I've gotten myself into. But why not stay? She's my birth-grandmother after all, and the tour won't be back from Itaewon until mid-afternoon. Maybe she has some answers for me. And what trouble could I possibly get into? I mean, if it gets too intense, I could just walk away and leave the comb with Mrs. Hong. Right?

Outside, it's turning hot and humid again. A breeze kicks up dirt on the street. The cab. I forgot about the cab. *Fifteen dolla' American every fifteen minute.* I grab my purse and tell Mrs. Hong I have a cab outside and should let it go. I have to give him a time to come back. "How long will your story take?" I ask.

"It's a long story," she says, picking up the photographs from the table. "A very long story."

I say I'll tell the cabbie to come back at 3:00. I wait for her to say okay but she just stares at her photos and says nothing. I tell her I'll be right back.

I go to the door, pull on my shoes, and run out to the cab. The driver rolls down the window when I get there.

He tells me he's been waiting twenty minutes and I owe him thirty dollars. "Fifteen dolla' American every fifteen minute," he says.

I take thirty dollars from my purse and give it to him. I tell him I need to stay and ask if he can come back to pick me up. He says okay and asks for a time.

"Three o'clock," I answer.

"Okay, three o'clock," he says. "If I wait, fifteen dolla' Amer…"

"Yeah, yeah. I know," I say. "Fifteen dolla' American every fifteen minute." The driver flashes his bad teeth in an amused grin and drives off.

*

Mrs. Hong's apartment door is open when I get back. She is standing by the table framed by the light from the window. She has changed her blouse and slacks for a yellow *hanbok* made from what looks like silk. It has long, loose sleeves and a hem a few inches above the floor. She has braided her hair and pinned it up with an ornate *binyeo*. She invites me in. "Granddaughter, *unlinahyi*. Are you ready to hear my story?"

I nod and say yes. I feel like I'm in a dream.

"Come," she says. "Sit, listen, learn."

I sit at the low table again. She moves the flower blossom and the photographs to the center of the table, next to the package containing the comb. She sits straight, with her hands in her lap. She takes a long breath and starts in a voice clear and strong.

"A young soldier on a rusty motorcycle delivered the orders from the Japanese military command in Sinuiju…"

FIVE

September 1943. North P'yŏngan Province, Northern Korea.

A YOUNG SOLDIER on a rusty motorcycle delivered the orders from the Japanese military command in Sinuiju. I was the first to see him, motoring up the hill toward our house. As he came near, I wanted to run outside and throw a rock at him. I wished I was strong like a boy or older—I was only fourteen—so I could throw a big rock and knock him off his motorcycle back down the hill.

I had seen him before. He had come the previous fall to deliver orders for my father. The orders said Father was to report the next day to the military headquarters in Sinuiju so he could work in Pyongyang in the steel mill there. The next morning, the sun had not yet climbed over the aspen trees and the morning air was cold when Father said good-bye to me, my older sister Soo-hee, and our mother. I think Mother cried a little as Father walked past our persimmon tree with his head held high and his orders in his pocket.

I loved my *appa*. He let me get away with things my mother never would. But after that day, I never saw him again.

As the soldier came near, I quickly gathered the *nappa* cabbage I had been washing. I wrapped it in a large cloth and stuffed it under the sink. I ran to the back door.

"Soo-hee!" I said to my sister who was digging up clay *onggis* of rice and vegetables we had hidden behind the house. "The soldier on the motorcycle is coming!"

Soo-hee stood and looked down the road. When she saw him she said, "Stall him." She dropped to the ground and began to push the *onggis* back into their holes.

I ran back inside the house and watched the soldier from the kitchen window. I hoped he would drive past to another house up the road, but he stopped and leaned his motorcycle against the persimmon tree. He took off his gloves and slapped the dust out of them across his legs. He reached into his leather satchel and pulled out a yellow envelope. He came up to the front of our house.

"Hello!" he called out in Japanese. "I have orders from military command. Come out! Come out!"

I pushed aside the gray tarp where our beautiful carved oak door had once hung. I folded my arms across my chest. "Go away," I said in Japanese.

The soldier eyed me. "Is that any way to treat me?" he asked. "I've come all this way to deliver your orders." He held out the envelope. "Here, take them."

"You should throw them into the Yalu River instead of bothering us with them," I said not moving an inch. "Why do we always have to do what you say?"

The soldier grinned and leaned against our house. "Because you are Japanese subjects. If you don't follow our orders, you will be shot."

"It would be better to be shot," I said.

The soldier's grin dropped to a scowl. "Soon, you will learn how to serve Japan."

I was about to tell him how I felt about serving Japan when Soo-hee came from the back, wiping her hands on her dress. "Yes? What is it?" she asked in Korean. She couldn't speak Japanese like I could.

"*Konnichi wa*," the soldier said. "I see you haven't learned to speak Japanese yet," he said switching to Korean. "Perhaps you should take lessons from your disrespectful little sister."

Soo-hee bowed her head. "I'm sorry for my sister. She is young."

"She is not so young," the soldier replied, eyeing me.

He straightened and lifted his chin high the way the Japanese do. "Your landlord is not pleased with the harvest this year," he said. "You are in debt to him now." He held out the envelope. "These orders are for you and your sister. They are what you must do to repay him. Take them." With a small bow, Soo-hee took the orders.

The soldier looked at me in a way that made me glad I hadn't told him what I thought about serving Japan. "You better take care of your little sister," he said to Soo-hee. "She could get you all in trouble." He gave a quick nod, and then went to his motorcycle. He turned it around and started it with a kick. He drove away down the road followed by a curl of dust.

"What is it?" I asked over the motorcycle's fading snarl. "What do the papers say?"

Soo-hee tucked the envelope inside her dress. "Don't worry about them, little sister," she said. "We must start soaking the vegetables soon or they won't be ready to make *kimchi* in the morning." She headed to the back of the house.

"But *Onni*, Big Sister, the soldier said they were orders for you and me. What do they say?"

"Hush, Ja-hee!" Soo-hee said turning on her heel. "You must learn to do the right thing. Mother will read them tonight when she comes home from the factory. *Ummah* should see them first. Now go back to your chores."

Soo-hee always sounded like Mother, and I didn't like being told what to do. So I stomped inside the house and pulled the *nappa* cabbage from under the sink. As I prepared it for the *kimchi*, I worried about the orders tucked away in Soo-hee's dress. I guessed they were orders to work in a factory during the winter months. When our skinny Japanese landlord with the big ears had come to collect that year's crop, he had told us the Japanese needed more workers to support their war efforts. "We are winning glorious battles against the Americans!" he had said climbing inside his truck filled with the vegetables we had worked so hard to grow. "If you do what you're told, the filthy Americans will be pushed back across the ocean, never to trouble us again." He started his truck and eventually found the right gear. As the truck began to roll down the road, he stuck his head out the window and I thought his ears might flap in the wind. "Then, you will be rewarded for the sacrifices you have made," he said. "You will be glad you are Japanese subjects!"

*

By the time the sun had set over the fields in the west and the evening turned cold, Soo-hee and I had two pots of vegetables soaking in brine. We had the biggest farm for miles around, but we didn't have enough to feed us through the winter. Then, Mother would have to beg for an extra sack of rice, just like our neighbors did every year.

It seemed like we had to wait forever for Mother to come home. Soo-hee and I sat at a low table and ate *nappa* cabbage and a handful of rice for our evening meal. Our

house had a large main room with a kitchen, eating area and family sitting area. It was here where Mother taught us how to read and write. In the back of the kitchen, an iron cook stove fed heat to the home's *ondol* under-floor heating system. The floor was wood plank, polished smooth from the feet of generations of my ancestors. In the kitchen were two wooden stools, and in the eating area a low table with mats on the floor. Mine was the blue one. Sliding latticed doors separated a sleeping room from the main room. The sleeping room had straw mats on the floor and an ornate cabinet that Mother had refused to sell, even though Father said we should. I was glad she didn't.

When we finished eating, Soo-hee set some rice and vegetables aside for Mother. She would soon be walking up the road with the other women from the uniform factory where she worked every day since the harvest. Mother was very smart—too smart to work in a uniform factory. Our house had many books that she and *Appa* were very proud of. We had books in Chinese and Japanese as well as a few in Hangul, even though the Japanese banned them. We had the great novels, the teachings of Confucius, Chinese poetry. Even western literature like Shakespeare, Tolstoy, and Dickens translated into Hangul or Chinese or Japanese. It was wonderful. After a long day of work in the fields, the four of us would read until we couldn't keep our eyes open any more. It was how I learned to speak Japanese and Chinese so well.

But Soo-hee wasn't good with languages like I was and that was a problem. The provincial government insisted that all Koreans speak Japanese. I didn't like Japanese—it was rough and harsh sounding—but Mother insisted we speak it when they were around and she told me I had to help Soo-hee. So to pass time, Soo-hee and I sat on the great room floor and I tried to help her learn Japanese.

"What is the word for sheep?" I asked.

Soo-hee thought for a while and then shook her head.

I snorted. "Why is it so hard for you to learn these? '*Hitzuji*' is the word for sheep. What about 'tree'?"

"I know that one," Soo-hee answered. "It's '*moku*'."

"Yes!" I said. "See? It's easy! You look for patterns, things you already know that you can connect the words to. And to pronounce them right, you pretend you're Japanese. It's like acting."

"Do you mean like this?" Soo-hee stood and puffed out her chest. "You must speak Japanese!" she said in Korean.

That made me giggle and I stood too. "Yes, like that!" I said. "But do it in Japanese." I puffed out my chest as Soo-hee had done. "You are now Japanese subjects!" I said in Japanese, wagging my finger. "You must learn to obey!"

Both of us laughed, careful to cover our mouths. But our laughing died quickly and Soo-hee turned melancholy. "You will have to speak Japanese for me, little sister," she said. "I can understand most of what they say, but I can't bring up the words when I have to."

"Why do I have to do it?" I said. "Why can I learn it and you can't? The white crane must have left you at the door. You're not my real sister."

Soo-hee smiled at me, but it was an embarrassed smile. I had hurt my sister's *kibun*—her feelings and honor. I quickly said, "I'm sorry, *Onni*."

"Ja-hee," Soo-hee said gently, "you are smart like *Ummah*. You are luckier than me, and prettier, too. And you were born in the year of the dragon. You must be careful with these things you have been given."

"I'm just mad that we always have to do what they say," I said.

My *onni* put her arm around me. "Don't be stubborn, little sister. We have to be careful with the Japanese."

"I hate them," I said.

*

A full moon was rising over the aspen trees when Mother trudged up the road, grimy from work. Soo-hee and I pulled aside the tarpaulin and ran to greet her. Our mother, her name was Suh Bo-sun, was dressed in her old wool coat and faded purple scarf. She smiled when she saw us. "My babies, *ye deulah*," she said. "How are my babies today?" Mother always called us 'her babies.'

"*Ummah! Ummah!*" I blurted out. "The soldier came on his motorcycle today with orders. He said they are for Soo-hee and me."

"*Ja-hee!*" Soo-hee scolded. "We must first show our mother respect!"

I sighed, but bowed to *Ummah* with Soo-hee. Then Mother led us inside the house. "Orders?" she said. "What do they say?"

"Soo-hee said we couldn't look at them until you got home," I said. "Can we look at them now?"

"Little sister, you must learn to hold your tongue!" Soo-hee scolded. "*Ummah* is hungry. Let her eat."

Mother slowly removed her scarf and sat at the table without taking off her coat. Soo-hee placed the rice and vegetables we had made in front of her.

"Let me see the orders, Soo-hee," Mother said, ignoring the food.

"*Ummah*, you should eat first. We can read them later."

"Daughter!" Mother scolded. Then, more gently she said, "Let me see the orders."

Soo-hee bowed. She was always more respectful than I was. She reached inside her dress and pulled out the yellow envelope. She handed it to Mother.

Mother read the orders to herself and her shoulders sagged. She gave the orders to me. "Here," she said, "you read Japanese, too. Make sure we understand them correctly."

The orders were signed by the same official who had signed Father's orders a year earlier. As I read them, I said aloud, "We are to report to the Japanese military headquarters in Sinuiju tomorrow where we will be sent to work in a boot factory. We will live in a dormitory. They will subtract rent and the cost of the meals from our wages. Anything left over will go to our landlord."

I pushed the papers back at Mother. "I am not going. They can't make me."

Mother stared at the orders in her hand. "You must go," she said, shaking her head. "We don't have enough food for the winter. And you must always do what the Japanese say."

"But how will we plant the crops in the spring?" I asked. Mother could not possibly plant them by herself.

Mother didn't answer. After a while, Soo-hee said, "Hush, Ja-hee. You ask too many questions." She was right. I always asked a lot of questions.

Eventually, Mother folded the orders into the envelope and laid it on the table. "Go, girls. Prepare for bed," she said, gently. "Prepare for bed and come back to me. Tonight, I will comb your hair with the comb with the two-headed dragon."

SIX

SOO-HEE AND I went out to the well and washed. When we came inside to change for bed, Mother was building a fire in the iron stove. That surprised me. We only burned wood on the coldest days of winter.

When we returned to the kitchen, the fire was high and Mother was kneeling on the floor. She had washed the grime from her face and hands, and had changed into her white *hanbok* that she only wore on special occasions, before the Japanese outlawed them. She held her back straight and her chin high as I remembered she did many years earlier. Next to her, on the table, was the comb with the two-headed dragon.

I had only seen it a few times before. When I was young, Mother would comb our hair with it during the Korean New Year, before we paid our respects to our grandparents. Father was always away when she did, visiting a friend in need or helping the village men butcher a pig for the New Year's celebration.

I had always wondered where Mother had gotten the magnificent comb with the gold spine and the strange two-

headed dragon. I asked her about it once and Soo-hee scolded me for asking too many questions. But I could tell Soo-hee wanted to know, too. Mother had said we were too young to understand.

Then, when I was eight years old, the Japanese forced us to give our land to the skinny landlord with the big ears. They told us we had to celebrate the New Year the Japanese way. Mother did not comb our hair with the special comb that year, and I never saw it again. I thought she had sold it along with our furniture to buy rice. But now there it was, on the table in front of me.

Mother told us to come and sit by her so she could comb our hair. Soo-hee was the eldest so she got to go first. She knelt in front of Mother, facing the fire while I sat close. As the fire danced on the wood in the open stove, Mother pulled up the sleeves of her *hanbok* and carefully combed Soo-hee's hair with the beautiful comb. Its gold spine gleamed in Mother's hand and the dragon was white as new snow. *Ummah* worked slowly, carefully teasing out Soo-hee's tangles.

"You never told us where you got the comb, *Ummah*," I said, as I watched her work on Soo-hee. "You always said we were too young. Will you tell us now, please?"

Mother didn't answer and I thought Soo-hee would scold me for asking questions again, but she didn't. *Ummah* combed Soo-hee's hair until it was smooth and shiny. And then it was my turn. I knelt with my back toward Mother. The comb pressed softly against my scalp. The fire threw black shadows against the kitchen walls. Our house was pleasantly warm and it smelled of burning aspen wood.

Then Mother began in a far-away voice. "My grandmother gave the comb to me after Soo-hee was born. Back then, our family owned the fields behind the house all the way to the tall trees. We raised pigs and cattle. We grew potatoes and *nappa* cabbage, and carrots, radishes, and

onions. When I was a young girl, my father had to hire twenty men to bring in the harvest."

I remained perfectly still as Mother combed my hair and told her story. Soo-hee, her hair smooth as silk, knelt off to my side facing mother as the fire softly crackled.

"My grandparents had two sons," Mother continued. "Their youngest, my uncle, went to Manchuria to join the forces there that opposed the Japanese occupation of our country. The Japanese killed him, so my father was the only child, and I was his only daughter. My grandmother told me that is why she gave me the comb—because I was her only female descendent."

"Where did she get it, *Ummah*?" I asked. "Who gave it to your grandmother?"

"Hush, Ja-hee," Soo-hee said. "Let *Ummah* tell the story."

Mother continued. "It was given to her by her mother. Your great-great-grandmother is the one who had it made. She was an important woman who lived in Seoul. When the Japanese became powerful, your great-great-grandmother sent her children here. She gave them this land and sent people along to watch over them. She visited from Seoul when she could, and one day, she gave her daughter this comb. Her daughter was your great-grandmother—my grandmother who gave me the comb.

"Our great-great-grandmother had it made?" I asked. "She must have been very rich. A *yangban*! Why did she give her daughter the comb?"

"She said the dragon had magic to help her," Mother said. "She told me it must be passed on to daughters to help them, too." Mother finished combing my hair and turned me around. She looked at me and then at Soo-hee. Her eyes were sad. "It was supposed to help me," she said.

"How was it supposed to help you, *Ummah?*" I asked.

She did not answer. After a while, Soo-hee said, "You can tell us when we come back from the boot factory,

Ummah. We must go to bed now. Tomorrow we have a long journey." Soo-hee pulled at my sleeve. I wanted to ask more questions but Mother just stared into the fire. Soo-hee and I bowed to her and went to our mats to sleep.

*

I lay on my mat next to Soo-hee and tried to picture my great-great-grandmother, the important lady, the *yangban*, who could afford to have such a fine comb made for her daughter. I decided that she must have been beautiful with long black hair down to her knees. She must have commanded the respect of even the most powerful men. I wished my great-great-grandmother was still alive so she could stop the Japanese from making Soo-hee and me work in the boot factory. I wondered how the comb was supposed to help my mother. I hoped it would help me someday.

I lay awake for a long time waiting for Mother to come to bed. The floor was hot from the *ondol* heating system in our house. I kicked a leg out from under the blanket but the air outside was hot, too. I peeked through an opening in the latticed doors and saw an orange glow coming from the kitchen.

I crawled off my mat and went to the kitchen. The fire was high and the room was hot. Mother sat next to the fire still dressed in her white *hanbok*. A stack of wood was at her side. I asked her why she was burning all the wood. She stared at the fire and didn't answer me.

I pulled on the sleeve of her *hanbok*. "*Ummah, Ummah,* what is wrong? Come to bed now. You have to go to work tomorrow."

Mother turned to me and ran a hand along my hair. "No," she said sadly, "I will not give them any more."

It frightened me to see my mother so sad, so I quickly went back to my mat. When I crawled under the blanket, Soo-hee was awake. "Soo-hee," I whispered, "*Ummah* is burning all the wood."

Soo-hee put a hand on my arm. "I know. Go to sleep, little sister."

I closed my eyes and eventually, I fell into a fitful sleep.

*

The next morning, Soo-hee tugged at me to get me out of bed. "Ja-hee, wake up!" she said. "We must make the *kimchi* before we leave."

The house was cold and I didn't want to get up. I rolled into my blanket but Soo-hee pulled it off of me. She yelled at me again to get up. "We don't have much time," she said.

I sat up and rubbed my eyes open. It was still dark outside and I couldn't see well. I peered into the kitchen. The fire was out and the wood was gone. The shadow of Mother, still in her *hanbok*, sat in the cold room staring at nothing. Her eyes looked like the eyes of old Mr. Lee when Soo-hee and I found him behind his house dead from starvation.

As daylight broke through the aspen trees, I helped Soo-hee drain the brine from the *nappa* cabbage and *daikons*. We only had time to rinse them twice instead of three times like we always did. We made a sauce from garlic, ginger, and hot peppers. The spices stung my hands. We tossed in the vegetables and put the mixture into two large *onggis*. We dragged them to the back of the house and buried them in deep holes. By the time we were done, it was daylight and Soo-hee said we had to go.

I washed the sting from my hands and braided my hair. I wrapped an extra set of clothes in a cloth sack and set it next to Soo-hee's sack bag. Soo-hee packed a handful of rice

and *kimchi* in a hide bag. She brewed some *bori cha*. All the while, Mother continued to stare into the cold stove.

I sidled up to Soo-hee. "What's wrong with *Ummah?*" I whispered. It wasn't at all like Mother to be quiet like that.

"She is very tired," Soo-hee said. "Now drink some *bori cha* and eat some rice."

I drank my *bori cha* and, though I wasn't hungry, I ate a little rice. The comb was on the table in front of me. It was the most beautiful thing I had ever seen. I stared at the two-headed dragon and it stared back at me. I brought my face close in and something made me turn an ear to it. For a moment, I thought I heard the dragon speak to me.

"Come little sister," Soo-hee said. "We must say good-bye to *Ummah.*"

The dragon had hypnotized me and I didn't respond. "Ja-hee!" Soo-hee said. "We do not have much time!"

"Yes, *Onni*, I'm coming," I said. I forced myself away from the comb and joined Soo-hee in front of Mother.

Soo-hee bowed low. "We are leaving to work in the boot factory, *Ummah*. We made *kimchi* and buried it in an *onggi* in the back of the house where the Japanese will not find it. We buried the rice, too. We will write if we can." She bowed again. Mother continued to stare into the ashes.

I stood in front of Mother to bow. Instead, I took her by the shoulders and shook her hard. "*Ummah*, wake up!" I insisted. "You have to go to work!" She didn't move and I took a step back, afraid that my mother's spell would never be broken.

Soo-hee took me by the arm and pulled me toward the tarpaulin door. She told me it was time to go. We gathered our sacks and walked out of our house leaving our Mother inside, alone.

*

The sun had climbed over the hills in the east and the morning air was warming as we walked past the persimmon tree onto the dirt road. I slipped my hand inside Soo-hee's and we walked down the road toward Sinuiju. We had gone only a little way when there was a rush of noise behind us. We turned to see Mother running toward us. Her feet were bare and her white *hanbok* billowed out. When she got to us, she stopped suddenly. I was glad to see that she was normal again. But then I saw she wasn't. Her eyes were wild and scary.

"Here," she panted, "take it!" In her hand was the comb with the two-headed dragon. She held it out to Soo-hee.

"*Ummah,* I am sorry," Soo-hee said. "I cannot. The Japanese will steal it."

"I do not want it anymore," Mother said.

When Soo-hee didn't take it, Mother took Soo-hee's hand and pressed the comb into it. "Do not let go of it," she whispered. "It has not helped me. Perhaps it will help you. And then you must pass it on to your daughter someday." She gave Soo-hee a firm nod.

She turned to me and took me by the shoulders. "Ja-hee, listen to your *onni,*" she said. "Do as she says. It is important that you do." She let go of me and stood straight. She looked from Soo-hee to me. Her mouth opened, her brow furrowed, and I was afraid that my mother might cry in front of me for the first time in my life. "My babies," she said. *"Ye deulah."* Then, she lifted her *hanbok* and walked to the house without looking back.

Soo-hee held the comb as if it were a baby bird that she didn't know where to put. Then, she pushed the comb into her sack and took my hand again.

"Come, little sister," she said. "We have a very long journey."

SEVEN

"WE HAVE COME to work in the boot factory," I said in Japanese to the soldier behind the desk. Soo-hee held our orders out to him. On the soldier's arm was a white armband with Japanese characters that identified him as *Kempei-tai*, the Japanese military police.

We were standing in a large room with high ceilings, wide plank floors, and many desks. Dozens of Koreans stood in lines, waiting to speak to soldiers sitting at the desks. Outside the window, the daylight was fading.

The *kempei* glanced up from his work. "Address me as 'sir'. I am *Kempei-tai* and you must show respect."

"Yes, sir," Soo-hee said in Japanese.

"Let me see your orders," the *kempei* said. He took the orders and scanned them. "Yes. You've come to the right place. The truck to take girls to the boot factory will be leaving in a little while. Wait over there with the others." He pointed to an open area where five other girls sat on the floor. Soo-hee and I went and sat with them.

We had walked all day to Sinuiju and hadn't arrived until the sun was low. Father always said he would take me to Sinuiju someday, but he wasn't able to before he left home. I had imagined the city having tall, shimmering buildings, shiny cars speeding along on paved boulevards, and elegant ladies on walkways carrying pink parasols, just like in the books I had read with Mother. But when we arrived, all I saw were low shabby buildings, noisy military trucks cutting ruts in dirt roads, and hundreds of ragged workers heading home.

We had stopped at the city's outskirts and asked a soldier where we should go with our orders. The soldier pointed down the road. "Military command," he had said. "The two-story building with the Japanese flag." We finally found the large stucco building flying the white flag with the red sun. We went inside with our orders and a soldier pointed to the *kempei's* desk.

As we waited for the truck to take us to the boot factory, I studied the other girls. Their eyes darted about nervously. I recognized a tall girl from down the road from our farm. Her name was Sun-hi. All the girls were pretty and young. It concerned me that I was the youngest. I moved closer to Soo-hee.

My *onni* leaned into the circle of girls and whispered in Korean, "Are all of you going to the boot factory, too?"

"Yes," whispered an older girl with light skin. "That is what our orders say."

"I thought the factory was here in Sinuiju," whispered Soo-hee, "but the *kempei* said we will be going on a truck."

"Quiet over there!" shouted the *kempei* from his desk. "No talking!"

We bowed our heads and stayed silent, sitting on the cold floor, waiting for the truck to arrive.

*

An hour later, the *kempei* approached us followed by a Japanese regular army soldier with dark eyes and a thick chin. "This man has come to take you to the boot factory," the *kempei* said. "Follow me."

We followed the soldiers outside. The sun had set making Sinuiju even grayer. In front of us was a large green truck with a canvas top. The soldier with the thick chin helped us into the back. Inside were crates of supplies and sacks of rice. There was only a small area for us to sit. He handed one of the girls a water jug and slammed the truck gate closed as the *kempei* walked back inside the building.

We huddled together and stared at each other wide-eyed. The boxes and sacks of rice hovered over us. The engine roared to life and the truck lurched forward. Several girls let out a squeal. We grabbed each other and held on. The truck rumbled down the street and I could see that it was heading out of the city. Soon, we were in the country rolling past farms and rice paddies. Sinuiju's lights faded in the distance.

"Soo-hee," I asked, "where are we going?"

"I don't know," Soo-hee answered. "But I don't think we're going to the boot factory in Sinuiju."

The older girl with light-colored skin shook her head. "I knew we weren't going there," she said. "My mother said that girls our age are sent to Seoul to work in the textile mill. At first, I didn't want to go but she told me I had to. She said it's easy work and we get as much rice as we want." She turned to me and Soo-hee. She asked what our names were.

I spoke up first. "My name is Ja-hee, and this is my *onni*, Soo-hee."

"My name is Jin-sook," she said. "My mother said that all we need to do is obey the Japanese," Jin-sook said to all the girls. "Listen to me and do what I say." Jin-sook looked like

she was the oldest so we all nodded. No one said anything more as the boxes and sacks of rice swayed over our heads.

The truck rolled on until the sky was dark and the stars twinkled. The smell of farmland and the diesel fumes made me sleepy. I was hungry, cold, and thirsty, too. I leaned into Soo-hee who pulled me close. Someone passed the water jug. When it came to Soo-hee, she handed it to me without taking a drink. "Take my share, little sister," she whispered. "I'm not thirsty." I took two swallows and passed the jug on.

Eventually, I fell asleep.

*

I jerked awake in the middle of an odd dream where the dragon from Mother's comb was chasing me. The truck had come to a stop and its engine was silent. It was completely dark and the air was still. I rubbed the dream from my eyes. "Where are we?" I asked in Korean. "What's happening?"

"Shush!" Jin-sook whispered. "You'll get us all shot."

A light came from around the side of the truck and pointed in at us. I raised my arm to shield my eyes. A hand behind the light reached in and lowered the truck gate. The driver said, "You, come with me."

I was terrified he was talking to me, but the driver reached in and grabbed the tall girl named Sun-hi. "The rest of you stay put," the driver barked, "or I will cut off your ears."

Sun-hi cried out, "Where are you taking me?"

"Quiet!" the driver commanded. There was a slap and a muffled cry. The light disappeared into the darkness. I sat close to Soo-hee and trembled. I could feel Soo-hee trembling too.

A short way from the truck Sun-hi cried out again. "No," she said. "Please, no!"

There was another slap and the sound of tearing fabric. "Quiet," the driver barked. "Better get used to it you Korean whore."

I tried not to listen to Sun-hi's cries, but it was the only sound in the dark night. After a few minutes, Sun-hi stopped crying and the driver grunted. He started breathing hard, then grunted again and again. Then he was quiet.

Eventually, the light came again and pointed in at us. I was terribly afraid. I looked out the back of the truck for where to run in case the driver came for me next. All I saw was smothering blackness. I pushed myself tight against Soo-hee and blinked back tears. All the girls sat perfectly still. The driver shoved Sun-hi into the truck and she flopped down next to me and curled into a tight ball. Her dress was ripped and her hair hung in strings over her face. A streak of blood ran down her chin.

The gate slammed closed and the light went toward the front of the truck again. The engine started and the truck jerked forward.

As we rolled along in the darkness, one girl started to cry. "I thought you said we would be all right," she said to Jin-sook. Jin-sook didn't answer. Two other girls began to cry. I was about to cry too, but before I could, Soo-hee drew me close and whispered, "Do not cry, Ja-hee. We must be strong. We must be strong or we will die."

For the first time in my life, I was going to have to be strong. Until now, my parents and Soo-hee had always taken care of me. But now I had to do what Soo-hee said, so I pushed my cries down and felt my insides harden a little. I brought my knees up and curled into a tight ball like Sun-hi. I thought about the comb with the two-headed dragon. I hoped that if I stayed strong the dragon would protect me and I would be spared Sun-hi's fate.

But as the truck rolled on toward our destination, I wondered if the comb was nothing. After all, Mother said it

didn't protect her. Maybe it was only a trinket she had bought in Sinuiju and the story about my great-great-grandmother was a tall tale to make Soo-hee and me less afraid about leaving home.

Maybe the comb with the two-headed dragon, hidden in Soo-hee's sack, was nothing at all.

EIGHT

FEAR KEPT ME awake for the rest of the night. By the time the sun rose, I was further away from my home than I had ever been before. Outside was a landscape I had never seen. There were only a few trees among the high rolling hills and brown wheat fields blanketed the flats. It was cold and the air was very dry.

I asked Soo-hee where we were. "I think we're in China," she answered.

By midday, we rolled into a town of low stucco buildings with gray-green tiled roofs. Men in strange clothing hauled carts down the narrow dusty streets. The truck stopped at a wooden building at the edge of the village. The driver came to the back of the truck and lowered the gate. I tried to hide behind Soo-hee.

He ordered everyone out and told us to form a line. I climbed out with the other girls and we formed a line facing the building. The driver pulled Sun-hi out by the arm and pushed her into the line. Standing before us was a thin Japanese officer in a gray army uniform and a white *Kempei-*

tai armband. He had sharp, black eyes, and a pointed nose. He slapped a *shinai* against his leg. The bamboo blade made a thwacking sound with each strike. Off to the side, a young regular army soldier with a rifle leaned against the narrow building.

"What happened to this one?" the officer said, pointing his *shinai* at Sun-hi.

The driver straightened. "The clumsy girl fell out of the truck when we stopped to piss, Lieutenant."

"Really? That had better be all that happened to her, corporal." I wanted to tell the *kempei* what really happened, but I stayed quiet.

"Lieutenant, sir," the driver said, "I must unload these supplies at once, and take injured soldiers to the hospital in Pushun." He gave a quick bow and ran back to his truck. The engine started, and the truck rumbled off.

Out of the corner of my eye, I saw Jin-sook step forward with her head lowered. "Honorable sir," she said in Japanese, "please forgive a girl for being so bold, but there has been a mistake! Our orders said we were to work in the boot factory in Sinuiju."

The lieutenant glowered at Jin-sook. "Come here," he said.

Keeping her head low, Jin-sook approached the officer. He lifted her chin with the tip of his *shinai*. "A mistake was made?"

"Yes, sir," she answered. "We were to go to the boot fa…"

With a quick motion, he punched Jin-sook in the stomach with the butt of his *shinai*. She gasped and fell to her knees. "I heard you the first time, girl. Stand up."

Jin-sook, holding her stomach, struggled to her feet. She gasped for air. The lieutenant pointed his *shinai* at her. "Your disrespect has earned you a beating. But I can't spoil you

now, can I? Not before the officers have you. Go back in line with the others."

Back home, I had heard other girls talk about how the Japanese beat Koreans who showed them disrespect, but I didn't believe them. I thought they were rumors started by the Japanese to make us obey them. But now I was seeing it with my own eyes. It was terrifying and it frightened me how disrespectful I had been to the Japanese. I worried about what else I didn't know about them.

Jin-sook, still holding her stomach, stepped back in the line. The lieutenant drew in a long breath through his nose and pointed his chin out. He began inspecting the line of girls. He slapped his *shinai* against his leg with each step. "I am Lieutenant Tanaka," he began in a clipped authoritative way. "I'm the *kempei* in charge of this comfort station. You are our new volunteers. You will only speak to me when I ask you a question. You will only speak Japanese." He came up to me. I lowered my eyes to the high black boots of the *Kempei-tai*.

The *kempei* lifted my chin with a finger. "You're a young one. Pretty, too. What's your name?"

"Hong, Ja-hee, sir," I answered.

The *kempei* grabbed my chin and pushed his fingers hard into my jaw. He forced me to look at him. "That is a Korean name and you are a Japanese subject," he said. "You have a Japanese name. What is it?"

"Namiko Iwata, sir," I said, quickly.

"Namiko Iwata. Yes." He let go of my chin and I lowered my eyes again. The *kempei* walked on.

"You will obey my orders without question," he continued saying to all the girls. "If you do not, you will earn a beating. If you run away, we will catch you, beat you, and then shoot you. Anyway, I assure you, here there is nowhere to run."

Jin-sook stepped forward again and dropped to her knees in the yellow dirt. She bowed her head. "Kind sir, please hear a worthless girl," she cried. "We should not be here! We are not volunteers for your comfort station. Please sir, send us back with the truck."

"Private Ishida!" Lieutenant Tanaka barked.

The young soldier leaning against his rifle snapped to attention. "Yes, sir?"

"Take these other girls to be examined by the doctor. Then, bring them to the courtyard." He pointed his *shinai* at Jin-sook. "I'll take this one. Surely the officers won't mind one spoiled girl to show them all discipline."

Lieutenant Tanaka grabbed Jin-sook by the hair and pulled her around the other side of the building. She twisted and sobbed. "I'm sorry, sir," she cried. "I will not say anything more. Please! I'm sorry."

Private Ishida ordered the rest of us to leave our packs against the building and follow him. I laid my sack next to Soo-hee's and followed the girls down a dirt path leaving Jin-sook pleading with the *kempei*.

*

I had never seen a doctor when I was young. Back home, when someone got sick, they called a woman from the valley who, after examining the patient, prescribed special herbs. But I never needed her. So I didn't know what to do when a nurse took me inside a white room with a bright light as the other girls sat silently in the infirmary's hallway. The nurse pushed me to stand in front of a fat Japanese doctor who sat on a wood chair next to a cot.

The nurse left and the doctor said, "Take off your clothes."

I wasn't sure if I had heard him correctly. "Sir?" I said, keeping my eyes low.

"I said, take off your clothes. Do it now."

"You want me to take off my clothes?" I asked.

The doctor leaned in and slapped me hard across my face. It was the first time anyone had struck me. The shock of it took my breath away. "I'm a doctor. I have to examine you," he said. "Do as I say now or I'll send you to Lieutenant Tanaka for a beating."

I didn't want to get a beating, so I slowly unbuttoned my shirt and pants. I untied my undergarments and let them fall to the floor. I had never been naked in front of a man before. I started to tremble. "Come closer," the doctor said. I took a step closer. The doctor ran his hands along my torso. He pressed his fingers into my neck, stomach and chest. I flinched with each touch. He made me turn around and he put his cold stethoscope on my back and told me to breathe in slowly. I couldn't stop trembling.

The doctor pointed at the cot and told me to lie there on my back. "Pull your knees up and spread your legs open."

I couldn't believe what he was telling me to do. "What are you going to do to me?" I asked.

"I need to see if you are a virgin. Now stop asking questions and do as you're told."

I still felt the sting from the doctor's slap and the *kempei* and his *shinai* were fresh in my mind. So I closed my eyes and did what the doctor told me to do. My body tensed as the doctor probed me with his fingers. I dug my fingernails into the palm of my hand and stifled a sob. After a few long seconds he stopped. "You're a virgin," he said. "I would expect it, someone as young as you, but you can never be sure. How long have you been bleeding?"

"Sir?" I asked.

"Your monthly bleed, how long has it been?"

"Five times."

"Good. You're clean. You have good skin and pleasing features. I'm sure Colonel Matsumoto will want you first,

someone so young, so pretty. Do what he tells you and you'll be all right. Now get dressed and go back with the others."

I quickly dressed as the doctor washed at a porcelain basin. "Doctor," I said, "what will the Colonel ask me to do?"

"Nothing you can't handle," he said without looking up.

"But what if I don't want to do it?" I asked.

The doctor turned from the basin. "Don't talk back, girl, and do what he tells you. Now go." I ran back to the hallway with the other girls and sat on the cold tile floor. I thought about what had happened to Sun-hi in the truck and how the *kempei* had punched Jin-sook in the stomach. I was terrified that awful things like that would happen to me, too. And I wasn't as sure as the Doctor was that I would be able to handle it.

*

Private Ishida, his rifle in hand, led us back to the barracks. "Listen to me," he said. "Do not cross the lieutenant or you will pay the price! Only speak Japanese. And don't disappoint the senior officers, either. Do you understand?"

"Yes sir," we replied in unison.

We came around the barracks to where the truck had dropped us off. Lieutenant Tanaka was waiting for us. Jin-sook was not with him. He ordered us to take our things and follow him. We gathered our sacks and followed him to where he had dragged Jin-sook. We came to a courtyard closed off by three long barracks, each with ten doors, closely spaced. Two wooden steps led to each door. There were no windows in the barracks. The yellow dirt in the courtyard was hard and dry.

In the center of the courtyard, Jin-sook stood with her wrists and ankles tied to a post. She was naked and she trembled visibly. She breathed in shallow sobs. We all

gasped and covered our mouths when we saw her. Sun-hi began to cry quietly.

Japanese women, some dressed in *yukatas*, lounged on the steps of the largest barracks. Others leaned against walls. When we came in the courtyard, they filed out.

Lieutenant Tanaka pointed his *shinai* at the ground twenty feet in front of the post and ordered us to form a line facing Jin-sook. I couldn't take my eyes off her as I stood at the end of the line next to Soo-hee.

Lieutenant Tanaka faced us. "You are all fortunate!" he said, strolling down the line. "You will learn what happens to a Korean girl who doesn't please her *kempei*. You will watch the lesson without closing your eyes. If you cry, you will earn a beating. If you faint, you will earn a beating. If you vomit or piss yourself or do anything other than watch the lesson, you will earn a beating. Watch now and learn from your *kempei*."

Lieutenant Tanaka approached Jin-sook with his *shinai* at his side. She sobbed and pleaded with the *kempei* not to beat her. She said she was sorry and wouldn't talk back. He didn't seem to hear her.

Lieutenant Tanaka stood in front of Jin-sook and slowly raised his *shinai*. Then he struck her across her thighs with a loud whack. Jin-sook's body stiffened. Her eyes went wide and her mouth opened, but no sound came out. Lieutenant Tanaka brought the *shinai* down again on the same place and Jin-sook let out a long, jagged scream. She shook violently against the post. Lieutenant Tanaka struck her thighs again. Then again and again and again. Jin-sook screamed and jerked with each blow. She pulled hard against the ropes and they cut her wrists. Angry red welts swelled on her thighs. Urine ran down her legs.

My own thighs jerked with each strike of the *shinai*, as if Lieutenant Tanaka was beating me. I wanted desperately to close my eyes and put my hands over my ears to make the

beating stop. But I was shocked at what I was seeing and so horrified, that I could not do either. Bile rose from my stomach and I was afraid I would vomit. I wanted to cry but I pushed it down inside my stomach as Soo-hee had told me to.

Then, Lieutenant Tanaka struck Jin-sook on her shins. With this blow, Jin-sook's body stiffened again, her mouth opened wide and she took in a short gulp of air. Lieutenant Tanaka hit her in the same place and Jin-sook let out a long, mournful shriek. Mucus ran from her nose, her hair was wild and tangled. Lieutenant Tanaka struck her shins over and over, each blow causing Jin-sook to scream horribly. Finally, Jin-sook slumped unconscious against the post, her black hair falling like a veil over her face. Lieutenant Tanaka lowered his *shinai* and faced us.

I couldn't breathe and the courtyard was spinning. Out of the corner of my eye, I saw Sun-hi faint. Lieutenant Tanaka pointed his *shinai* at her. "That girl has earned a beating," he said. "Private, make a note. We will do it tomorrow."

Lieutenant Tanaka walked down the line of girls. "I have given you a valuable lesson. What do you say to your *kempei* for this lesson?"

No one answered.

"I asked a question!" Lieutenant Tanaka barked, slapping his *shinai* hard against his boot. "Someone answer, or you will all earn a beating."

No one said anything and I was afraid I was going to faint like Sun-hi did. Finally, Soo-hee took a step forward and bowed low. "*Kempei*, sir," she said in broken Japanese, "thank you for this lesson."

Lieutenant Tanaka looked down his pointed nose at Soo-hee. "What is your name, girl?"

"Okimi Iwata, sir," Soo-hee said with another low bow.

"You're welcome, Okimi Iwata. Go back in line." Soo-hee stepped back.

"Now," Lieutenant Tanaka said, "all of you, wash and change into *yukatas*. The *geishas* will assign you to rooms. The senior officers return from maneuvers tonight."

As Lieutenant Tanaka headed out of the courtyard, he said over his shoulder, "Be ready for them."

NINE

AFTER LIEUTENANT TANAKA left the courtyard, I gripped Soo-hee's hand hard. I asked her what was happening to us.

"Quiet!" Private Ishida barked, untying Jin-sook from the post. "Don't talk! If Lieutenant Tanaka hears you, you will get a beating!" I lowered my head.

"Seiko! Maori!" the private shouted. "Get the others and come help with the new girls." The Japanese women reappeared from behind their barracks.

Sun-hi, lying on the ground, moaned and grabbed at Soo-hee's leg. Soo-hee helped her to her feet. When Sun-hi saw Jin-sook slumped at the post, she began to sob uncontrollably. "No!" Soo-hee said in a sharp whisper. "Do not cry." The tall girl drew in an uncertain breath and fell quiet.

Private Ishida ordered Maori to get water for Jin-sook. "She needs to go to the infirmary," he said. He kneeled next to the unconscious girl and untied from the post. He told the other *geishas* to show us our rooms and where to wash. "They need *yukatas* for the officers tonight," he said.

A Japanese woman in a dark blue *yukata* grabbed me by the arm. "I am Seiko," she said. "Come with me." She was at least seven years older than Soo-hee. She had shoulder-length hair, long eyelashes, and a petite nose. She walked with short, deliberate steps. She led me to a narrow door at the end of one of the barracks. "Listen to me. This is where you work. From one o'clock to five, it's the enlisted men. They get ten minutes each. From five to seven, you have the non-commissioned officers. They get a half hour. At eight, you will go to one of the senior officers' quarters and stay as long as he wants you. Today you're lucky—you only have the senior officers. The troops return from maneuvers tomorrow. Then you will put in a full day's work."

Seiko continued. "You wash in the latrine next to the infirmary. Get a *yukata* in the room by the latrine. You must wear it when you work. We prepare food in the kitchen next to the *geisha's* barracks. You will be assigned cleaning, cooking and laundry duty tomorrow."

"And one more thing," Seiko said, poking me in my chest with her finger. "Always remember you are a Korean. Do as we say or you will get a beating just like your friend over there. Now put your things in your room and follow me to the latrine."

I went inside the room. It was dark and small and stunk like a toilet. Strips of sunlight showed through gaps between the boards in the floors and walls. The door hung loosely on leather hinges. Covering the floor was a small, thin mat. There was a chamber pot in one corner and in the other, a stool.

I placed my sack on the mat. I turned to Seiko. "What kind of work do we do here?"

Seiko scoffed at me. "You *are* a stupid Korean. You're an *ianfu*—a comfort woman. You are here to service the soldiers."

Ianfu. I had heard the word once before, years earlier when I overheard Mother and Father talking in hushed tones about what had happened to an older girl who lived near us. I wondered what it meant so I asked Soo-hee. She told me to forget I heard the word, but I never did.

Now I was beginning to understand and my stomach turned into a knot. I had never been with a man before. I had never even imagined what it would be like. I thought about what had happened to Sun-hi in the truck only hours earlier. I could still hear her cries and see how she rolled up into a tight ball when the driver threw her back in the truck after he had used her. She hadn't been the same since. And I knew I would not be the same, either.

I looked beyond the barracks over the brown wheat fields. The distance between the hills was much greater than in the hills outside of Sinuiju. I remembered Lieutenant Tanaka's words; *there is nowhere to run.* I glanced at the post in the middle of the courtyard and a shiver of pain went through my legs.

I looked back at Seiko who glared at me. "Thank you, ma'am," I said with a respectful bow.

*

An hour later, I had washed and even though I wasn't hungry, I had eaten a small bowl of broth with a few mushy *azuki* beans. Seiko had given me a green *yukata* with small, white and pink flowers. She gave me white *tabi* socks and *zori* sandals. The *yukata* was too large for my slender frame and I tripped on the hem while walking back to the courtyard. Lounging on their steps, the Japanese women laughed at me without covering their mouths.

"Look at that poor little chicken," one of them said. "She will squawk when the officers pluck her."

The women laughed again, except for Seiko who stared at me and said, "Yes. And the officers will be here soon."

When I entered the courtyard, the other Korean girls were standing awkwardly in front of their barracks. They were all wearing *yukatas* and there was terror in their eyes.

Soo-hee, wearing a yellow *yukata*, was on a step at the end of the barracks. I ran to her. I told her I was scared.

"We all are," Soo-hee said. She scanned the other girls and told me to follow her.

As the Japanese women and Private Ishida looked on, Soo-hee gathered the girls around her. Then she said in a low voice, "We're in a terrible place. We have to do what they say, or we will die. But we have each other and we must stay strong."

"But I do not know what to do!" a younger girl cried.

Soo-hee nodded. "What's your name?"

"Midori Sato," she answered.

"No, no. What's your Korean name?"

"Mee-su," the girl said.

"I don't know what to do either, Mee-su," Soo-hee said. "The doctor said we would be all right if we do what they say. I think we should."

"But I don't know how," Mee-su said.

Soo-hee put a hand on Mee-su's shoulder. "You have to try. Remember what I said. Be strong." Mee-su choked back a sob and Soo-hee looked at each of the girls in the eye. "We must be strong. We must help each other."

We all nodded. Mee-su wiped her eyes and no longer cried. The girls went back to their steps. Sun-hi still trembled.

Soo-hee led me back to my step. She tugged at my sleeve and told me to come closer. "Take this," she whispered. She lifted a fold of her *yukata*. In her hand was the comb with the two-headed dragon. "*Ummah* said that it will protect us."

"But *Onni, Ummah* gave it to you."

"You were born in the year of the dragon," Soo-hee said. "This comb with the dragon is a sign for you. Take it little sister."

I wrapped my hand around the comb. It was the first time I had ever held it. It was heavy and cool in my hand, and felt like something important. But after what had happen to Jin-sook, I doubted if a comb could help me.

"Where will I hide it?" I asked.

"In your chamber pot," Soo-hee said. "No one will find it there. Put it there now."

I slid the comb inside my *yukata* and went to my room. I did as Soo-hee said and dropped it inside my chamber pot.

*

We waited in the courtyard exchanging nervous glances. Then, Lieutenant Tanaka walked in with his *shinai* at his side. Private Ishida grabbed his rifle and stood straight. The Japanese women continued to lounge on their steps. Now that the sun had set, it was cooling quickly. There was no breeze and I could hear the rumble of trucks in the village. We huddled close except for Sun-hi who stood off to the side and stared at the ground.

With his *shinai,* Lieutenant Tanaka pointed at the yellow dirt in front of him. He ordered us to form a line and stand straight with our hands at our sides. He said we were not to talk. "The officers are coming," he said.

I heard voices and the laughter of men from behind the barracks. The voices grew louder and a group of men entered the courtyard led by a man a half head taller than the rest. I had seen Japanese senior officers before, but never anyone like him. He had square shoulders, smooth skin, and a strong chin. Just by the sight of him, I feared him like I'd never feared anyone before.

"Attention!" Lieutenant Tanaka barked. He and Private Ishida snapped to attention. The Japanese women stayed seated on their steps.

The square-shouldered officer approached Lieutenant Tanaka. "Lieutenant, I see we have new girls," he said.

"Yes, Colonel," Lieutenant Tanaka said crisply and with a slight bow. "One was disrespectful and had to be disciplined. She is in the infirmary. The doctor reports all the rest are virgins except the one at the end." He pointed at Sun-hi.

"Let's take a look," the Colonel said. With his hands behind his back, he slowly examined each one of us. He stopped at me. I bowed my head low and looked at his feet. His boots were polished, clean and tied tight. Under my *yukata*, my knees shook.

"This is a young one," he said. "Is she clean, Lieutenant?"

"Yes sir. She is the youngest. Her name is Namiko Iwata."

The Colonel lifted my chin with a finger and examined my face from side-to-side. The shaking in my knees spread to my legs. The courtyard spun around me and thought I would faint. "You have a pretty face, Namiko Iwata," he said, his eyes fixed on me. "Pretty and delicate, like an aristocrat."

He turned to Lieutenant Tanaka and said, "This one."

TEN

August 2008, Seoul, South Korea

"HE RAPED ME," my birth-grandmother says, glaring at me from across her table. I want to look away but I don't dare. "They took me to his quarters where he raped me. I was fourteen years old. I didn't know what sex was. I had only been menstruating for five months. Five months! How could I know? How could I know?"

"You couldn't possibly," I say. It's hot and humid inside the apartment. I need to fan myself, but I don't dare. Not now. Not with Mrs. Hong reliving her horrible rape. The agony of it is written on her face and is deep in her eyes.

"He raped me in the cruelest way," she continues. "I'm sorry to tell you this, but you must know. First, he told me to take off my clothes in front of him while he watched. I wanted to say no, but I had just seen how they'd beaten Jin-sook. I was terrified so I did what he said. I stood there naked and helpless like a baby. I shook with fear. Then he made me undress him. I had to start with his boots—those

polished, clean boots that he tied so tight. I had to unbutton his shirt, then his trousers. He made me kneel and take off his undergarments as he stood over me, naked. He told me to look at him. He thought I would be impressed. I had never seen a naked man before. I had only imagined what they were like. I desperately wanted to run away, back to the hills behind our farm where Soo-hee and I used to run in the aspen trees."

She locks her hands into a single fist and places them on top of the table. Her eyes never leave me. "Then he touched me. Everywhere. He ran his hands over my hair, my face, my neck, my breasts, my stomach, my legs, my genitals. He pushed me down and forced himself inside me. He pierced me and made me bleed. He pushed over and over again. Each thrust hurt more than the previous one. I cannot describe the pain. It was worse than pain. It was pain and terror and humiliation and shame all together. I wanted to die. I tried to resist but when I did, he just laughed at me. He was a strong man. I was a girl. And he was the Japanese Colonel."

She clenches her fingers so hard I think they might break. The pain on her face never eases. She continues. "But what made the Colonel so cruel was that as he raped me he made me stare into his eyes. When I shut them, he ordered me to keep them open. 'Look at me, girl,' he ordered. 'Keep your eyes open and look at me!' So I looked into his eyes as he raped me. Can you imagine how humiliating that was? Can you?"

"No, ma'am," I answer, "I can't."

"He did not use a condom," she says. "He didn't have to. I was a virgin and he was the first to rape me. So, when he orgasmed I felt his slime crawl inside every cell of my body like maggots. I could feel it spoil me, turn me rotten. And I knew he would always be in me. Always.

"Do you know what the worst part of it was?"

"I'm sorry," I say, "I don't."

"The worst part is I thought it was my fault. I had always been so proud and stubborn and sure of myself. But when the Colonel raped me, I lost everything. I could only think of my grandparents, my mother and father and Soo-hee. I was overcome with shame but I did nothing wrong, nothing wrong. It doesn't make sense, does it?"

"No," I answer, "it doesn't make any sense at all."

She places her hands in two curves on the low table and turns to the purple flower in the glass bowl. "Do you know what I did when it was over, when he was done with me and told me to leave?"

"No, ma'am."

"I bowed and thanked him," she says in a whisper. "I don't know why I did that. I wanted to spit on him, scream at him, tell him how much I hated him and all the Japanese. But I had to do the right thing, like Mother said. So I thanked him. It seemed to please him that I did."

We're silent for a long time. My birth-grandmother, who earlier was so proud, now looks completely humiliated. I don't know what to say. I'd never met anyone who'd been raped before. I never even got close to it. Of course, sometimes I get nervous when I'm alone on the street at night or when there's a sketchy-looking guy in a hallway. But I never knew how devastating rape could be. Until now.

Eventually, the pain in her face goes away and she straightens up. "Would you like some *bori cha*, Ja-young?" she asks.

"*Bori cha?* You mentioned it in your story. I don't know what it is."

She frowns. "Americans think all Koreans drink the same tea as the Chinese and Japanese. However many traditional Koreans, like me, prefer *bori cha*. It is roasted barley tea. You must have some."

"Sure," I say. "Thank you."

She puts a pot on the stove and tosses in a handful of what looks like black tea. She takes two cups from the cupboard and brings them to the table. She moves gracefully in her *hanbok*. "I like my *bori cha* strong," she says. "That is the way we used to drink it when I was a girl. It has become fashionable for our young people to drink coffee like the Americans. I don't like coffee. It isn't Korean and I am afraid I'm a traditionalist. I think Korea needs to hold on to its traditions, don't you?"

"Of course."

"What do you know about our traditions, Ja-young?"

"Not much, I guess," I confess.

"You should know more about Korea. Yes, you were raised in America. But an important part of you is here," she says, tapping a finger on the table. "You cannot escape it."

I can't escape it? I'm not sure I want it. I'd rather be just an American, like my friends and family. But when I'm alone in my room and look in the mirror, I see someone different. The woman in the mirror is Korean. It's in her face, her eyes, and her hair. Maybe it's in her blood, too.

The teapot starts whistling and she gets it from the stove. She pours the tea through a strainer into our cups. The aroma fills the room. I take a sip and it's really strong and bitter. It isn't anything like the weak tea served on our tour. As I drink it, I feel cooler and more relaxed.

"Tell me, what do you think of my story so far?" Mrs. Hong asks over the top of her cup.

"It's… horrible," I say. Outside, the wind is blowing sending a breeze through the window. It gives some relief from the heat—or maybe it's the *bori cha*.

She stares at me. I sense that she's sizing me up to see if she's made the right decision to give me the comb. I don't want to disappoint her so I say, "Go on, please. Tell me the rest of your story."

She smiles but her eyes turn hard. "I have only just begun!" she says. She puts her cup on the table and her hands in her lap.

She continues. "The day after the Colonel raped me, the troops came, and I quickly learned what to do. I had become an *ianfu*—a comfort woman. I learned a trick, too. I examined the men's boots before they raped me. As I said, the Colonel had his boots tied tight. It was a warning sign. His type of cruelty was the worst. It was psychological as well as physical. After that, whenever I saw someone with boots tied tight, I knew I would be humiliated.

"But there were many others. A soldier with dirty, untied boots would be careless and quick. A soldier who kept his boots on would often hurt me. If his boots were clean and polished, it would be someone who wanted me to pretend I was enjoying him.

"Examining their boots was just something I did. But knowing what was going to happen to me did not help. In fact, it made it worse. It was like a torturer telling you what he was going to do to you next. By looking at their boots, I knew how they would rape me.

"And," she says, "I was raped thousands of times."

ELEVEN

August 1945. Dongfeng, Manchuria

WHEN THE SOLDIER with the dirty, untied boots left my room, there was only one more waiting at my step. There was always a long line at my door before the soldiers went off to their maneuvers. *Kempei* told us the soldiers needed to purge themselves so if they died in battle, they could enter the afterlife pure. "You're doing a great service for these men," he said. "And for Japan and for the Emperor."

I had been serving Japan and the Emperor nonstop since midday and it was now early evening. Even with the six new Korean girls Lieutenant Tanaka had brought in, my line was always the longest. At ten minutes apiece—the soldiers' allotted time—I had serviced over thirty men that day. I was sore and exhausted and had to force myself to serve one more soldier.

That man was Corporal Kaori. He was a big man and he liked to hurt me. He always said he wanted to be the last in

line so no one would rush him. But I knew it was because being last, he could do what he wanted to me.

When Kaori entered my room, I saw he had his boots tied tight and that there was a hardness in his eyes. I knew I had to be careful.

As Corporal Kaori unbuttoned his trousers, I washed off the condom the last soldier used. I bowed as I gave the cleaned condom to the corporal. I lay back and opened my *yukata*. My tiny room was hot and humid and reeked of sweat and semen. My sweat dripped into my bedding, already drenched from the sweat of dozens of men. The foul bedding clung to my back. Kaori pulled down his trousers without taking off his boots. He pulled his large penis through his underwear and I stroked it to get it stiff. It wasn't working.

"Faster, girl," he ordered. "Don't you know how I like it?" He pulled my hair, sending spikes of pain into my scalp.

I knew what I had to do to get him going. "Come on, big man," I hissed. "Hurt me some more."

His eyes flashed excitement and he slapped me hard.

"Yes, that's right," I said clenching my jaw. "It's what you want." I stroked him faster and his huge penis grew. He fumbled with the condom. I took it from him and put it on. He mounted me and tried to push inside me, but he wasn't stiff enough.

"Pinch me," I said. He pinched my nipples hard and slapped me again. My eyes filled with tears. I continued to stroke him. He grew stiff and finally was able to push inside me. His bulk overwhelmed me and my body jerked with each of his thrusts. He slapped me again and put his hand around my throat. His eyes grew wide and he grinned lasciviously.

He was choking me. Hard. I gasped and could feel my face turn red. I tried to tell him to let go, but I couldn't push the words past his grip. I grabbed his arm and squirmed but

his weight kept me pinned to the mat and my struggles only aroused him more. I saw stars and everything started to go dark. Then with a convulsion that banged my head in the wall, he was done. He released his hand from my neck and climbed off of me. I turned to the side and coughed. I took in air in big gulps. Eventually the stars went away. I clung to the wall and forced myself to stand in the corner.

Kaori removed his condom and dropped it inside my chamber pot. As he pulled up his trousers, I bowed and said a weak thank you. The corporal grunted and left my room.

I clutched the clothes hook on the back of the door to keep myself from collapsing. It took several minutes until I could breathe normally again. Then I picked up my *obi* and looked at the clothes hook. I admit I thought about doing it. One end of the *obi* around the clothes hook, the other around my neck. After all, Sun-hi had done it not more than a week after we arrived at the comfort station. She had tied the knots, relaxed her legs, and let herself go. It must have taken great strength for Sun-hi to let herself hang until her *obi* choked the life from her. I wondered if I could do it, too.

I let go of the clothes hook. I wiped the sweat off my forehead and rubbed the pain from my neck. I wrapped myself in my *yukata* and tied it closed with my *obi*. I reached inside my chamber pot and among the used condoms and semen, I felt for the comb with the two-headed dragon. I took it out and wiped it clean on my bedding. I looked at the two-headed dragon. Mother had said that it would protect us. I was keeping it hidden from the Japanese but so far, it had not protected me from anything.

I slipped the comb under my mat and gathered the sweat-soaked bedding. I picked up the chamber pot and headed out the door. Outside the sun was bright. It was hot and the sky was hazy blue. Swarms of big black flies buzzed around the barracks. In the courtyard, the slick mud of

spring had turned hard from the sun and the boots of thousands of men.

Seiko and the other Japanese geishas were lounging on their steps fanning themselves when I walked by. "You have another night with the Colonel," Seiko said to me. "I don't know why he wants a Korean whore like you when he could have a good Japanese *geisha* like me. He must like the way you use your stone face on him." The other Japanese women laughed without covering their mouths.

I blushed at Seiko's taunting. The Colonel had only forced me to do that once. He had just returned from visiting his family in Japan and was upset about something. I never found out what it was. After I undressed him like I always did, he pushed my face into him. I fought back but he was so strong, and I was afraid he would break my neck. So I did it. I had to.

Afterward, the Colonel had turned quiet almost as if he was ashamed. When I rose to leave, he asked me to stay. That was the first time I stayed the entire night with the Colonel. Since then, we spent more time talking than having sex. He gave me Japanese books to read during the long breaks when the soldiers were away. I think the other *ianfu* and the *geishas* were jealous of me.

As I walked back to my room, Private Ishida was resting in the shade. He nodded to me and I returned a small bow. I liked the private. He only used the *geishas* for himself and warned the Korean girls when the *kempei* was coming. He always carried his rifle, but I was sure he had never used it.

When I got to the latrine, I emptied my chamber pot and rinsed it out. I washed my hands. In the room next to the latrine, I left my bedding on the pile of dirty laundry and took a clean set. I headed back to the barracks. Seiko and the other Japanese women glared at me. I made sure to keep my eyes low. When I got to my room, I set the chamber pot at the foot of my mat and spread the clean bedding so it

would be ready for the next day. I retrieved the comb from under my mat and dropped it inside my chamber pot.

*

I went to the latrine to wash before dinner. The latrine was an open outhouse fifty feet behind the barracks. There was a wooden deck with three holes for the girls to squat over. To the side, on wooden frames, were three chipped and stained ceramic washbasins. Soo-hee, dressed in her yellow *yukata*, was washing laundry at a basin. I went to the basin next to her.

"I think Kaori will kill me someday," I said, staring into the washbasin.

"I will talk to the *kempei* about him again," Soo-hee said.

"No don't," I said quickly remembering the times Soo-hee had been punched for asking the *kempei* for something. "It is not so bad." I began to wash in the gray water.

"I hear the war is going badly for the Japanese," Soo-hee said. "The Americans are winning in the east. Maybe it will all end soon."

"Then what will we do?" I asked.

"We will go home." Soo-hee said.

"I do not want to go home after what we've done here," I said, "What will Mother and Father think? We have dishonored them."

Soo-hee put a hand on my arm. "Don't worry about what Mother and Father will think. You just need to stay strong a little while longer."

Stay strong? What for? So I could be raped another day? Growing up on the farm, I thought I was strong. I could work all day in the fields alongside Father and Mother and Soo-hee and go days without a full meal when the rice was low. But for the past two years, the effort to make it through each day took everything out of me. I was nothing more

than a toilet to the Japanese, and that's exactly how I saw myself. I was doing my best to stay strong, but I wasn't sure how much longer I could.

Soo-hee returned to her basin and looked at me out of the corner of her eye. "This dirty water reminds me of the day that pig got away from Father and Mr. Lee from up the road. They were butchering it for the New Year's feast. Do you remember?"

"Yes, I think so," I answered.

Soo-hee continued. "It was raining that day and the pig slipped out of their arms. Mr. Lee said they should put out cabbage for it and catch him that way. But *Appa* was impatient and chased after it."

Soo-hee began to chuckle and I could feel a smile forming on my face. She continued. "Father chased that pig all around the pen. He slipped and fell in the mud twice before he caught him. And Mr. Lee refused to help."

Soo-hee laughed. "*Appa* was covered with mud when he got home. *Ummah* was angry with him for tracking mud inside the house. She made him take off all his clothes and wash outside at the well. He was so mad, he had three helpings of roast pig that night!"

We laughed together, careful to cover our mouths as we did. But our laughs quickly went away. As I dried my hands, I looked at my *onni's* face. "How is your cheek?" I asked.

"It's healing," Soo-hee answered, turning to the basin.

The ugly purple and yellow bruise on Soo-hee's cheek made my heart sink. Three days earlier, Lieutenant Tanaka had punched Soo-hee when she asked the *kempei* if a new girl could see the doctor about a pain in her stomach. It was only the latest cruelty that my *onni* had had to suffer at the hands of Lieutenant Tanaka.

"I'm sorry," I said.

"What for?"

"You should have kept the comb. Then, you would have better luck and the *kempei* wouldn't be so mean to you."

"No, it is better that you have it. It has given you good luck. You are the Colonel's favorite."

"It is not so lucky that I am," I said.

Soo-hee stared vacantly at the basin. "Little sister," she said, "I have something to tell you."

"Oh?" I said. "What is it?"

Soo-hee took in a long breath. "I've missed my monthly bleed. My breasts are sore. I'm sick in my stomach in the morning. I think I am pregnant."

My heart stopped. "*Onni*, are you sure?" I asked.

"Yes. I have to tell Lieutenant Tanaka. He's the only one who doesn't use a condom with me. There is no saying what he will do."

I felt like the ground was opening up and swallowing me in. "Soo-hee, they will give you an abortion with a wire, just like they did with Maori and Yo-ee before they died."

"Not everyone who has an abortion dies, Ja-hee. Bo-yun and Mee-su were just fine after their abortions. And Jin-sook was only sick for a month before she came back to work."

I gripped Soo-hee's arm. "You have to take the comb! It will give you good luck like it has for me."

Soo-hee shook her head. "No. You keep it."

"But Soo-hee, if you die I will die, too. I'll hang myself with my *obi* like Sun-hi did."

"Do not talk like that!" Soo-hee snapped. "You will do no such thing."

I lowered my eyes and took a few deep breaths. "When will you tell Lieutenant Tanaka?" I asked.

"I'm supposed to be with him tonight. I will tell him before then. The longer I wait, the riskier the abortion will be. I should have it tomorrow."

"I'm with the Colonel tonight," I said. "I'll ask him to send you to the hospital in Pushun."

"He will not do that. Doctor Watanabe will do the abortion."

"Soo-hee, you cannot die. You cannot!" I wanted to cry.

Soo-hee put her hand on me. "I will be all right, little sister. I will not leave you here alone."

*

As I sat on my step in the fading light waiting for my time with the Colonel, I tried not to think about what life at the comfort station would be like if Doctor Watanabe's abortion killed Soo-hee. I wouldn't be able to do it anymore. I could not possibly go on. I desperately wanted the doctor to send her to the hospital in Pushun for the abortion. But I knew he would not. He didn't even send the *geishas* there when they got sick.

Suddenly down the barracks, a roar came from Soo-hee's room. It was Lieutenant Tanaka. I stepped out to the courtyard and watched Soo-hee's door. The door swung open and Lieutenant Tanaka backed out dragging Soo-hee by the hair. He pushed her down to the dirt and kicked her in the chest. Soo-hee quickly got to her hands and knees, and lowered her head to the lieutenant. "I'm sorry, *Kempei*," she said.

I brought my hand to my mouth to stifle a cry. I watched in horror as Lieutenant Tanaka kicked Soo-hee a second time and growled, "You whore! We must take care of this." He grabbed my *onni* by the hair and marched toward the infirmary. Soo-hee got to her feet, stumbled and fell, and scrambled to her feet again. Lieutenant Tanaka never slowed as he dragged Soo-hee to the infirmary to see Doctor Watanabe.

TWELVE

COLONEL MATSUMOTO'S MEN said he was a brilliant military tactician. It was rumored he was being considered for an even higher office. He worked long hours and I never saw him when he wasn't deep in thought about something. He could be cruel to me, but he could be surprisingly gentle, too. He no longer humiliated me when he raped me and almost seemed ashamed afterward. But he still raped me nearly every night he was in Dongfeng.

I lounged on the daybed alongside the Colonel in his private quarters near the center of town. I hadn't slept the night before thinking about how to convince him to send Soo-hee to the hospital in Pushun for her abortion. I ran a finger over the rosewood table next to the bed. "Colonel Sir, have you gotten a letter from your family in Nagasaki?" I asked.

"I received a letter yesterday," he answered.

"That's wonderful. What do they say?"

"Nothing you need to know."

I wrapped my *yukata* around me and reclined on the silk bed covers. Next to the bed was a picture of the Colonel's family—his wife with an upper-class smile, a pugnacious-looking boy about eight years old, and a girl only a few years younger than me dressed in a pretty white *kimono*. Next to the picture was a bowl containing two round *amanatzu*. Their citrus smell filled the room. I laid my legs alongside the Colonel's muscular frame. The smooth skin on his chest shimmered with the afterglow of sex. His head lay on a *dakimakura* pillow and he stared at the ceiling where a fan slowly turned.

"When will you see your family again?" I asked.

"I do not know," he said. "I cannot see the future. It might not be for a long time. Why do you care?"

"I have heard the war is ending."

The Colonel glared at me. "Who told you that?"

"I'm sorry, sir. It is just a silly rumor."

The Colonel turned his eyes to the ceiling again. He folded his arms over his bare chest. "Eat some *amanatzu*," he ordered. "They were shipped from Kumamato for the senior officers. I doubt you get much fruit at the comfort station."

I put a hand on the Colonel's leg. It was warm and dewy. "Thank you for taking care of me." I picked up one of the yellow fruits. "What will happen when the war ends? I mean, when Japan has defeated the Americans?"

"We will rule all of Asia of course," the Colonel said.

"Yes of course. I mean sir, what will happen to the *ianfu* when the troops return to Japan?"

The Colonel pulled his head off the pillow. "Why do you ask such questions? Am I a prophet? How do I know what will happen to anyone when the war ends?"

He was right. I was asking too many questions again. I lowered my head. "Please forgive a silly girl for asking stupid questions," I said.

The Colonel reclined on the *dakimakura* pillow. "You haven't eaten any *amanatzu*. Eat some. You are too thin."

"Thank you, sir." As I peeled the *amanatzu*, I let my *yukata* slip open revealing my breast.

The Colonel eyed my breast and the fan in the ceiling turned. "I don't eat *amanatzu* this time of year," he said staring. "They are sour. Take as much as you want." He returned his gaze to the ceiling.

I ate a section of the fruit. It was indeed sour, but I ate it anyway.

"Colonel Sir," I said, "may I ask for something?"

"Ask."

"Sir, my sister is pregnant. Doctor Watanabe is giving her an abortion. Please sir, have her sent to the hospital at Pushun for the abortion. She will be better off there."

The Colonel shook his head. "I will not do that."

"Please sir, as a favor to me."

With a powerful swipe of his arm, he pushed me off the bed. I fell on the floor with a thud and what was left of the *amanatzu* tumbled across the floor. "Why should I care about what happens to a Korean girl?" he said. "I only serve the Emperor."

I scrambled to my knees and crawled to him. I brought my face over his thighs and began to unbutton his underwear. He looked down at me as I pulled his penis from beneath his underwear and began to stroke him. He didn't respond, so I brought my face in close. The musty smell from the sex we'd had earlier was strong on him.

The Colonel leaned back and grabbed a bottle of *sake* off the nightstand. "It will not work," he said evenly.

"Please sir," I pleaded, "I will do anything."

The Colonel pulled the cork from a *sake* bottle and reached for a glass as if I wasn't there. "Leave me. Now," he said.

I removed my hands from him and slowly stood. As the Colonel poured a glass of *sake*, I bowed and pulled on my *tabi*. At the door, I slipped on my *zori* and left the Colonel alone in his quarters.

I walked between the low stucco buildings toward the comfort station with my head down. I took the path next to the infirmary. I stopped and put a hand on the infirmary wall. Inside was Soo-hee, waiting for her abortion.

I had tried. I had been willing to do anything. But I had failed and now my *onni's* life was in the fat hands of Doctor Watanabe.

*

"You're clean," Doctor Watanabe told me as I lay on his cot inside the infirmary's tile inspection room with my legs spread. "I don't know how you do it. All *ianfu* eventually get pregnant or contract some kind of disease, but not you. You're lucky."

I was seeing the doctor for my monthly inspection for venereal disease. Every month the fat doctor would poke and probe each girl looking for signs of disease. The soldiers were supposed to use condoms with us, but the Japanese were low on supplies and we had to reuse condoms until they broke. They usually lasted only two or three times and all of the girls got venereal disease except me. Perhaps the comb was giving me luck after all.

"Doctor Sir," I said as I stood from the cot and pulled on my short pants, "may I see my sister before the troops come back tomorrow? I will be too busy to see her after that. She is only upstairs from here. Please, sir?"

"No. She is too sick for visitors," the doctor answered from the washbasin.

"Sir, she is my sister."

"Don't talk back girl," the doctor said over his shoulder. "I said no."

I lowered my eyes. "Will she be all right?" I asked. "Will she recover from the abortion?"

"She's bleeding inside," the doctor answered drying his hands on a towel. "I don't have time to do an operation. If she doesn't stop bleeding on her own, she will die."

The doctor's words hit me like a punch in the stomach. I stopped buttoning my shirt. "She must go to the hospital in Pushun!" I cried. "Please doctor, send her there."

The doctor turned his fat frame toward me. His eyes were red and his face sagged. "Do you think they will take an *ianfu* when they have so many Japanese soldiers to care for? They will laugh at me for sending her."

"Can anything be done? Please, doctor."

The doctor motioned for the nurse to send in the next *ianfu*. He ordered me to go back to the comfort station. "There is nothing I can do for your sister," he said.

THIRTEEN

THE LAUNDRY WAS four poles supporting a corrugated metal roof next to the latrine. Three metal washtubs rested on low wooden tables. Behind the laundry were wire clotheslines strung from posts. Several sets of bedding dried in the warm sun.

As I washed a stack of bedding, Jin-sook and Mee-su came in, each carrying an armful of the *geisha's* laundry. Mee-su asked me what I had heard about Soo-hee.

"She is no better," I answered.

"She's a fool," Jin-sook said dropping bedding into a tub. "She pushes the *kempei* too much. She should do as I do. Make friends with them."

"The Japanese are not our friends, Jin-sook," I said.

"You pretend they aren't," she said, "but you have become friends with the Colonel. He gives you books and you never get a beating. I became friends with Lieutenant Tanaka and haven't gotten a beating since we came here. I have made friends with the *geishas*, too."

"You are their slave," Mee-su said, kneading the laundry into the water. "You do everything they say."

"That's not true," Jin-sook said. "I just... respect them."

"Well, I'm glad Soo-hee stands up to the *kempei*," Mee-su said. "We will all be in trouble if she dies."

"She will not die," I said, looking at the tub. "I have a plan."

Jin-sook looked from the laundry tub. "A plan? What is it?"

Yes, I had a plan, but I was not going to tell anyone, especially Jin-sook. Without answering her, I gathered my laundry and headed to the clothesline. "Be careful," Mee-su said. "*Kempei* is watching you."

I hung the bedding on the line and took a clean set for my room. When I got to the courtyard, Lieutenant Tanaka was sitting in a chair leaning against the *geisha's* barracks. His *shinai* rested in his lap. Private Ishida looking bored as usual, leaned against a wall. Tanaka bent forward as I walked by. "Come here girl," he said.

I walked to him and lowered my head. His high, black boots were freshly polished.

"Look at me," he said. I looked at him. His eyes were small and sharp. "You're not going to cause trouble for me if your sister dies, are you, Namiko Iwata?" He stroked my thigh with his *shinai*.

"No, *Kempei*," I answered.

"You won't do something stupid like run away or hurt one of the men?"

"No, *Kempei*."

"Good, because Colonel Matsumoto cannot help you if you do. I am *Kempei-tai*—military police. The Colonel has no authority over me. So do as I say or you will earn yourself a beating." He tapped my thigh with his *shinai*. "And I will give you a good one. Understand, girl?"

"Yes, *Kempei*."

"Go on now. The troops are returning tomorrow. They need you. It is a great service you do for them." He leaned his chair back against the stucco wall.

As I carried my laundry to my room, I glanced at Private Ishida who turned away.

*

After I had spread my bedding, I went to the courtyard. It was humid and clouds were forming in the west. The *ianfu* had put on their *yukatas* and were waiting on their steps for the soldiers to arrive.

I went to the *geisha* barracks and inched open Seiko's door. "Seiko," I said with a slight bow, "I need your help." Inside, Seiko was preparing her room. The room was twice as large as mine and had a table and a light. Instead of a mat on the plank floor, there was a low bed with a mattress.

"Why should I help you?" Seiko asked.

"Please. I need to see Soo-hee. She's dying."

"I don't care," Seiko said.

"Seiko, you and I, we are not so different. I heard you crying in your room the night Maori died."

Seiko spread clean bedding across her mattress. "Maori was a good Japanese woman. Soo-hee is a Korean."

"I promise to be your servant for a month if you help me. Please, Seiko."

"I will not do anything that will get me in trouble."

"You are Japanese and Doctor Watanabe is a regular customer of yours. Talk to him. Tell him if Soo-hee sees me, she will recover and return to work. He will listen to you."

Seiko raised an eyebrow. "If I do that, you will be my servant for a month?"

"Yes, I promise. I'll do anything you say."

"What if the doctor says 'no'?"

"You are his favorite. If you ask, he will agree."

Seiko turned to her bed. "Okay. I will talk to him. I'll let you know what he says."

"Thank you, Seiko." I bowed as I backed out of her room.

*

A while later, Seiko came to me from across the courtyard. She told me she had good news. She said she talked with Doctor Watanabe and persuaded him to let me see Soo-hee. She said she cleared it with the *kempei* too. "And now you must be my servant for a month," she said.

My heart skipped. "Thank you, Seiko."

"Lieutenant Tanaka said you should go before the soldiers come. You have a half hour. And then come back here. You can start working for me right away."

I bowed and thanked Seiko again. I ran to my room and closed the door. I took the comb with the two-headed dragon from inside my chamber pot. The dragon was so white and the gold spine so bright that I knew it would give Soo-hee good luck. I slipped it inside a fold of my *yukata* and quickly headed for the infirmary. In the courtyard, the comfort women rested on their steps, fanning themselves in the summer heat. Mee-su and the other girls watched as I crossed the courtyard. Mee-su slowly shook her head at me.

When I got to the infirmary, I didn't see Doctor Watanabe or Lieutenant Tanaka. I hadn't seen Seiko talk with the doctor or the *kempei*. I thought Seiko might be setting me up, but I didn't care. I was already in the infirmary and Soo-hee was on a bed on the second floor. I had to give her the comb.

I hurried up the stairs to the infirmary ward. At the end of the hallway, a Japanese nurse sat at a desk writing on a chart. I snuck across the hallway to a large, white room with a long row of evenly spaced cots. Sheets hanging from metal

rods surrounded several cots. High on the wall, small windows opened out to the town. I did a quick scan of the cots, but didn't see Soo-hee.

A bandaged soldier sitting on the floor next to his cot lifted his head. He asked if I had come for him. I told him I was here to visit my sister.

"When you're done, come see me," he said. "You can help with my recovery."

I walked down the long room. My *zori* slapped against the tile floor. Another soldier lifted his head off the pillow and nodded at me. A third rolled over and pulled his blanket over his shoulders.

In a corner, separated from the soldiers by a white sheet, I saw someone lying on a mat on the tile floor. I went there and saw it was Soo-hee. My poor *onni's* face was pale except for gray circles around her eyes. Her lips were chapped, her hair, greasy and tangled. I knelt and took her hand. It was clammy and cold.

Soo-hee opened her eyes. "Little sister," she said weakly, "why are you here? You will get in trouble."

"Seiko talked to the doctor and he said it was okay."

"Do not trust her, Ja-hee."

I brushed a strand of hair from Soo-hee's face. "*Onni*, you look so sick."

Soo-hee's eyes became cloudy and she pushed her head in the pillow. "Ja-hee, I do not think I will recover. I said I would never leave you. I'm sorry." Tears welled in her eyes.

I came in close. "No, you will not die," I whispered. "I've brought the comb." I scanned the room and saw that no one was looking. I reached inside my *yukata* and pulled out the comb. I slipped it into Soo-hee's hand. "Here," I said, "take it."

Soo-hee shook her head. "No. If I die, they will take it. And then the dragon can't protect you." She pushed the comb back at me.

"But, Soo-hee, *Ummah* gave it to you. If you have it, it will help you. It has not helped me."

"It has helped you, little sister. You must believe in it."

Suddenly Soo-hee's eyes grew wide.

"What do we have here?" a voice boomed from behind me. I spun around, and saw the high, black boots of the *Kempei-tai.*

"*Kempei* sir," I said with a gasp. "The doctor gave me permission to visit my sister."

Lieutenant Tanaka stepped past me and peered down at Soo-hee. "What do you have there in your hand?" Soo-hee wrapped her hand around the comb. He bent down and slapped her hard. He pulled the comb from her hand.

"No!" I cried, lunging for the comb.

Lieutenant Tanaka grabbed a fistful of my hair and held me away. I ignored the pain and fought for the comb but he was too strong. He held the comb up and examined it. "My, my," he said. "You have been hiding it all this time? You should have given it to your *kempei.*"

I stopped struggling but Lieutenant Tanaka held on to my hair. "Please sir, let Soo-hee have it," I pleaded. "It will help her get well."

"Oh, no, I cannot do that. Colonel Matsumoto should see it, don't you agree? I'll give it to him when I tell him why you will not be with him tonight."

"*Kempei*, Seiko asked the doctor for permission for me to come here. He said I could."

"That's not what Seiko told me. She said you asked her to watch for me so you could sneak in here against orders. Come," he said with a jerk of my hair, "let's go see Colonel Matsumoto."

As Lieutenant Tanaka dragged me away, Soo-hee pushed herself up on an elbow. "*Kempei*, Sir," she said, "the comb is mine, not Ja-hee's. I should be punished for hiding it."

Lieutenant Tanaka looked down at Soo-hee. "If you're going to die, girl, do it more quickly," he said evenly. "And don't worry about your sister. I will take care of her."

FOURTEEN

LIEUTENANT TANAKA HAD a firm grip on my arm as we stood in Colonel Matsumoto's office. The Colonel studied maps spread across his desk. Dark, rough-hewn wooden beams crisscrossed the high ceiling. Windows with Chinese latticework overlooked a courtyard in the center of Dongfeng. A photograph of Emperor Hirohito hung on a wall, a map of Manchuria hung on another. The white and red military flag of Japan stood in a corner. The Colonel had not bathed after his return from the battlefield and his field uniform was dirty. There were dark circles around his eyes and fatigue creased his once-smooth face.

"Colonel, sir," Lieutenant Tanaka said, "this girl disobeyed orders and must be punished."

"What did she do?" he asked, without looking up from his maps.

"She was in a restricted area against my orders."

"Where?"

"In the infirmary, sir."

"The infirmary?"

"Yes, sir. Visiting her sister."

"That is not a serious offense, Lieutenant," the colonel said. "Why do you bother me with it? I have much more important matters to attend to."

"Sir, you asked for her tonight. I thought you should know why she won't be available."

"Really Lieutenant, is this necessary?"

"Sir, there's something else you should know. This one has been hiding a comb." He pulled the comb with the two-headed dragon from his jacket pocket and put it on the desk.

The Colonel gave the lieutenant a hard look. "A comb, Lieutenant? With what is happening in the war, you are concerned that this girl has been hiding a comb?"

"Sir, it shows a lack of discipline."

The Colonel pushed away from his desk and paced across the wood-planked floor. "Our homeland is under attack, Lieutenant," he bellowed. "We fight the Americans in the east, the Chinese in the south, and now the Russians in the north. They are less than one-hundred miles away and they are advancing with ten divisions." He placed his palms on the desk and leaned toward Tanaka. "The Russians are well equipped and well trained. We do not have the forces or the equipment to… " The Colonel held his eyes on the lieutenant for a moment, and then he took a quick look at me. He sat down and stared at his desk.

Eventually, he noticed the comb. He picked it up and examined it. He asked me where I got it.

I bowed. "From my mother, sir. It has been in our family for a long time."

The Colonel brought it close to his face. "It… it has a two-headed dragon and its feet have five toes," he whispered.

"Sir?" I said.

"Five-toed dragon, with two heads." He looked at me wide-eyed, then turned to Lieutenant Tanaka. "Do not discipline this girl, Lieutenant."

Lieutenant Tanaka stiffened and pointed to his white armband. "Sir, I am *Kempei-tai* and I am responsible for the comfort station. I take orders from my own officers. I'm only telling you because she is scheduled with you tonight."

"Yes, you are *Kempei-tai*," Colonel Matsumoto said with a glare, "and I am a colonel, Lieutenant."

"Yes sir, but I must maintain discipline. For the Emperor. For Japan."

"For the Emperor. For Japan," the Colonel repeated slowly. He looked at the comb and ran his finger along the gold spine. He slipped it into his shirt pocket and looked away. Then he said, "I will take Seiko tonight, Lieutenant."

Lieutenant Tanaka gave a small nod. "Yes sir." He grabbed me, pushing his fingers hard into my arm. As Lieutenant Tanaka dragged me to the door, I looked over my shoulder at the colonel. Behind his huge desk and alongside the flag of Japan, he looked small.

*

Lieutenant Tanaka called for Private Ishida as he led me into the comfort station courtyard. "Get the rope," he said. "I have a lesson to give." The private jumped to his feet. Our eyes met and he hesitated a moment. Then he quickly disappeared around the back of the barracks.

Lieutenant Tanaka pushed me toward the post. I fell to the yellow dirt and he stood over me with his *shinai* at his side. He ordered me to take off my clothes.

I had always been terrified of getting a beating from Lieutenant Tanaka. I almost fainted when I watched Jin-sook scream and urinate on herself the first day at the comfort station. And I had to fight to stay upright all three

times the *kempei* had beaten Soo-hee. Now for the first time, it was my turn at the post. But I wasn't afraid. I had turned hard over the previous two years.

So I untied my *obi* and let my *yukata* fall to the ground. As I slipped off my *zori* and *tabi*, I looked out over the courtyard past the road, over the wheat fields, south toward Korea. I tried to remember the place where Soo-hee and I made *kimchi* in the kitchen of our home, where our mother had combed my hair in front of the fire. But no images came, only the gray of this place where I had been dying each day for the past two years.

Private Ishida returned with the ropes and handed them to Lieutenant Tanaka. The private didn't look at me as I untied my undergarments and let them fall to the ground.

Lieutenant Tanaka ordered the private to gather the other Korean girls. Then he pushed me against the post. I offered no resistance as he tied my hands and ankles tight to the post. A cool breeze swept over my body. It honestly felt good. The earth, warmed by the afternoon sun, was soothing on my bare feet. The air tasted sweet. I closed my eyes for a minute and heard soft booms to the west. I wondered if it was the Russian cannons. But the Colonel had said the Russians were still far away.

The other girls gathered in the courtyard and stood in a line facing me. When Mee-su saw me tied to the post, she brought her hand to her mouth, but quickly took her place with the others. Seiko and a few other Japanese women sat on their steps and watched as Lieutenant Tanaka finished with the ropes. He began pacing in front of the girls.

"This girl has earned a beating," he said, slapping his *shinai* against his boot harder than usual. "When will you learn that you must not displease your *kempei*? Do you think I enjoy this? Do you think I *want* to beat you? No! I give you these lessons for your sake, so you will learn to be good Japanese subjects. Soon, we will win the war and you will be

glad you are on our side. Now you will watch the punishment without closing your eyes."

Lieutenant Tanaka approached me. His thin lips were curled up at the ends, but his eyes were like a doll's eyes, cold and lifeless. I looked past him, south toward Korea.

Then he raised his *shinai* and brought it down hard on my thighs. The blow shot white-hot flames down my legs and up my back. My stomach clenched hard and my lungs and throat seized sending sharp needles of pain into my head and nose. The Lieutenant struck me again in the same place and the flames from the first blow exploded into a thousand more. My lungs let go and a huge, jagged cry boiled up to my throat. But before it could escape, I grabbed it and choked it back down. And as the *kempei* beat me, I kept my cries inside where I was dead like stone.

*

I could barely make out Private Ishida's face as he carried me to the infirmary. He kept his eyes forward and muttered something under his breath about Lieutenant Tanaka. As he carried me up the stairs, the fire in my legs made me moan. The private stopped and carefully shifted my weight in his arms. He slowed his pace and carried me across the ward. He laid me next to Soo-hee.

I couldn't move my legs and my eyes didn't focus. My head was heavy on the mat.

"*Onni*," I said weakly, "I'm sorry."

"Don't be sorry, Ja-hee," my *onni* said. "You did not do anything wrong."

"I was strong," I said. "I didn't cry."

Soo-hee reached over and stroked my hair. "I know," Soo-hee said. Her eyes were red and her face was pale. A tear ran down her cheek. "You were strong."

"Soo-hee," I said, "they've taken the comb."

"Hush, little sister," Soo-hee whispered. "Hush and go to sleep."

*

Four days later, I lay on my mat in my tiny, stinking room as soldier after soldier raped me. The bone-deep ache in my legs from Lieutenant Tanaka's beating combined with the fiery pain between them was almost too much to bear. To protect my thighs, I had to spread my legs wide, which made the soldier's thrusts more painful. Eventually, I found a position that delivered the pain evenly between my bruised thighs and raw vagina so I could keep going.

For the past two days, an endless line of soldiers circulated in and out of our courtyard as cannon fire boomed in the distance. The soldiers were crueler than usual. They slapped me, pulled my hair, and mounted me roughly, desperate to purify their souls before they went off to battle.

As another filthy soldier climbed on top of me, I thought of Soo-hee. I had been able to spend only one night with her on the infirmary's cold tile floor before Lieutenant Tanaka saw that Private Ishida had placed us together. He made Doctor Watanabe put us at opposite ends of the ward. When I saw her last, my *onni* was pale and weak, but she was still alive, fighting for her life.

At last, there were no more soldiers at my step. I struggled to make my aching legs work as I pushed myself off my mat, wrapped my *yukata* around me and picked up my chamber pot that no longer hid the comb with the two-headed dragon. When I pushed the door open, Lieutenant Tanaka was at the foot of my steps with his *shinai* at his side. "You have the Colonel again tonight, Namiko Iwata."

"Yes, *Kempei*," I said trying not to show how weak I was.

"Oh, and I'm sorry to tell you, Doctor Watanabe reports that your sister is not doing well. He says she has

only days to live. And in case you're thinking about sneaking out to see her again, I've told Private Ishida to keep a close eye on you and shoot you if you get near the infirmary."

"Yes, *Kempei*."

"Now go clean up for the Colonel," Lieutenant Tanaka said, walking away. "Do your job well. He is under a lot of stress and needs to stay strong for Japan."

And then I finally saw the end. If Soo-hee died, I would die, too. I would hang myself with my *obi* like Sun-hi did. I had only enough strength left to do that. The end did not make me sad or anxious. It only made me glad that soon my nightmare would be over.

As I pushed myself toward the latrine, I saw that Seiko and the other Japanese women were gone. Private Ishida leaned against the barracks wall and watched as I walked by. He looked in the direction of Lieutenant Tanaka and then at me again. I thought he wanted to say something, but he stayed silent. I went to the latrine and as I washed, I could hear trucks on the road and movement in the village. The cannons in the distance were louder than they were in the morning.

FIFTEEN

WHEN I WENT to be with the Colonel, he was sitting in a black, short-legged chair with an ornate carved back. Over his square frame, he wore a white dress uniform with a stiff collar and red insignia. An empty bottle of *sake* lay on its side on a rosewood table next to him. There was another full bottle and two glasses next to it. He had moved the picture of his family from the bed to the table where he sat. The latticed windows were open to the street below and a breeze blew in.

I had never seen the Colonel in a formal uniform. I wondered if there had been a mistake and I was supposed to be with someone else that night. But when he saw me, he ordered me to come in. He nodded toward the rosewood bed and ordered me to sit. I removed my *zori* and placed them by the door. I sat on the edge of the bed and lowered my eyes.

"I see you are walking with a limp," the Colonel said. "Lieutenant Tanaka must have given you a good beating the other day."

"Yes sir," I said.

He shook his head lazily. "He says he is doing his job like an honorable Japanese soldier. But he does not know what honor is. Perhaps someday, I will show him." He lifted the glass to his mouth and drank the remaining *sake* in it. He grabbed the full bottle, uncorked it, and poured more *sake* into his glass.

The Colonel laughed lightly. "Drink some *sake* with me. It will ease your pain."

"Sir?" I said. He had never offered me *sake* before.

He poured *sake* in the other glass and held it out to me. "Here," he said. "*Sake*. Drink it."

I took the glass and returned to the bed. I held it in my lap. Outside the window, the wind made the trees sway.

"Drink it!" the Colonel ordered. "It's white *sake* from Japan, not the yellow swill they have here. Drink!"

I took a sip. I'd never had liquor before. It cut my tongue and burned my throat. I would have spit it out but I no longer cared about anything anymore, so I swallowed it.

"Good Japanese *sake*," the Colonel said, lifting his glass and admiring the clear liquid inside. "I've been saving it for someone special and you are it! Drink more, girl."

I took another drink. This time, it didn't burn as much and I started to feel warm.

The Colonel lifted the picture of his family and gazed at it. "Have you ever been to Japan, girl?" he asked. His speech was slurred. "No, of course you haven't. I will tell you about it. It is beautiful, not like this godforsaken country. My country has snow-capped mountains, blue seas, beautiful green islands, modern cities teeming with people and automobiles. We were the greatest country in the world!" He carefully set the picture down on the table and smiled sadly. "Drink to Japan, girl."

I took another drink.

He leaned toward me unsteadily. The glass of *sake* dangled between his middle finger and thumb and he pointed at me with his index finger. "It was a compelling idea," he said. "An empire from the Indian Ocean to the Bering Sea. From the Pacific Islands to China and India. Think of what we could have had! Think of what we could have done! We would have ruled the East for a thousand years!" He grinned at the thought, leaned back, and downed the contents of his glass. He filled it again.

He waved his free hand. "Everyone would have prospered. Not just the Japanese but all Asians. Especially you Koreans. The sacrifices we asked of you were no greater than our own. And you would have been rewarded!" The Colonel glared. "But you did not appreciate what we were doing for you."

"I'm sorry, sir," I said. "I do not care." I had never spoken to the Colonel like that, but I was feeling lightheaded. And I really did not care.

The Colonel laughed. His face was red and his eyes swam. The wind outside blew hard making the window bump against the wall. He swayed as if the wind were blowing him, too. "Of course you don't care. You are a stupid Korean! Let us drink a toast. Let's drink to Korea! Big drink this time." He raised his glass to me and together, we drank.

He grabbed his glass and the bottle and came to the bed. He loomed over me. "Here, more *sake* for you," he said, and poured more of it in my glass.

The room was starting to move and I was getting nauseous. I wasn't thinking clearly. "I do not want any more of your *sake*, sir," I said.

He took a step toward me and struck me with the back of his hand. I fell to the floor, spilling the *sake* on his Chinese rug. The blow hurt, but in a strange, dull way. I tasted blood in my mouth.

The Colonel picked up my glass and filled it to the top. "I said drink!" he roared. "I will drink to Korea and you will drink to Japan." I lifted myself onto the bed and he handed me the glass. I brought it to my mouth and took a drink. The *sake* no longer burned.

The Colonel leaned toward me unsteadily. He unbuttoned his collar. "Lieutenant Tanaka. *Kempei*," he said, slurring the word. "His job was to turn you into good Japanese subjects. He did not do a very good job, did he?"

"Yes sir. I mean, no sir," I said.

"Ha, ha, ha!" the Colonel laughed again. He swayed in front of me. Or perhaps it was me who was swaying. He slid into a chair. "It is unfortunate for him. And for you and for Japan. Take another drink," he ordered.

We drank together, the Colonel emptying his glass.

"Korea had things Japan needed," he said. "Minerals, protection from the Chinese and mongrel Russians! You are ignorant peasants and needed us, too. If you had done what we asked, it would have worked. It would have worked!" He pointed a finger at me. "It's your fault, you whore. You and your damned comb."

I wasn't sure I had heard him right. "My comb, sir?" I heard myself say. "Maybe I should go back to the comfort station."

"You cannot go there," he said. "You must stay here tonight. Do you hear me?"

I didn't understand what was going on. I didn't want to be there with him anymore and I didn't care if my impudence got me shot "Sir, I am going back to the comfort station now." I tried to stand.

He stumbled toward me with the *sake* bottle and a scowl on his face. He grabbed my cheeks with his thumb and fingers. He pushed me down and opened my mouth. He shoved the bottle in. "Shut up and drink with me, girl!" He emptied the *sake* down my throat. I swallowed what I could

and choked on the rest. He pulled the bottle away and I coughed and sputtered. *Sake* dribbled down my chin and onto my *yukata*.

"Please sir," I heard myself say, "let me go."

"No! Didn't you hear me? Don't you understand what I'm doing? I am saving you."

"I don't want to be saved," I said.

He threw the bottle aside, and it shattered against the wall. He struck me in the face with his fist. The pain was dull like something hard had hit me softly, or something soft had hit me hard. I wasn't sure. "You whore," I heard him say. "It's your fault! You made us do it! You made *me* do it." He hit me again and the room spun.

I thought I should say I was sorry—sorry for being a stupid Korean whore, sorry for not being a good Japanese subject, sorry for not being strong enough—but I really didn't care.

Outside, the trees swayed in the wind. I felt another blow against my face. There were stars in my head and then everything went dark.

*

I heard rain falling on the street outside the window. I opened my eyes and turned to the side. It was daylight. My head pounded and my mouth was dry. I pressed a finger against my lip. It was tender and puffy. I couldn't see well out of my left eye.

I lifted my head and looked around. I couldn't tell if I was alone. A strong wind blew in from the window behind the Colonel's desk. I stood unsteadily and wrapped my *yukata* around me. It stunk like *sake*. I tried to focus on the door, but the room moved. My stomach convulsed and I fell to my knees next to the bed and retched. Green bile spewed from me onto the Chinese rug. I retched three times more.

My head pounded so hard with each one, I was afraid I would pass out again. I spit sour bile from my mouth. Eventually I caught my breath and the room stopped moving.

I looked up and thought I saw something on the bed. I forced my eyes to focus on it. On the white linen, where I couldn't miss it, was the comb with the two-headed dragon.

I stood uneasily and looked around the room. I thought I might be dreaming. The desk chair was on its side. Empty drawers were scattered around the room. The military flag of Japan lay on the floor, ripped in half.

The pounding in my head eased a little. I looked again at the comb. The gold spine glistened and the dragon reached for me like it did the day I left home. I picked it up and slid it inside my *yukata*. I stumbled to the door. I slipped my feet in my *zori* and went out into the rain. The shower of cold rain brought me out of my fog a little and I saw that the entire village was on the move. Military trucks rumbled slowly along the narrow streets. Lines of soldiers walked alongside the trucks with their heads down and rain dripping from their helmets. They were all marching east.

I dragged myself through the muddy streets toward the comfort station. I smelled something burning as I came to the back of the latrine. I peered around the corner at the comfort station. One of the barracks was on fire and Private Ishida was setting fire to another. Lieutenant Tanaka paced in the middle of the courtyard. The Korean girls stood in a line, facing the back end of a green, canvas-covered truck. The rain made their hair and clothes cling to their bodies.

"Where is Namiko Iwata!" the lieutenant shouted above the rain. "Where is Ja-hee? I want to know!"

Jin-sook stepped forward and bowed. "She did not come back last night, sir."

Lieutenant Tanaka took a step toward Jin-sook. He lifted her head with the tip of his *shinai*. "You wouldn't lie to me, would you girl?"

"No, sir," she answered. "Not me."

The *kempei* lowered his *shinai*. "Ja-hee was with the Colonel last night," he said. "Well, well. I think our leader has gone soft. I had better see about that. Carry on, Private," he said to Private Ishida. As he walked away, he threw his *shinai* in the burning barracks.

Private Ishida went to the truck and lifted the canvas flap. He stepped away and from inside the darkness, a machine gun opened fire.

SIXTEEN

THEY KILLED FIVE of my *ianfu* sisters immediately. Three girls froze in fright and soon, the thundering, heavy-caliber gun found them and put them down like the first five.

Jin-sook fell to her knees. "No!" she cried. "Why me?" The gunner put several bullets in her, throwing her body into the mud with her legs twisted underneath her. Mee-su ran screaming toward the latrine with her hands over her ears. Private Ishida lifted his rifle and shot her square in the back. She flopped to the mud, arms out, limp like a rag doll. Then the machine gun was silent and there was only the smell of gunpowder and the splatter of rain falling on mud.

Private Ishida lowered his rifle and stared at the lifeless body of Mee-su. His mouth was open and his head cocked to the side as if he was trying to understand what he had just done. He stared for several seconds. Then he looked directly at me. I held his eyes, stepped out from behind the latrine, and faced him without fear. He raised his rifle but he did not shoot. I reached inside my *yukata* and pulled out the comb. I held it in my hand. As I looked down the barrel of Private

Ishida's rifle, I saw all the women in my family who like me, had once held the comb in their hands, too. I saw them all the way back to my great-great grandmother, the *yangban* who'd had the comb made. And they told me to run.

So I ran. As fast as my sore legs could carry me, I ran behind the latrine toward the village. To my left was the laundry and in front of me the white walls of the infirmary. I slipped in the mud, pushed myself up and ran inside the infirmary. I ran up the stairs to the ward. It was empty except for Soo-hee. I went to her and grabbed her arm. "Soo-hee," I panted. "They're shooting us! We have to run!"

Soo-hee's eyes were sunken and her skin was as pale as snow. "I can't," she said weakly.

I tugged harder. "You have to. They will kill us!" Soo-hee winced in pain and I let go of her arm.

I stood over Soo-hee with the comb in my hand and saw that she was too weak to move. And then I knew it was over. I lay on the cold tile floor next to my *onni*. "Okay," I said. "We will die together."

Soo-hee lifted her head off the mat and took in a pained breath. "Ja-hee," she said. "You must go without me."

I shook my head. "No Soo-hee. I cannot." I was finally at peace. I was ready to die.

With effort, Soo-hee rolled toward me. "Yes you can, Ja-hee. You have the comb with the dragon, there in your hand. You were born in the year of the dragon. You can survive this. The comb will protect you."

I opened my hand and looked at the comb. "I do not believe in the comb," I said. "It didn't help *Ummah* and it did not save us from this."

"You can still be saved," Soo-hee said, "and then you can tell them what happened here."

"I don't want anyone to know what happened here," I said.

"Then," Soo-hee said, "they will get away with it."

I heard footsteps from the stairway at the other end of the ward. Men were talking in clipped voices. Soo-hee touched my arm. "You must go," she whispered. "Please do this for me. Do it for all of us."

I glanced down the long corridor, then back at my *onni*. Her eyes were sunken and sad. I so wanted to stay with Soo-hee, to let it all be over.

The footsteps grew louder. "Oh, Soo-hee," I said.

"Goodbye little sister," Soo-hee said weakly. "Go now. Hurry!"

I reached over and stroked Soo-hee's hair. I gave my *onni* one last look and pushed down another cry. Then, with the comb in my hand, I ran for the door. My legs no longer hurt and my head didn't pound. I ran down the stairs and out into the street. The rain was falling hard among the colorless procession of soldiers. I didn't see Private Ishida or Lieutenant Tanaka. I cut between two buildings and the roofs dripped rainwater on me. I ran through a courtyard and between two more buildings. I came to a grass strip separating the village from a wheat field. I looked to my left, then to my right and ran for the field.

From somewhere behind me, Lieutenant Tanaka shouted, "There she is! Shoot! SHOOT HER!" A rifle shot rang out and mud splattered a circle near my feet. I ran as fast as I could and reached the wheat field as another shot rang out. The bullet snapped through the stalks alongside me. I ran into the field. Mud grabbed at my *zori*, so I let them slip off. I ran and ran but the stiff, sharp wheat stalks cut my feet. I dropped to my hands and knees and crawled, gripping the comb as I went. Boots splashed in the mud behind me. I crawled with all my strength, but I kept slipping in the mud. The footsteps came closer. Over my shoulder, I saw Private Ishida scanning the wheat field for me, his rifle in both hands. He spotted me and ran up to me. I rolled over on my back. The private aimed his rifle at me.

I held the comb in front of me. Rain struck my face and ran in my eyes. I blinked it away and met the eyes of Private Ishida. "Private," I said, "your people have already killed me many times. Let me live this once."

He held his aim. Rain dripped off the rifle barrel and the bill of his cap. He held nervous eyes on me for several seconds. Then he whispered, "They'll shoot me if they find out. Stay here until we leave." He pulled the rifle barrel a few inches to the left and fired twice into the ground making mud splatter on my face. He ran back to the village.

I couldn't breathe. My ears rang from the rifle shots and I wondered if I was still alive. Eventually, the ringing went away and all I heard was rain patting on the ground next to me. I pulled my arms and legs to my chest. I wanted to cry but I hadn't allowed myself to cry for so long I didn't know how so tears never came.

*

Darkness. The rain had stopped and the air was still. I lay on my side, my knees to my chest, shivering in the cold, sticky mud. Inky clouds slid away revealing bright stars in a moonless sky. The only sound I heard was a dog barking from somewhere in the village.

I pushed myself to my knees, and then unsteadily to my feet. There was no movement in the village and no lights. I held the comb with the two-headed dragon tight in my fist.

I walked barefoot through the wheat field, across the grass to the village. The pain in my thighs from Lieutenant Tanaka's beating had come back making it difficult to walk. The bruises on my face from Colonel Matsumoto's blows had turned into a sharp ache. I stumbled down an abandoned street to the infirmary. I pulled myself up the dark stairs to the ward and went to where Soo-hee had been. I pulled aside the white sheet. My *onni* wasn't there.

I left the infirmary and went to the comfort station. They had burned the barracks to the ground. A few lonely flames danced among the smoldering remains. And there I saw the bodies of the eleven girls lying in a jagged line, lifeless, like mounds of dirt.

I stood in the courtyard and all the cries I had pushed down for so long roiled and raged inside me. I felt the stone in my stomach crack. I closed my eyes, fell to my knees, threw back my head, and opened my throat. And all my cries burst out.

I kneeled on the muddy ground with my face to the sky and a thousand cries met a thousand stars in the moonless Manchurian night. I cried for my innocence and for each time they called me a whore. I cried for the dead girls who had been my sisters. I cried for my mother and father. And I cried for Soo-hee. The cries ripped out my stomach, my lungs, and my heart until there was nothing left inside and I collapsed, empty, to the mud.

*

Daylight. The smell of burned wood. The sticky wet of mud underneath me. A crow cawed nearby. I felt the stillness of death.

I drew a breath and opened my eyes. The sun was at its mid-morning angle. The air was calm. Here and there, thin lines of smoke drifted up from the barracks' charred remains. A crow perched on the dead body of Mee-su pecking at her eyes.

I heard the sound of a truck behind me. A truck door opened and I heard footsteps in the mud. The crow cawed and slapped its wings in flight. I heard voices in a strange language.

A boot like I had never seen before—dirty and well used—kicked me. A voice said something in a language I

didn't understand. The boot kicked again sending pain into my ribs. I lifted my head and looked to where the voice had come from. I saw a man's face.

His eyes were blue.

SEVENTEEN

August 2008. Seoul, South Korea

MRS. HONG IS giving me an "I-told-you-so" stare. I look inside my empty teacup. I tell her I didn't know anything about the comfort women. After I say it, I realize I sound incredibly lame.

"I am telling you," she replies, "because you must know."

"To fulfill your promise to your sister," I say. "To tell what happened to you."

"Yes, but you must also know because you are a Korean. You should know what happened to your country. You need to know your people. Anyway, you have only heard part of my story. There is more, much more I have to tell you."

There's more? She's still dressed in her yellow *hanbok*, sitting upright in her chair, ready to go on. Me? I need to stop. I'm tired and confused. I now have more questions than when I got here. It just doesn't make sense—the gold comb in the hands of this poor woman, her incredible story. I need time to process this.

A breeze blows through the window and clouds are forming outside. It smells like it does before it rains. I look down at the street. I check my watch. It's 12:45. The cab won't be here for over two hours and I have no other way to get back to the hotel. I have to stay.

"Ma'am," I say, "I'll listen to the rest of your story. But what is it about this comb? I mean, it's just an heirloom right?"

Mrs. Hong shakes her head. "It is important that you take the time to understand what it is so you know what it means for you."

"I'm sorry, but I don't know if I should take it," I say. "I don't want to break any laws."

Suddenly there's a loud knock on the door. A man's voice shouts something in Korean. My eyes snap to Mrs. Hong. "The police," she whispers. Her weird smile rattles me as much as the knocking at the door. "They're here for the comb!"

I look at the table where Mrs. Hong set the package with the comb. It isn't there. The knocking turns into pounding. My heart starts racing. "Anna," Mrs. Hong says, "listen carefully. Tell them that you went to an address that came with the comb and gave it back to the person who gave it to you. Then you came to visit me. Do you understand?"

"Why?" I ask.

"They cannot have the comb," she says.

Mrs. Hong goes to the door and opens it. In the hallway are two men. Mrs. Hong bows, but the men push past her into the apartment. The taller one is dressed in a smooth suit and looks like a government man you see on TV. The other guy is bald and looks like an Asian version of Bruce Willis. He's wearing a sports coat a size too small that shows off his impressive biceps. Two policemen follow them in. I quickly stand as Government Man comes up to me.

"Are you Anna Carlson?" Government Man asks. His English is well practiced with only a slight trace of an accent.

I shoot a nervous look at Mrs. Hong. "Yes," I say.

"And this is your grandmother, Hong Ja-hee?" Government Man asks pointing at Mrs. Hong.

"Yes it is? Who are you?"

"My name is Mr. Kwan," he answers. "I'm here for the comb you showed Mr. Kim yesterday. It might be a valuable Korean artifact. I wanted to talk to you at the hotel this morning, but your father said you were sick and had to stay in bed. But now we find you here. You lied. So, where is the comb?"

"I… I don't have it. I gave it back. Are you with the police?"

Mr. Kwan takes out his I.D. and shows it to me. It is in Hangul so I can't read it, but it looks official enough. He tells me he's with the National Police. He asks who I gave the comb to.

"There was an address with it," I say quickly. "I went there and gave it back. Then I came here to visit my grandmother." My knees are shaking and I don't want Mr. Kwan to see so I move closer to the table.

"I don't believe you," Mr. Kwan replies clearly noticing my move into the table. "Anyway, it doesn't matter. If the comb is here, we will find it." He motions Bruce Willis over to me. As the policeman start to search the apartment, Bruce motions for me to raise my arms.

"Are you going to frisk me?" I ask unsteadily.

"Yes we are," Mr. Kwan answers. Bruce has a metal-detecting wand so thank God he doesn't have to touch me. He waves the thing over my entire body. When he's satisfied that I don't have the comb, he turns to Mrs. Hong. Her twisted grin makes me even more nervous. Bruce says something to her in Korean and waves his wand over her. He doesn't' find anything on her, either.

Mr. Kwan points to the table. "Both of you sit," he orders.

We sit at the table and Mr. Kwan stands over us with his arms folded as the policemen search the apartment. They're amazingly thorough. They disassemble parts of the stove, pour the *bori cha* down the drain and look inside the pot, remove the trap in the sink, wave the wand over every inch of the bed mat. They wand all of Mrs. Hong's clothing, pour out the rice from the burlap bag in the cupboard, examine the light fixture in the ceiling, turn over the table and chairs. They look everywhere but when they're done, they haven't found the comb. I begin to wonder myself where it is.

Finally, the police are done and Bruce Willis shrugs. Mr. Kwan turns to me. He asks me if I remember the address where I took the comb and how I got there. I say I don't remember and I don't know where it was. He asks me to describe the comb and I give him a general description of it. He writes everything I say on his pad.

Then he asks, "Did the dragon have five toes? Try to remember. This is important."

I remember Mrs. Hong's story that Colonel Matsumoto was amazed that the dragon had five toes but I didn't notice it myself. "I don't remember seeing that," I say.

"So you gave the comb back and then you came here?" he asks. "Why?"

"To meet my grandmother. To hear her story."

"Her story?" he says. "I can only imagine what she is telling you. But you should know that if she was an honorable woman, she would live in the comfort woman home in Gwanju instead of this place."

He turns to Mrs. Hong. "I have read your papers Hong, Ja-hee. What are you hiding? Why do you live in this place and not at the House of Sharing? You would be honored there along with the other comfort women."

Mrs. Hong glares at him but doesn't say anything. Mr. Kwan says, "Perhaps it is because you were a *chinulpa?*"

He turns back to me and I swallow hard. "Is she the one who gave you the comb? Answer me."

I'm starting to panic. I don't want to tell the truth, but I don't want to lie either. Mr. Kwan motions to Bruce who comes and stands behind me. Mr. Kwan puts his hands on the table and looks at me straight in the eye. He's scowling making me wish I'd never come here. He tells me people have stolen Korea's national treasures from for hundreds of years. He says it's illegal to take artifacts out of Korea and that I'll be in a lot of trouble if I do. He says the comb might be very important to Korea. "Now I want answers," he says. "I ask you again. Is this the person who gave you the comb?"

I feel the hulking presence of Bruce behind me and I'm about to cry. "I... I," I stammer.

Mr. Kwan slams his fist on the table making both me and the teacups jump. "Answer me!" he barks. "You know where it is and I want you to tell me. Now!"

Tears are welling in my eyes. I can't breathe. If these men want to hurt me, there's nothing I can do to stop them. I take a deep breath and prepare to tell them everything they want to know.

Then in a flash, Mrs. Hong is on her feet pushing Mr. Kwan toward the door. "Get out!" she screams. "Get out of my apartment this minute!"

Mr. Kwan steps back, surprised at her rage. "Ma'am, do not get in our way. This is an official matter."

She takes an angry step toward him. "Do you think I'm afraid of you?" she growls. "Do you think you can do anything to me that has not already been done? You are nothing! I have suffered all my life for Korea. I can suffer a lot more." She steps in to Mr. Kwan's face. "She doesn't have the comb and you have searched my apartment. Now

go, find who has it instead of threatening me and my granddaughter!"

Mr. Kwan locks eyes with Mrs. Hong. Then he blinks twice. After a few long seconds, he turns to me and asks what my plans are for the rest of the day. I tell him after I'm done here, I plan to buy a celadon pot and then go to the hotel to catch the bus for the airport.

"Good," he says. "Be sure you are on your flight tonight or I will have you arrested. Is that clear?"

I assure him he's very clear and he shoots another look at Mrs. Hong who hasn't backed away an inch. He turns to leave but stops mid-step. "Oh and by the way, the best place to buy a celadon pot is at Kosney's Department store, not from the shops on the streets. The quality is much better. It's worth the higher price."

"Thank you," I say. He gives me a diplomatic smile and then he and the others leave.

Mrs. Hong comes back to the table. All the anger she showed only seconds earlier is gone. She asks if I'm alright.

I shake my head. My heart is pounding. The apartment is shrinking in on me and I'm suffocating. "They… they were going to hurt me," I gasp. "I have to go." I grab my purse and push away from the table.

"No, stay," she says. "You will be fine."

"No I'm not fine!" I cry. "I have to get out of here." I head for the door.

"If you leave now Ja-young, you will prove that I was wrong about you," she says.

I quickly turn back. "Look, my name is Anna and I'm sorry if I'm afraid, but I can't do this." I fight back tears as I march to the door and pull on my shoes.

As I reach for the door handle, she says, "It is your fear that will prevent you from becoming who you are meant to be." I grip the door handle hard but don't turn it.

"Don't you want to know, Anna?" she asks, gently.

EIGHTEEN

MRS. HONG TELLS me to come back to the table. "You are safe here," she says. I let go of the door handle and slowly push my shoes off. I go back and sit with her. She's perfectly composed which is only a little reassuring. She points at the blossom in the bowl on the windowsill. "It's beautiful in the sunlight, don't you think?" she asks.

"Yeah, I guess," I say.

"Every two or three days I get a new one at the market even though I can't afford it. Notice how the sun brings out the colors. You can see the veins in each petal." I don't look at it that closely.

"That blossom started as a seed," she continues. "It was buried deep in the cold, dark ground. One day when the soil was warm and moist, the little seed split apart and began to climb to a world it could not see. Imagine the courage it had! It did not know what it would find when it broke through the surface. The scorching sun? The gardener's blade? The crushing hoof of a cow? But the seed courageously pushed on so that one day, it could become a beautiful flower."

She points a finger at me. "You must have the courage of the seed, Anna. Without it, you will stay buried. You will rot and die. It does not matter how smart you are, or how pretty, or if you have money and many friends. If you do not have courage, you will never blossom into the flower you were meant to be."

"I don't have much courage," I say.

She raises an eyebrow. "You have more than you think. It took a great deal of courage to come here today. And you didn't tell that awful man what he wanted to know."

"I was about to tell him everything," I admit.

"Perhaps. But you didn't."

She goes to the stove to put on another pot of *bora cha*. "Tell me Anna," she says from the stove, "do you know what kind of flower it is?"

I glance at it. "It looks like a hibiscus," I say. "We have a bush in our back yard."

"Very good. You are correct. It is in the hibiscus family." She turns on the stove and comes back to the table. "In Korea we call it a *mugunghwa* blossom. Have you ever heard of it?"

"I think one of our tour guides told us it's used in Korean architecture. Something about the House of Yi."

"Did the guide tell you anything more?"

"I don't remember," I say. I'm losing the battle against my nerves. I don't want to talk about the *mugunghwa* blossom or the House of Yi. I'm afraid that Mr. Kwan and Bruce Willis will come crashing back in and arrest me. I just want to get away.

Mrs. Hong frowns. "You need to pay attention. The *mugunghwa* was the symbol of the Chosŏn Dynasty of Korea. The House of Yi was our ruling family from the fourteenth century until the Japanese annexed our country in 1910 and turned Korea into a slave state."

"Yes, it was a terrible thing the Japanese did," I say.

"The Americans, too," Mrs. Hong says.

"The Americans?"

She sighs. "Ja-young, for all of our history, world powers, including America, have exploited us." Do you remember how the Russo-Japanese war ended?"

"No. I haven't studied history."

"You should," she says. "The U.S. negotiated the treaty in 1905. However, to get the Japanese to sign, and so Tokyo would not challenge America in the Philippines, your President Roosevelt secretly agreed to let Japan occupy Korea. And that is just what they did. They took our country and said Korea was now part of Japan. Of course, because of that secret agreement, America did nothing. The result was thirty-five years of horrible oppression of my people— like being raped by their soldiers

"But Americans didn't rape you," I say.

"No," she snaps back, "but they let it happen to protect their own interests."

She lets her point sink in. Then she goes to the stove, pours two cups of *bori cha* and brings them to the table. The aroma fills the room. I take a sip and immediately the strong, bitter liquid calms my nerves. Mrs. Hong sits in her chair, relaxed and poised.

She turns her attention to the blossom again. "The *mugunghwa* is not only beautiful, it has a pleasant fragrance, too. Smell it."

"What? You want me to smell it?"

"Yes," she answers.

I lean over and take a sniff.

"No, no," she says. "Take the bowl in both of your hands and smell it that way."

I lift the bowl from the sill and bring it to my nose. The fragrance is earthy and sweet. "I see what you mean," I say.

Before I can put the bowl back, she lifts an end of the windowsill. There's a small compartment underneath. She

reaches inside and lifts out the package of coarse brown cloth. I have no idea when she put it there. It must have been sometime during her story about the comfort station when I wasn't looking. Dumbstruck, I continue to hold the bowl with the *mugunghwa* blossom in my hands.

She giggles like a kid who just got away with something. "I have lived in this apartment for thirty-five years," she says. "Practically since the building was new. I have hidden the comb here all that time. I knew they wouldn't find it."

She sets the package on the table and pulls on the twine. The cloth falls open, and there's the comb with the two-headed dragon.

"By the way," I say setting the blossom back on the sill, "you said there were two things you wanted me to do. One was to hear your story. What's the other thing? You haven't said yet."

She moves the *mugunghwa* blossom to the table next to the comb and the two photographs. "Listen to the rest of my story first."

I'm still a bit shook up but her confidence reassures me. I lean back, ready to listen again.

"Where were we before we were so rudely interrupted?" she asks.

"The Japanese left and the Russians had come."

"Ah yes," she nods. She holds her teacup in both hands. "The communists. How disappointing."

NINETEEN

September 1945. Dongfeng, Manchuria.

FOR TWO YEARS in Dongfeng when I dared to dream, I dreamed of the day I'd be free and could go back home. I thought it would be the happiest day of my life. But when the day finally came, I was lost and alone. With the Japanese, I always knew what I had to do—laundry in the morning before the soldiers came, cooking on the days the *geishas* assigned it to me, servicing the soldiers all afternoon and night. I wasn't allowed to go anywhere outside the comfort station except the infirmary for my monthly inspection and the officer's quarters at night. My routine was simple and my world was small. But now it was gone and I didn't know what to do.

And I was afraid. I was afraid of the Russians with their strange, guttural language. I was afraid the Japanese might come back and kill me.

So for days I hid among the low stucco buildings of Dongfeng still dressed in my green *yukata*. I snuck from

empty house to empty house, always staying far away from the comfort station. I ate what food I could find and each night I took shelter in one of the abandoned houses, curled up in a dark corner, and tried to sleep.

One day, I went inside a house that had a mirror and I saw my reflection. At first, I didn't recognize myself. But gradually, I could see it was me who was dressed in the green *yukata*. I was horrified. I immediately stripped off the *yukata* and searched the house until I found regular clothes.

I do not know how many days I lived like that. It might have been weeks. But eventually, the Russians caught me and took me to their headquarters in Colonel Matsumoto's old office. The thick-browed Russian officer sitting at Colonel Matsumoto's desk spoke Japanese and asked me what I was doing in Dongfeng. I couldn't answer his question. I honestly didn't know what to tell him. He asked me where I was from.

"Korea," I answered.

"You were one of the Korean girls," he stated.

"Have you found Soo-hee?" I asked. "She is two years older than me."

"We only found the bodies by the burned out barracks. You're the only one we found alive."

I was too numb and confused to put together all that had happened those last days at the comfort station. I must have looked confused, too, because the officer said, "The Japanese have surrendered. They're gone. Go back to your home. You can't stay here."

I didn't know exactly where my home was from Dongfeng, so I asked the Russian officer. He told me it was two-hundred-eighty miles to Sinuiju and there was no transportation there. Apparently, I'd have to walk the entire way. The Russians gave me some rice which I wrapped along with the comb in a wool blanket.

I was afraid to go back home where I would have to tell my mother and father I had been an *ianfu*. How could they possibly understand? But I longed to see them again and have things the way they were before. So on a clear morning, I lifted the blanket sack to my shoulder and asked an old Chinese farmer which way it was to Korea. The farmer nodded down the road and I set off.

After a mile, I turned onto the main road. I looked back at the low, tile-roof buildings of Dongfeng and thought of the eleven girls I knew there, my *ianfu* sisters. I thought of my *onni,* Soo-hee. Somehow, I had survived and I wondered why. Perhaps it was because I had been born in the year of the dragon. Maybe the comb had brought me good luck after all. Whatever the reason, I had to go on. I had to go on for them. So I joined a thin gray column of refugees with bundles on their backs, pots and utensils tied to their waists and children in tow. There were young and old, Chinese and Koreans, bent under their loads, going east, going south—going home.

*

I walked for many miles each day. Then on the third day, a Russian soldier offered me a ride on the back of his flatbed truck. I was tired and my feet were sore so I climbed up and hung on. After a few miles, the driver stopped where there was no one on the road. He pulled me off the truck and led me to the ditch. I lay in the dewy grass and opened my dress as the driver unbuttoned his trousers. He went to mount me, but he wasn't stiff yet.

"Slap me," I said in Japanese.

He looked at me confused. "Slap me hard!" I yelled. I took his hand and made him slap my face. "Pinch me!" I demanded. I brought his fingers to my breasts and made

him pinch me. "Come on!" I screamed at him. "I know what you like. Aren't you a man?"

He pulled back confused and started to button his trousers. I flew into a rage. I jumped on him. I scratched his face and spit on him. I screamed at him, nasty words that I learned from the Japanese *geishas*. I punched him in the nose making it bleed. He punched me back throwing me hard to the ground.

"What's the matter?" I said looking up at him. I'd never had anyone pull away like that before. He walked backwards to his truck mumbling something in Russian. He climbed in and drove off, leaving me alone in the ditch.

I sat in the tall grass and watched the truck disappear down the road. And then I laughed. I laughed out loud at the stupid Russian driver who thought I wouldn't know what to do. I faced toward Dongfeng and laughed at the thousands of Japanese men who had raped me, slapped me and pulled my hair. I laughed at the arrogant *geishas* who did exactly what we did, only they volunteered. I laughed at all of them without covering my mouth. And then I stood up and screamed. I screamed so hard that it hurt my throat. My scream echoed off the hills, and I laughed again at the echo of my scream, this time careful to cover my mouth as I did. After a while, standing there in that field with my dress wide open I wanted to cry. Instead, I buttoned my dress and lifted my sack and I marched on.

On the eighth day, I ran out of food. My legs ached from walking. My feet were on fire with blisters and bleeding, and my stomach growled constantly. I was weak with fatigue. I stopped for the day along side two elderly Chinese women. They told me they were going to Dandong, China, across the Yalu River from Sinuiju. I spoke Chinese to them and they were nice to me. They gave me some rice and a pair of *tabi* for my raw feet. They said I could travel

with them. At night before they went to sleep, one of the women asked, "What did you do in Dongfeng?"

I didn't know what to say. I was exhausted and confused and nothing about the past two years made sense. After a few long moments, I said, "My sister and I worked for the Japanese."

"What did you do for them?" the woman asked.

"I...I..." I stumbled, "we were supposed to work in the boot factory," I finally said.

The other woman raised an eyebrow. "You worked for the Japanese in a boot factory?"

"We did not volunteer," I said quickly. "We were not *chinulpa*. They made us do it."

The women exchanged glances and said nothing more. They crawled under their blankets to go to sleep. When I awoke the next morning, they were gone.

*

Midday on the fourteenth day, I arrived at the outskirts of Sinuiju. I had run out of food and water again. My stomach had stopped growling a day earlier and my tongue was thick and dry. But I didn't go to the city. Instead, I turned up the road that Soo-hee and I had taken to Sinuiju two years earlier. I was desperate to get home. I wanted to see my mother and father again. I wanted Soo-hee to be there too. But the last time I had seen my *onni*, she had been close to death. It wasn't possible that she had recovered and found her way home. No, it wasn't possible at all.

I forced myself up the long road to our farm. My heart raced when I saw our big, stucco house with the tarpaulin door. The gray-green roof tile was crooked and broken from neglect. Someone had cut down the persimmon tree and weeds grew in the yard. The front window was broken.

I stood in the road a long time looking at our house. I tried to think of what I would say to my mother and father if they were inside. I thought about turning around and going back to Sinuiju.

Finally, I went to the house and stepped inside. It was musty and dark. "*Ummah?*" I called out hesitantly. " *Appa?*" My calls echoed off the walls. There was no answer. Cobwebs grabbed at my face. "Soo-hee?"

I went to the back of the house. In the field, tall weeds cast long shadows in the setting sun. I went to the well and took a long drink of water. I filled the bucket with water and took it to the kitchen. I took off my clothes and washed myself. I scrubbed and scrubbed until my skin was raw, but I didn't feel clean. I washed my clothes and laid them out to dry. I wrapped a blanket around myself and laid on the floor of the big room. I curled up and went to sleep, alone.

The next morning, hunger pains knotted my stomach. I dressed, went out back, and dug up the *onggis* of rice and vegetables that Soo-hee and I had buried two years earlier. They had not been touched. I opened one. The brine and spices had not preserved the vegetables and they were rotten. The stench of it almost made me retch. I opened the other *onggi*. The rice was unspoiled, so I dragged it inside the house. I made a fire with dried weeds and brought some water to boil in a pan I had found inside the stove. I threw in some rice. As the rice cooked, I went out and found some carrots and potatoes growing in the field. I dug them up and took them to the house. I washed them and sliced them with a rusty knife from the kitchen drawer. When the rice finished cooking, I ate it with the raw carrots and potatoes. Eventually, my hunger pangs went away.

I looked around the house. There was a thick coat of dust on the floor and cobwebs in the ceiling. In the main room, only one chair and the low table remained. I went to the sleeping area. Mother's cabinet was gone. But where it

once stood, I saw an old photograph of my family taken during the New Year's celebration when I was just four years old. My family, dressed in *hanboks*, stared out at me from the photo. Father stood tall with his beautiful young wife at his side. Soo-hee and I, innocent young girls, stood in front of our parents holding hands. I was so happy to have found the photograph, but for some reason, it made me cry.

I put the photograph inside my dress and went out to the field to dig up more potatoes and carrots. I found some garlic and dug it up too. I gathered dried weeds and sticks. I took it all back to the house and made a fire in the stove. Soon, the home's *ondol* system warmed the floors. Next to the stove, I found some ground *bori cha* and Father's tin cup. I filled the cup with water and a handful of *bori cha* and put it over the fire to seep. Soon, I had *bori cha*, bitter and strong.

I went to work cleaning the house. I swept the floor and spent an hour scrubbing the kitchen sink. I brushed the cobwebs from the ceiling and spent another hour cleaning the soot from the stove. I made several trips to the field, all the way back to the tall aspen trees, and gathered wood and brought it back to the house. I stacked it neatly next to the stove.

Then I scrubbed myself again until my skin was raw like I had done the day before. I braided my hair and washed my clothes again. When night came, I sat at the table drinking *bora cha* and stared out the window. I desperately tried to remember what it was like when Father and Mother and Soo-hee were still there and we read books by the firelight, but the images never came.

TWENTY

THE NEXT DAY I went to work on the outside of the house. I pulled weeds in the yard and climbed up on the roof to straighten the tiles. I scrubbed the stucco walls until my knuckles bled. I raked the yard smooth with a tree branch.

In the mornings of the days and weeks that followed, I searched on my hands and knees for the tiniest speck of dirt in the house and when I found one, I cleaned the entire house again. And each day I pulled weeds and picked stones from the field behind the house until not even a pebble was out of place. I gathered wood and vegetables until I had as much as we used to put up for the winter. And every night, I scrubbed myself raw and washed my clothes and carefully braided my hair and waited by the fire trying to remember my life the way it was before.

Then one gray afternoon as I was raking the yard, an old woman came up the road and stopped by where the persimmon tree had been. *"Anayehaseyo"* the woman said. "Are you the girl who used to live here?"

"*Anayehaseyo*," I said with a bow. "Yes I am. Do you know where my family is?"

"I'm cold and need to rest," she said. "May I come into your house?" I showed her in and invited her to sit at the table. I thought I had seen her before. She was bent from age and too much hard labor. Her clothing was tattered and stained. She coughed deeply several times and collapsed in the chair.

I offered her some rice and a few carrots. She devoured them as if she hadn't eaten in a week. After she finished, she sat a while as if she had to gather strength. Then she eyed me. "I live down the road," she said. "What is your name?"

"I am Hong, Ja-hee," I answered. "My father is Hong Kwan-bae and my mother, Suh Bo-sun. The Japanese sent my *onni* and me away to work in the boot factory. The Russians told me to come home and wait here. Please tell me what you know about my family."

The woman had another coughing spell, making her face turn purple. It took her a full minute to recover. "I knew your mother," she said finally. "We worked at the uniform factory together."

"You know my mother?" My heart pounded. I moved closer to the woman. "Where is she? Please tell me."

"I am sorry to tell you young one, when you and your sister went away, your mother..." The woman lowered her eyes. "Your mother knew before you left home, that your father had been killed in the Philippines. The Japanese never sent him to Pyongyang like they said. They forced him to be a soldier and fight for them. She never told you that he had died.

"And," the woman said, "your mother is dead, too."

I clearly heard the word 'dead' but it was only a sound floating in the air. "Dead," I repeated, trying to understand what it meant.

"Yes," the woman said. "One very cold day about two years ago, your mother hadn't been to work for many days. The women from the factory found her sitting under the persimmon tree, dead from the cold. We buried her in the field with the tall grass just north of your house."

"No," I heard myself say. "You must be mistaken. It couldn't be my mother you buried." Then I remembered Mother had burned all the wood the night before Soo-hee and I had left for Sinuiju. I remembered her saying she refused to give the Japanese anything more. And I knew the woman was not mistaken.

The old woman stood to leave. "Go to Sinuiju," she said. "The new government is taking a census. You have to give them your information. Perhaps you can find work there." The woman thanked me for the rice and carrots and left through the tarpaulin door.

For a long time I sat alone inside my perfectly clean house and let the woman's message sink in. At first, I was glad that my parents were gone so I wouldn't have to tell them about Dongfeng. Then I was overcome with loss. My family was gone. Everyone I once loved was gone and I knew my life would never again be like it was, like I so desperately wanted it to be again. And I cried. Through my tears, I tried to see my future without Soo-hee by my side or my parent's gentle love. But all I could see was the darkness of being alone. I wondered how I could go on, what I had to live for. I wished I was dead like the rest of my family.

And as I sat at the table, I finally remembered. I remembered the meals that my family had shared after a hard day's work in the fields. I remembered my joy in seeing my grandparents when they visited during the New Year. I remembered how Soo-hee and I played in our front yard and my mother teaching us to read in the great room. I remembered trying to teach Soo-hee to speak Japanese and

getting frustrated with her. And I was sad, but thankful that I could remember again.

And after I had remembered it all, I retrieved the comb from underneath my blanket and took it to the fire. I looked at the dragon with its claws and two heads. I thought of my great-great grandmother and my ancestors who had passed the comb to their daughters. Their spirits had brought it to me and I was now responsible to all those who had carried it before me.

I sat in front of the fire and let down my hair. And I combed it with the comb with the two-headed dragon.

*

Growing up, I never thought much about Korean traditions. I participated in them of course, because that was what my family did. Being young, I saw them as just something we had to do because we were Korean. But now that my family was gone, our traditions were important to me.

So the next day I rose before dawn and didn't clean the house for the first time in weeks because Koreans do no work during the time of mourning. I didn't cook rice and I didn't eat. I wore my hair down as we did when my grandparents died.

I took a handful of rice and carrots and my father's tin cup out to the field with the tall grass and found the mound of dirt where they had buried my mother. I tossed three handfuls of dirt on my mother's grave, the *chwit'o* ritual that I had seen done at funerals when I was young. I took great care to smooth the ground and clean it of pebbles. With my eyes low, I placed the rice and carrots on the grave to nourish my mother's spirit for its long journey. I put my father's cup on the mound so she could give it to him when their spirits met.

I touched the cool earth and raised my eyes up. And in the aspen trees beyond the field I had so perfectly cleaned, I saw the faces of my father and my grandparents and all my ancestors. And in front of them all, I saw the face of my mother.

"Thank you, *Ummah*," I said softly. "Thank you for all you did for me and for teaching me to read and write. I am sorry for what I did in Dongfeng and I'm sorry I couldn't save Soo-hee. I have the comb you gave Soo-hee. I will take care of it as you said we should." I took a handful of dirt and let it trickle through my fingers. I stayed a minute more, quiet and respectful as I should have been when I was young.

I went back to the house, made a sack out of my blanket, and packed it with rice, carrots, potatoes, the photograph of my family, and the comb. I dragged the *onggi* of rice to the front of the house where the old woman would find it. And then I set off.

The sun had climbed over the hills in the east and the morning air was warming when I walked past where the persimmon tree had been. I turned toward Sinuiju. After a week of meals and hard work, I was strong and made good time. I was in Sinuiju by early afternoon.

I walked to the two-story military headquarters where the Japanese had been two years earlier. A Korean flag had replaced the white flag with a red circle. I went in the building to the large open room with the wood-planked floor. A few uniformed Russian soldiers worked at desks, but most of the people inside were Korean. There was an expectant buzz. I was glad the Japanese were gone. But honestly, it felt a little strange.

I approached a middle-aged, female clerk sitting at a desk under a sign that read 'Records' in Hangul. It was the first time since I was a little girl I had seen a sign in Hangul. "My name is Hong Ja-hee," I said in Japanese. "I have come for the census."

The clerk peered over glasses perched on the end of her nose. "Why are you talking in Japanese?" she said.

I lowered my eyes. "I am sorry," I said in Korean.

She turned back to the papers on her desk. "We only take census in the morning," she said without emotion. "You will have to come back tomorrow."

"Please excuse me, ma'am," I said. "If I must wait until tomorrow, do you know where I can stay tonight? I don't have anyone here."

"I don't know," the clerk said.

As I turned to leave, a man stood from a desk behind the clerk. "Wait," he said. "Perhaps I can help."

The clerk lowered her head as the man approached.

"I'm in charge of the census," he said. "Come to my desk. I'll take your information." He smiled. It was the first time a man had smiled pleasantly at me in over two years.

TWENTY-ONE

THIS MAN WAS like no other I had ever seen. His skin was smooth, his hair long and shiny. Over his medium build, he wore an unusual, loose cotton shirt. He wore leather slip-on shoes the likes of which I had never seen before.

He pointed to a chair next to his desk and told me to sit. He asked my name as he retrieved a sheet of paper and pen from his desk. I sat straight-backed with my hands in my lap. I gave him my name and he wrote it down.

He asked my age. "I'm sorry," I said. "I don't know. What month is it?"

"September," he said with a smile that reminded me of Father when he laughed at me for saying something funny. "Almost October."

"Then, I am just seventeen."

"Where do you live?"

"On my father's farm, up the road, north about twenty miles."

"Father and mother's name?"

"They are dead, sir," I said.

He looked at me and I saw kindness in his eyes. "I'm sorry," he said. "The Japanese killed many people. I'm in charge of gathering information about what they did here in Sinuiju. Please, tell me their names and how they died."

I did and the man wrote it down, careful not to miss any details. Then he asked, "Do you have any brothers or sisters?"

"Yes, a sister, Soo-hee. She is... was my *onni*. She was two years older."

"Where is she?"

"I think she is dead, too, sir."

"I'm sorry. How did she die?"

"The Japanese took her away," I said. "To China."

"I see," he nodded as if he understood and wrote something on the paper. "What did you do during this time?"

I hesitated. I didn't want to lie, but I couldn't tell him I was an *ianfu*. So I said, "I worked in the boot factory."

"The boot factory?" he asked.

"Yes, sir," I answered.

"I see." The man smiled his smile again and this time, he didn't write anything down. He put the paper on top of a large stack, then put his pen in the holder on the desk. "I heard you say you don't have anywhere to stay here in Sinuiju," he said.

"Yes, sir. I came for the census and I was told I could find work here."

The man leaned back and folded his arms across his chest. "The city is full of people with nowhere to go. And there's not much work, either."

He eyed me for a long time making me feel as if I had done something wrong. I thought he might be looking at me sexually like the soldiers at the comfort station. Finally he said, "Perhaps you can help me and I can help you too. My wife is pregnant. It's been difficult for her. She gets tired easily. We have an apartment with one of our friends near

the river. If you would like, you can work for us for food and a place to stay."

I thought of all of the men I had known over the past two years—Colonel Matsumoto, Corporal Kaori, Lieutenant Tanaka. I wondered if this man was like them. But I couldn't walk back home, not this late in the day. And there was honesty in him. "I would be grateful for the work," I said with a bow.

"Good. My name is Pak Jin-mo. Wait over there on that bench. I'll be done here soon."

*

Thirty minutes later, Jin-mo stuffed some books in a canvas satchel and threw it over his shoulder. He led me from the military headquarters to an area of town by the shipyards on the Yalu River. An evening breeze blew from the south and the day was pleasantly warm. The shipyard was crawling with men unloading supplies and military equipment from large gray ships. The ships were flying the same Russian flag that had flown over Dongfeng after the Japanese had fled. There were Russian soldiers in this area of Sinuiju and to my surprise, Korean men in military uniforms.

We came to Jin-mo's apartment. As we pushed through a door leading to a set of stairs, Jin-mo stopped and said in a low voice, "Don't tell anyone you worked in the boot factory. Just tell them you lived on your parent's farm. Okay?"

I nodded. I looked up the stairs and wondered what I would find behind the door. I thought about running back to my home in the hills. But Jin-mo's eyes met mine and he said. "It's all right. Don't be afraid." I decided I had to trust him.

He led me up the stairs to a two-room apartment overlooking the river. When we stepped through the door, I

was relieved to see a woman at the stove. A man about Jin-mo's age sat on the floor in front of an old radio. "Hello, comrades," Jin-mo said kicking off his leather shoes. When they saw me, the man lifted himself onto a crutch and the woman turned from the stove. Her pregnant belly protruded from underneath her blue blouse.

"This is Hong, Ja-hee. The Japanese killed her family and she has nowhere to go. She can help Ki-soo." He pointed at the pregnant woman. "This is my wife, Choi Ki-soo. And that's my comrade, Park Seung-yo."

I bowed to them. Choi Ki-soo, tall and pretty with hair down to the middle of her back, was expressionless as she said, "*Anyeonghasayo.*" She wore simple pajama-like pants that went to just above her ankles. She wore *zori* without *tabi*. I could see in her face the weathered hardness that I had seen in the comfort women in Dongfeng.

Park Seung-yo stood in front of the radio and nodded his greeting. He had only one leg and the wooden crutch he leaned on was worn smooth and shiny. After I bowed to him, he curled his leg and stump underneath him. Then he began to fiddle with the knobs and antenna on the radio. Faint whistles and static came from the speaker.

Jin-mo pointed to the floor next to Seung-yo. "You'll have to stay in this room with Seung-yo," he said. "Ki and I have the other room. After dinner, we'll find a mat for you." Jin-mo walked over to Ki-soo and put his arm around her bloated belly. I was surprised and embarrassed at the open display of affection. It was not how proper Koreans behaved.

As Ki-soo continued to stir the rice, Jin-mo disappeared through a door into the other room. I took off my *tabi* and put my cloth sack on the floor next to the wall. The apartment was neat and clean with windows overlooking the street below and the harbor beyond. The wooden furniture

was simple. On one wall was a cabinet filled with many books like we used to have at home.

I went to Ki-soo. "May I help?" I asked.

She didn't look up. "It's almost done," she said. "I was able to get a chicken on the dock and onions for *bulgogi*. I need to eat meat for the baby. Where are you from?"

"I lived on my parent's farm east of here."

"Jin-mo said your family is dead."

"Yes, they are."

Ki-soo pressed a hand into the small of her back. "How did they die?"

"My father was sent to fight for the Japanese and died in battle. They sent my sister to China and she died there. My mother was killed by the Japanese."

"Japanese pigs," Ki-soo said. Then, she looked sideways at me making me uncomfortable. "And you, so young and pretty, you stayed at the farm after your mother died?"

"Yes," I answered.

After a few moments, Ki-soo said, "Get chopsticks and bowls from the cupboard. Jin likes to eat right away when he gets home."

*

 During the meal, Jin-mo, Seung-yo, and Ki-soo fell into a passionate discussion about the rich, the poor, property and workers. Mother always said that it was an insult to the cook if young people talked while the elders ate. Soo-hee often pinched me under the table when I did. So I didn't talk and concentrated on my food. Over the past few years, I had forgotten what good food tasted like. In Dongfeng, the comfort women rarely ate meat and when we did, it was often tough, boiled horsemeat. But here, the chicken *bulgogi* was delicious. It felt like the meals I'd had with my family when I was a young girl.

Jin-mo sat close to Ki-soo at the low table. He did more talking than eating and the meal lasted a long time. Ki-soo kept looking at me out of the corner of her eye. Seung-yo, with his good leg tucked underneath him and his stump out front, devoured his food and talked with his mouth full. Then, when Jin-mo, the eldest male, finished eating, everyone stopped. I helped clear the table while Jin-mo and Seung-yo tinkered with the radio antenna. Finally, Jin-mo exclaimed, "Got it!" A faint voice came over the radio's speaker.

The high-pitched voice was saying something in Korean. Ki-soo lowered herself to the floor next to Jin-mo and I sat behind Seung-yo. I could only catch a few words above the static but the others listened carefully, especially Jin-mo. Every once in a while, he nodded in agreement with what the person on the radio was saying. Eventually, the voice signed off and in its place tinny music played.

Jin-mo turned off the radio. "We have to go to Pyongyang soon," he said, looking pleased. "The party is gathering there. The Russians are supporting us. We will be the new government of Korea."

"I'm not going," Seung-yo said, lighting a cigarette.

Jin-mo leaned forward. "Seung-yo," he said, "why not?"

"I can't go to Pyongyang with one leg. It was all I could do to make it to Sinuiju. Anyway, this is my home. It's where I grew up. Maybe my family will come back someday." He took a pull on the cigarette and blew smoke toward the ceiling.

Ki-soo pushed herself off the floor without expression. She went to the other room and closed the door. Jin-mo continued to stare at Seung-yo. "I can get a car to go to Pyongyang. You must go. The party needs you. Korea needs you."

Seung-yo returned Jin-mo's stare. "I have given plenty to Korea already," he said. "I just want to rest a while. I'll

find something to do here. I'll stay in this apartment." He took another puff from his cigarette.

"But Seung-yo, this is our opportunity! It is what we've been fighting for. All those years in the hills and now Korea will be free and we will be the leaders. You cannot quit now."

"I'm staying," Seung-yo said simply. He pulled himself over to the corner and curled up on his mat. He took a book out from under the mat and began to read, his cigarette dangling from his lip.

*

Jin-mo and I sat in front of the radio. He sighed and regarded me with his liquid-soft eyes. "What do I do with you?" he said.

I lowered my head. "Perhaps I should leave."

"And go where?"

There was a long, uncomfortable silence. Then, Jin-mo asked, "Can you read?"

"Yes, sir," I said. "My mother taught me to read Hangul and Chinese. I know Japanese, too. Mother always said I had a good ear for languages."

"Oh? Do you speak them well?"

"I speak Japanese and Chinese fluently," I said, looking up. "I have already learned some Russian and English, too."

A sly smile spread over Jin-mo's face. "Okay," he said in Chinese, "tell me, what did you think of our dinner tonight?"

I could feel the corners of my mouth turn up. "I thought it was delicious," I answered in Chinese, careful to pronounce the words correctly. "I haven't had chicken in a long time."

Jin-mo's grin grew to a full smile. In Japanese, he asked, "What do you think of our apartment? Is it... um..." in Korean, "what's the Japanese word for 'satisfactory'?"

I straightened and put out my chin. "*Juubun* is the word." Then in Japanese, I said, "And I think your apartment is indeed satisfactory. I like the view of the river."

Jin-mo laughed with delight and my heart skipped a beat. "And you're learning Russian, too?" he asked, switching back to Korean.

"I haven't heard it much but I already know many words. Their sentences come together in a strange way. When I hear more, I will learn it quickly."

Jin-mo shook his head. "You have a remarkable talent indeed. Perhaps you can come to Pyongyang with us. We could use your help."

"Why are you going to Pyongyang? Why don't you stay here?"

"Because with the Japanese finally gone, Korea will be free and independent for the first time since they took our country from us. We can do it with a new kind of government, one that represents all Koreans—not just the wealthy, not only the landholders, but the working people, too."

"I don't know anything about governments," I said.

The door from the other room opened and Ki-soo leaned out. "Jin, are you coming?" She had a hand on her belly.

"In a minute," Jin-mo said. Ki-soo's face flashed disapproval. She slipped back inside the room and shut the door.

Jin-mo turned back to me. "I have something for you," he said. He went to the bookshelf and took out a small, well-used book. "This is my most prized possession. It is one of the few copies of *The Communist Manifesto* translated into Hangul. It's by a man named Karl Marx. Read it and we can talk more." He handed me the book.

"Thank you," I said.

Jin-mo moved toward the room where Ki-soo was. "We won't leave for Pyongyang for a few weeks. In the meantime, help Ki-soo around the apartment and read that book. Then you can decide if you want to go to Pyongyang with us and join the Communist Party."

I took the book and a blanket Jin-mo handed me and went to a corner. Seung-yo curled up on his mat. Soon he was snoring softly. I wrapped the blanket around me. I felt out of place in this apartment with these strange people. But I had nowhere else to go.

TWENTY-TWO

TWO WEEKS LATER, Jin-mo, Ki-soo and I drove to
Pyongyang in a tiny, beat-up Fiat that Jin-mo had borrowed
from a government official he knew in Sinuiju. He had
bartered with a Russian soldier for just enough gasoline to
make the 150-mile trip. We packed the car, said a heartfelt
goodbye to Seung-yo, and set off. Jin-mo drove and Ki-soo
sat in the passenger side with her hand on her belly. I was
wedged in the back seat next to several old suitcases, two
bedrolls, pots and pans and Jin-mo's duffle bag stuffed with
his books. On my lap was an old suitcase that Jin-mo had
given me. Inside were some old clothes from Ki-soo, Jin-
mo's copy of *The Communist Manifesto,* the photograph of my
family and, tucked within the lining where no one could see
it, the comb with the two-headed dragon.

It was my first ride in a car. Of course, I had ridden in
trucks before—you cannot very well grow up on a farm
without riding in a truck once in a while—but never a car.
The Fiat smelled of exhaust fumes and the ride over the
rutted road was bumpy.

At first, I was scared to be going so far from home again. But the further south we went, the better I felt. Every mile was another mile away from Dongfeng and the comfort station.

And then, many miles out of Sinuiju, I saw the Yellow Sea for the first time. I had learned about the sea from my parent's books and Father's stories. I had always tried to picture water stretching so far that it looked like it was spilling off the edge of the earth. Now it was there in front of me, outside the car window.

It was wonderful. The blue-green sea sparkled under the morning sun and the sea air smelled fresh and clean. A large freighter with its stacks trailing thick black smoke, steamed along on the horizon. Closer in, dozens of fishing boats bobbed and pulled their nets. Still closer, great waves reached for the shore liked white foamy fangs, then crashed against the cliffs with a thunderous roar, only to retreat back again to the sea, gathering themselves for another surge. I could not take my eyes off it.

After a while, the road turned south. We traveled across a broad plain with rice paddies all the way up the hills. Dozens of workers in pointed straw hats, their black pants rolled over their knees, skillfully swung long cane poles knocking the rice grains into baskets. Others balanced baskets full of rice on their shoulders and carried them to carts waiting on the edge of the fields.

Eventually, the road rose from the rice paddies into farm fields like those behind my home. The smell of onions and garlic filled the air. It made me feel like a girl again. Workers stuffed sacks with carrots and beets and I remembered my mother saying how grandfather had to hire twenty men to bring in the harvest on our farm. In another field, cattle grazed lazily on the fall grass. I felt a surge of pride for this land and for my country and I realized Colonel Matsumoto was right. Korea was indeed a great country.

Now I understood why the Japanese wanted it for themselves and had to be forced to leave. And now that they were gone, I was sure Korea would be great again.

"How much have you read of Marx?" Jin-mo asked with an elbow over the front seat. I snapped out of my spell. *The Communist Manifesto* had been difficult to read. It was dense and filled with words I didn't know. Jin-mo and even Ki-soo had helped me with the new words. However, I had read so much growing up that I was able to finish it and understand most of the ideas. But I was afraid of exposing too much of myself so I didn't let them know that I did.

"It is very difficult," I answered.

"Don't worry," Jin-mo said. "It was difficult for me when I first read it. I got through it and you will, too."

Ki-soo let out a snort. "Why do you bother? She's too young."

Jin-mo slid his elbow off the seat and gripped the steering wheel with both hands. "I was her age when I first read it. You were only a year older. Anyway, we'll build the party on the shoulders of the young. They are the future of Korea."

Ki-soo turned her pretty face to the side window and didn't say anything.

During the two weeks in Sinuiju, Jin-mo, Ki-soo, and Seung-yo had passionate discussions at night in the apartment about governments, workers and the future. They used each other's shortened names—'Ki,' 'Seung,' and 'Jin'—which sounded strange and impolite to me. It was not the way proper Koreans addressed each other. They discussed what would happen to Korea now that the Japanese were gone. Jin-mo tried to include me in their discussions and I had tried to participate as much as I could. The ideas were new, but they seemed to make sense. The discussions felt like the discussions my family had about one of our books after a hard day's work on the farm.

I had learned that Jin-mo, Ki-soo, and Seung-yo were rebels and had fought the Japanese with other Koreans in the mountains of northern China. It had been a dangerous, hardscrabble life that had cost Seung-yo his left leg and many of their friends their lives. They had been part of a group led by a man named Kim Il-sung who they said had fought bravely and who had convinced the Russians to enter the war against the Japanese. The radio in the apartment had given them news that Kim Il-sung, with Russia's support, was in charge of a provisional government in Pyongyang. Jin-mo had been close to comrade Kim and was going to Pyongyang to secure an important position in the new government there. He had said he could get a job for me, too.

Jin-mo turned to me. "It's an exciting time in Korea, Ja-hee. A new beginning. Soon, the party will take over and Korea will become a modern country. You'll see."

Ki-soo folded her arms across her bloated belly and continued to look out her side window. "I wouldn't be so sure," she said under her breath.

Jin-mo tensed. "Why do you have to be that way, Ki?" he demanded. "Why are you always so cynical?"

"Because I don't trust them," she said, suddenly facing him. "I don't just believe everything they say."

I sank low in my seat. I had never heard a woman talk back to a man like Ki-soo did to Jin-mo. My mother never talked to my father like that. But Jin-mo and Ki-soo argued often and it usually ended with Ki-soo slamming the door to her room and Jin-mo staring blankly at Seung-yo and me.

"Look Ki, this isn't going to be easy," Jin-mo said. "We'll have to work together or other countries will push us around just like they always have. Communism is our chance. No more Japanese, no more Chinese. And the Russians and the Americans have agreed to leave once we establish a government."

"I'm not sure it will work," Ki-soo said.

"What's the alternative? Capitalism? Money and power in the hands of a few greedy men? It plunged the world into a ten-year depression that the Japanese and Germans took full advantage of. It caused the World War. We have to find a better way. Communism is it."

"'A classless society based on common ownership of the means of production,'" Ki-soo said, as if she were reading from Marx.

"Exactly," Jin-mo said. "It's what has made Russia powerful. And there are communist movements in a dozen other countries, too. China will be next, and countries in Asia and Europe will follow. There's even a communist movement in America. And right now in Korea, we can make it happen without a civil war."

"Changes like this are never bloodless, Jin. And who will lead this new government, your friend Kim Il-sung? I don't trust comrade Kim," Ki-soo said, twisting the word 'comrade'.

"He fought against the Japanese, Ki, when others ran away to America or Europe."

Ki-soo faced the window again and said nothing more for a long time. The car climbed into hills terraced with more rice paddies.

Finally, with a nod to me, Ki-soo asked, "What are you going to do with her in Pyongyang?"

"She can help with the baby."

"I don't need help with the baby."

"Then, she can help in the new government. She is great with languages. She speaks Japanese better than I do. Chinese, too. I've never seen anything like it."

"Is she going to live with us?" Ki-soo asked. Her eyes flashed.

"She lost her family, Ki."

"Half of Korea lost their family during the Japanese occupation. You aren't going to invite all of them to live with us, are you?"

Jin-mo gripped the steering wheel hard as the car bumped along the road and crested another hill. Pyongyang loomed in the distance. I hoped we would get there soon so I could get out of the car, away from Ki-soo.

Finally, Ki-soo said, "I have to piss again. This traveling isn't good for the baby."

Without a word, Jin-mo pulled the car to the side of the road and let it idle while Ki-soo got out and squatted in the ditch.

*

Pyongyang. I had heard about the great city with tall buildings on the Taedong River. *Appa* had been there once and had told us all about it. But after my disappointment in seeing Sinuiju for the first time, my expectations were low. But Pyongyang was different. It was a marvelous city teeming with people on bicycles, on foot, in cars, in trucks, on boardwalks and on the streets all rushing to get somewhere. Hundreds of electric wires on tall posts ran along the streets. Buildings—some several stories tall—were everywhere. The sounds, the sights, the smells, the *energy* was like nothing I had ever imagined.

Jin-mo produced a map from the glove box and gave it to Ki-soo. She did her best to decipher it and help Jin-mo navigate around the trucks and bicyclists on the busy streets. The Fiat rolled through the heavy traffic before we finally came to a stop in front of a massive, four-story, stone building. "This is it!" Jin-mo said excitedly. "You two stay here while I check in."

He changed his shirt, brushed his hair, and slipped on his leather shoes. Then he disappeared inside the building while Ki-soo and I stayed in the car. Ki-soo kept her back to me, staring out the car window at the people on the street. After a while, she said into the window, "I will not let Jin-

mo destroy me and my baby." I sank in my seat among the suitcases and bedrolls and prayed that Jin-mo would return soon.

An hour later, Jin-mo came running out of the building and jumped into the car. He held some papers in his hand. "It's all arranged," he said with a nod. "We have a furnished apartment close to here. I report to work the day after tomorrow. I think I will be able to get a job for you too, Ja-hee."

As he started the car, he turned to Ki-soo, then to me. The joy in his smile made my heart beat fast. "Welcome to the new Korea," he said.

TWENTY-THREE

Sixteen months later

IT WAS ANOTHER late night in the provisional government headquarters building. I sat at my desk, helping translate documents into Hangul for the meeting two floors above. The meeting was between delegations from the American-controlled South and the Russian-controlled North. The two sides were trying to reconcile their differences and unify Korea under one government. It was the third day of meetings and, according to Jin-mo, a delegate for the North, the meetings were not going well.

My desk was surrounded by a dozen others in a large bullpen on the second floor. The bullpen was dark except for the area around me. The head of my department, Mr. Chee, paced behind me reading the translations aloud. He was a middle-aged, bookish man who had been educated in London. He always wore reading glasses on a chain around his neck. When I had first started in the translation department eighteen months earlier, he had been angry that

Jin-mo's friends forced him to work with someone so young, so he put me on low-level translations. But Dongfeng haunted me and I was determined to put my shame behind me. I desperately wanted to prove that I could do something more than lie on my back and let men rape me. And I didn't want to disappoint Jin-mo. So I worked very hard at learning languages.

I studied every day and late at night when I should have been sleeping. I never took a day off. I learned dozens of new words every day and researched their precise meanings and pronunciations. I was obsessed with grammar. I read everything I could get my hands on in English and Russian and Japanese. I snuck away to the cinema to watch foreign films. I saw *Gone with the Wind* three times and read the book in English twice, making long notes in the margins of every page. I practically memorized a book on English grammar that Jin-mo gave me. I used my dictionaries so much, they fell apart.

And I had a gift. It's hard to explain, but I only needed to hear a word once and I was able to recall its meaning, remember the context, the correct pronunciation, and everything about its usage. People said I was a genius, and I suppose I was. But they didn't see how hard I worked at it. Eventually, Mr. Chee had to make me his top translator.

But my success didn't help. I often woke up at night from nightmares about the comfort station. I could still clearly see the machine gun cut down my *ianfu* sisters that last, horrible day. I could feel the sting in my thighs where Lieutenant Tanaka had beat me and the ache between my legs where Colonel Matsumoto and a thousand men had raped me. And every day I yearned for my *onni*, Soo-hee.

"What do they mean by this phrase?" Mr. Chee asked. "*A dictatorship of the proletariat through which the socialization of the means of production can be realized?*"

"It's the basis for a communist government," I said. "It means the workers will build a government that controls economic production for the benefit of everyone."

"Why do they call it a dictatorship?" he asked.

"It's a Marx idea," I answered. "He believed the workers need to take complete control from the proletariat capitalists for a more fair economy."

"How do you know all of this?" Mr. Chee asked, shaking his head. "Never mind," he said quickly with a wave. "Let's just get the translation done. They're waiting for it upstairs."

We worked for a while longer, tossing phrases and words back and forth. When we finally agreed on the translation, I wrote it out and handed it to Mr. Chee. As he read it, he said, "You need to stay. They could go all night again." I bowed and said I would. He smiled a tired 'thank you' and hurriedly headed to the stairs to deliver the translations to the delegation.

I leaned over my desk and laid my head on my arms. I closed my eyes, and words in three languages danced awkwardly in my head. Soon, I fell into a restless sleep.

*

"Ja-hee!" someone said, over the impossibly long line of Japanese soldiers in my dream. "Wake up! It's time to go." I forced my eyes open and lifted my head. Jin-mo's handsome face replaced the faces of the Japanese soldiers in the comfort station. "You fell asleep again," he said. "Come, we have to go. Ki will be worried about us."

I walked with Jin-mo through the empty street toward our apartment six blocks from the provisional government headquarters. We had made this walk together nearly every night since we'd started working for the provincial government. At first, I was uncomfortable being alone with

a man who was not my husband. But over time, I realized that Jin-mo was a gentle, kind man. He had a way of talking to me that made me believe that I was someone important. His passion for Korea and his ideas for a new kind of government were infectious. I felt alive around him and had feelings for him I had never known before.

As we walked in the cool spring air, I asked, "How did the meeting go today?"

Jin-mo sighed. It worried me how sunken his eyes had become and how his back was beginning to bend. "Not well," he said softly. "Both sides feel they have the legitimate right to rule the entire peninsula. Neither is willing to give ground."

"What is going to happen?"

"If the Americans and Russians would leave us alone, maybe we could work something out," he said. "They have both agreed to leave this year if we can form a unified government. But the Russians want a communist government and the Americans won't tolerate it. They want to make a stand against communism here in Korea. It's turning into a stalemate."

We walked for a while in silence. The huge fronds on the weeping willows that lined the street swayed in the gentle night breeze.

"What side do you think is right?" I asked. As soon as I asked it, I wished I hadn't. I was asking too many questions again, especially in Pyongyang where questions were discouraged. But it did not appear to bother Jin-mo.

"I used to think it was the North. This is where Korea was born. We have more industry here than they do in the South. And as you know, I believe a socialist government would be right for us. But what is most important is that we come together under *one* government. We've been divided our entire history—the North always aligned with the Chinese, the South with the Japanese. This is our chance to

be one nation if the Russians and the Americans don't keep us divided."

"What must we do?"

"I've presented ideas, but my *comrades* won't listen. They're inflexible. They won't compromise and I think they are wrong." Jin-mo raised an eyebrow. "Of course, my comments are just between you and me."

I nodded, pleased that he had taken me into his confidence. "Of course," I said.

When we came to the apartment there was a black car with a driver inside parked out front. Jin-mo gave the car an uneasy look. He quickly opened the apartment door and I followed him inside.

The government had given Jin-mo a furnished, western-style apartment across the street from a park filled with the giant willow trees that Pyongyang was famous for. There were four rooms—a large main room with European upholstered furniture and a fireplace, a bedroom, a kitchen with a cast-iron stove, and a small room off the back where I slept.

Jin-mo and I removed our shoes and stepped inside the main room. Ki-soo sat on the sofa with her legs folded underneath her. Her eyes were red. On the sofa next to Ki-soo was her winter coat and on the floor in front of her was a suitcase. Lying next to her was their sixteen-month-old son, Suk-ju. The little boy was leaning against his mother, sleeping. He wore a traveling coat.

Jin-mo saw the suitcases and stopped. "What is this?" he asked.

Ki-soo said, "I can't risk it anymore, Jin. I'm leaving and I'm taking Suk-ju with me."

"What do you mean?" Jin-mo asked. "What can't you risk anymore?"

Little Suk-ju pressed his face into his mother's side and moaned.

Ki-soo said, "I don't want to talk about it. You will wake Suk-ju."

"If you're leaving, when *will* we talk about it?" Jin-mo asked, trying to keep his voice down.

Suk-ju opened his eyes and reached his little hands to Ki-soo. "*Ummah?*" he said.

I stepped forward. "I will take him so you can talk." Ki-soo looked at me angrily, but let me take the boy.

Suk-ju wrapped his arms around my neck as I carried him to my room and closed the door. I sat on my mat and held him close. The boy was warm against my breast. Over the previous year and a half, I had come to love this little boy as if he were my own. I took great delight in everything he did—the way he clung to my finger when he was just a few days old, his first steps, his first words, his mischievous toddler grin, his eyes, soft and intelligent like his father's.

Suk-ju fell back to sleep while the voices of Jin-mo and Ki-soo—low at first—argued in the living room. I tried not to listen, but the voices grew loud and clear.

"I said you could not reason with these people, Jin-mo!" I heard Ki-soo say. "It's going to be a bloody dictatorship, just like in Russia with Stalin."

"I'm being careful, Ki. We have to try."

"You have made too many compromises."

"Look, the Russians have agreed to leave in a few months. It will be different then."

"Different? Your leader is murdering people, Jin-mo! Once the Russians leave, it will only get worse."

"The South is murdering people too, Ki."

"So that makes it right? What happens when the murdering comes here, to our home? I will not let that happen."

"I work for them. They won't do anything to us."

"Don't be so sure. You have enemies. You are on the wrong side of this."

"I'm not the only one. And I won't stop trying. It's the only way we can bring the North and South together. We cannot give up. We can still make it work."

There was silence for a while. Then, there was a crash of porcelain breaking. In my arms, Suk-ju jerked but didn't wake up.

"You and your ideals!" Ki-soo cried.

"Keep your voice down, Ki."

"No, I will not! You said you were going to get rid of her a year ago."

"She doesn't have anywhere to go. Anyway, she loves Suk-ju and he loves her. I'm not going to just throw her out."

"I told you I will not allow it!"

"Ki-soo, nothing has happened between us."

"I don't care. Go ahead. Live with your pretty little *chinulpa*, your comfort woman whore."

Every nerve in my body snapped to life. Had I heard Ki-soo right? Had she just called me a comfort woman? I hadn't told anyone about what I had done in Dongfeng. How had the secret I kept for nearly two years possibly have gotten out? *How could they know?*

There was another crash from the living room. "Shut up, Ki! We have to help each other."

"That's not why you won't get rid of her."

"What do you mean by that?"

"You know what I mean."

"Okay, go ahead. Leave."

"I'm taking Suk-ju." I heard the sound of footsteps marching to my door. The door flew open and Suk-ju jerked awake. Ki-soo took her son from me. She marched out to the living room. She grabbed her coat and suitcase and stomped out of the apartment.

*

For a long time, I sat on my mat with my knees to my chin. Ki-soo's words, 'comfort woman whore' rang in my ears. I hadn't heard those words in nearly two years. I put my hands on my head and tried to make them go away, but they stayed, like the insults the Japanese had thrown at me every day at the comfort station.

Finally, I rose, cracked open my door and peeked into the living room. Jin-mo was in a chair in the shadows looking at nothing. Outside the window, the willows swayed gently in the night breeze.

I went to the kitchen and got a broom and dustpan. I started to sweep up the shards from the broken celadon pot. "Leave it," Jin-mo said from the darkness. "It's my responsibility."

I set the broom down and went back to my room. I shut the door and sat on my low bed as the horrors of Dongfeng surrounded me again.

TWENTY-FOUR

"YOU RUN THIS upstairs while we start on the other one," Mr. Chee said. "Hurry!"

I grabbed the proclamation that the translation team had just finished and ran to the stairs leading to the fourth floor of the government headquarters. It was midday and the building was abuzz with activity. People in the translation department examined documents or talked on telephones. Others flitted from desk to desk, carrying file folders. They all stopped and stared when I ran by with the papers.

As I climbed the stairs, I sensed a pending doom for the meeting on the fourth floor—and for the chance to unify Korea. The document in my hand was a proclamation from the Southern delegation declaring they were going forward with national elections as directed by the United Nations. And they would do it with or without the North's consent. It further stated that as far as the South was concerned, these elections would determine who had the right to govern all of Korea, North and South.

The translation department was feverishly working on a similar proclamation from the North. It stated that the North would not recognize the elections in the South which they believed the Americans would rig to elect the pro-American puppet, Syngman Rhee. It said the North would hold separate elections under the supervision of the Soviet Union. And just like the South, as far as the North was concerned, *their* elections would determine who had the right to govern the entire peninsula. It was, as Jin-mo had feared, a stalemate.

I reached the fourth floor and ran to the huge, two-story, mahogany-paneled anteroom of the great meeting hall. I heard voices arguing on the other side of the giant wooden doors. A clutch of bureaucrats sat at desks, shuffling papers or talking softly to each other. They looked up as I approached. I went up to a desk by the door, bowed to the man sitting there, and offered the translations. The stern-faced man took the proclamation, read it over, and said, "Where's the one from the North?"

"Sir," I said with another bow, "we have not finished it. It will be done soon."

Suddenly, the huge double doors swung open and a group of men carrying briefcases came marching out with their eyes resolutely forward. I quickly stepped aside to let them pass. Half the bureaucrats in the anteroom scrambled to their feet, stuffed papers into their briefcases and ran after them.

Inside the great hall, Jin-mo and the other delegates from the North stood at the door staring at the backs of the men who were leaving. Jin-mo ran his hands through his hair. A bureaucrat asked aloud, "What do we do now?"

Jin-mo and the others turned to their lead delegate. The man said, "Issue our proclamation."

I watched Jin-mo as he went to his desk and stuffed papers into his briefcase. Then he headed out of the great hall. As he walked past me he said, "Let's go home."

*

"It's over," Jin-mo said, sitting with me on a bench in the park outside our apartment. There were new lines in his face and the circles under his eyes were darker than before. "There will be no reconciliation. Korea is officially a divided nation."

It was a glorious spring day. The willows had just leafed out and were bright green against a cloudless sky. The sun was high and warm but the sadness on Jin-mo's face made it feel like midwinter.

"You did your best," I said, facing him.

He scoffed. "My best was not good enough. Now the only way to unify Korea is through a civil war. With the Americans and Soviets involved, it might lead to another world war. And they both have nuclear weapons. Fools! Why wouldn't they listen to me?" He closed his eyes and shook his head.

How could I know what to say? I had read about the global conflict called the Cold War. I knew that Korea was an important battleground. I had also read about nuclear bombs and their ability to destroy entire cities. But could Korea be the cause of another world war? Surely Jin-mo was exaggerating.

Jin-mo stared at his hands. He was so handsome with his smooth skin and shiny black hair. It made me sad that he never smiled any more. I wondered if his sadness was from losing the fight for a unified Korea or from losing Ki-soo and Suk-ju.

I asked him if he had heard from Ki-soo. Perhaps I shouldn't have asked—I still asked too many questions—but

I wanted to know. He told me he hadn't. "She will not change her mind," he said.

"I am sorry, Jin-mo."

He turned to me. "I've been avoiding asking you this, Ja-hee. How much did you hear of our argument the night Ki left?"

I looked out over the park. "I heard everything," I answered.

"Then, you heard what she called you."

"Yes." It was then that I knew that I had heard Ki-soo correctly two weeks earlier. She had called me a comfort woman and a *chinulpa*. Apparently, they had known all along the secret I had tried so desperately to hide.

"How did you know?" I asked.

"I knew when I first met you. You said you worked in the boot factory at Sinuiju. Ja-hee, there was no boot factory there. It was a cruel joke by the Japanese. When they said they were sending a girl to the boot factory, they meant they were sending her to a comfort station. When you told me you worked there, I knew you had been a comfort woman."

I felt so stupid for not knowing this. Boot factory. How fitting. It was like the Japanese were humiliating me all over again. I exhaled a sob. "I'm sorry I lied," I said. "I did not want anybody to know."

Jin-mo turned to me. "I only told Ki because she told me to kick you out. She said she didn't want a marriage like that. I thought she would feel sorry for you when I told her what you'd been through, but it only made her angrier."

"I was tricked into it," I said quickly. "The Japanese sent orders for me and my sister to report to work at the boot factory. We didn't know they were sending us to work in a comfort station. We were not *chinulpa*. We did not want to do it. They forced us to. We would have been shot."

"I know," Jin-mo said. "I know. They forced tens of thousands of girls into their comfort stations. You have nothing to be ashamed of."

I had nothing to be ashamed of? Now that I had learned that Jin-mo knew all along, all I felt was shame. For two years, I had let the Japanese use me like a toilet. And Jin-mo knew what I had done! I couldn't bear to look at him.

"I should go," I said. "I should find another place to live. It would be the right thing to do."

"I don't want you to leave," Jin-mo said.

He reached out and gently touched my arm. At his touch, the images of the men who had slapped me, punched me, and raped me for two years flashed in my mind and I recoiled.

He quickly took his hand away. "I'm sorry," he said. "Please know Ja-hee, I will never hurt you."

I knew he wouldn't. My reaction had been instinctive and I wished I had not pulled away. But I had been an *ianfu*, a comfort woman whore, and Jin-mo was a respectable man.

"I'm sorry I made Ki-soo leave," I said.

"You aren't the reason she left. I am. We weren't meant for each other. I'm an idealist and she is a cynic. I wanted to bring Korea together and I put it above everything else, including my family. I'm not going to change, Ja-hee. Neither is she."

Jin-mo sank onto the bench. I could still feel the place on my arm where he had touched me. I hoped he would touch me again someday, and if he did, I would not recoil. After a few seconds I asked, "Shall I stay?"

"Yes," he said. "I want you to very much."

*

That night as I prepared for bed, I sensed a change in the apartment. In a strange way, I was glad that Jin-mo knew my

terrible secret. He had said I had nothing to be ashamed of but I couldn't believe a man like Jin-mo thought it was true. But he had asked me to stay...

I put on clean bedclothes and stood before my mirror combing my hair with the comb with the two-headed dragon. I had left my door open to the main room. Jin-mo had a fire going in the fireplace. The apartment was comfortably warm.

Then, beyond my reflection in the mirror, I saw Jin-mo leaning against the doorjamb, watching me. My stomach jumped. The horrors of the comfort station began to rise in my mind, but I pushed them away. I put the comb on the dresser and turned to him. Our eyes met and my heart beat fast. He came and stood in front of me. He reached out and stroked my hair. His touch was so tender and this time, I did not recoil. I pressed my cheek into his hand and closed my eyes. He moved his hand to my shoulder and down my arm. And then he stopped. He was looking at my comb. He asked me where I got it and I told him it was my mother's.

"It's beautiful," he said. He took his hand from me and picked up the comb. As he examined it, his eyes grew wide. "The dragon," he whispered, "it has two heads and its feet have five toes."

"Yes," I said. "It has been in our family a long time."

"How long?" he asked.

"For generations."

He looked at the comb again, then handed it to me with a weak smile. He went back to the living room.

I didn't understand why he didn't stay in my room. I wanted him to touch me again. I wanted him to make love to me. I followed him with the comb in my hand. I asked him what was wrong. I asked what the comb meant to make him react the way he did.

He sat in a chair and I sat on the sofa across from him. The fire in the fireplace crackled. He told me to tell him

what I knew about the comb. I told him the story Mother had told me and Soo-hee years earlier. I told him that women in my family had passed the comb on to their daughters for generations. I told him how Mother had given it to Soo-hee and how Soo-hee had given it to me at the comfort station.

"You have had it all this time?" Jin-mo asked.

"Yes. Why?"

He didn't answer right away and I thought he was angry with me for not telling him about the comb. Finally, he said, "A dragon is a powerful symbol as you know. But in Korea, a two-headed dragon is extraordinary. You see the two heads are facing opposite directions, east and west. The head facing east protects Korea from Japan. The head facing west protects us from China. And the dragon protects those who possess it so they can serve Korea."

I wanted to ask questions, but I stayed quiet and let Jin-mo continue. "When the Japanese annexed us, they forbid anyone from having that dragon. They said we were Japanese now and did not need protection from them. So when they found something with the two-headed dragon, they destroyed it and arrested whoever owned it. Nothing with that dragon was thought to have survived."

"I didn't know. It must be very valuable."

"Valuable?" he said. "It is beyond value." Jin-mo focused on the comb as if it had put him under a spell.

I stared at it too. "Do you believe it?" I asked. "Do you believe a dragon can protect someone?"

He shook his head. "I am an educated man," he said. "I believe in science and history and observation and careful analysis. I am not given to superstition. Normally I would not believe such a thing. But honestly, I do not know what to believe anymore."

Then he looked at me with his mouth slightly open as if he wanted to say more. Instead, he took a step back and forced a smile. "I should go to bed," he said. "I'm very tired."

My heart sank. I so wanted him to come with me to my room, but I could tell he wouldn't, not tonight. Perhaps not ever. "Yes," I said. "I am tired too."

I closed my hand around the comb, bowed and said goodnight. I went to my room and shut the door. I hid the comb in the lining of the old suitcase Jin-mo had given me. I curled up in bed and pulled the blanket to my chin. The familiar guilt I had carried with me since the first day Colonel Matsumoto had raped me came flooding back.

The dragon protects those who possess it so they can serve Korea, Jin-mo had said. I closed my eyes. Just like mother, it had not protected me. I had been a comfort woman whore. And surely someone like me would never have the love of a man like Jin-mo.

TWENTY-FIVE

Months Later

I WAS COOKING rice flour at the cast iron stove to make *dduk* with *jujube* for Jin-mo. I hoped the sweet rice cakes and jelly would entice him to eat something. It was morning and snow fell among the bare willows in the park outside.

Jin-mo sat at the low table in the kitchen and stared vacantly into his *bori cha*. His hair was a mess and his wrinkled, unwashed clothes drooped on his thinning frame. He had stayed up all night reading his books, scribbling on paper, pacing the living room and talking aloud to no one.

"Jin-mo, you have to go to work," I said. "You've missed too many days."

"I do not feel well," he said.

"They are asking about you. I'm running out of excuses."

"Why do they care?" Jin-mo scoffed. "They don't listen to what I say."

"What should I tell them when they ask about you?"

Jin-mo sighed. "Tell them you don't know anything. Tell them we never talk. Tell them you just have a room here. I'm serious. That's what you should say."

I continued to steam the *dduk* as Jin-mo stared into his *bori cha*. After a long silence Jin-mo said, "Tell me about your sister."

"What do you want to know?" I asked.

"She was your *onni*, right?"

"Yes. Two years older."

"And the last time you saw her, she was still alive?"

I set the spoon on the stove. "You've asked the same questions three times this past week, Jin-mo. Yes, she was still alive but she was almost dead. And the Japanese *Kempei-tai* killed all the Korean girls. I'm sure they killed her, too. Why? Why do you want to know?"

Jin-mo turned away.

I went back to stirring the rice. "I'm making *dduk* for you. You should eat."

"I'm not hungry."

"Jin-mo, you have to eat."

"No!" he said angrily. He marched into the living room and flopped in the upholstered chair. He picked up a book.

I removed the rice from the stove. It hadn't finished cooking but I knew Jin-mo wouldn't eat it. I poured myself a cup of *bori cha*, sat at the table and stared out the window at the snow on the willows. Months earlier, Jin-mo had asked me to stay with him and I had hoped we would become a couple. It never happened. After he saw the comb with the two-headed dragon, he regarded me with caution, as if I was a fragile thing not to be broken. I yearned to have him touch me, kiss me, make love to me the way it should have been done before the Japanese had raped me. Instead, he had fallen into fits of depression and had lost himself in his books. I orbited around him and felt like a fool.

I finished my *bori cha* and went to the living room. Jin-mo had curled himself up in his chair, reading. His books and papers were in stacks all around him. I picked up one of his papers and began to read it.

"What are you doing?" Jin-mo asked from behind his book.

"I'm reading this."

"Leave it," he said. "Put it back exactly where it was."

"I want to see what you're working on." I held on to the paper.

Jin-mo slammed his book closed. "Put it back!" he yelled. "You're messing up the order."

His tone startled me. He had never talked to me like that before. "I'm messing up the order? What order, Jin-mo? I do not see any order at all."

Jin-mo looked around the room and his shoulders sagged. "You think I'm mad, don't you?" he asked.

I sat on the couch across from him. "I am worried about you."

He set his jaw. "I wasn't wrong. The compromises I proposed were right for Korea. It was the only way to have one government."

"You cannot compromise with a dictatorship," I said.

"Dictatorship?"

I pushed myself to the edge of the couch. "The way I see it," I said, "Marx's revolution of the proletariat is not possible. That much power will always turn into a dictatorship. It is human nature. In Korea, the dictator will be Kim Il-sung, just like Stalin is in Russia."

"Yes," he said. "That is a problem, isn't it?" He picked up his book and fell into it again.

As I stood to go to the kitchen, he said, "I'm sorry."

"For what?"

"I'm sorry about me... about you and me."

"You and me?"

"Yes," he said. "I'm sure you wanted more. From our relationship, I mean."

I let his words sink in. He was right, I had hoped for more. But as the weeks and months passed without anything happening between us, my hope had faded. And when his depression came and deepened, my hope died completely. I had tried everything, but I couldn't reach him. I had lost him before I ever had him.

"Yes, I did," I said. "But I understand why you cannot love me."

"No you don't," Jin-mo said, setting his book down. "You think it is because of what you did... because of what you were forced to do by the Japanese."

A lump grew in my throat. I turned away.

"That's not why, Ja-hee," he said. "You were just a girl when the Japanese tricked you. How could you know?"

"I could not possibly," I said quickly.

"The Japanese did unspeakable things. They murdered our children and the elderly. They forced our women to work long hours in their factories and made our men fight their war. They raped girls like you. It's not your fault. Do you understand? It is not your fault."

I looked at Jin-mo. "Then why don't you want me?"

"I do," he said.

I had never had a man say he wanted me before. Not like this. And the man who said it was my beloved Jin-mo. "I want you, too," I heard myself say.

"I'm sorry. I can't," he said, shaking his head. "I cannot fall in love with you."

But I was already in love with him and couldn't wait any longer. I went to his side and took his hand. I lifted his chin so our eyes met. "I love you, Jin-mo."

"Ja-hee. No."

I leaned into him and we kissed. The sublime tenderness of Jin-mo's lips on mine pushed away the demons of the

thousands of men who had raped me. And where the demons had been, a warmth rose. Jin-mo lifted a hand to my back and gently pulled me in close. I ran my hand along the muscles of his smooth back and the warmth in me grew into a fire. I pushed myself into him and kissed him harder. He wrapped his arms around me and our bodies met, chest to breast. I fell into his embrace. He lifted me in his arms and carried me to his room.

And there, I made love for the first time in my life.

*

I lay next to Jin-mo and ran my fingers across his bare chest. I had never felt this way before. I had never even imagined it. I'd had sex thousands of times with thousands of men, but this, this was the first time I felt anything other than pain. For years, I worried that if true love came, the demons of my rapists would haunt me and make love impossible. But in Jin-mo's embrace, the demons never came and I knew I was meant to love him.

And he loved me too, I could feel it. It was in his hold, in the way he said my name when we made love. It was in the way he touched me so tenderly, kissed me and held me close. Maybe what I did in Dongfeng, as shameful as it was, was not my fault after all.

I thought about my *onni*. Poor Soo-hee never knew the joy of making love. She had only known the pain of forced sex and the humiliation of rape. Perhaps it was because Soo-hee had given me the comb. *I am sorry, Soo-hee*, I said to myself. *This should have been you.*

I asked Jin-mo why he was asking so many questions about my sister. He said he was just curious and that it was nothing for me to worry about.

"Jin-mo," I said, "she is dead."

"You don't know that for sure," he said.

I thought for a moment. He was right—I didn't. Of course, I had often wondered what had happened to Soo-hee after I left her for dead in the infirmary. I knew it would have taken a miracle for my *onni* to survive. And it was best not to hope for miracles.

"I do not think it is possible she's still alive." I said.

"It *is* possible," he said. "And I can find out. I am an official in the provisional government. I have access to records."

I pushed myself up on an elbow. "You've looked? What have you learned?"

"Nothing yet."

"Why do you want to know?"

Jin-mo sighed. "I want to find her, so you will not be alone."

"Alone? But I have you," I said putting a hand on his shoulder.

Jin-mo pushed me away. He sat on the edge of the bed with his bare back to me. "Listen to me, Ja-hee," he said over his shoulder. "This... this was a mistake. We should not have done it. I should have been stronger."

I pulled the blanket over my shoulders. "So everything you said before, about it not being my fault was a lie?"

He turned to me. "No. I meant what I said. This, what we did, it was beautiful. I have wanted you for a long time. Don't you see? Didn't you feel it?"

"Yes, I did," I answered. "So why was it a mistake?"

He shook his head. "Because I am a marked man. Those fools think I'm their enemy. They want to kill me. But you, Ja-hee, you must go on. That is why I want to find your sister."

"If they kill you, they will have to kill me, too," I said.

"I believed you would do that, but I will not let you."

I pushed myself straight. "Then we should run away, Jin-mo, escape to the South. Thousands of people are doing it."

"They will never let me escape, Ja-hee. If you go with me, they will kill you, too. And then they will get your comb."

"My comb?" I said, surprised. "What does my comb have to do with this?"

"They cannot have it. I don't want the dragon to protect them."

"I don't believe what you said about the dragon. It did not protect me."

"Maybe it did," Jin-mo said. "You survived, Ja-hee. Do you understand? When your family and the other comfort women died, *you survived*. And now you must go on."

"But you said the dragon protected those who possessed it so they could help serve Korea. I haven't done anything for Korea."

"Yes you have," he said simply. "You've done something very important. You survived. And we should never do this again."

He started to dress. At that moment, I felt Jin-mo slipping away like my family had years earlier. I couldn't imagine not lying with him again, not feeling his touch, not making love to him. Without Jin-mo, my terrible loneliness would return, and I was convinced that next time it would kill me. "I do not care about the comb," I said.

He turned to me angrily. "Don't say that. You have to keep it, Ja-hee."

"But why me? Why am I responsible for it? Why can't I throw it away and be with you?"

Without answering, Jin-mo finished dressing and went to the living room. I lay on the bed with the blanket to my chin. I loved Jin-mo more than I ever loved anyone. And I did not want the cursed comb anymore. If I had to, I would destroy it to hold on to the man I loved.

TWENTY-SIX

WHEN I PUSHED my way out of the apartment to go to work, my stomach churned. I moved to the street in case I had to vomit again. I had to wait a full minute to let my stomach settle.

I had decided not to tell Jin-mo about my morning sickness or that my breasts were swollen and sore. I didn't want to burden his troubled mind with the fact that I was pregnant. Over the past few months, we had made love sporadically, and after each time, Jin-mo berated himself and called himself weak. It frightened me to watch him slip deeper and deeper into his depression. When my morning sickness began, I did my best to hide it. Jin-mo was missing a lot of work. He slept during the day, and at night, he read his books or filled sheets of paper with notes. He rarely ate and had turned pale and weak. I worried about him.

That morning, the March wind was sharp. I wrapped my scarf tight, dropped my shoulder to the wind and headed to work. I dreaded going to work. My manager in the translation department, Mr. Chee, had disappeared months

earlier. Some said government officials took him away because he had lived in England and might have had capitalist's ideas. Others said he had escaped to the south. After he left, the documents and contracts I worked on became increasingly absurd. I didn't want to do it anymore. I wanted to be home with Jin-mo. But with the way things were in Pyongyang, I went to work every day and kept my feelings to myself.

As I rounded a corner onto the boulevard leading to the government building, a convoy of gray-green army trucks belching black smoke in the air rumbled south. In the back of the trucks, young soldiers clutched rifles and looked out at the pedestrians with fatalistic eyes.

Outside the government building, a group of workers clung to scaffolding around a newly installed granite base on the boulevard. Next to it was a tall crane. A government official dressed in a black wool coat and fur hat stood next to the scaffolding. The pedestrians bowed to him as they walked by. From behind the scaffolding, the crane lifted a huge iron statue of a man. Its back was to me and its arms stretched out to the street below. As it rose to the pedestal, it slowly turned toward me and I saw they were erecting another statue of Kim Il-sung. The massive figure smiled down at me benevolently.

I went inside the building and climbed the stairs to the second floor. In the bullpen area, a man whom I had never seen before was sitting in my chair. He wore wire-rimmed glasses and a black military coat with a major's insignia. Standing next to him was a soldier in a green uniform. The pistol on his belt made me swallow hard.

I wanted to run but went to my desk as my coworkers glanced at me nervously. Without getting up, the man asked if I was Hong, Ja-hee. I told him I was. He ordered me to follow him. He picked up his briefcase and marched toward

the stairs. His footsteps echoed off the walls. The soldier with the pistol motioned me to follow the major.

They led me to a windowless room on the third floor. Inside was a metal table and two chairs. The soldier stood with his back against the door. The major told me to sit. He took off his coat, laid it on the table, and sat in the chair across from me. He took out a pencil and paper from his briefcase. "My name is Major Lee," he said. "I have some questions. I expect you will answer them truthfully."

"Yes sir," I said.

Major Lee observed me coldly which sent a shiver through me. "You are Hong Ja-hee from near Sinuiju. Correct?"

"Yes, sir."

He wrote on his paper. "Your father died in battle fighting for the Japanese and your mother worked in a uniform factory. Correct?"

"Yes, sir."

"And during this time, your sister Soo-hee was sent to a comfort station in Dongfeng, China. Correct?"

I was stunned. How did this man know about Soo-hee? I wondered if he knew about me, too. "Yes sir," I answered quickly.

"What did you do during this time?"

My stomach began to roil again. I wanted desperately to keep what I did in Dongfeng a secret, but his question hung heavy in the air.

The major leaned over the desk toward me. "I asked a question. You will answer."

My stomach turned into a knot. I tried to think. Ever since the Russians had left North Korea and Kim Il-sung had taken power, people who lied to the new regime had disappeared. The Communist officials expected North Koreans to cooperate and always to tell the truth. And there were rumors that the officials always knew if someone was

lying. "I worked in the comfort station in Dongfeng, too," I said finally. I lowered my eyes.

Major Lee nodded and wrote something on his paper. The soldier at the door glared at me.

The major continued to ask his questions. He asked me why I came to Pyongyang and he asked about my relationship with Jin-mo. I told him I came to work for the provincial government, that Jin-mo and I only shared an apartment, and that we were not married. "We rarely talk," I said, truthfully. He asked why Jin-mo wasn't coming to work anymore and I told him it was because he was sick.

And then the major asked, "Do you know why he has been inquiring about your sister?"

My stomach jumped again and my mind raced. "Sir," I said, "I asked him to. He has learned nothing. I do not think it is possible my sister is alive."

The major nodded. "Yes, I don't believe he found anything about her." The major wrote some more on his paper, folded it, and pushed it inside his briefcase.

"Very well," he said. "There is one more thing and we will be done."

From his briefcase, he took out a two-page document, a pen, and an inkbottle and placed them on the table. He stretched his lips into a polite smile but his eyes remained cold behind his wire-rimmed glasses. "It has been determined that you are valuable to the Worker's Party of Korea. You have the physical qualities of an ideal Korean woman, and apparently, you have great skill with languages. Your supervisors report that you are an obedient worker. We need someone with your skill in the department of education where you will translate literature supporting our Great Leader. It is an important assignment and you are fortunate to have been selected for it."

He pushed the document and pen toward me. "First, we must be sure you are qualified. This is a statement of

support for Chairman Kim. It states that you believe he alone is the rightful leader of Korea, North and South. It further states that you agree to give him your devotion and are even willing to die for him if asked."

Major Lee's smile stretched thinner. "The party is willing to overlook someone's past if that person agrees to support Chairman Kim. I'm sure you will agree with this statement. Please sign where indicated." He uncorked the inkbottle and pointed it at me.

I dipped the pen in the ink and signed the document without reading it. Major Lee blew once on the ink to dry it and put the document in his briefcase. He told me I had made a wise decision. "And now," he said, "this man will show you to your new assignment."

The soldier with the sidearm led me to the Ministry of Education on the third floor. I sat next to a stern woman with thick ankles who regarded me with disdain. I spent the entire day translating into English and Japanese propaganda about Kim Il-sung. The documents expounded upon the Dear Leader's incredible bravery when he fought the Japanese during their occupation. They said that he alone had the skill and vision to bring the Korean people together as one nation. The documents made him sound like a god.

I did not question a word and made the translations as accurately as I could.

*

That evening when I left the government building to go home, the wind was still blowing cold. I wrapped my coat tight around me and walked quickly to the apartment. I was anxious to talk to Jin-mo about Major Lee and his questions.

I pushed the apartment door open and took off my shoes. The books and papers that Jin-mo had stacked in the living room were gone. Jin-mo crouched in front of a blaze

in the fireplace. What remained of his books and papers was in a small stack next to him. The orange flames threw shimmering shadows against the wall.

As I took off my coat, I asked Jin-mo what he was doing. His face reflected the orange flames. He had changed into clean clothes, and had brushed his hair smooth.

"I'm burning them," he said in an odd voice. He tossed another book in the fire.

"Why?"

"Because these books do not mean anything anymore."

"Jin-mo," I said, coming to his side, "someone came to talk to me today. Major Lee was his name. I had to tell him what I did in Dongfeng."

Jin-mo stared into the fireplace as the flames caught the pages of the book and rose high. "It's a good thing you did," he nodded. "They probably already knew."

I took his hand. I looked in his face, still handsome through all his pain. "Jin-mo, let's leave Pyongyang. Let's run to the South where no one knows us. We can go tonight."

"It's too late for me," he said.

"Jin-mo, they will kill you here."

"Yes, they will," he replied matter-of-factly. He tossed another book on the fire.

The flames were hot against my face. "What should we do?" I asked.

"You have to go without me."

I pushed his hand away. "No, I won't go alone," I cried. I could feel a tear overrun my eye. "I will not leave you!"

"Ja-hee," he said, "they are probably outside right now. They will not let me get one block from this apartment. And if you're caught trying to escape with me, they will kill you, too."

"I don't care. I will not go without you."

"You have to. They will destroy you here; first your mind, then your soul. In the end, you will not care when they kill you."

He picked up a book and admired it. After he tossed it in the fire, I said, "Jin-mo, I'm pregnant."

He looked into the fire and smiled sadly. "How long?" he asked.

"Three months."

"It is a girl," he said simply.

"How could you know?"

"Because of your comb."

"I don't care about the comb," I said. "I do not believe in the dragon. And I will not have this baby without you."

"Yes," he said. "That's how I will do it."

I shook my head. "Jin-mo, what are you talking about?"

Suddenly Jin-mo grabbed my shoulders and forced me to look at him. "Ja-hee, promise you will do this for me. Promise you will keep the comb and let the dragon protect you."

"No. I will not."

He gripped me hard. "You must do it. Don't you see? You must survive this. Then, someday you can tell them what we tried to do here. Do it for me. Do it for Korea."

I must have winced from his grip because he let go of me. He nodded oddly and smiled a sad smile.

"I thought you didn't believe in the dragon," I said.

"I said I didn't know," he said, picking up the last book. "But now, it's all I have to believe in. At least it's something. And who knows? It might be true." He tossed the book in the fire.

Eventually the flames consumed each page and all that remained of Jin-mo's beloved books were glowing orange embers. He watched as the embers faded to ash and then looked at his feet.

I took him by the arm and led him to his room. I stripped off his clothes and put him in bed. I took off my clothes too, and slipped beneath the blankets next to him. He pushed his head into my breast and cried.

TWENTY-SEVEN

THEY CAME FOR him when the night was darkest. They were inside the bedroom and were on him before I knew what was happening. Two soldiers dragged him naked from the bed and made him dress. He offered no resistance.

"What are you doing?" I cried, as I pulled on my clothes. I scrambled to the living room as they led Jin-mo toward the front door. "Where are you taking him? No! He's sick. Let him go!"

"Halt!" came an order from beside the fireplace. Poking at the ashes of Jin-mo's books was Major Lee. The soldiers stopped at the front door and turned Jin-mo to face him.

The major wore a black coat and fur hat. I hated the way he looked sideways at me through his wire-rimmed glasses. "It has been determined that Mr. Pak is sick and needs rehabilitation," the major said. "Yesterday, you told me you were not married to this man. You signed a paper in support of Kim Il-sung and agreed to die for The Great Leader if asked. In return, we have given you an important job in the Worker's Party of Korea. You have a fine

apartment here. You have done well for someone with your… history. Certainly, you do not want to give it up for a disillusioned man, do you?"

Jin-mo pulled himself from the soldiers' grip. "Ja-hee," he said, "remember your duty to Korea." For the first time in months, his eyes were clear. He looked like the man he was when I first saw him in charge of the census in Sinuiju. He looked like a man who believed in ideas. "You can do it," he said. "Do it for Korea. Do it for me." He smiled sadly. "Goodbye, Ja-hee." He turned and walked out the door as the soldiers scurried after him.

I loved Jin-mo, I truly did. And I was not afraid to die for him. I desperately wanted to curse at Major Lee and run to Jin-mo's side. But as I watched the man I love disappear out the door, my insides turned to stone just as they had in the comfort station in Dongfeng. The stone took hold of me and froze me in place like the Pyongyang fountains in the winter. I couldn't feel and I couldn't move. And I let them take my beloved Jin-mo away.

Major Lee slowly placed the poker back in the stand. "You've made the right decision," he said pressing his lips into a smile. "Our Great Leader will not forget. And now I must see to Mr. Pak's care. I hope the rest of your night is quiet." Major Lee followed the soldiers out the door.

I dragged myself to the sofa and covered up with a blanket. I stared into the fireplace and wanted to cry. But my stone-hard heart imprisoned my sobs. And I thought about what kind of person I had become. I had tried so hard to put Dongfeng behind me and heal Jin-mo with my love. But I was a comfort woman and I could never have a man like Jin-mo.

My stomach roiled and I became nauseous like in the mornings. My skin turned clammy and I shivered. I threw off the blanket and built a fire in the fireplace. When the flames had taken hold of the wood, I marched to my room

and pulled out my suitcase. I reached under the lining and took out the comb with the two-headed dragon.

I took it to the fireplace. In the flame's flickering light, the gold spine glimmered and the two-headed dragon mocked me with its tongues and claws. I decided I hated it. The comb was nothing more than a cheap heirloom and the power of the two-headed dragon was just a myth. It had brought me only sorrow and loneliness and death to the ones I loved. How could I have been so naïve to believe it would protect me?

The baby inside me kicked and I cursed it. I kneeled on the hearth and poked the wood in the fireplace. The flames rose high. I added another log, then another. Soon, the flames reached past the flue. I held the comb close to the fire. The heat burned my hand and brought tears to my eyes.

You must pass on the comb, my mother had said. *Do this for me,* Soo-hee had said. *Do it for Korea* Jin-mo had said. I could see their faces dancing in the flames. "Damn you!" I shouted at them. "Damn you for making me do this. I am not the one who should!" The baby kicked me again, hard this time. I cocked my hand to toss the comb in the fire. And then the faces in the fire changed to those of Colonel Matsumoto, Lieutenant Tanaka and Major Lee. They laughed and mocked me. I dropped my arm and the faces changed back to flames.

Confused, I took the comb to the couch and wrapped myself in the blanket again. My nausea was gone and my stomach was settled. The baby no longer kicked. I watched the fire for a long time, trying to make sense of all that had happened to me.

Soon, I was warm and a profound weariness took hold of me. I lay on the couch to sleep. As I was about to close my eyes, I noticed something on the bookshelf. On the lowest shelf was one lone book that Jin-mo had not burned.

I went to the bookshelf and picked it up. It was Jin-mo's copy of *The Communist Manifesto* in Hangul.

I took it to the couch and opened it. Near the back was an envelope. Inside was money and a note. I took the note out and read it.

> *My dear Ja-hee,*
>
> *You must leave the North as soon as you can. Go to the Gimhae Hotel just off the Taedong River south of the great square. Ask for a man named Mr. Gah. Tell him you want to see the world. Use those exact words. Pay him what he asks and he will take care of you.*
>
> *Please forgive me for loving you.*
>
> *Jin-mo*

I thumbed through the money. It was a substantial sum. I read the note again and memorized the hotel and phrase I would need to say. Then, I took the money and tossed the note and book in the fire. I took the comb to the kitchen. I found some cloth, wrapped it around the comb and tied it closed with twine. I went to my room and laid out my dress for work the next day. I put the comb, the money, and the photograph of my family in my dress pocket. I went to bed and waited for morning to come.

*

The next day, I didn't have morning sickness for the first time in a month. I washed and dressed and went to the kitchen. The apartment was eerily still without Jin-mo and his books. I finally cried a little when I realized I would never see him again, lie by his side, or talk to him about his ideas. I wondered what was happening to him, if he was being tortured or if they had simply killed him right away.

I hated them. The communists killed my beloved Jin-mo and they would kill Korea, too. Like the Japanese, they wanted all of you. It was just like Jin-mo said—first they

take your mind, then your soul and then your life. Well, I wasn't going to give them anything more.

I ate a breakfast of *dduk* and strong *bori cha*. I wondered if I should make *dduk* cakes to bring with me but thought better of it. Jin-mo's note said Mr. Gah would take care of me. I had to trust that he would.

I put on my coat and went out the door. The sun was shining making everything bright again. The willows filtered the sun like lace. It was almost warm. I headed to the provincial government building, careful not to look over my shoulder or do anything out of the ordinary. When I got there, I looked at the huge new statue of Kim Il-sung. He beamed down at me with outstretched arms. I threw a silent curse at him.

I walked inside and climbed the staircase to the Ministry of Education. I sat at my desk and bowed a greeting to my supervisor with the thick ankles. I began to work on a translation proclaiming that Kim Il-sung would be Korea's supreme leader for all eternity.

When my supervisor left the room, I went to the service staircase and down to the street level. I pushed the door open to an alley jammed with military trucks and official government cars. I wound my way to a side street and turned south toward the Taedong River.

TWENTY-EIGHT

"I WANT TO see the world," I said to Mr. Gah, sipping green tea in a back room of the shabby Gimhae Hotel. He was thin and balding and had a lazy lower lip, but his eyes were sharp.

He asked me if I was in trouble with the authorities. The words bumped across his lip, making him sound drunk. I said no I wasn't in trouble and I wanted to go because I didn't have anyone here in the North. He asked me if I had someone in the South.

"No sir," I said. "I have no one."

Mr. Gah raised an eyebrow. "So you want to leave because you have no one here. But you have no one there, either? Are you sure you want to go?"

"Sir," I said, "I believe they will kill me here."

"And do you think it will be better for you in the South?"

I held Mr. Gah's stare and thought about his question for a second. Then I said, "I honestly do not know."

Mr. Gah's face spread into a sloppy grin. A chuckle rose from his chest and spilled from his mouth. After a few seconds, he turned serious again.

"There is a fee to see the world," he said in a professional tone.

"I understand. How much?"

"One thousand won."

One thousand won was nearly all Jin-mo had left me. I counted out the money and laid it on the table in front of Mr. Gah. His lip curled unevenly into a smile. He took a sip of tea. "When do you want to go?" he asked.

"I have to leave right away," I answered. "I cannot go back."

Mr. Gah took the money and folded it into his pocket. "You're lucky. We have a truck leaving tonight. Behind the hotel is a shed. Go there and wait."

*

The shed was an old lean-to with a tin roof built against the hotel wall. I pulled opened the door and slipped in. It was dark. A man and woman and a young boy, huddled close to each other. I sat on the floor next to a sack of rice. I could smell the dampness of the Taedong River a few blocks away. Outside the shack, trucks rumbled over the cobblestone street.

After a few minutes, I could make out the others' faces. I could see fear in their eyes. The man's jaw was set at a defiant slant. The woman clung to his arm and held the boy close.

I smiled at the boy. He reminded me of Suk-ju. "What is your name?" I asked.

He blinked at me, then at his mother.

"It's okay," I said. "I'm going on a trip, just like you."

The boy eased a little. "My name is Sang-dong."

"Hush," scolded his father. "Children should not talk to strangers."

My heart went out to the frightened boy as he pushed his face into his mother again.

Sang-dong's father looked at me suspiciously. "Why are you leaving the north?" he asked.

"They killed the man I loved," I answered.

The man nodded. "There will be a civil war soon and the South will win. Maybe Korea can finally be united."

"Yes," I said, "although I hope it can be done without a civil war."

The man said, "I have a brother in Taejon. His name is Yaeng Il-dak. He works for an American contractor there. I haven't heard from him in over two years. I'm hoping he can help me get work. What will you do there?" he asked.

I hadn't thought about it. Jin-mo's note had only told me how to escape. It hadn't told me what to do after I did. I had very little money and nothing except the clothes I wore, the comb with the two-headed dragon, and a baby growing in my belly.

"I don't know what I will do in the south," I answered. "All I know is that I will not stay here."

We said nothing more and waited in the shed all day. My bladder grew painfully full and I was thirsty. My muscles ached from sitting, but my pregnant stomach was calm. Finally, the door opened. By the sun's angle, I could see it would be dark soon.

Mr. Gah leaned in. "Go inside and use the toilet," he said. "Hurry, the truck is coming."

I followed the others inside the hotel. I waited until they were done in the toilet and then used it myself. I took a long drink from the tap in the basin. When we went back to the lean-to, a military supply truck was waiting for us. Mr. Gah stood at the tailgate, watching the street. "In here," he said. "Quickly!" He lifted the tarp and helped each of us in.

Mr. Gah held up the corner of the tarp. "Listen carefully," he said. "In four hours, the driver will stop and knock on the cab three times. It is the signal for you to get out. Find a tire on the side of the road. Take the path by it until you come to a fence. Don't go off the path. When you get to the fence, go right fifty yards. There's an opening in the fence. You'll have to look for it. Go through it and follow the path on the other side to the road. Wave down the first truck you see. It will be the South Koreans."

Mr. Gah jutted his lip at us. "Be quiet, stay low, and move quickly. Be sure you stay on the path on both sides of the fence. Understand? Stay on the path. There is a quarter moon tonight, so your chances are good. If you get caught, do not tell them about me or I will never be able to help anyone again," he said. He dropped the flap closed and pounded on the truck side.

The truck lurched forward and rolled through the city. After a while, the ride smoothed out over what felt like a paved road. Sang-dong's mother pulled him close and eventually, the boy fell asleep. As evening gave way to night, the back of the truck grew dark and cold. I wrapped my coat tight around me. I wondered if I was making the right decision to escape to the south. What the communists said about it made it sound evil. But I knew the north *was* evil and I didn't want anything more to do with it. I had no choice. I had to make it to the south. I had to trust that my baby and I would be better off there.

Several hours later, the truck came to a stop. Three thuds came from the cab. Sang-dong's father jumped up and crawled out. He helped his wife and son get down. As I stood to jump out, the truck began to roll. I placed a hand on the tailgate and jumped. When I landed, my ankle twisted and I fell. A sharp pain shot up my leg. I stifled a yell and pushed myself to my feet. I tested my ankle. The pain was

almost unbearable. I hobbled over to the others who were crouching low in the ditch.

The truck disappeared over a ridge and we were alone in the darkness. We were next to a large, open field filled with dead waist-high weeds. It was very dark and deathly quiet.

"We have to find the path," the man whispered. "Do you see the tire?"

He looked along the ditch one way, then the other. "It's too dark. I'll have to find it," he said. He crawled along the ditch and a few seconds later, he came back. "This way!" he whispered. "Follow me." He lifted his son and took his wife by the hand. They disappeared into the blackness.

I tried to follow them as fast as I could, but each step sent spikes of pain up my leg. A few yards down the ditch, I found them crouched next to an old truck tire. Together, we crawled to the top of the ditch to a path among the weeds.

Then, on the other side of a ridge, came bright lights from a vehicle heading toward us. My heart stopped as the faint sound of a truck engine broke the stillness of the night. "Quickly!" the man said, darting forward. I followed them, but the pain in my ankle made me fall behind. I glanced over my shoulder just in time to see a truck crest the ridge and slowly come toward us. On top of the truck was a searchlight sweeping over the field.

I gritted my teeth and quickened my pace. Soon, I caught up to the others. The truck came closer. The searchlight cast its beam across the field to our left. The man stopped and crouched low. "I see the fence. It's only a short distance if we go straight for it." He handed Sang-dong to his wife. "I will lead the way. Come quickly."

"No!" I whispered. "Stay on the path." But the man had already disappeared. The woman lifted the boy to her hip and followed him.

I was about to follow too when the night sky exploded in a blinding light throwing me to the ground. The explosion

echoed off the hills. I lay there for what seemed like several seconds, then pushed myself to my hands and knees. I shook my head to clear the ringing in my ears. I thought I heard screaming. The searchlight swept through the weeds next to where the explosion had been. Something moved in front of me.

The woman burst through the weeds with the boy in her arms. Blood covered them both. The woman's eyes were wild. She thrust the boy at me. "Take him," she cried. I was still dazed and didn't understand what she wanted. The woman pushed the boy into my arms. "Take him!" she said through clenched teeth. I took him and she ran back into the weeds.

The searchlight scanned the area around us. Men were shouting from the road behind. The boy's eyes were wide. His face was splattered with blood. He reached for where his mother had gone. "*Ummah!*" he cried. "*Appa!*"

I put my hand over his mouth and he squirmed and fought. I lifted my head above the weeds. In the distance, I saw the outline of a high fence topped with barbed wire. I left the path and ran for it. The boy continued to wriggle, but I held him tight. When I got to the fence, I tried to remember Mr. Gah's instructions. I couldn't remember if he said to go left or right. I went right as the voices behind us grew louder.

I looked along the fence for an opening but in the darkness, I couldn't see anything. The searchlight swept the ground behind us. I dropped among the weeds. My hand came off the boy's mouth and he cried out. I found the boy's mouth again with my hand. "Shhh," I whispered. "Please be quiet." The boy, his eyes wide with fear, stopped struggling. When I took my hand away from his mouth, he stayed quiet.

As the searchlight moved closer, I felt inside my pocket for the comb with the two-headed dragon. It wasn't there. I

frantically searched the ground among the weeds, but I could not find it. The searchlight swept over us exposing something a few feet from me. It was the comb. Then I looked beyond the comb and followed the path of the searchlight. For a split second, the light illuminated the fence and I could see an opening next to a post. It was small, barely big enough for one person to squeeze through. I grabbed the comb and with the boy on my hip, I crawled for the opening.

The voices behind me grew louder. "Sergeant, over here!" a man said. There was the sound of boots running. The footsteps stopped where the explosion had been.

"You killed him!" the woman screamed. "You pigs, you killed him!"

At the sound of his mother's voice, the boy jerked up. "*Ummah!*" he shouted.

"Someone else is over there!" a soldier yelled.

With the comb in one hand and the boy in the other, I ran for the fence. The boy squirmed and shouted for his mother. "*Ummah!*" he cried again. "*Ummah!*" I got to the fence and lifted the wire. I pushed the boy through. I crawled under the fence, grabbed the boy, and ran.

Be sure you stay on the path on both sides of the fence, Mr. Gah had said. I looked at my feet and saw I wasn't on the path. I was terrified, but I kept running. The weeds slapped at my legs and my ankle screamed in pain.

A shot rang out, ripping through the weeds next to me. Then the searchlight found me. Another shot rang out, but this one came from in front of me. "Halt! Stay where you are," a voice said. I stopped and crouched among the weeds. The searchlight stayed on me. There was the sound of footsteps approaching from in front of me. Suddenly, three sets of boots, black and polished, surrounded me. I looked up. Soldiers pointed rifles at the fence behind me.

The searchlight went out. A soldier reached down and took the boy. Another helped me to my feet.

"Be very careful to follow exactly where I step," he said. "Welcome to the Republic of South Korea."

Twenty-nine

August 2008. Seoul, South Korea

MRS. HONG DOESN'T seem to notice me as she stands at her apartment window telling her story as if the entire world is her audience. The sun has moved around and it shines on her. The *mugunghwa* blossom basks in its rays. Still dressed in her yellow hanbok, she has clasped her hands behind her back and she sways slightly. I notice the lines on her face are deeper than before, as if her story is aging her.

She tells me she was able to give young Sang-dong to his uncle in Taejon, one week after she escaped from the North. She said the uncle was not pleased to have another mouth to feed and as a reward for saving his nephew, he gave her a few grains of rice. Then, when she finished eating, he told her she had to leave. "I was on the streets of Taejon with nothing more than the clothes on my back, the comb, and a baby in my belly," she says.

She stays quiet for a while and then turns from the window. She tells me she was able to work for food until

several months later, when she gave birth to a girl. It was September 15th, 1950, three months to the day after the North invaded the South that started the Korean civil war. It was also the day General MacArthur landed at Inchon to repel the invasion.

"The baby girl," I say, "she was my birthmother?"

Mrs. Hong nods. "Yes she was. I named her 'Soo,' for my sister Soo-hee, and 'Bo,' for my mother, Bo-sun. In Korea, it is not proper to name a child after an elder. But I did it anyway to regain a little of what I had lost. It was selfish, I suppose." She flashes a mischievous grin. "But who would know? Would you like more *bori cha*?"

"Yes, ma'am," I answer. I'm beginning to get a taste for it.

She goes to the stove and fills our cups. She hands me mine and sits at the table across from me, upright with both hands around her cup. "Soo-bo was born prematurely," she says. "It was a difficult delivery. I was in labor for eighteen hours during the Battle of the Pusan Perimeter. The North had almost won the war. I was terrified that if they did, they would find me and kill me. So I went to Pusan with the retreating South Korean Army.

"Pusan was the war's defining battle," she continues. "The American Air Force turned the war for the South. There were bombs going off day and night. Thousands died. There was an equally violent struggle inside me. But finally, Soo-bo was born. She was sick for a long time. An American army doctor cared for her. Captain Charles Keegan was his name. He was young, not even thirty years old. He was able to find a cotton blanket for Soo-bo and gave me food from the American mess so I could nurse. I heard he was killed by a mortar a few months later."

I take a sip of *bori cha* and try to imagine what it was like back then. "The war must have been awful," I say.

She looks into her teacup and shakes her head. "It should not have happened. The Americans and Russians should have let us be after World War II. Perhaps then we could have resolved our differences."

I push to the front of my seat. "When we visited Panmunjom they told us that the Russians gave the North weapons and pushed them to invade the South. The Americans only came in later. To prevent the communists from taking over."

She glares at me. "Yes. But then they drove all the way to the Chinese border. Your General MacArthur's insolence and disrespect for the Chinese made them believe the Americans were going to invade them, too. So they entered the war on behalf of the North. As a result, the war in my homeland went on for three more bloody years."

"So you think we should have let the communists win?"

"I think the Americans should have been more careful with my country," she says. "Understand, Ja-young, millions died in that war. Millions! They are not just numbers in a history book. They were families, entire villages, people I knew, my friends and countrymen. And millions more were left homeless with nothing to eat. After centuries of being torn between the Chinese, Japanese and Russians, and after thirty-five years of a brutal Japanese occupation, all we wanted was to be one country, at peace. Instead, we were a pawn in a game fought to a draw by the world's superpowers."

She looks at me like a teacher trying to get through to a stubborn student. I have to look away. I'd never had much interest in history before, but now I'm seeing it from someone who lived it. I'm beginning to see why Dad says I should take a few history classes in college.

"To answer your question," she says, "we are better off having not let Kim Il-sung rule all of Korea. He became a

despot, just like I had predicted. Although the corrupt American puppet Syngman Rhee was not much better."

"What happened to you during the war?" I ask.

She sits back and looks into her *bora cha* again. "I was one of the homeless and destitute. I was fluent in English, as I said, and that helped. But I still struggled. Soo-bo and I were always close to starving. In the middle of a war, a poor young woman with a sick baby is a nuisance to everyone. You need know nothing more, other than we survived through effort and luck."

I think about how hard her life had been at my age and feel guilty for feeling sorry for myself and for being afraid. I mean, really. Compared to what she had to go through, what do I have to be afraid of? "You're life was tough," I say. "I'm sorry."

"Yes, but I survived," she says. "And for me, that is what was important."

She eyes me for a few seconds and then she asks, "And what about you? What is important to you?"

"Well, I'm not sure. I used to think it was being successful, you know? Doing well in school. But I'm not in school anymore," I confess. "I had to drop out when Mother got sick."

"Do you plan to go back?"

I shake my head. "I really don't know. I haven't got a clue what for."

She continues to stare at me and I can see she's expecting more of an answer. I fidget and then tell her that at one time I was thinking about medical school. I tell her I took the pre-med classes and I did enough to get in, but I'm not sure if I want to be a doctor. I say then I thought about law school and that I made a pros and cons list for each one, medical school versus law school. I tell her that after all that, I thought maybe I should do something completely different. "Now," I say, "I don't know if I should even finish school."

"You made a pros and cons list?" she asks. "Do you always think things through that way?"

"Yes. I try to."

"And, does it work for you?"

"I guess."

"You have a very good mind, Anna, that is obvious. But you are a Korean and Koreans make decisions differently. We use our hearts as well as our heads. When we say, 'I think,' we point to our hearts.

"So let me tell you what I think," she says, pointing to her heart. "I think you are trying to find what is in your heart, but your head keeps getting in the way. You came to Korea to try to discover something about yourself, something you cannot simply make a pros and cons list for. After I gave you the comb, you came to meet me for the same reason. You did not give in to those government officials even when they threatened you. If you had thought through those decisions—if your heart wasn't tugging at you—you would have never done them.

"So tell me, Anna Carlson," she says, "what does your heart say about your future?"

I shrug. "I really don't know."

She smiles and says she understands. She says that after she finishes her story, we'll talk more. She asks if I'm ready to hear the rest of her story. I say that I am.

She straightens and puts her hands in her lap. She tells me that after the Korean War, South Korea was in chaos and that everyone was angry, looking for people to blame. She says there was a backlash against anyone who might have been sympathetic to the communists and that she was caught in that backlash. People knew she had worked for the North so she was blacklisted, unable to get work. They cut her off from assistance. She was in real danger and had to disappear for a while.

She takes in a breath as if she's about to start again, but she hesitates. She gives an embarrassed smile. I wonder if she'll be able to continue.

Finally, she says, "I'm sorry. This last part is hard."

"It's okay," I say. "Maybe we should rest a while."

She shakes her head. "No. I must do this."

THIRTY

April 1954. U.S. Military Base Camp Humphreys, South Korea

I STOOD IN the backroom of a bar with three-year-old Soo-bo clinging to my side. I could feel my daughter's bones pressing through her dress. Soo-bo's sunken cheeks and eyes worried me. And she was feverish again. It had been three days since we'd had anything to eat. I was terrified that my daughter was going to starve to death.

American jazz pulsed from the barroom on the other side of the wall. A man in his early thirties with green eyes and a deep scar in his cheek reclined in front of me with his feet on a desk. He had his blonde hair cropped short, in the style of a U.S. military man. His name was Alan Smith.

Alan leaned back and inspected me professionally. "We don't give away food here. You hafta earn it. It's called capitalism."

I had read all of Jin-mo's books written by the world's greatest economists that argued the merits of capitalism

versus socialism. I doubted if Alan had read even a single word on the subject. "I see, sir," I said. "How does it work?"

"We give you a loan for your first and last month's rent. We also give an advance for food and clothing. That's the 'capital' part of capitalism, understand? I charge ten percent interest every month. Rent is due at the beginning of the month, no exceptions. A hundred bucks. Another twenty for the bed and chair. Anything you buy we charge against your account. You'll also have to pay for food and laundry."

I was anxious to end the interview so I could get something to eat for Soo-bo. But I didn't want to appear too desperate. "What do I have to do?" I asked.

Alan kept his eyes on me as he worked a toothpick between his teeth. "Well, some girls start by helping out around here—working the bar, cleaning, laundry, running errands and such. You're lucky. I need someone for that."

"I see. How much will I be able to earn?"

He took his toothpick out and pointed it at me. "Depends on you. That's how capitalism works, see? The more you do, the more you make. I pay fifty cents an hour."

"I understand," I said. I pressed Soo-bo close.

Alan eyed Soo-bo impassively. "'Course, if you can't earn enough just by helping out, you can be a juicy girl. You're older, but you're pretty and you speak English good. Could make a lotta money. Here's how that works. If a customer wants to spend some private time with you, they pay what's called a bar fine to take you upstairs. On top of the bar fine, they give you a tip for your services. I get half of your tip. It's the same deal for everyone. It's the same at every bar in this *kijichon*."

I could hear Soo-bo's stomach growl. My stomach clawed at me, too. "No. I won't do that," I said. "I would like the other job please. Can I start right away?"

Alan grinned and the scar on his face twisted. "Sure. If that's what you wanna do."

Alan led me and Soo-bo up a set of wooden stairs to a long, dimly lit hallway on the second floor. At the end of the hallway, he opened a door and pointed inside. "Your room," he said.

I stepped inside the room, leading Soo-bo by the hand. It was small. A grimy window looked over the only street in the *kijichon*. It reeked of stale sweat and semen. I recoiled at the all-too familiar stench.

Before I could pick up Soo-bo and run out the door, Alan held out a dark green can and an opener. "And here's your lunch," he said. "Should be enough for you and the kid."

Soo-bo grabbed at the can. "*Umshik, Ummah!*" she cried. "Food! I'm hungry."

I closed my nose to the stench in the room and took the can and opener. "Thank you," I said.

Alan Smith jammed the toothpick in his mouth. "I need help at the bar this afternoon. Get yourself an outfit at one of the tailors on the street. Can't work dressed like that. This is a classy joint." As he headed down the hallway, he said over his shoulder, "I need the can opener back when you're done with it."

I closed the door and pushed my rucksack beneath the American-style bed. I sat on the floor, pulling Soo-bo's scrawny frame into my lap. As Soo-bo anxiously watched, I opened the can. Inside was a gelatinous, gray-green mass. I picked at it with my fingers and tasted it. It was salty and slimy, but it was something to eat. I scooped out a finger full and fed Soo-bo who greedily slurped at it. In less than a minute, we had eaten the can's entire contents.

Soo-bo, her starving body finally satisfied, drooped with fatigue. I laid her on the bed. I kissed my daughter on the head, and soon she was sound asleep.

The meal made me tired, too, but as I listened to the American servicemen gathering in the bar below, I knew I

had to start earning money right away. I left Soo-bo and went downstairs to the street. At the end of the street was a paved road and a gate to a military base with an American flag flying atop a flagpole. Above the entrance, a sign read 'Camp Humphreys'. The shabby bars that lined the street advertising Korean girls reminded me of the comfort station. I wondered how I had come to this. I thought I had put places like this behind me. But here I was again, and I wondered if I'd ever be free of the comfort station.

I walked a few doors down and turned into a tailor shop. A balding man wearing half-glasses was at a sewing machine. "Do you need an outfit?" he asked without looking up.

"Yes, sir."

"What bar are you with?"

"The Hometown Cat Club."

The man examined me over his glasses. "You need something that makes you look younger," he said. "I recommend a short black dress."

"No," I answered. "I'm not doing that."

He shook his head and laughed. He pointed to the back. "You can choose from that rack. The prices are in dollars. Sizing is extra."

I went to the rack. Hanging from metal hangers were all sorts of provocative women's outfits—long, formal dresses; short sequined dresses; several Japanese kimonos and even an American cowgirl outfit. At the end was a green *yukata* with pretty white and pink flowers.

I ran my hand across the cool, green silk of the *yukata* and tried to think of what I could do other than this. I couldn't think of anything. I was trapped. But if I stayed here, I would be able to hide for a while and feed Soo-bo. I would have a roof over my head and, if I worked hard enough, perhaps I could pay off the debt I now owed. Then, I could move to Seoul once things settled down.

I turned away from the *yukata* and looked for an outfit more appropriate for me. On the rack was a simple blue dress with a knee-high hem that was about my size. It was thirty dollars—the cheapest on the rack. I took it and presented it to the balding man. He looked from his sewing machine. "You sure you want that cheap one? You would be better off with…"

"I want this one," I said.

The man shrugged. "Okay. Do what you want. What's your name?"

I gave it and he wrote it down. "I'll charge your account at the bar," he said, and returned to his sewing. "Good luck."

THIRTY-ONE

SOO-BO WAS IN a deep sleep when I returned to my room.
From the rucksack, I took a blanket and laid it in the corner
on the floor. I carried Soo-bo from the bed and put her on
the blanket. She moaned and rolled toward the wall. I was so
relieved to see her sleep like that again.

I took a rag from my rucksack, cleaned the window and
wiped the floor. I placed the photograph of my family next
to the bed. I grabbed the rucksack to push it under the bed
and the flap opened. Inside was the coarse brown cloth
package of the comb with the two-headed dragon. I
wondered how much it was worth. Perhaps enough to go to
Seoul and stay low until I could find a job there. After all, I
had a gift for languages and South Korea was beginning to
rebuild after the war. Surely, someone could use a person
like me.

But I had promised Soo-hee and Jin-mo to carry on and
tell their story. I promised to keep the comb. So I closed the
rucksack and slid it under the bed. I stripped off my clothes

and put on the blue dress. I pulled on my *tabi* and *zori* and went downstairs to the Hometown Cat Club bar.

Beer and cigarette smoke had stained the bar's plywood floors brown. Behind a long, flimsy bar was the red and black emblem for the United States Eighth Army. Red linoleum tables, chipped and leaning, were scattered in front of a large, dirty window that looked out at the *kijichon's* dusty street. A jukebox played jazz music and a soldier danced cheek-to-cheek with a young Korean girl. The room smelled like stale beer.

When I came into the room, sixteen servicemen and six working girls studied me. I pushed myself to the bar. Alan Smith, his toothpick jammed in the corner of his mouth, was behind the bar pouring drinks. He motioned for me to come over. He nodded toward three soldiers at a table. "Get their drink orders," he said. "Your job is to keep them drinking. Go."

I approached the table. A young, uniformed lieutenant with thick, dark hair and a slim build, smiled at me lasciviously. "Hey baby," he said, curling an arm around my waist. "You speak-e English?"

Instead of bowing like I should, I faced him straight on. "As a matter of fact, lieutenant," I said, careful to pronounce each word correctly, "I am fluent in English."

He smiled broadly at the two soldiers next to him. "Holy shit! D'ju guys hear that? She speaks English like a damn school teacher." The soldiers grinned at me expectantly.

"You from America or somethin'?" a stocky sergeant asked. He clutched a mug of beer in one hand, and a cigarette in the other.

"No, sergeant. I have never been to America. I just have a good ear for languages. My name is Ja-hee. I'm here to get your drink orders."

"Fuckin'-a," the sergeant said. "Good ear for languages, eh? We got ourselves a regular Margaret Mitchell juicy girl here. You ever write a book like *Gone with the Wind?*"

The other soldiers laughed at the sergeant's joke. A man in civilian clothes who had been sitting alone at a table by the window came over and joined the group. I hadn't noticed him when I came into the bar. His left arm was missing. "What's going on, men? Who's the new girl?"

"Name's Ja-hee, Colonel," the lieutenant said, still clinging to my waist. "Says she's good with languages. She talks like a goddamn English professor, even though she's never been to America."

I was surprised the man was a colonel. He looked young for that rank. He inserted himself between me and the lieutenant. "Where'd you learn to speak English?"

I looked back at four sets of eyes eagerly awaiting my answer. It was a careless thing what I did next, but I wanted them to know I wasn't like the other girls there. So I said, "I was a translator for the government for four years. I worked on important contracts, statements and speeches. In fact, in 1948, I helped translate into English the declaration that established the Republic of South Korea, the country you now occupy. Now, what can I get you men to drink?"

The soldiers looked at each other wide-eyed for several seconds, then burst into laughter. The sergeant knocked over his beer and dropped his cigarette on the floor. The lieutenant almost fell down. Everyone in the Hometown Cat Club stared at me.

"Where'd you get this one, Al?" sputtered the lieutenant. "She's good!"

The Colonel pushed himself further between me and the others. He stood inches from me. "Come join me at my table," he said.

I bowed my head. I noticed the Colonel was wearing polished shoes tied tightly and my *ianfu* instincts kicked in.

Be careful, I said to myself. "I'm sorry, sir," I said. "I have to help at the bar."

The Colonel said, "Don't worry, Al won't mind. Get these men what they want and put it on my tab. Then come sit with me." He went to his table.

After the soldiers stopped laughing, I took their drink orders and gave them to Alan. I told him the Colonel asked me to sit with him.

"Do as he says," Alan replied.

I brought the soldiers their drinks, then went to the Colonel's table next to the big, dirty window. He told me to sit with him for a while.

The Colonel was tall and trim. His eyes were the blue-green of jade and his hair the smooth, dark brown of polished rosewood. He wore pressed khaki slacks and a white safari shirt. The empty sleeve, where his left arm had been, was neatly pinned to the front of his shirt. He was well tanned.

He told me his name was Colonel Frank Crawford. He had a light Southern accent. He asked what my family name was and I told him.

"*Anyahasao*, Hong, Ja-hee," he said. He continued in Korean, "What brings you to the Hometown Cat Club?"

I kept the conversation in Korean. "I've come here to work. It's difficult to find work in Korea right now."

"What will you do here?"

"I'm helping Mr. Smith at the bar and with his chores."

"You won't make it just doing chores," the Colonel said, switching to English. "You'll have to be a juicy girl like the rest."

"I'm a very hard worker," I replied.

"It doesn't matter. There aren't enough hours in the day to earn what you need. Everyone who starts like you is forced to be a juicy girl."

I did some quick math in my head and realized the Colonel was right. At fifty cents per hour, I would earn less than ten dollars per day. I was already in debt for the first month's rent, my blue dress, and for the food that Soo-bo and I had for lunch. I would never be able to catch up.

The Colonel raised a brown eyebrow. He asked me if it was true what I said about being a translator before the war. "Your English is certainly good enough," he said.

I knew I had to be careful what I told the Colonel. As a senior military officer, he would know the names of people that I would have worked with. I told him no, that I was only making a joke.

The Colonel looked out the window and said, "I've seen a lot of Korea over the past several years. It's a beautiful country, although it's hard to see anything through this filthy window. Where are you from?"

"I'm from the North. I escaped to the South after World War II."

"Do you have family there?"

"No, sir. They were killed by the Japanese."

The Colonel took a sip from his glass and held it in his hand. He was drinking what looked like bourbon. "I'm sorry to hear that. If it wasn't for the damn communists, we would have the entire peninsula on the right track."

"You mean we would all be capitalists under the American system," I said.

The corners of the Colonel's mouth turned up and his blue eyes sparkled. "Do I detect cynicism in you, Hong Ja-hee?"

"With all due respect, Colonel, I do not think it's as simple as you say."

"Ah, you're a philosopher. How interesting."

The Colonel set his glass on the table. He regarded me for a moment making me feel like I was someone special, but also like someone who he could buy. Finally he said,

"Would you like to dance with me? I'm a very good dancer, even with just one arm. My mother insisted I learn. 'A Southern gentleman should know how to dance with a lady,' she always said. And a Southern gentleman never disappoints his mother." He smiled pleasantly.

"I don't know how to dance," I said quickly.

The Colonel stood and held out his hand. "Come," he said. "I'll teach you."

"No, I shouldn't. It isn't right. What about your wife?"

"She divorced me when I volunteered for a third tour in Korea." The Colonel took my hand. "Come with me."

When we took the dance floor, the soldier and girl who had been dancing there moved to the bar. The Colonel leaned over the jukebox and punched a few buttons while I stood alone. Soon, the jazz song ended and the jukebox began to play a waltz.

He faced me. "I had Al put in some records just for me. The men don't like it. Razz me about it all the time. But I outrank them," he said with a grin. "Now, let me show you how to do a Viennese waltz."

He wrapped his one arm around me and pulled me close. He told me to put my hands on his shoulders. He said it was a three-count step that I could hear it in the music. One, two, three. One, two, three. He instructed me to move my feet with his.

He began to step with the music, taking a step back with his right foot on 'one', putting his feet together on 'two', and taking a side step with his left foot on 'three.' Looking down, I tried to imitate his steps. I missed a beat and nearly tripped on his feet. He held me firmly. He told me it was okay and that I should try again. He moved once more and I moved with him. After a few more tries, I could feel the music flow through me. I stepped to its rhythm. When I made a mistake, the Colonel pulled me back in step with the poise of a self-assured leading man. "You're doing fine," he said. "Keep

going. Good," he said when I got it right. His support melted away my self-consciousness and I began to move with the Colonel across the floor as if we were a single dancer.

I looked up from my feet. The room spun around as we moved and I became light-headed. My steps became more natural. I began to surrender to the moment, to the dance with this soldier who embraced me with one arm. I felt free and alive, like I did in the arms of Jin-mo.

Then he said, "Look at me. Look into my eyes."

I looked into his jade-blue eyes. Suddenly, the image of Colonel Matsumoto flashed in my mind. *Look at me,* he had said as he raped me. *Look into my eyes.* I stopped dancing and pushed back. "I'm sorry, sir," I said. "I cannot do this."

"Is something wrong?"

"Yes... I mean, no. I should get back to work."

The Colonel nodded politely. "Thank you for dancing with me, Hong Ja-hee," he said with a slight bow. "We'll do this again, I hope."

I bowed back to him and went to join Alan at the bar.

THIRTY-TWO

"*UMMAH*, WAKE UP!" Soo-bo said, inches from my face. I blinked sleep from my eyes. Standing in front of me was my daughter, ready to begin her day. The morning light was still low and I needed more sleep. I ached from long hours of hard work. But I didn't mind. I had saved Soo-bo from starving.

My daughter had filled out since we arrived at the *kijichon* ten months earlier. She was still thin and often had long spells of fever. But at the *kijichon*, she was able to eat every day and I was greatly relieved. I loved her more than I had ever thought possible. I took sublime joy in dressing her, her playfulness, and her four-year-old mannerisms. Still, Soo-bo struggled with the simple lessons I gave her. Sometimes she slipped into dark moods and I worried about her strength.

I stroked Soo-bo's hair. "You're awake so early, little one."

"I'm hungry, *Ummah*," my daughter said. "Will you tell me more of our story?"

I swung myself to the edge of the bed. "Yes," I said. "Where did we leave off?"

"The rich *yangban* had come from Seoul with a present for her daughter. What is it, *Ummah*? What is the present?"

"You will have to wait to see," I said. "Let's eat breakfast first."

I pulled on a shirt and slacks. I took Soo-bo's hand and we went down the stairs to the small, plywood-walled kitchen in the back of the bar. It had a newer army refrigerator that Alan bartered a juicy girl's time for, and a propane countertop stove. As Soo-bo waited at the table, I made *bori cha* and poured myself a cup. I poured Rice Krispies in a bowl with milk and gave it to Soo-bo. After I had worked for Alan for a while, I encouraged him to trade bar tabs for supplies, so we usually had American foods available. Rice Krispies was Soo-bo's favorite. She loved the characters of Snap, Crackle and Pop on the box and delighted in the sounds that the cereal made. She wouldn't eat anything else for breakfast. As Soo-bo ate her cereal, I cleaned the kitchen and washed out dozens of foul mugs with stale beer and cigarette butts inside.

As Soo-bo finished her breakfast, a juicy girl shuffled into the kitchen. She was dressed in baby-blue lingerie and her hair was a mess. Her name was Dae-ee and I guessed she was not much more than seventeen years old. She poured herself some *bori cha*. She looked at Soo-bo, then at me and I could tell she wanted to talk.

I told Soo-bo to go to our room and wait for me and that we would have more of our story when I got back.

Soo-bo hurried out of the kitchen and Dae-ee slumped into a chair at the table. Four months earlier, Dae-ee had strolled into the Hometown Cat Club on the arm of an American corporal who had told her he loved her and that he would take her to America and marry her. She'd looked with disdain at the juicy girls, and only talked to me to order

drinks for her man. Days later, when the corporal went back to America without her—undoubtedly with a few hundred dollars in his pocket from Alan—she was alone, penniless and scared. She had to accept Alan's offer to help me at the bar. One month later, she was a juicy girl.

"I can't do this anymore, O*nni*," Dae-ee said staring at her *bori cha*. "But I don't know what else to do."

I set the towel on the counter and took the chair across from her. "You should go back to your family," I said. "Chonan is not far from here."

"I cannot. I have shamed them. And I owe Alan too much. I thought if I worked as a juicy girl, I would be able to make more money. But now I owe more than when I started." She began to cry. "What should I do, O*nni?* Tell me, what should I do?"

My heart went out to her. She reminded me of myself when I was young—stubborn and a little too proud. So when Dae-ee started working at the club, I had taken her under my wing and helped her get by. I warned her about becoming a juicy girl, but she didn't listen to me. Now she owed Alan so much, she would never get out from under her debts. Dae-ee, like most other juicy girls, had become nothing more than a sex slave for the Americans, just like I had been for the Japanese.

I reached over and touched Dae-ee's hand. "Don't worry about what you owe Alan. Go back home and face your family. You have to find the strength to do the right thing."

Dae-ee had tears in her eyes. "I can't. I just can't do it."

I looked at my hands. "I have felt that way several times. Honestly, sometimes I feel like it here, too."

Dae-ee's jaw tightened. "You've never had to do what I do here," she said.

I gave her a stern look which put her back. "Do not ever assume you know how others have suffered."

Dae-ee lowered her eyes. "I'm sorry, *Onni*." She set her *bori cha* aside and sighed heavily. "I wish I was strong like you." She left the table and trudged up the stairs.

*

Thursday was the Colonel's day off and I hoped to see him in the bar that evening. I gave Soo-bo to Dae-ee. Without Soo-bo in tow, I was able to finish my chores by early afternoon. I washed my blue dress and hung it on the line behind the club to dry. I took a hot bath, washed my hair and combed it smooth with the comb with the two-headed dragon.

Late afternoon, I put on my blue dress and went down to the bar. It was early. Only a handful of soldiers were there and only two juicy girls were working. Alan had an elbow on the bar and rested his square head on his thick hand. "When are you going to make some real money, Ja-hee?" he asked. "Been ten months and you ain't making progress on your debt. You're popular with the men. Any one of them would pay top dollar to have a poke with you."

"I do make money for you, Alan. You just don't pay me for it. Business is way up since I started here. I have offers from other bars."

He plucked a toothpick from a shot glass and examined it. "You'd make a lot more as a juicy girl."

"Who would do all the cooking and cleaning? Who would take care of the girls? This place would fall apart."

"I'd find someone."

No, he would not. Not anyone as good as me and he knew it. I leaned against the bar. "Dae-ee wants to leave. Let her go."

"Can't. She has debts."

"She can't pay it off."

"'Cause she's lazy. And she's just another girl. You, on the other hand, you got somethin' the men want. You'd make a lot of money. Wouldn't be so bad. You'd get used to it."

I shook my head. The girls in the Hometown Cat Club served three or four men per night. In Dongfeng, I'd had forced sex with as many as thirty men nearly every day for two years. I never got used to it then and I certainly would not get used to it now.

Alan chuckled. "Shit, I bet the Colonel'd pay five hundred bucks for a night with you. Maybe more. He likes you and he's got money. Comes from a real rich family in Atlanta. They build houses or somethin'."

"Commercial construction," I said.

"What?"

"His family owns the biggest construction company in Georgia. They build skyscrapers. He told me all about it."

"Is that what you two talk about all the time? Skyscrapers?"

"We talk about a lot of things. He gives me books to read. We talk about those. You told me I should spend as much time with him as he wants."

"You shouldn't be wastin' time with your damn books. I wish you'd do more than talk to the Colonel. You'd be able to pay off your debt."

"You and your debt," I sniffed. "This is nothing more than indentured slavery."

Alan pointed his toothpick at me. "Be careful, Ja-hee. I have a good guess why you're here. A few calls and I'd know for sure. Then what'd you do?"

He jammed the toothpick in his mouth. "Beginning of the month," he said, "you owe another rent payment. I ain't letting you out of here until you pay me off, so you better think about how you're going to make more money." He went to the other end of the bar and picked up a magazine.

*

Disgusted, I grabbed a rag and went to the front window. I stood on a chair and wiped the window clean. I cleaned it every day—on most days, inside and out. I told myself I did it because it was my job to keep the club clean. But inside, I knew it was because the Colonel liked to look out the window.

The bar started to fill with soldiers and the girls came from their rooms to work them. I went from table to table taking drink orders. Jazz music pulsed from the jukebox while the girls started their nightly trek up stairs with men. The Hometown Cat Club ran smoothly because of me. It was clean, I had the bar stocked with good liquor, the beer was always cold, and the jukebox played the latest American records. The most attractive girls wanted to work at my club. I was proud that I had made it the most popular brothel in the entire *kijichon*. But when I thought about what I was doing, I was ashamed, too.

It was bustling when the Colonel came in. I smiled when I saw him. He was wearing the same khaki slacks and safari shirt that he always wore. His empty sleeve was pinned to his shirt. He took his table in front of the window. I poured some Old Fitzgerald Kentucky bourbon into a spotless glass and took it to him. Months earlier, he told me that he drank Old Fitzgerald at home in Georgia. "It's what they serve in the White House," he had said. So, I asked the man who sold us liquor to get a case and I convinced Alan to pay the higher price for it. The bourbon had come three days earlier and I couldn't wait to surprise the Colonel with it. I took the glass to his table.

He said good evening to me in his soft Southern drawl. And asked how business was in the Hometown Cat Club. I

told him it was busy as usual and took a seat across from him.

"Yes, it is that," he said.

He raised his glass and took a sip of bourbon. He looked in the glass, lifted an eyebrow and took another sip. His jade-blue eyes went wide. "Ja-hee, what have you done? I do believe this is Old Fitz!" he exclaimed.

I grinned and nodded. "Alan was upset at how much it cost. I had to convince him to buy it. He's charging you double."

"Well worth it, well worth it. The drink of presidents. They say General Ulysses Grant drank a glass every day. He was a great warrior, but, as you know, my favorite is Robert E. Lee."

"Yes. You have told me many times," I said.

The Colonel sipped more bourbon and took a long look at me. "Thank you," he said. "You always treat me well."

"You are a good customer."

"Good customer? Is that all I am?"

"Okay. A special customer," I said.

"So why don't you ever dance with me? You only did that one time."

"I cannot."

"Why not? We've spent a lot of time together, Ja-hee. We've shared a lot. At least, *I've* shared a lot. I think I've earned a dance, don't you? As I recall, you caught on quickly to the Viennese waltz."

I looked into the Colonel's eyes. He was a decent man. He was always polite, always a Southern gentleman. He was well read on a host of topics. We spent hours talking about his family and friends back home in his beloved Georgia. He went on and on about "General Robert E. Lee of the Southern Confederacy" as he always said. We talked about politics, World War II and the Korean War. He gave me books to read—his favorite was Ayn Rand's *The*

Fountainhead—which we discussed every Thursday night at his table for a month. I honestly enjoyed our talks. They reminded me of the long talks I'd had with Jin-mo about his books. But just like the juicy girls and their customers, there was no future for me with the Colonel. I knew he would go home someday and I would stay trapped in the *kijichon* thinking about him, wishing I had not gotten involved with the handsome southern gentleman.

"It is not proper for a Korean woman to dance with a man who is not her husband," I said. "I'm sorry."

"We're in a *kijichon*. All sorts of improper things go on here. Dancing is relatively tame, don't you think?"

"It depends on what your ulterior motives are."

"My ulterior motives?" he exclaimed. "With you?"

"Yes."

He shook his head. "I just want to dance."

"And then?"

"There doesn't have to be an 'and then'. We can dance to enjoy dancing." He set his glass on the table. "Why don't you trust me? Is it me or do you distrust all foreigners?"

"I distrust people who have their soldiers in my country," I answered. "I distrust a military that supports the trafficking of women for sex."

"We don't support it."

"Oh? Then what are you and these men doing here?"

"We're not the Japanese, Ja-hee," the Colonel said.

"What's the difference?" I pointed my chin at the girls in the room. "For them, for the girls, what's the difference between you and the Japanese?"

He looked annoyed. "What would you have us do? Leave? Let the Communists take over? It's us or them, Ja-hee. Take your pick."

"So here we are, a divided nation," I said.

The Colonel shrugged. "Like I said, take your pick." He took another sip of Old Fitz and regarded me with a long

stare. "So if you feel that way, what are *you* doing here serving drinks to American soldiers?"

"I'm trying to pay my debt to Alan."

The Colonel sighed. After a long pause, he grinned at me and told me I should try some Old Fitz. I said no, but he was already halfway to the bar. He got the bottle and another glass from Alan and brought them to the table. He filled my glass, then his own.

"Come on, try it. Good Kentucky bourbon, not like the swill they have here." I refused.

The Colonel looked at me as if I was one of his men. He said, "If you won't dance, then have a drink with me."

I decided I could give him that, so I took a sip. The bourbon cut my tongue and burned my throat.

The Colonel lifted his glass and admired the liquid inside. "Good Kentucky bourbon. Liquor like this should only be drunk with someone special, and that's you, Ja-hee! Have another sip."

I took another drink. This time, it didn't burn as much, and I started to feel warm.

"Someday, you should go to America," the Colonel said, pointing his glass at me. "It's beautiful. It has snow-capped mountains, blue oceans, modern cities teeming with people and automobiles. We are the greatest country in the world."

He grinned to himself, and raised his glass. "Let's drink a toast. I'll drink to Korea and you drink to America."

I looked at his handsome face and remembered the night I drank *sake* with Colonel Matsumoto. Suddenly, everything about this place—the soldiers who took advantage of Korean girls, the Eighth Army emblem above the bar, Alan and his book where he kept track of the girls' debts—it all sickened me. I set my glass down and bowed my head. "Thank you for the drink, Colonel, but I should not have any more of your bourbon. And, I must get back to work."

I went to a table of soldiers and took their drink orders. As I brought the orders to the bar, I glanced at the Colonel. He sat alone, drinking his Old Fitzgerald Kentucky bourbon, looking out the window that I had cleaned for him.

THIRTY-THREE

IT WAS VERY late at night when I hauled a sack full of dirty linens toward the laundry at the far end of the *kijichon*. The cheap cafés had switched off their outside lights hours earlier and light shone from inside only one bar. Here and there, a drunken soldier staggered toward Camp Humphreys or slumped against a wall in a stupor.

On the other side of the street, the bartender of the last open bar shoved three drunken soldiers out to the street. One stumbled to the ground. His companions pointed at him and laughed. As the soldier climbed to his feet, the bartender closed the door and switched off the lights.

"What the fuck?" said the soldier who had fallen. He carried a bottle in one hand and clung to his companion with the other. "Ain't there nothin' open in this goddamn place?"

"All shut down with nothin' to do," his companion said. I kept walking toward the laundry trying not to be seen.

"Well, look-e there," a soldier said, pointing at me. "It's a juicy girl."

One shouted, "Hey, you. Wanna make some money?"

I quickened my pace in spite of the heavy load. The three crossed the street toward me.

"Hey, don't go away," a soldier said. "I'm talking to you."

They caught up to me and surrounded me. I dropped the laundry sack and faced them.

"I'll be damned," one said. "It's Ja-hee from the Cat Club. She don't screw anyone. Not even Crawford." He took a step closer. "Why don't you fuck, girl? You too good for an American?"

"Let me be," I said.

"Shit, you talk like an American. You should be willing to fuck one."

"Yeah," another said, "I need someone new."

The three pressed in close and I could smell beer on their breaths. "I am friends with Colonel Crawford," I said quickly. "You don't want to get in trouble. Now leave me alone!"

One of the soldiers laughed. "Colonel Crawford? He ain't the colonel here no more. He shipped out."

"Yeah," another said. "Won't be much help to you now."

A soldier reached for me and I punched him hard.

He rubbed his nose and said, "You bitch!" And then all three jumped on me. I fought as hard as I could, but I couldn't fight off all three of them. I tried to scream for help but they covered my mouth. One of them straddled me and started to unbutton his pants.

"Get off of her!" shouted a voice from behind the soldiers. I saw a hand reach in, grab a soldier and throw him to the ground. One of the two others wheeled around and a fist slammed into his stomach. He collapsed to his knees.

The third soldier backed away. "What're you doin'?" he said.

"Leave her the fuck alone!"

"Jesus, Alan!" the third soldier said cowering. "Don't hit me."

Alan Smith stood a few feet away, his fists clenched and pure rage in his eyes.

"Take these other two assholes and go back to your barracks!" Alan ordered. "And if you pricks ever touch her again, I'll fuckin' tear your heads off and shit down your throats. Understand?"

"We're just havin' fun," the soldier said, helping his friends to their feet.

"Get outta here!" Alan roared. They scurried away keeping a wary eye on Alan as they stumbled down the street toward Camp Humphreys.

Alan helped me to my feet. "You all right?"

"Yes, I think so," I said. "They were going to rape me."

"Ah, they're just drunk," Alan said. "Probably couldn'ta done it if you let them."

I blinked at Alan. "What are you doing here?"

"Came to get you. Colonel wants to talk to you. He's in a car outside the club."

"The Colonel?"

"Yeah. Wouldn't tell me what it's about. I'll take the laundry. You go."

"Alan," I said, "thank you."

"Better hurry," Alan replied, hoisting the sack of laundry. "He said he didn't have a lotta time."

*

A big black Cadillac sat underneath a streetlight outside the Hometown Cat Club. A sergeant leaned against the car, smoking a cigarette. "Are you Hong Ja-hee?" he asked as I approached.

"Yes sir," I replied.

The sergeant dropped his cigarette and ground it out with the toe of his boot. He opened the car door. "Get in," he ordered.

"Where are you taking me?" I asked.

"Nowhere. The General wants to talk to you."

I climbed in and sat next to Colonel Crawford. In the darkness, I could see that he was wearing a traveling uniform with several rows of service bars and medals above his breast pocket. He held his dress cap in his lap.

"Hello, Ja-hee," he said. His soft southern accent made my heart beat a little faster.

"The driver said a general wanted to talk to me."

"A general *is* talking to you. They've made me a general, Ja-hee. I'll be one of the army's youngest. I'm heading to the Pentagon now. I don't have much time."

"I see," I said.

"I was going to tell you last night, but you cut our conversation short."

"Yes, I did. I'm sorry."

A beam of light from a street lamp shone through the car window and fell across the Colonel's face as he analyzed me. "Hong Ja-hee," he said. "There's more to you than you let people know. I've done some research."

"Research?"

"You grew up on your family farm outside Sinuiju. You had a sister named Soo-hee who was in China during World War II. I wasn't able to find out what she did there, but I have an idea. I didn't find out what you did either."

"I worked on my family farm," I said quickly.

"No you didn't," he said. "You were in China, too."

My heart sank that he knew about China. I wanted to jump out of the car and let him leave and take my secret to Washington. But for some reason, I stayed in the car with him.

He looked out the window. "The goddamn Japanese. It was reprehensible what they did to Korea. And I fear that we all let them get away with it."

He turned back to me. "You shouldn't blame yourself."

"I'm trying not to," I said.

"Good," he said.

Then the Colonel continued. "After World War II you worked as a translator in the North and eventually, you escaped to the South. A few months after the Korean War, you showed up here. I presume it was because you had worked for the communists."

"It was because Soo-bo was starving," I said.

"Yes," the Colonel said with a shake of his head. "War is cruel."

"More for some than others," I replied.

There was an uncomfortable silence. Then the Colonel asked, "Do you think we could have fallen in love, you and me?"

The Colonel's bluntness surprised me. "I... I don't know," I said.

"I'd be a damn liar if I said I didn't think about it. You're a beautiful woman. Intelligent. Graceful. And you have something... something special. Maybe in a different time and place."

I kept my eyes low. "A different time and place," I said.

"I'm sorry," the Colonel said with a wave. "I don't mean to embarrass you. I guess I'm just saying I'll miss our talks." He smiled tenderly and I realized I would miss him very much.

"By the way," he said, "I talked to Alan about your debt. I told him to forgive it and let you go. He agreed."

"He did?"

"I didn't give him a choice," the Colonel said with a glint in his eye.

"You didn't need to do that," I said.

"It's done. Oh, and I have something else for you." The Colonel reached inside a briefcase at his feet, took out an envelope and handed it to me. "Inside is the name and address of the head attorney of a construction company in Seoul. They need a translator. Tell them I referred you." He pointed at the envelope. "There's also a few hundred dollars in there to get you started. It's all I could get my hands on with such a short notice."

"I can't take this," I said.

"Don't let your pride hold you back, Ja-hee. The money is nothing to me. Just take it and leave the *kijichon*. You don't belong here."

I looked at the envelope for a few seconds. The Colonel was right, I had always been too proud. And I didn't belong here. I tucked the envelope into my pocket. "Thank you," I said.

The Colonel let out a sigh. "I wish we could've danced just one more time. I don't imagine I'll get to do it much with my new responsibilities."

I looked into his handsome face and his jade-blue eyes. Then I took his hand and said, "Come with me." I opened the car door and we got out. I led him to a place under the streetlight. I faced him and put my hands on his shoulders. "Show me again," I said.

He smiled broadly as he wrapped his arm around my waist. "It's a three-step, remember? One, two, three. One, two, three." He moved his feet and I moved with him as I had done when we first met. He pulled me in and swung me around. I quickly remembered the steps and soon we were moving as one. The sergeant, smoking a cigarette and leaning against the car, grinned at us.

The Colonel beamed. "Good," he said. "This is good."

We danced for a while and then he said, "I have to go." We stopped dancing, but held on to each other for a moment longer. "Thank you," he said finally, stepping away.

He gave me a Southern gentleman's bow. "Goodbye, Ja-hee," he said and went back inside the car.

The driver flicked away his cigarette and took his place behind the wheel. The Cadillac pulled onto the road next to the *kijichon*. And as the car's taillights disappeared into the blackness, I whispered, "Goodbye, Frank."

*

"You're leavin'?" Alan Smith asked me, standing in my doorway the next morning. Soo-bo clung to my side as I shoved my belongings inside my rucksack. It was morning and downstairs, the barroom was quiet. "But we made a lotta money, you and me," he said.

"No, *you* made a lot of money, Alan. I did all the work, you did nothing. It's like Karl Marx said in *The Communist Manifesto*: 'The bourgeoisie, veiled by political illusions, control the means of production and instinctively, brutally, exploits the proletariat.'"

Alan cocked his head. "What the fuck are you talkin' about?"

I shook my head. "You should read more, Alan."

"Look," he said, "I'll double your wages. And you'll never have to be a juicy girl. You're a real capitalist, Ja-hee."

"I want you to let Dae-ee go, too," I said.

"Why in the hell would I do that?" Alan asked with a twist of the scar on his face.

"Because I'm telling you to."

"You're nuts," Alan said.

I finished stuffing my belongings into my rucksack. "I'm leaving my dress. Give it to your next girl." I took Soo-bo's hand and turned to leave.

"Wait! Okay, look. You can live here for free." Alan said. "I'll even give you a percent of the profits. You're right. I need you."

I tugged at Soo-bo to follow me. I pushed past Alan out the door. "Please stay, Ja-hee," he said.

I went to Dae-ee's door and knocked. After a few seconds, she answered. Her black hair was a mess and there were dark circles around her eyes. "Do you need me to take Soo-bo?" she asked sleepily.

"I'm leaving," I said.

Dae-ee ran a hand through her hair. "What? You can't leave."

"Yes I can and you should, too. Don't worry about your debt to Alan. Just leave. Today." I pushed a twenty-dollar bill at her. "Here, this is enough for bus fare to Chonan. There is one this afternoon."

Dae-ee looked puzzled. "But I can't pay you back."

"You don't have to. Go back to your family, Dae-ee. It will be hard, but they will take you back. Go home and never fall in love with an American again. Now take the money."

Dae-ee stood in the doorway looking from me to the twenty-dollar bill and back at me again. She took the money. "Thank you, *Onni.*"

"Go home," I said.

I took Soo-bo's hand and went down stairs. I walked out of the Hometown Cat Club into the morning light. Without looking back, I walked down the dirt street to the bus idling at the gate of Camp Humphreys military base.

THIRTY-FOUR

SEOUL. IT WAS MY first time in South Korea's capital city. I was thrilled to finally see it. But I was scared, too. As the bus—a wobbly antique filled with poor farmers and American enlisted soldiers on R and R—weaved through the city under the April sky, there were signs that South Korea was rebuilding from the rubble left by the Korean War. On the sides of buildings, workers carrying bricks and mortar crawled on scaffolding. Cranes lifted building materials high in the sky. But in the dark spaces between the construction sites, I saw ragged, homeless people staring vacantly from the shadows. They looked like I did only a year before.

It was mid-afternoon when the bus came to a stop outside the Yongsan U. S. Military Garrison in the Itaewon district of Seoul. I lifted Soo-bo to my hip and my rucksack to my shoulder. I followed the line of soldiers off the bus. A swarm of filthy children and women dressed in rags confronted us. They reached out to us with grimy hands and begged for our spare change.

I pushed into the crowd. The beggars took one look at Soo-hee on my hip and let me pass. A half dozen taxis waited nearby. I approached a taxi driver. He asked me what I wanted.

I took the address of the construction firm from my pocket and read it to him. I asked if he could take me there. The taxi driver looked past me at the American soldiers trying to escape the beggars and told me to go away.

I put Soo-bo on the ground, reached inside my rucksack and pulled out a five-dollar bill. I showed it to the taxi driver. "I can pay just as well as they can," I said.

The driver looked at the money, then at me. He grinned and told me to get in.

Less than ten minutes later, we stopped in front of a two-story concrete building on a wide boulevard not far from Itaewon. Above the door was a new sign that read 'Gongson Construction'. After Soo-bo and I got out, I asked the driver how much I owed.

"Five dollars American," he answered.

"That's too much," I said.

"That's your fare," he answered firmly.

I sighed and gave him the five-dollar bill. I took Soo-bo by the hand and we went inside the building.

Inside, painters on upside-down v-shaped bamboo ladders brushed paint on the walls. A handful of workers scurried from desk to desk. I approached a middle-aged woman at a makeshift reception desk and told her who I wanted to meet. She said that Mr. Han was on the second floor and pointed at Soo-bo. "You shouldn't take your child up there. Can you leave her with someone and come back?"

"No ma'am," I answered. "This is my first time in Seoul. I don't know anyone here."

The woman looked around the office. "Well, I don't have much to do right now. I can watch her for a while."

I sized up the woman and decided I had to trust her. "Thank you," I said.

The woman came from behind the reception desk. "My name is Mrs. Min. What's your daughter's name?"

"Her name is Soo-bo. I am Hong Ja-hee."

"It's nice to meet you. Come with me, Soo-bo," Mrs. Min said extending a hand.

"*Anyeonghasayo*," Soo-bo said as she took Mrs. Min's hand.

Mrs. Min pointed at my rucksack. "You should leave your pack with me, too. You can wash in the bathroom before you see Mr. Han."

I swung my rucksack off my shoulder and put it on the floor behind the reception desk. Inside was everything I owned—my clothes, the money Colonel Crawford had given me and the comb with the two-headed dragon. Mrs. Min sat Soo-bo at a desk behind her and gave her some paper and a pencil. Soo-bo went to work on a drawing and Mrs. Min watched with obvious delight and I could see Soo-bo was in good hands. I headed off to the bathroom to wash and then to the second floor to meet Mr. Han.

I approached a man at a desk. When I told him what I wanted, he scoffed. "You want to work as a translator for our firm?" he asked. He wore thick glasses, a white shirt, a dark blue tie and a worn suit coat.

"Yes sir," I said. "I read, write, and speak several languages. I was referred here by Colonel Crawford of the American Eighth Army."

He cocked his head, then shook it. "I don't know him."

"Aren't you Mr. Han?" I asked.

"No, I am Mr. Park, Mr. Han's assistant. Which languages do you know?"

"English, Chinese and Japanese. I learned Japanese and Chinese as a young girl and when the Americans came, I learned English, too. I also know some Russian."

Mr. Park raised an eyebrow. "All of them?"

"Yes, sir."

"Fluently?"

"English and Japanese, yes. Colonel Crawford said I should see Mr. Han."

Mr. Park leaned back and eyed me. "Mr. Han is not here," he said in English. "Where have you worked before?"

Mr. Park's English was dreadful. His grammar was wrong and his accent was so bad, I could barely understand him. "I worked as a translator for the government," I responded in my best English. "I worked for a negotiator during the talks between the North and South."

I could see that my excellent English intimidated Mr. Park. He switched back to Korean. "Did you work for the North or the South?" he asked.

"The South, of course," I said.

"Okay. We need a translator, so let's find out how fluent you really are." He reached inside his desk and took out some papers and a pencil and handed them to me. He gave me a contract. He pointed to a wooden table in a corner and told me to do my best at translating it into English. "You have one hour," he said.

I thanked him, and took the papers to the table. The language on the contract was similar to the declarations and decrees I had helped to translate for the North Korean government. There were only a few words I didn't know and I burned them into my mind where I would never forget them. Thirty minutes later, I handed the translation to Mr. Park.

"Are you done already?" he asked.

"Yes sir."

"And you know Japanese, too?"

"Yes, sir. Even better than English."

Mr. Park scratched his head. "We will have to look this over. Come back in a week and we will let you know."

"Thank you, sir. Will I be able to see Mr. Han then?"

"It depends on how good your translations are."

I bowed again and went downstairs to get Soo-bo. When I got to the reception desk, Soo-bo was still drawing pictures and Mrs. Min was working on some papers.

"You're back so soon," Mrs. Min said without looking up.

"Yes. Thank you for watching my daughter." Mrs. Min kept her eyes on her work.

Soo-bo showed me one of her drawings. "Look, *Ummah*," she said. "Here's where we used to live." Within the scratching and scribbling, there was a picture of a bar and me in my blue dress. On top, Soo-bo had written 'Cat Club.'

I quickly stuffed the drawings into my rucksack and picked up Soo-bo. I thanked Mrs. Min again. She didn't look up.

I hurried outside. I looked one way down the boulevard, then the other way. It was late in the afternoon. I was tired and hungry and didn't have anywhere to stay for the night. Soo-bo, even as thin as she was, was heavy on my hip. I could tell that she was tired and hungry, too. I started walking. The boulevard was full of workers going home. I noticed construction workers were heading in one direction while well-dressed office workers were heading in the other. I lowered Soo-bo to the sidewalk and we joined the line of construction workers.

After many blocks, the line began to thin. We walked into an area of cheap-looking boardinghouses. I scanned the windows and doorways for a sign offering a room to rent. I didn't see any.

Soo-bo tugged on my hand. "*Ummah*, I'm hungry," she said.

"I know, little one," I said. "I am too. We will find something soon."

We walked several more blocks to where the boardinghouses were shabby. Hopeless-looking people watched us from windows. I quickened my pace. Finally, in the doorway of a dirty, two-story house was a sign, 'Room for Rent.' I went to the door and knocked. An old woman with several missing teeth answered.

"Forty-five dollars a month, American," the woman said without introducing herself. "First month now and another forty-five dollars as a down payment. If all you have is *won*, the price is higher and will change every month because of the inflation. Take it or go away."

I did some quick math in my head. Ninety dollars was nearly half of what Colonel Crawford had given me. I would need clothes, food, and a sleeping mat for Soo-bo and me. If I didn't get a job, I would be broke in just a few months.

I looked down the street at the shabby buildings. My stomach growled. Soo-bo leaned against my leg.

"I will take it," I said.

THIRTY-FIVE

"WE HAVEN'T GOTTEN the results in yet," Mrs. Min said from behind the Gongson Construction Company's new reception desk. The painters had finished their work in the lobby a month earlier and they had brought in new furniture. Everything in the lobby was new and there was a feeling of prosperity.

"It's been two months," I pleaded. "Mr. Park told me you would know in a week."

Mrs. Min pressed her lips together and picked up some papers. I could tell she only pretended to read them. "I'm sorry," she said. "I have work to do."

Dejected, I walked out the door. Seoul's summer rains had come and with it, the humidity. The air was heavy and the skies were a seamless gray. It smelled like it would rain again soon. I turned down the boulevard toward the market in Itaewon. I had left Soo-bo with a neighbor, a young woman named Yon-lee who watched Soo-bo for four *won* per day. I always dropped Soo-bo off when I went to the market to look for work. So far, I hadn't found any.

I had hoped to have the translating job from Gongson by now. A week after I had taken their test, I had come back as Mr. Park had told me to. But when I asked Mrs. Min if I could see Mr. Park, the receptionist told me that they hadn't been able to check my translation yet. She gave me the same answer for seven weeks now.

I was desperate. Food, clothing and a mat cost much more in Seoul than I had expected. My landlord demanded the rent on the first of each month. This month's rent was past due and I didn't have it. In fact, I was nearly broke. I was terrified that if I didn't find work soon, Soo-bo and I would be out on the street like the people dressed in rags who begged for my spare change.

I walked to the market in Itaewon. The clouds turned dark and a breeze kicked up. I searched for 'Help Wanted' signs in the stores, restaurants, tailors and souvenir shops that catered to the American military men. I saw nothing.

I went to the seedier section of Itaewon where bars and cheap restaurants advertised their goods with sad signs in English. One bar named The Queen of Hearts had a sign next to its door that read, 'Girls Wanted.' I stopped on the sidewalk facing the bar. On the second floor, a young woman wearing too much makeup stared impassively out of a window.

Next to the bar was a pawnshop. Behind its yellowed windows were old watches, jewelry, leather goods, radios and cheap antiques. A sign in the window said, 'Will Buy Anything.'

The breeze swelled and the dark clouds opened up. Rain poured down with a hiss at first, then in loud splatters. Shoppers ran for cover and soon, I was the only one on the sidewalk. I was getting drenched, but I didn't care. I stood facing the bar and pawnshop and let the hard rain wash over me. My hair matted against my head and my dress clung to me. After several minutes, I took a step forward.

I pushed open the pawnshop door. Glass cases filled with goods surrounded a small, energetic man. "Good morning, pretty lady. Do you want to buy a watch for your husband? A radio? Jewelry? I have a good price for you."

I stepped to the glass counter. Inside were several antiques. My hair dripped rainwater on the glass. "Do you want something for your home?" the man asked, scooting behind the counter. "I have valuable antiques and a good price for you."

"Your sign says you will buy anything," I said.

The merchant sagged. "What do you have?" he asked.

"I have an antique comb."

"A comb? That's all?"

"Yes."

"I am not interested in an old comb."

"It has a solid gold spine and an ivory inlay of a two-headed dragon."

The man froze for just a second, and said, "Are you sure the dragon has two heads?"

"Yes, I'm sure. And its feet have five toes."

The man gasped. "The dragon has five toes?" he whispered. "Are you sure?" He pulled back and smoothed his hair. He smiled professionally. "Now that you mention it, I might be interested in a comb. Do you have it with you?"

I glared at the man. "It's valuable, isn't it?" I asked.

The man shrugged. "It might be. I would have to see it."

I leaned over the counter pressing both hands on the glass. All of my frustration over the past two months boiled over. "Tell me," I snarled. "It is an antique comb with a two-headed dragon whose feet has five toes. It's valuable, isn't it?"

The man frowned and nodded. "Yes," he said. "If it is what you say, it is very valuable. Do you have such a comb to sell? I'll give you a lot for it."

"What does it mean?" I demanded. "A two-headed dragon with five toes. *What does it mean?*"

The man said, "The dragon... it protects Korea and the one who possesses it so they may serve Korea."

I stood with my hands on the counter as the merchant stared at me. So what Jin-mo had said years earlier was true. The dragon with one head facing east and one facing west protected Korea. And I could get a lot of money for it—certainly enough to live on until I could find a proper job, and perhaps enough for a long, long time.

I headed for the door.

"Wait!" the merchant pleaded. "I will give you good money for it!" He followed me outside into the pouring rain. "Bring me the comb," he shouted. "I will give a lot for it. More than you can imagine!"

I walked all the way home in the rain. As I entered the boardinghouse, my landlord came shuffling up to me. "Rent is past due," the old woman said, through the gaps in her teeth. "Forty-five dollars. I have others who can pay. Don't make me kick you out."

"Yes, ma'am. I understand."

"I will come with you to your room. You can pay me now."

I growled at the woman. "I have to get my daughter. And I need to change. I will pay you later."

The old woman turned away with a huff. "Rent is past due," she hissed over her shoulder. "Pay me tomorrow or I will kick you out."

I went to my neighbor's apartment and knocked. Soo-bo opened the door. "*Ummah!*" she squealed. She grabbed my leg and quickly let go. "You're wet!" she said.

I waved a thank you at Yon-lee.

"You still owe from last week," Yon-lee said from inside her room.

I took Soo-bo down the hallway to our tiny room. I asked her about her day as I changed into dry clothes.

"I read books in English," Soo-bo said proudly. "Mrs. Kim is trying to learn, and I helped her."

I smiled at my daughter. "Someday soon little one, I will buy you books and teach you many English words. Other languages, too." Soo-bo beamed.

I went to the closet and took out my rucksack. I opened it and picked up the envelope where I kept my money. There was only fourteen dollars in it. I put the money back into the rucksack. The brown package containing the comb with the two-headed dragon was in the corner. I took it out and held it in my hand.

I shoved the rucksack into the closet and lowered myself onto my mat. Soo-bo sidled up next to me. "What's that, *Ummah*?" she asked, pointing at the package.

"It is a comb, little one."

"Can I see?" Soo-bo said.

I pulled on the twine and opened the cloth. Soo-bo's eyes went wide when she saw the comb. "Is it the comb our story is about, *Ummah*?"

"Yes it is."

"It's pretty. Can I comb my hair with it?"

I ran my hand over Soo-bo's hair. "No, little one. This comb is too valuable for combing hair."

"Is the story true, *Ummah*—the one about the *yangban* and her daughter?" Soo-bo asked.

I carefully folded the cloth around the comb and tied it closed. "No," I said softly, "it is only a story."

Soo-bo went over by the window and bounced a red ball. Lately, she had started to cling after I picked her up from Yon-lee. It worried me that she was eating less, growing thinner and asking questions about money. I was doing my best to keep my despair hidden from her, but I knew she was sensing it. If we ran out of money and had to

live on the street, Soo-bo, with her poor health, would suffer terribly and maybe even die.

I looked at the package containing the comb. What should I do with it now? If I sold it to the pawnshop merchant, Soo-bo and I would not have to live on the street. And if the comb was what Jin-mo said, then why didn't it protect me? Why did I have to suffer just to survive?

Soo-bo stopped bouncing the ball and grew quiet. I could see she was falling into one of her dark moods again. I took the comb from the brown cloth and slipped it inside my dress pocket. I extended a hand to Soo-bo. "Come, little one," I said. "We have to go somewhere."

*

Outside the rain had stopped. Silver puddles glistened in the street. People were starting to come out of their rooms to breathe the rain-cleaned air. Soo-bo and I headed toward Itaewon. We walked several blocks into the neighborhood where the boardinghouses were not as shabby. A few blocks further was the business district, and beyond that, the Itaewon market. I walked with my back straight and my eyes focused ahead. Soo-bo had to run to keep up with me.

I came to a corner. In one direction was the Gongson Construction Company, in the other was the pawnshop. I reached inside my dress pocket and felt the comb. It was smooth and cool in my hand. And then I turned toward the Gongson Construction Company. When I got to the door, I pushed my way into the lobby. I marched up to Mrs. Min and said I wanted to see Mr. Han.

"You... you can't," Mrs. Min said. "He is busy. Anyway, I told you this morning, we do not have the results."

"I do not believe you," I said. I lifted Soo-bo to my hip and marched to the staircase.

"Wait," Mrs. Min shouted. "You can't go there. Stop!" She swung around the reception desk and came after me.

I kept walking and was at the top of the stairs before Mrs. Min could catch me. Mr. Park was at his desk. With Soo-bo still on my hip, I marched to him and bowed my head. Mrs. Min came up from behind.

"Sir, I want to see Mr. Han," I said.

"I'm sorry, Mr. Park," Mrs. Min said, panting. "She came in without permission."

Mr. Park frowned. "You can't come in here like this. You have to..."

The office door opened and a tall, graying-haired man in a smooth, blue suit stepped out. Mr. Park stood and bowed. "What's going on out here?" asked the man.

"This woman has come in here without permission, sir," Mr. Park said.

The tall man looked at me. "What do you want?"

I lowered Soo-bo to the floor and bowed. I reached inside my pocket and gripped the comb. "Sir, several weeks ago, Mr. Park gave me translations to do as a test for a translator position. I have been waiting to hear the results. Colonel Crawford of the American Eighth Army told me that I should give you his name."

"I know the Colonel well," the man said. "Tell me what you know about him so I know you're telling the truth."

"Sir, he enjoys Old Fitzgerald bourbon and his hero is General Robert E. Lee of the Confederacy of the South."

The man smiled. He looked at Mr. Park. "We still need a translator. Why haven't you checked her work?"

"Sir," Mr. Park said, "Mrs. Min told me this woman was no longer interested in the position."

The man glared at Mrs. Min. "Well, obviously Mrs. Min is wrong." Mrs. Min bowed low and scurried away.

"Do you still have this woman's translations?" the man asked.

"Yes sir," Mr. Park answered.

"Check them immediately," the gray-haired man said over his shoulder, as he walked back inside his office.

*

I was nervous as I sat in a leather chair in the attorney's newly carpeted office while Soo-bo waited outside. An enormous bookshelf behind Mr. Han's rosewood desk dominated his office. In it were hundreds of books. At the desk, Mr. Han was reading my translations that, moments earlier, Mr. Park said I had done perfectly.

"I should ask how you met Colonel Crawford," Mr. Han said, over the top of his reading glasses, "but I probably don't want to know."

"Sir," I said, "I will do a good job for you."

"I believe you will." He set the translations on the desk and took off his glasses. "Ja-hee, a company lives on the honorable conduct of its employees. I am going to hire you based on Colonel Crawford's recommendation. You might have done things in your past that we should leave in your past. But from now on, you need to uphold the honor of this company."

"I understand. I will. Thank you, sir."

"Good," the attorney said. "Welcome to the Gongson Construction Company."

THIRTY-SIX

Ten years later. November 1964; Seoul, South Korea

I SAT AT a low table in my new apartment and watched with pride as Soo-bo grabbed her book bag, pulled on her coat and headed for the door. Soo-bo would be fifteen soon and, though she was still thin, she had filled out like a woman. She would never be strong like me, or brilliant like Jin-mo, but she worked very hard at school and had progressed in her studies.

It hadn't been easy to get her into school. Since Soo-bo did not have a father, she was unable to get a family registration. I'd had to go to the local elementary school and pay a bribe to get her admitted. Then, on her middle school entrance exam, I made Soo-bo study long hours and she had passed. The middle school administrator had assumed that Soo-bo had a family registration and let her in. Soon, she would take the exams for placement into high school and I hoped Soo-bo would pass again. But the exam would be more difficult and in high school, the officials would be

careful to check for a family registration. Without one, they would not admit Soo-bo and her formal education would be over.

"Soo-bo," I said as my daughter opened the door to leave, "shouldn't you say goodbye to your mother?"

"Oh," Soo-bo said, "I'm sorry, *Ummah.*" She bowed. "Goodbye, mother. I am going to school now." She hurried out the door.

I watched Soo-bo leave and smiled to myself. At her age, the only education I'd had was from my mother who taught me to read and write in Hangul, Chinese, and Japanese. If it weren't for my skill with language, I would have stayed poor as South Korea flourished after General Park Chung-hee overthrew the corrupt government of Syngman Rhee. Now, South Korea was hard at work building a modern nation while our children went to school. In a few years, Soo-bo would come to adulthood in a nation with endless promise—but only if she passed her exams, and only if I could somehow get her admitted to high school.

I stuffed the translations that I had worked on the night before inside my bag. I was thankful that I had such a good job at the Gongson Construction Company. I worked very hard at it. I went to the library every week and checked out books in Japanese, Chinese and English. I read every night after work, just like I did on the farm. I watched foreign films whenever I could. With my language skills, I was a highly valued employee at Gongson. And I no longer thought of myself as a comfort woman. Yes, I'd let the Japanese exploit and brutalize me for two years, but that was no longer who I was. I was now one of millions of proud South Koreans helping to build my nation.

Today I wanted to get to work early. Gongson was expanding, along with the rest of South Korea and I had a lot of work to do. Before I left, I looked at the black and

white photograph of my family sitting in a new frame on the table.

I picked up the photo. *"Ummah, Appa, Onni,"* I said to the images as I did every morning before leaving for work, "thank you for sending your spirits to help me. I will always do my best to honor you." I set the photo on the table. I left the beige, eight-story apartment building and headed to work.

*

I greeted Mrs. Min in the lobby of the new glass and steel, four-story Gongson building. "Good morning, Mrs. Min. "Isn't it a lovely day?" As usual, she pretended not to notice me.

When I got to my desk, Mr. Han, the senior attorney for Gongson, was already outside his office waiting for me. The gray-haired man wore his customary smooth blue suit and a worried look below his thick, gray hair. He held a stack of documents out to me and said we had to finish translating them today. "This is the most important deal our firm has ever done," he said. "If we can get this loan at a favorable rate, we can expand into other industries and become a conglomerate, a true *chaebol.* Then you will see our company prosper!"

"Yes sir," I said with a respectful bow. I took the documents to my desk. "Are we doing them in English when we are done with the Japanese?"

"No, we do not need them in English. We're only dealing with the Japanese on this one. We want to keep the Americans out of it. Anyway," he said slyly, "Diashi Bank is anxious to do business with us. Hopefully, they will give us a good rate."

"I will get them done today, sir," I said.

"Good," Mr. Han said with a quick nod. "Oh, by the way, the bank's negotiators will be here tomorrow morning. We need your help interpreting. You're good at reading Japanese men."

Mr. Han went inside his office and closed the door while I sat at my desk and seethed. Yes, I knew all about the Japanese. They were ruthless and cruel and arrogant and bigoted. Even atomic bombs on Hiroshima and Nagasaki and a seven-year American occupation did not subdue their conceit. And now that Korea and Japan had normalized relations, Korean businesses were turning to the Japanese to help build their industries. *Why are we doing business with these people?* I fumed. *Don't you remember what they did to us? Don't you know what they did to me?*

I closed my eyes and the images of the machine gun murdering the Korean girls in the comfort station courtyard burned in my mind. My stomach turned. I wanted to throw the contracts on the floor and storm out the door. I wanted to march into the South Korean Ministry of Foreign Affairs and tell them what the Japanese had done to me. I wanted to reach out to thousands of other women who I had heard the Japanese had also raped and tortured as *ianfu*.

Then I remembered Soo-bo and the long hours she had to study to pass her exams. I remembered how I had promised my ancestors I would honor them. So, I went to work translating the contract. I took my time and consulted my dictionaries and made sure I got everything just right. In the margins, I made notes where the language was ambiguous and where Mr. Han should be careful.

By mid-afternoon, I was done and gave the contract to Mr. Han. "Good work, Ja-hee," he said. "Don't forget, we need you to interpret tomorrow. Wear something the Japanese men will like. You know how they are."

"Yes sir," I said, taking care to hide my disgust as he disappeared into his office.

The telephone on my desk rang and I answered it.

"Ja-hee," the caller said, "I want to see you after work. Can you meet me?" The caller was Choi Chul-sun, a senior manager at Gongson and I was sure he was in love with me. He was a friend of the founder's son. We had been dating for nearly two years, going out to dinner and to the movies on the weekends. He was always painfully polite. Lately, he had been cautiously dropping hints about taking our relationship further.

"Chul-sun, I can't see you tonight. I have an important meeting tomorrow."

"Yes, I know about the meeting with Diashi Bank. But this is important, too."

"I also have to get home to Soo-bo."

"I will pay for a cab. You'll be home at your usual time."

"Well, okay," I said. "For just a little while. Where shall we meet?"

He told me to meet him outside, at the corner in twenty minutes. I told him I would see him then, and hung up the phone. Over the next twenty minutes, I worked on a translation of a letter to an American subcontractor and put it in my 'out' basket. I put on my coat and headed to the lobby. On the way out, I passed the steno pool. Moon-kum, a thick, middle-aged woman looked up as I walked by. "Are you going to see Choi Chul-sun again tonight, Ja-hee?" she teased. "When are you going to marry him and make him a real man?"

The other women looked from their typewriters and smiled. "He is not so handsome," Moon-kum continued, "but he makes good money. He will be a vice president someday. What more do you want?" The other women covered their mouths and giggled.

"Why do I need a man?" I said, throwing my head to the side. "I have everything I need. Men are nothing but a

burden to a woman. And," I whispered loudly, "they have bad odors."

The women laughed careful to cover their mouths. I smiled at them and took the stairs down to the lobby.

When I got to the corner outside the building, Chul-sun was already waiting for me. As a senior manager in the accounting department, Choi Chul-sun was always well dressed but it didn't help his looks. His expensive suit, white shirt, and red tie hung awkwardly on his boney frame. His skin was pocked and his thin hair was graying prematurely.

He blushed as I approached. "Ja-hee," he said. "Seeing you pleases me." He motioned down the street. The sidewalk was crammed with people heading home. The November air was dry, but not too cold. Chul-sun took my arm. "I thought we could go to Namsan Park," he said. "I will pay a cab to take you home. It's not too cold for you, is it?"

"No, I am comfortable."

We walked six blocks to Namsan Park. All around, the city was under construction. Office buildings and apartment buildings were springing up everywhere. Workers laid new streets. Cars motored about. Seoul was pulsing with growth.

Chul-sun and I exchanged small talk as we walked. I could see he was nervous and I did my best to make him relax. It had been that way ever since we first went out two years before. That day, he picked me up in a cab and took me to an expensive new restaurant near the Han River. At first, he was terribly nervous and blushed a lot. But I used my skill at talking with men to put him at ease. Since then, we had gone out on dates nearly every weekend, and Chul-sun had become more comfortable around me. He told me that he was from a wealthy merchant family from Seoul and had gone to school for accounting after World War II. He had worked in procurement for the South Korean army during the Korean War and, for the past ten years, had

worked for Gongson Construction. He was a proud, respected senior manager and had a bright future.

I had told him about my family farm outside Sinuiju, how the Japanese had sent my father and sister away, and how my mother had died. I told him about Soo-bo's father and how I had escaped to the South. I told him how I got my job with Gongson. But I never told him about the two years I had spent in Dongfeng, or that I worked for the communists, or about the year I had worked in the *kijichon*. I prayed that he would never find out.

We entered the west end of Namsan Park. To the east, Mount Namsan rose gracefully in the low November sun. Young couples walked side by side over the gravel pathways. In an open field, an old man dressed in white, practiced *taekkyeon* with slow, graceful movements.

An old man in a shabby coat sat hunched on a park bench. He extended his hand for spare change as we walked by. Chul-sun kicked gravel at him and scoffed. "Why do they let these people in the park?" he said.

"He doesn't have anywhere to go," I replied.

"It does not look good for Korea," Chul-sun said. "They should get rid of them."

We walked on. Eventually, Chul-sun let go of my arm. "Ja-hee," he said, his lanky frame tipping forward, "um… how was work today?"

"It was very busy. We reviewed the Diashi contracts."

"Good! Good," Chul-sun said. "That is an important meeting tomorrow." We started walking again.

We walked in silence for a while longer. Finally, I said, "What is it, Chul-sun? You did not bring me here just for a walk."

"Yes, there is something. Something very important I want to ask you."

"I see," I replied. "What is it?"

Chul-sun drew his hand over his balding head and he blushed. He scanned the path in front of him as if the question he wanted to ask was lost among the gravel.

I took his arm and turned him to face me. "Chul-sun, ask your question."

He shook his head. "I want to do this right like a proper Korean man should, but you have no father so I can't ask him first, so I have to ask you directly, which is not the way it should be done, and now I cannot remember what I was going to say."

I gently touched his arm. "I understand. Just ask."

He gathered his courage and said, "Ja-hee, I would be honored if you would marry me. I will make a good husband."

I looked at Chul-sun and smiled to myself. I did not love him, not like I loved Jin-mo. But he was a good man and he wanted me very much. With him as my husband, I would have a good life in the new, prosperous South Korea. Soo-bo would have a family registration so she could go to high school. With luck, maybe she could even go to the university someday. Given my history, a man like Chul-sun was more than I could have ever expected.

I lowered my eyes. "Yes, Chul-sun," I said with a respectful bow. "I will be honored to be your wife."

THIRTY-SEVEN

THE NEXT MORNING, I put on the dress that best showed off my slender legs. I applied more makeup than usual and carefully brushed my hair, flicking my wrist with the brush to make it curl at the end. I looked at my reflection in the mirror. At thirty-four, I was still able to turn men's heads. But I was disgusted to have to put on such a display for the Japanese men. They made my stomach turn.

I walked out of my apartment along with Soo-bo. We said goodbye at the street and I watched my daughter march off to school. I pulled my coat tight against the November chill and headed for my bus. As I walked, I pushed aside my anger about dealing with the Japanese. After all, for the first time in my life, my future looked good. The night before, I had agreed to marry Chul-sun.

A block from the bus stop was a dress shop. I stopped at the window and peered in. In the back were colorful wedding *hanboks* with long *chima* skirts and *jeogori* blouses. I spotted a red one. I always looked good in red. Off to the side were intricate ceremonial headdresses and wedding

sashes with brightly embroidered flowers. I pressed against the window to get a better look. My heart beat a little faster as I tried to picture myself dressed in the red *hanbok* holding the arm of a proud Chul-sun in front of his family and our friends from Gongson. I smiled as I imagined an excited Soo-bo, wearing the blue *hanbok*, and the young men at the wedding staring at her when they thought no one was looking.

I heard the bus to Itaewon pull up a quarter of a block away. I ran and caught it as it started to pull out. I thanked the driver for stopping for me and then took a seat near the back. When I settled in my seat, I quietly laughed at myself for almost missing my bus to look at wedding dresses.

As the bus wound its way through the Yongdungp'o-gu district and crossed yet another new bridge over the Han River into Itaewon, I prepared myself for the meeting ahead. It was always difficult working meetings with the Japanese. They used word tricks and deception to gain an edge. Even though Mr. Han and the executives of Gongson spoke Japanese, they depended on me to read their counterpart's body language and catch the nuances of what they were saying. I was good at it, and today, I was determined not to let the Japanese get away with anything.

*

The Gongson Construction Company had designed their fourth floor conference room to impress people. It had mahogany paneling, red carpeting and a western-style table that sat twelve people with enough room to spread papers around. I stood in the corner while the company's executives took their places at the table. Mr. Han caught my eye and gave me a firm look to remind me how important this meeting was. I bowed my head to indicate I understood.

Three Japanese executives from Diashi Bank entered the room. I kept my eyes respectfully low as the executives greeted each other and exchanged business cards in a grand show of respect. I carefully examined the shoes of the Japanese bankers. One wore shoes that were coming untied and I knew he would be sloppy in his negotiations. Another had shoes that were smudged and unpolished and I knew that what he said would be inconsequential. The third wore shoes that were perfectly polished and tied tight. He would be the one to watch out for.

The executives took their places at the table. I stood behind them, keeping my eyes on the red carpeting. The meeting began with a short speech in Japanese from the president of Gongson, about how honored they were to have an opportunity to do business with a firm as respected as Diashi Bank. I cringed when he said Korea was lucky to have such good friends as the Japanese, but I pushed my disgust aside.

Next, the Japanese executive with the smudged shoes stood to introduce their head negotiator. I smiled to myself at their grandstanding. While Gongson's president merely gave a speech, the Japanese had to introduce the head of their team. I had to admit, they knew how to take the upper hand.

I stepped forward, ready to interpret. "Gentlemen," the junior executive said bombastically, "you are very fortunate to have one of Diashi Bank's top executives to meet with you today. Normally, he would not get involved in a transaction this small. However, since you are a new customer, he has graciously agreed to be here. He is a man of great intellect and importance. I am pleased to introduce to you, Diashi Bank's Senior Vice President, Mr. Tanaka."

Every nerve in my body snapped to life. Had I heard the man correctly? Had he said, *Tanaka*? I slowly raised my eyes and watched as the executive stood to make his speech.

When I saw him, my heart stopped. He had filled out in the past twenty years and his hair was gray and thinning. But he still had the pointed nose, the cold sharp eyes and the air of authority. It was my *Kempei*, Lieutenant Tanaka. I could almost see him slapping his black boots with his *shinai*.

I stood in the Gongson conference room with my eyes low and began to tremble. My breathing was difficult and the walls closed in. My legs ached where he had beaten me that last week in Dongfeng. I squeezed my eyes closed and forced myself to take a deep breath.

At the head of the table, Lieutenant Tanaka paced back and forth while he delivered his speech in his clipped tone, just has he had done in front of the Korean girls in Dongfeng. Only a few words of his speech registered with me; "You are fortunate... discipline... obey." The *kempei's* words swept me back to the comfort station. I could picture the terror in Jin-sook's eyes when he tied her to the post that first day. I could hear the girls' sobs as they lay in their tiny rooms at night. I could see Soo-hee's ashen face as she lay dying on the infirmary floor. And there, standing in the opulent Gongson conference room, I was a comfort woman again.

I took another glance at the *kempei* strutting and posturing in front of his audience and another fear gripped me. I had never told anyone except Jin-mo about my two years in the comfort station. Lieutenant Tanaka could reveal my terrible secret or use it as an advantage in these negotiations. But I had been just a girl in Dongfeng and now I was a mature woman. Perhaps he wouldn't recognize me. I struggled to keep my composure and kept my head bowed low.

Lieutenant Tanaka finished his speech and took his seat. I moved to a place out of his line of sight and the negotiations began. The Japanese carefully answered questions about the loan contract and they themselves asked

pointed questions about how we would use and repay the money. Several times, Mr. Han asked me to clarify what the Japanese meant in a phrase or statement. Each time, as I stepped forward and answered, I glanced at the *kempei*. He never looked at me.

The meeting progressed, each side angling for an advantage and gaining none. After two hours, both sides agreed to the final contract language. They decided to reconvene later that evening to celebrate with drinks and dinner at Seoul's most expensive restaurant. As they rose and bowed to each other, Mr. Han, standing next to Lieutenant Tanaka, motioned for me to come to them. I approached with my head lowered. Lieutenant Tanaka was talking to the president of Gongson with his chin raised and chest out, as he did to the girls in Dongfeng.

"Yes, sir?" I said softly.

"I want to be sure we are clear on the maturity dates. Please look them over in both languages. That will be all, Ja-hee."

I froze. Mr. Han had said my name aloud. I glanced at Lieutenant Tanaka and our eyes met for a split second. He showed a flash of recognition. I quickly went to my place behind the executives. Soon, all the men left leaving me alone in the mahogany-paneled conference room.

I took a seat at the table to collect myself. I was sure Lieutenant Tanaka had recognized me. It was in his eyes. For just a flash, a look of surprise replaced his cold arrogance. And… what else did I see? Was it fear? Could it be that he, too, didn't want anyone to know what had happened in Dongfeng twenty years earlier?

I quickly gathered my papers. As I was about to leave, the conference room door opened and Lieutenant Tanaka stepped in. He closed the door behind him. I lowered my eyes as he took a seat at the table and stretched his legs out in front of him.

"Namiko Iwata," he said, punctuating each syllable of the name. "I suppose I should call you 'Ja-hee'. Imagine my surprise at seeing you here." He nodded toward the door. "I told Mr. Han that I wanted to talk to you alone about the contracts. They probably think I'm courting you for sex. How ironic."

I kept my head lowered. I tried not to show any emotions, but under my dress, my knees shook.

"Don't worry," *Kempei* said. "It would be in both our interests if no one knew what happened in Dongfeng."

"Yes *Kempei*," I heard myself say.

"Good. As long as you hold your part of the bargain, I will see that your company gets a favorable rate on this contract. I will even tell them I am impressed with your work."

"Thank you, *Kempei*."

He slowly traced a circle on the table with his finger. "I have a wife now, and a daughter. Her name is Miwa."

"How old is she, sir?"

"Fourteen."

"That is how old I was when... when we first met."

He stopped tracing the circle and looked down his sharp nose at me. "It was a war, Ja-hee. We had a duty to fulfill. I had mine, and you had yours."

I looked up. "My duty, *Kempei?*"

"Yes, of course! The comfort women had a duty to the men, and to Japan." He pointed his chin at me as if I should naturally agree.

I returned his stare. "Then why did you kill them, sir?"

There was a sudden blankness in his face. He blinked twice and said, simply, "I do not remember doing that."

It took him a moment to come back. Then he rose to leave. "Do you still have that comb with the two-headed dragon?" he asked. "Colonel Matsumoto said he gave it back to you."

I thought about the comb hidden under the windowsill of my apartment. I looked at my feet. "No, *Kempei*. I had to sell it to feed my daughter."

"Too bad. I remember the dragon had five toes. I didn't know what it meant at the time. But it does not matter, now. I hope you got a very good price for it."

"I did, *Kempei*."

"Good. I better get back. They'll start to wonder what we are doing in here." He turned to leave and then turned back. "One more thing," he said. "Give my greetings to your sister. I always did like her. I trust she is well."

I quickly lifted my head. "Sir," I said, "Soo-hee died in Dongfeng. Didn't she?" My knees stopped shaking.

A thin smile stretched across Lieutenant Tanaka's face. He shook his head. "You don't know, do you?"

"I don't know about what, *Kempei*? Please tell me, sir."

Lieutenant Tanaka laughed quietly and put his hands on the back of the chair. He told me that when the Japanese left Dongfeng, Doctor Watanabe insisted that they take all his patients to Pushun, including Soo-hee. No one thought she would make it, but in Pushun, Soo-hee had an operation and eventually made a full recovery. He told me that when he went home to Japan several months later, Soo-hee was trying to get back to Korea. "Don't tell me after all these years, you never knew," he said.

"No *Kempei*, I didn't."

"My guess is she's in the North somewhere. So there you go. Your old *kempei* has given you valuable information to reward you for a job well done."

"Thank you, *Kempei*."

Lieutenant Tanaka regarded me for a moment. "Remember our agreement, Ja-hee. No one needs to know about Dongfeng."

"Yes, *Kempei*," I said.

Lieutenant Tanaka tapped the back of the chair twice and went out the door.

I lowered myself to a chair and stared at the door. Was it possible that Soo-hee was alive? Or was this a cruel joke by the cruelest man I had ever known? And why, I wondered, why hadn't I screamed at him, scratched his eyes, cursed him for what he had done to me? Why did I have to be a good Korean and keep it all inside?

After awhile, I gathered my papers and left the conference room. It *was* possible my *onni* was alive. I hadn't seen my sister after I fled from Private Ishida. And when I returned to the infirmary, she was gone. Lieutenant Tanaka might be telling the truth. I had to find out. But how? The North and South were bitter enemies with an impenetrable border between them. Yet, there were rumors of underground networks that families could use to pass letters to each other.

As I went back to my desk, I resolved to find my sister whom I hadn't seen in twenty years.

THIRTY-EIGHT

"WHAT DID YOU and your sister do in Dongfeng?" Mr. Lee asked, peering over his glasses from his metal desk in the Department of Records. Mr. Lee's desk sign identified him as the Administrator of Records. He had a slight paunch and his white shirt was gray from age. His office was on the first floor of one of South Korea's new government buildings. For the past fifteen minutes, he had been asking me questions so he could complete his form. He hadn't even bothered to look up until I mentioned Dongfeng.

I told him we worked for the Japanese hoping he would accept my answer and move on, but he asked me to be more specific. He held his pen over his form.

I wondered what I should tell him about the comfort station. What people had done during the Japanese occupation was something proper Koreans did not discuss. But I had come here to see if Lieutenant Tanaka had told me the truth about Soo-hee and if there was information about her. So I had to tell Mr. Lee about Dongfeng.

"My sister and I received orders from the Japanese military command to report to work at a boot factory in Sinuiju," I said. "The orders were a trick. They put us in a truck and shipped us to Dongfeng. They forced us to become comfort women. That's what we did there. We were *ianfu*."

Mr. Lee glared at me for several seconds and then pushed the papers to the side of his desk without writing anything more. "I cannot help you," he said flatly.

"Why?"

"Because we have no records of that sort of thing happening."

"It is what happened," I said, keeping my voice low. "I spent two years there. If we had not done it, we would have been shot."

Mr. Lee looked from side-to-side as if he were afraid someone was listening. "You should not talk about it," he said. "The Japanese are our allies now. They're helping us. There is no need to bring up what happened twenty years ago. I'm not putting it in the records."

"That's fine, but please see if you have anything about my sister. Her name is Hong Soo-hee. She was from Sinuiju."

"Look," Mr. Lee said, leaning forward, "families were scattered after World War II and again after the Korean War. Millions died. The chances of your sister still being alive are small. The chances of you finding her if she is alive are even smaller."

I moved to the edge of my chair. My jaw tightened. "Mr. Lee, isn't that what this department is for? Helping family members find each other? You have thousands of files here. Can't you at least look? Just because the Japanese forced me to be an *ianfu*, does not mean you don't have to help me. Why do you make me suffer for what the Japanese did to me?"

Mr. Lee sighed. "Okay, I will look if it will get you to leave. I doubt if I'll find anything. What was your sister's name again?"

I gave it to him and he wrote it down. He said it will take some time and I told him I would wait.

Mr. Lee disappeared into a huge open area filled with tall, beige file drawers and long shelves packed with boxes. I looked at the form on Mr. Lee's desk. I was glad he didn't want to write down what Soo-hee and I had done in Dongfeng. But as I waited for him to return, I wondered why it had to be that way. For years, there had been hushed talk throughout Korea about tens of thousands of women who the Japanese had forced to be *ianfu*. Apparently, there were many more women like me who the Japanese had raped and tortured. Now, the Koreans and Japanese were allies and we were sweeping aside the atrocities of their brutal occupation. No one wanted to hear about our suffering. I knew why. Just like me, Koreans did not want to admit what the Japanese had done to us. Simply put, we were ashamed.

Twenty minutes later, Mr. Lee returned scratching his head and holding a stained envelope. "I found something," he said. "Before the Korean War—in May of 1949, to be exact—there was a letter delivered to our department by a Park Seung-yo from Sinuiju who had escaped to the South. Apparently, Mr. Park lived with you at one time. He delivered this letter." Mr. Lee looked at me over his glasses as he handed the envelope to me.

The letter was water-stained and yellowed with age. On the back was a government label with the name 'Hong Soo-hee: Sinuiju' and a file number. On the front, handwritten in smudged ink, was; "For Hong Ja-hee, born twenty miles east of Sinuiju, last seen in Sinuiju, October 1945."

I pressed the envelope to my chest. My heart beat fast knowing my *onni* was alive. Lieutenant Tanaka hadn't lied.

Soo-hee had recovered from her botched abortion and was living somewhere in North Korea.

I opened the envelope. Inside was a letter dated April 1949.

>*Ja-hee,*
>
>*If you are reading this letter, you know I survived my illness in Dongfeng. After several years in China, I returned to Sinuiju to look for you. I made inquiries and found this man, Park Seung-yo, who said he knew you. So, I am sending this letter with him, hoping to find you some day.*
>
>*I have learned that Mother and Father are dead. You and I are all that is left of our family. Please write to me in Sinuiju. Perhaps we can be together again soon.*
>
>*Take care Little Sister,*
>
>*Your* onni, *Soo-hee.*

I read the letter twice more. I nodded to myself and asked Mr. Lee how I could get a letter to my sister in Sinuiju.

He shook his head. "It is impossible. Communicating with people in the North is prohibited."

"But my sister is alive," I said. "I must get a letter to her. I've heard it can be done. Help me. Please."

Mr. Lee eyed me carefully, and then looked from side-to-side. He motioned for me to lean in close. "I'm not supposed to tell you this, but... there is an underground network. It is not cheap and, if you are caught, you will be arrested."

"I understand. How do I do it?"

He told me about a Chinaman named Dr. Wu that I would find in a warehouse in Songdong. He wrote down an address and gave it to me. He told me to tell Dr. Wu that he sent me. "Don't get caught," he said, "and do not tell anyone where you got this information."

I thanked him and assured him I would be careful. I took the address and letter, then left the government building to catch a cab for Songdong.

*

The address was for the Daegu Refrigerated Warehouse and the taxi driver drove right to it through the late-afternoon traffic. As the cab waited for me, I entered the building through an open loading dock door. Workers on the warehouse floor noisily moved crates of vegetables from trucks to refrigerated rooms. The warehouse had the pungent smell of onions, which reminded me of our family farm. I climbed a set of open wooden stairs to a second floor office filled with file cabinets and cardboard boxes. A thin man sat at the office's only desk. When he saw me, he asked who I was.

"My name is Hong Ja-hee. I am looking for Dr. Wu. Mr. Lee sent me."

"What do you want with Dr. Wu?" he said without looking up.

"I was told he could help me get a letter to a family member in the North."

"Contact with people in the North is against the law. Go away."

I started to leave, but turned back before I got to the door. "I have money," I said.

The thin man didn't respond and I went to leave again. As I opened the door, the man said, "It will cost a lot of money," he said, still not looking up.

"I will pay whatever it takes," I said.

The man finally looked at me. "How do I know you aren't from the police?"

I thought for a moment, shook my head and said, "I guess you don't. But I assure you, I only want to find my sister. I just learned she is alive. I have not seen her in twenty years."

The man licked his lips. He told me to wait and went through a door. After a minute, he came out and pointed to the office. "Dr. Wu will see you in there," he said.

I walked inside the office. It was dark inside and it took a minute for my eyes to adjust. There was the sweet smell of incense in the room. Persian rugs covered the floors, and beautiful Chinese tapestries with scenes of cranes and snow-capped mountains hung on the walls. In the center of the room was a massive rosewood desk with thick carved legs. In front of the desk were matching chairs with embroidered cushions. Sitting in the shadows at the desk was a rotund man wearing a maroon smoking jacket. Between his stubby fingers was a long cigarette holder tipped with a thin cigarette. Smoke drifted up from the end.

I went to the desk and bowed. The man motioned to the chair in front of his desk. "What is your name, woman?" he asked in a husky voice. He had no trace of a Chinese accent.

"Hong Ja-hee," I answered.

From inside the shadows, the man nodded. "The Hong clan. From the North. Mostly farmers, if I'm not mistaken." He took a puff from his cigarette. The tip glowed orange.

"Yes, my family had a farm outside of Sinuiju."

"Sinuiju. I cannot say I like the place." He angled his head and blew cigarette smoke toward the ceiling. "I prefer the Chinese city of Dandong across the Yalu River. The Great Wall begins there and it has a lovely park at the base of Jinjiang Mountain. I am told you have a sister who you want to find."

"Yes, sir. The Department of Family Records had a letter on file. I think my sister might be in Sinuiju. I want to get a letter to her."

Dr. Wu leaned his bulk over the rosewood desk and his round face came out of the shadows. His eyes were white and lifeless. "It costs a lot of money to get a letter to

someone in the North. We do not know where she is or if she is even alive. We have to avoid the authorities on both sides of the border. It is all very... complicated."

"I understand, sir."

He leaned back into the shadows and took in a long draw from his cigarette. He angled his head in the manner of a man who has been blind all his life. "If I agree to do this for you, it will cost two-hundred thousand won or one thousand American dollars if you prefer. And I make no guarantees. The chances are your sister is dead. So many of your people died in the civil war. Are you sure you want to do this?"

"Yes, sir. I think I can get the money."

He took another pull from the cigarette. "Where will you get that kind of money, woman?"

"I work for the Gongson Construction Company."

"What do you do there?"

"I am an interpreter."

"What languages?"

"Japanese and English. I also speak Chinese."

"Impressive! When did you get separated from your sister?"

I peered into the shadows at the bulk of Dr. Wu. I hesitated only a moment and then answered, "We were *ianfu* in Dongfeng. The Japanese tricked us into working for them. I thought they had killed my sister, but as I said, today I learned she is alive."

Dr. Wu pointed his cigarette in my direction. "I doubt you earn enough as an interpreter for the Gongson Construction Company, but if you can raise the money, I will help you. When you have it, bring it here with your letter and everything you know about your sister. We will get back to you if we find her."

"How long will it take?" I asked.

Dr. Wu leaned forward exposing his lifeless eyes again. "Months," he said with a blind man's grin.

"Thank you, sir." I bowed and hurried out.

*

I climbed in the cab and gave the driver the address of my apartment. Two hundred thousand won. I didn't have that much money. But I was hopeful and excited because I knew one person who could give it to me.

THIRTY-NINE

CHUL-SUN AND I planned our wedding as we ate at an expensive restaurant in Itaewon. Since I had agreed to marry him, Chul-sun walked with his shoulders back and his chin held high. The pockmarks on his face didn't show as much, and his clothes seemed to fit better. He hadn't blushed all night. At the restaurant, he had ordered a bottle of plum wine and an elaborate meal. Several dishes of *banchan* were spread before us on the low table. We sat close to each other on mats.

Chul-sun took a sip of wine. "I want a traditional wedding," he said, holding his glass out. "I do not care what it costs. I want both of us to wear new *hanboks*. I want a *moja* for my head, just like the *yangban* wear. We will have a formal tea ceremony and a wedding feast at a hotel. *Bulgogi, galbi, mandu, bibimbop, gamjatang* and *jajagmeon, banchan* and all the trimmings. We will invite my family, our friends, and people from Gongson. It will be a grand wedding."

I picked at my food. "Maybe we shouldn't spend so much," I said. "It could be expensive."

"It *will* be expensive," he replied.

I took Chul-sun's hand and gave it a squeeze. A flash of excitement crossed his eyes. "We will have other expenses too," I said. "We will need money to send Soo-bo to school... and for other things."

"Yes, yes, I know. Don't worry. We will have enough."

After a long silence, Chul-sun said quietly, "Ja-hee, now that we're engaged, it would not be wrong if you went home with me tonight."

I lowered my eyes. "I have to get home to Soo-bo."

"It's still early. I'll pay a cab to take you home. You will be back to Soo-bo in plenty of time. Come home with me, Ja-hee, just for a little while."

I peered into his face and saw how deeply he wanted me. But I wondered if he would still want me if he knew my secrets. Would he still want to take me home, make love to me, go through with the elaborate wedding and take me as his wife?

I looked at my hands. "Chul-sun," I said softly, "I have to tell you where I went yesterday. I went to the Department of Family Records and discovered that my sister is alive and living in the North. I want to get a letter to her, but it costs a lot of money."

"You told me your sister died when you lived in Sinuiju."

"Yes, Chul-sun, that is what I told you."

"I don't understand."

I put down my chopsticks. "Let's go for a walk," I said.

A cold wind was blowing from the north as we left the restaurant. I took Chul-sun's arm and pulled myself close to him. He stayed focused on the sidewalk. I pointed down a side street away from the crowded Itaewon marketplace. I told him I wanted to marry him and have a grand wedding with a reception, a tea ceremony, and all of our friends, just like he wanted.

"But there is something you have to tell me first," he said.

"Yes, there is," I replied.

"Okay, tell me."

I could have made up a story about how Soo-hee had been taken away to work in a comfort station while I had stayed on the family farm. But I had to know if Chul-sun loved me for who I really was, just like Jin-mo had. If he did, perhaps I could love him, too.

So as we walked, I told Chul-sun everything I had kept secret for so long. Everything—the comfort station, working for the communists, the *kijichon*. For the first time since I had escaped to the South, I exposed my true self, my ugly history. And when I finished, I knew that I had done the right thing. I prayed that Chul-sun would understand.

At the end, I said, "If you still want to marry me after what I have told you, I will be happy to go home with you tonight."

I waited for his answer. After a while, he said, "You should have said no."

"What do you mean?"

He stopped and turned to me. His chin was set hard. "You should have said no, Ja-hee. When you realized the Japanese had tricked you, you should have let them shoot you. You should not have worked for the communists and you should have never gone to the *kijichon*."

"I should have let them shoot me? Chul-sun, listen to what you are saying."

"I know what I'm saying," he said angrily. "I am saying the honorable thing to have done is to have said no!"

As we stood on the sidewalk, the new streets and buildings of Seoul began to melt away, and in their place, I saw the comfort station, the huge iron statue of Kim Il-sung and the bar of the Hometown Cat Club. The people on the sidewalk became the Japanese soldiers who had raped me,

the North Korean soldiers who had carried Jin-mo off to prison, and the American soldiers in the *kijichon*. "Chul-sun," I begged, "please understand. If I had refused any of those times, I would have died. I was only fourteen years old in Dongfeng. I was too young to know. In Pyongyang, everything was so... so confusing. And at the *kijichon*, Soo-bo was starving. I could not let her die. Please, please accept my confession. Love me for who I am and I will love you too. Then we will be married and have a grand wedding."

I searched Chul-sun's face for his answer. He wiped his nose on the back of his sleeve. "I told my family about our engagement," he said with a voice jagged and hard. "I made a big show of it! And now, I have lost face. They will think I am a fool! I will never be able to look them in the eyes again."

"We do not need to tell them," I said. "Only you need to know. But you *had* to know. Don't you see? It is the only way I can be sure you accept me for who I really am. It is the only way I can marry you."

Chul-sun shook his head. "The receptionist, Mrs. Min, knows too. She told me you worked in a *kijichon*. I did not believe her. I didn't think it was possible, but she was right. She knows!"

My head began to spin. Chul-sun grabbed me and pushed me into a wall. His fingers dug into my arm. "How can I love you after what you've done?" he shouted. "You have dishonored me."

"Chul-sun, you're hurting me," I said.

He glared at me, squeezing my arm harder. Then with a shove, he let go and stepped back. He looked down the street. "I cannot marry you. You are not who I thought you were."

The faces of my past swirled around me. I closed my eyes to make them stop. But Chul-sun was right, I was not who he thought I was. I had tried to keep everything a secret, but my past would always be part of me. I wished I could go

back and refuse to obey the orders to work in the boot factory. It had set my life on an arc that years of honorable living could not bend straight. "Chul-sun," I pleaded with my eyes still closed, "how could I have known the right thing to do? How?"

"You should have said no!" he said. "And you should have said no to me, too." He gave me a long, pained look and then he walked away.

Eventually, the people and buildings in the street returned to normal and I turned for home. As I slowly walked through the busy streets of Itaewon and then over the long Map-o Bridge, I thought about my life and all that I had done. Had I made the right choices?

I stopped halfway across the bridge and looked back at the city. The lights of Seoul twinkled all around me. Below, the Han River slowly rolled to the sea. There I decided Chul-sun was wrong. Yes, I needed his money to get a letter to Soo-hee. I wanted to marry him so Soo-bo could go to high school. I even wanted to get married for myself. But if I denied that I had been a comfort woman, I would betray my *onni* and all of my *ianfu* sisters who had died in the comfort station. No, I had a higher duty to fulfill than to uphold Korea's reputation. After all, important men like Chul-sun and those who wanted to bury the Japanese atrocities so they could build their nation were doing a fine job of that. But telling what happened to us—how we struggled and how we were able to survive—was the only way Korea would become a great nation. I could not bury it.

And I finally realized how I was to serve Korea. The two-headed dragon had protected me so I could tell my story as Soo-hee and Jin-mo said I should. It was a grave responsibility and I didn't know how I would do it. But as I walked the rest of the way home, I vowed I would find a way.

*

The next day, the final loan agreement with Diashi Bank came through and the terms were more favorable than anyone at Gongson had hoped for. One reason given was that the chief Japanese negotiator was impressed with me. For one day, I was a hero among the women in the steno pool. "You will be made a manager soon," Moon-kum teased as I walked by. "Then you won't talk to us anymore."

"Yes," I replied. "Someday I will take over the company. And when I do, I will fire all the men." The women laughed at my joke, covering their mouths as they did.

All that day, Mr. Han smiled openly at me the way a proud father smiles at a successful son. At noon, I ate my lunch on a bench in Namsan Park near where Chul-sun had proposed. I did not hear from him or see him all day. In the afternoon, Mr. Han told me that I could go home early, so I left Gongson and took a cab home instead of the bus. That evening, I helped Soo-bo with her English homework and went to bed early.

The next morning, when I walked by the steno pool, Moon-kum and the other women kept their eyes on their typewriters. When I said hello, no one returned my greeting. When I got to my desk, there were no contracts to work on.

Mr. Han leaned out of his office. His face was cheerless. He told me to come in his office and close the door.

The firing was quick and perfunctory. Mr. Han gave no reason. He just said that the Gongson Construction Company no longer wished to employ me. I received no severance pay for my ten years of service. I had no pension. At the end, Mr. Han held out an envelope. "Here is your back pay," he said. "You must leave immediately."

I took the envelope and looked directly at Mr. Han. "I always did my best, sir. Ever since I was fourteen, I have tried to do the right thing."

The great, gray-haired attorney's eyes softened and he nodded. "The actions that society deems respectable—what Confucius called *li*—is not always the most righteous. We must be loyal to the duty we have to our families, our ancestors and our country first—your *yi*—and only you can determine what your *yi* is."

He smiled sadly. "Thank you for your good work, Ja-hee. Personally, I am sorry to see you go."

I knew then that Mr. Han was a great man, like Jin-mo and Colonel Crawford, and perhaps even like young Private Ishida in some way. It made me sad that I would never see him again. I bowed low and then smiled back at him. I got my coat and headed home. I held my head high as I walked through the Gongson Construction Company lobby past Mrs. Min.

FORTY

Eight years later

I HANDED OUT yellow pamphlets in front of the new
history department building at Seoul National University.
There was a spring breeze blowing through campus and I
had to hold the pamphlets tight to my chest so they
wouldn't blow away. The *akebia* were in bloom and the air
was heavy with their chocolate smell. All around me,
students carrying books braced themselves against the
breeze as they rushed to their classes. I pushed pamphlets at
them as they walked by. Every so often, a student reached
out and took one. It was my third day at the university and I
had only a small stack of pamphlets left.

I'd had the four-page pamphlets printed in a shop not
far from my apartment. When the shop owner read it, he
refused to do the job. I agreed not to tell anyone where I
had them printed and gave him one hundred extra *won*. He
quickly printed them and gave them to me in a plain paper
sack.

I was pleased with what I had written. The headline read,
"Japanese Sex Slaves. We Were Not Volunteers." The

pamphlet explained how the Japanese military had forced me and thousands of others to be comfort women. It proposed that the Korean government force Tokyo to acknowledge their war crimes against Korean women and make reparations. So far, however, no one had responded to my pamphlets.

I pushed a pamphlet at a female student with short black hair. I wanted to scold her when she stuffed it in her bag without reading it. I watched her as she walked to her class. She looked bright, happy and confident. Of course she did. She had her entire life before her. Her prospects in the modern Republic of Korea were good.

As she disappeared inside the history building, I thought about how different my own life was at her age. I was smart and had an exceptional gift for languages. I would have thrived at a great university like this. Perhaps I could have become an attorney, a negotiator or a diplomat. But fate had other plans for me.

And fate had other plans for my daughter Soo-bo, too. Without a father to get a family registration, Soo-bo had to quit her studies after Chul-sun broke off our engagement. And without an education, Soo-bo, thin and plain, had to work menial jobs to supplement my government welfare check. Even with her income, we barely got by.

The breeze kicked up and I held the pamphlets tight. A middle-aged man in a suit trotted toward me down the concrete stairs of the history building. He held one of my pamphlets in his hand. He asked me what I was doing.

"I am telling the truth," I answered.

The man's hair was thick and gray and he wore scholarly glasses. "I don't want to get you into trouble," he said, "so I'm asking you to leave."

"Why?" I asked. "This is the perfect place to hand out my pamphlets. It talks about an important part of Korea's

history. These students should know. All Koreans should know."

The man glared at me. "Do not tell me what these students should know. I am the head of the history department here."

I felt my jaw tighten. "You are?" I said. "Then certainly you understand how important it is to expose what the Japanese did to me and thousands of other Korean girls. It is your history too, professor."

"What is or is not our history is what historians like me say it is," the professor said, jabbing a finger at me. "And I say it did not happen."

"But it *did* happen," I said. "It happened to me and my sister. Why do you deny it?"

The professor looked around. "Because we are a modern nation now. If the rest of the world doesn't respect us, we will never become a world power. So I insist that you take your pamphlets and leave or I will have to call the police."

"I will not," I said. "I won't leave and I will not stop. I refuse to be a proper Korean and suffer in silence for the rest of my life. As a nation, we're a little too good at being the victim, Professor. Korea will never be great until we stop letting others use us. And it begins with making those who raped us admit what they did."

The professor sighed. "Very well," he said. "I warned you." He turned and trotted back up the stairs.

I watched as the head of the history department of Korea's most prestigious university disappeared inside the building and my blood boiled. Honor? To my fellow Koreans, honor was more important than the truth. But we would never have honor if we based it on a lie. And anyway, what did I do that was so dishonorable? Read the pamphlet. *We were not volunteers!*

I turned to look for more students to hand my pamphlet to. Standing several steps away was an attractive, middle-aged woman. She looked both ways and then came to me. Our eyes met for a second and she handed me one-hundred *won*. Then, she quickly walked away.

I went after her. "Wait!" I said, holding the money out. "Why are you giving me this?"

The woman quickened her pace. I ran and caught up to her. "Stop a minute," I pleaded. "Please. I just want to talk to you."

I placed a hand on the woman's arm. She shrugged it away. "Leave me alone," she said. "I gave you the money, that's all I can do."

I kept pace for a few steps and then I stopped. The breeze let up for a moment and the air was still. And then I said loud enough for the woman to hear, "They told me I was going to work in a boot factory. How did they take you?"

The woman stopped with her back to me. She stood for several seconds, and then dropped her head. She turned and looked at me and said, "They came for me in the middle of the night. My grandfather tried to stop them but they hit him with their rifles and knocked him unconscious. They sent me to the Philippines where they raped me for three years. I was only fifteen years old."

I went to the woman and put a hand on her arm. "I hear there are thousands of us," I said. "Maybe hundreds of thousands."

"Yes," the woman said looking down. "I have heard the same thing."

"If we work together, we can make the Japanese admit what they did."

The woman shook her head. "I have a husband," she said simply. Then she turned and walked away.

I clenched my teeth and marched to my spot in front of the history building. I thrust my yellow pamphlets at

students. A male student looked at me disapprovingly. I pushed a pamphlet at him. "You have to know about this," I said angrily. "If you don't, it could happen to your wife or daughter." The student walked away shaking his head.

A female student came by and looked at me questioningly. "Korea will never be great until we admit this," I said to her. "Take this and read it." She took a pamphlet. She read the headline on the front. She thumbed through the pages.

"I've heard rumors about this. Did it really happen?"

"Yes," I said. "It happened to me."

"Why don't they want us to know about it?" the young woman asked.

Before I could launch into a lecture about truth and honor, a man shouted at me from the stairs of the history building. "You there with the pamphlets," he said, "stop what you're doing." Two policemen ran down the stairs to me. The young woman shoved the pamphlet back into my hand and hurried away.

The policemen came up to me and took my pamphlets. "What are you doing?" I protested. "I'm not doing anything illegal."

They took me by the arm and led me toward the street. "Someone wants to talk to you," one said.

As we walked past a trashcan, they threw away my pamphlets and I could see there were already dozens of my yellow pamphlets inside.

*

I sat in a small, windowless room in the central government building. Across from me was an average-looking man who introduced himself as Mr. Cho, an agent for the national police in the Department of National Security. He told me I was not to hand out my pamphlets anymore. "In fact," he

said, "you are not to go to the university ever again. Am I clear?"

I pushed myself to the edge of my chair. "I am only telling the truth about what happened to me."

Mr. Cho tapped on the table and said, "Ms. Hong, you have an interesting record. It seems you've had a dishonorable past.

"I have not done anything dishonorable, sir. That is what I'm trying to say."

"I see. And how does your family feel about what you're doing?"

"My family?"

"Our records show that you have a sister living in the North," said Mr. Cho. "She is probably a Communist, too. Have you been in contact with her?"

"I have not seen my sister for twenty-seven years. She might not even be alive."

"And then there is your daughter, Soo-bo."

I hesitated for a second. "What about her?"

"According to our records, she was born five months after you escaped to South Korea. That means her father must be your lover in the north, Pak Jin-mo. She is the daughter of a well-known communist."

"Leave Soo-bo out of this," I said quickly.

Mr. Cho nodded. "We will gladly do that. All you need to do is stop stirring up controversy. If you do, no one needs to know who your daughter's father was."

I glared at Mr. Cho, and then I looked at my hands. Poor Soo-bo had suffered all her life. She didn't have a father and she was the daughter of a comfort woman. She was an outcast and she lived in poverty. She had suffered enough. I nodded my agreement.

"Good," Mr. Cho said. "And now Ms. Hong, you may go."

FORTY-ONE

Twelve years later

I SHOULD HAVE found a husband for Soo-bo. I tried, but she was so sickly and I was so poor that no one—certainly no one worthy of my dear Soo-bo—would have her. So when Soo-bo got pregnant by a man she met near where she worked, it was my fault. I should have met the man, but I never did. Soo-bo never talked about him. And she never saw him again after she became pregnant.

When we visited the hospital, the doctors recommended Soo-bo have an abortion. Her heart was weak, they had said, and they warned that a difficult delivery might kill her.

I was afraid that Soo-bo was considering having the abortion so I decided to take her to Gyeongbok Palace. I had to dig to the bottom of my satchel for the *won* I had been saving for food until my government check arrived. I counted it out. There was just enough for cab fare. Of course, the bus would cost far less. But it would require two

transfers and take over an hour each way, and that would be too much for Soo-bo.

It was a clear spring day when the cab dropped us off at the Gwanghwamun Gate. Behind its drab concrete entranced was the massive Japanese Governor General building that the Japanese built during their occupation. Its towering brass dome and massive stone walls obscured the palace behind it.

We walked around the unsightly building into the palace courtyard. There, trees and grass were green and flowers were in bloom. Before us were several buildings, some old, and a few under construction. The buildings' tiled roofs curved gracefully upward, like the wings of giant gray herons rising into the sky. The walkways and courtyards were paved with stones.

"Why did you bring me here, *Ummah*?" Soo-bo asked as we walked.

"I wanted you to see this place," I answered. "It was the home of the Chosŏn dynasty for five hundred years."

"I know. It is where Empress Myeongseong was murdered by the Japanese."

"On October 8th, 1895," I said. "Tell me if you get tired."

"I'm okay for now."

We slowly strolled past a pavilion with a long porch. Here and there, tourists took snapshots of each other or gazed in awe at the colorful buildings.

Finally, I said, "I want to talk to you about something."

"Oh? What is it?"

"You cannot have an abortion."

"But the doctor said I could die if I have the baby."

I looked at my feet. "Yes, I know."

I pointed at the palace grounds. "See this place? One hundred years ago, there were many more buildings here. Hundreds more. I have seen pictures and a map of what used to be here. Beautiful, majestic buildings for the

Emperor and Empress and the royal family. They said there was no other place like it in all of Korea."

"Hundreds of buildings?" Soo-bo exclaimed. "I can't imagine. What happened to them?"

"The Japanese destroyed all but ten during their occupation. There is talk of rebuilding every one. They also want to tear down the Japanese Governor General building and rebuild the Gwanghwamun gate. I hope they do."

"What does this have to do with me having an abortion?"

I looked up at Mount Bukhansan while we walked. "Do you remember the comb with the two-headed dragon?"

"Yes, of course."

"Do you remember the story I told you about it?"

"Yes. The one about the rich *yangban* who sent her daughter away and gave her the comb."

I took Soo-bo's arm. "Come. I want to show you something."

We walked to a series of connected buildings dominated by a tall tower with five pagoda roofs, one on top of the other in layers like the branches of a great pine tree. We entered a building. Inside was the National Museum of Korea. Glass cases filled with artifacts lined the corridors and folk art hung on the walls. Each had a plaque describing its history.

"I come here on Tuesdays," I said. "It's free and I can spend as much time as I want. There are things in here that remind me of my childhood."

I led Soo-bo down a corridor filled with exhibits of Korean treasures and armament. We stopped at a glass case containing a sword with detailed etchings and a gold rim along the scabbard. "See this sword?" I asked. "Look at the etchings."

Soo-bo examined the scabbard. "It has the same dragon as your comb!"

"That is right. Read the plaque. Read it aloud."

Soo-bo leaned in and read, "In 1967, this sword was found hidden in the walls of a home once owned by a wealthy merchant. Historians believe the two-headed dragon with one head facing east and one facing west, protects Korea and those who served our country. Some believed Empress Myeongseong created the symbol of the two-headed dragon, although there is no evidence she did. During their occupation of Korea, the Japanese destroyed all items they could find bearing the two-headed dragon. This sword is the only known surviving artifact."

Soo-bo stepped back. "What does it mean, *Ummah*?"

"Before you were born, your father saw me using my comb. He told me what the dragon stood for. I didn't know if it was true, but I kept the comb for years. When I discovered this sword, I knew that what he said was true."

I pointed at the sword. "Look at one more thing. How many toes does the dragon have?"

Soo-bo pressed against the case. "Four. It has four toes."

"Correct." I said. "Come. You look tired. Let's find a place to rest."

We went outside to the courtyard and sat on the steps of the tall building with five roofs. We looked south over Seoul and the towering new office buildings and apartments. A lazy haze hung over the city. People strolled across the grounds in front of us.

I let a few people pass. I reached inside the pocket of my dress and took out a package. I loosened the twine and unfolded the brown cloth. Inside was the comb with the two-headed dragon.

"You still have it!" Soo-bo whispered. "I thought you sold it years ago."

"The story about the *yangban* from Seoul," I said, "I didn't make it up. My mother gave this comb to my sister and me. She got it from her grandmother and her grandmother got it from her mother. My mother's great

grandmother, your third great grandmother, was the one who had the comb made."

"Who was she?"

"Look at the dragon," I said. "How many toes does it have?"

Soo-bo examined the comb. "Five," she said.

"That is right," I said. "A five-toed dragon." I faced Soo-bo. "I didn't know what it meant until one day I asked a docent why the dragon on the sword had four toes. She told me that most dragons on artifacts have only three. They knew the merchant who owned the sword was a very important man because the dragon had four toes. I asked her, 'What if a dragon had five toes?' She said that dragons with five toes were only used for items belonging to the Emperor and Empress."

Soo-bo cocked her head. "Does that mean...?"

"Yes, Soo-bo. The comb is proof that Empress Myeongseong created the two-headed dragon and that we are her descendents. Through this comb, she has given us a responsibility to serve Korea."

Soo-bo took a few minutes to take in what she had just learned. Then she asked, "But how can I serve Korea, *Ummah*?"

I took my daughter's hand. "Soo-bo, you are my joy. You are the only thing that has given me lasting happiness since I was a young girl. I love you and it would break my heart if I ever lost you. But we are royalty my daughter, and our first duty is to our people. I think perhaps you were meant to have this baby. The dragon will protect you."

I folded the cloth around the comb and gave it to Soo-bo.

She took it and stared at the package. "Do you really believe in the dragon, *Ummah*? Do you believe it will protect me?"

Looking back on my life, I saw that I had survived even the most dangerous situations while others had perished. Perhaps the dragon had protected me after all, like Soo-hee and Jin-mo had said it would. I had to believe it would protect Soo-bo, too. "Yes I do," I said.

Soo-bo nodded. "Then I will have the baby," she said.

We sat for a long time without talking. Eventually, I stood and extended a hand to Soo-bo to lead her home so she could rest. We walked arm in arm under the Gwanghwamun Gate, back into the great city of Seoul.

FORTY-TWO

IT SCARED ME how weak Soo-bo became as her stomach swelled with the baby. It was as if it was sucking the life from her and I wondered if I had done the right thing when I talked her out of having an abortion. The doctors grew increasingly worried too, and insisted that Soo-bo end her pregnancy. She refused. She slept long hours and forced down food when she wasn't hungry. Every morning and night, she did the breathing exercises the nurses had taught her. She studied books on how to deliver a healthy baby. I was so very proud of her.

One night after a meal of rice and vegetables, Soo-bo went into labor. As she held her stomach and tried to breathe like she did in the exercises, I ran to the payphone in the lobby and called a cab. It came in less than five minutes.

Earlier that afternoon, there had been a rain shower, and when I helped Soo-bo into the cab, the city lights twinkled off inky-black puddles. The rain had brought in cool air and everything smelled clean. As the cab wound through traffic on its way to the hospital, Soo-bo grimaced

in pain from a contraction. I held her hand. "The doctor will give you something for the pain," I said.

"It's okay, *Ummah*," Soo-bo replied. "It is a good pain."

As the cab pulled up to the emergency room door, Soo-bo's water broke. There was a lot of blood. A nurse helped her into a wheelchair. When she saw how weak Soo-bo was, the nurse called for the doctor immediately. She pulled me aside and asked how long Soo-bo was in labor.

The concern on the nurse's face filled me with fear. "Less than an hour," I said. "We came as soon as it started."

"She shouldn't be in this much pain," the nurse said. "And there should not be this much blood."

They wheeled Soo-bo inside a blue-tiled delivery room with a large bank of lights. The nurse stripped off Soo-bo's clothes, dressed her in a hospital gown and laid her in a bed with stirrups for her feet. She gave Soo-bo a shot for her pain and spread a blue sheet over her. I stood at my daughter's side and held her hand.

As another contraction started to build in Soo-bo, the doctor entered the room. He asked about Soo-bo's condition.

"She's in a lot of pain," the nurse replied, "and she's been in labor for less than an hour. Her blood pressure and heart rate are very high."

As the doctor took Soo-bo's pulse, he asked me, "What can you tell me?"

"Her heart is weak," I answered.

The doctor dropped Soo-bo's arm. "Yes it is," he said gravely. He ordered the nurse to get a heart monitor and some help. "Now!" he barked.

As the nurse ran out, the doctor lifted the blue sheet and looked between Soo-bo's scrawny legs. "The baby is breached," he said, "and the mother has lost too much blood for a Cesarean."

Soo-bo arched her back from a contraction and her body shook. The twisted pain in her face made me hate myself for making her have this baby.

"Breathe!" the doctor ordered from under the sheet. "Get her to breathe."

I leaned over my daughter. "Soo-bo, you have to breathe. Deep breaths like the book said."

Soo-bo closed her eyes and tried to take in deep breaths but she could only breathe in gasps. She gripped the bed with both hands. Beads of sweat formed on her head.

"Nurse!" the doctor yelled toward the door. "Get that heart monitor in here!"

I squeezed Soo-bo's arm. "Breathe, Soo-bo. Please, breathe."

After a few minutes, the contraction subsided and Soo-bo sunk into the bed. Her face was ashen and sweat matted her hair. The doctor put his stethoscope over her heart. "We need to turn the baby," he said. "But the mother's heart is arrhythmic. We have to change our approach before the next contraction. I'll be right back."

The doctor ran out of the room, angrily barking orders at the staff outside. Soo-bo blinked her eyes open and looked at me.

"Am I doing it right, *Ummah*?" she asked.

I stroked her sweat-soaked hair. "Yes, my daughter. You are doing it just right."

"Good," she said. "What should I name my baby?"

"Her name should be Ja-young."

"Why should she be named Ja-young, *Ummah*?"

I leaned in close and wiped my daughter's brow. "Because it is a royal name. She should have a royal name."

Soo-bo smiled and nodded. "Ja-young. Yes, that is a good name. I will name my baby Ja-young."

Then, as I held Soo-bo's hand she asked, "Do you have the comb? I should hold it so the dragon will protect me."

My heart stopped. In the panic to get to the hospital, I had forgotten to take the comb from its place under the windowsill in our apartment. I couldn't give it to Soo-bo.

Suddenly the door to the delivery room flew open and the doctor and nurse rushed through. Another contraction began to build in Soo-bo. She closed her eyes and gritted her teeth. Her back arched high.

"We're too late," the doctor said from between Soo-bo's legs. "We do not have time for anything else. What's her pulse?"

The nurse held Soo-bo's wrist, and answered, "I can't get a reading."

I watched in horror as Soo-bo's body convulsed as if an unseen spirit was shaking her. She gripped the bed hard. Her eyes rolled back and her mouth opened. She did not breathe and neither did I.

"Her heart stopped!" the nurse said.

I stared at my precious daughter. "Soo-bo," I whispered.

A second doctor and two nurses burst into the room with a heart monitor and oxygen. The doctor went to Soo-bo's side and hooked up the monitor while one of the nurses slipped the oxygen mask over Soo-bo's face. The other nurse took me by the arm. "You have to go outside now, ma'am," she insisted. "Quickly."

I looked at Soo-bo as the nurse led me to the door. "My baby," I said. "*Ye deulah.*"

*

I was numb as I stared at the delivery room door. I didn't know how long I sat there. On the other side, the doctors and nurses worked on Soo-bo. Medical staff rushed in and out. Time seemed to stop and I was afraid that I had made a tragic mistake. I had convinced my daughter to have her baby. I told her the dragon would protect her, but I didn't

know if it would. And sometimes it was hard for me to believe that Soo-bo and I were direct descendents of Empress Myeongseong, responsible to carry on the legacy of the two-headed dragon. Certainly, I believed in the spirits of my ancestors. I could feel them inside and see them in the people and land of my country. But if Soo-bo and I were a part of their grand scheme, why didn't they help us? Why did we have to suffer and die for Korea? I prayed to my ancestors, to my great-great grandmother, the powerful Empress who gave her life for Korea, to spare my daughter.

Eventually, the doctor pushed his way out the door and slowly walked toward me. His clothes hung loosely on him and his eyes were sunken. He bowed to me. "We did everything we could," he said. "Her heart just wasn't strong enough. We could not save her."

I was unable to move or to breathe or to see anything beyond his words. My sweet, sweet Soo-bo. The child I carried close in my womb, who suckled and slept at my breast, who I taught to walk and to read, who I loved so much that the loving hurt me inside. My daughter was dead and I had killed her because of the cursed comb and my duty to Korea. I wished I could go back and refuse to take the comb from Soo-hee in the comfort station. I had accepted it and it had cost me everything.

But there was still the baby. I heard myself say, "The baby?"

"She is fine," the doctor answered. "Strong, in fact. A beautiful girl. Would you like to hold her?"

The doctor stepped aside and I saw a bundle wrapped in yellow in a nurse's arms. Slowly, I rose to my feet. The nurse stepped forward and gave me the baby. I pressed her to my breast. Beneath the yellow blanket, I could feel her short breaths. I gently ran my hand over her smooth, warm head. With a finger, I traced the lines of her high cheekbones and her delicate nose. I pressed my finger into the baby's hand

and she gripped it with long fingers. I could feel the spirit of Korea strong inside her.

"She is an empress," I said. "Her name is Ja-young. Be sure she is given that name."

I held my gaze on the baby and reached to the depths of my soul for one last bit of strength. "And an empress needs a family where she can grow strong so that she can do what she must do." I pushed down one last cry and held the baby out to the nurse. "Please," I said, struggling to push the words out, "I would like to put my granddaughter up for adoption."

FORTY-THREE

August 2008. Seoul, South Korea

THE COMB WITH the two-headed dragon sits on the table between Mrs. Hong and me. The amazing comb with the gold spine and ivory dragon gleams in the evening light. Next to it are the *mugunghwa* blossom and the photographs of Mrs. Hong's family and her daughter—my birthmother, Soo-bo.

"Now do you understand why I sent you away?" Mrs. Hong says. "I had nothing left to give. I died the day Soo-bo died, just like my mother did the day Soo-hee and I left home. So I made the decision to have you adopted. I didn't know if I would ever see you again. But I believed that if the dragon was true, if everything I had suffered through was part of a grand enterprise to make Korea great, then the spirits of my ancestors would bring you back to me someday. And here you are, my granddaughter, here you are. I believe in the two-headed dragon and I believe it is your destiny to have the comb."

I shake my head. "I don't know."

Mrs. Hong sighs and looks at me. "Why did you come to Korea?" she asks.

"To see where I was born. To meet my birthmother. To learn what it means for me to be Korean."

"And what have you learned?"

I think of Mrs. Hong's story and all the things I saw on our trip. Nothing adds up to any real answer. "I can't say for sure," I say.

"You should know about Empress Myeongseong," Mrs. Hong says. She folds her hands in her lap. "Her name was Min, Ja-young. She was born in 1851 to a poor clan from Seoul. She was very beautiful and quite intelligent. At fifteen years old, her family arranged for her to marry Yi Myeong-bok, the boy king of the House of Yi. The king was lazy and incompetent, so Ja-young taught herself history, science, politics, and religion. She had a good ear for languages and learned to speak Japanese, Chinese, English, and Russian. Eventually, she acquired great power. She promoted education, modernization, freedom of the press, the arts, and equality for women. They say she modeled herself after Queen Victoria of England."

Mrs. Hong puts her hands around the *mugunghwa* blossom and admires the purple blossom inside. "The Empress took power during a time when Korea was being fought over by the Chinese and Japanese. She was a skilled diplomat and was able to keep both powers in check. That is when she created the two-headed dragon. She employed skilled artisans to make artifacts with the dragon for members of her family. She had shamans instill magic in them."

She takes her hands from the bowl and picks up the comb. "Isn't it interesting that the Empress had a comb made for herself instead of a sword or some other kind of armament? Look at it. It is a woman's comb. You can tell by

the long tines. The Empress knew that if her secret got out, the Japanese would kill her and persecute her son. So she gave the comb to her daughter."

"At the history museum, they told us she only had a son," I say.

"You are correct. You were paying attention. Good. Yes, history books say she only had a son. But it's not true. You see, back then, it was common for the royal family to say the first child died if it was a girl. Then, they would keep the girl cloistered in the palace. It turned out to be a fortunate thing. When the Empress learned the Japanese planned to assassinate her, she moved her daughter to our family farm and gave her this comb with the two-headed dragon."

She sets the comb on the table. Her eyes narrow. "On October 8th, 1895, the shameful Japanese murdered my great, great grandmother, your fourth great grandmother. Assassins snuck into Gyeongbok Palace where the Empress was sleeping. They dragged her out of bed and hacked her to death. The assassination marked the beginning of Japanese dominance in Korea and our darkest hour."

"When you learned about the two-headed dragon, why didn't you just give the comb to the government?" I ask.

"Because it was as Mr. Han said when he dismissed me from Gongson Construction, my *yi* was what was most important. I have a duty Korea and to my ancestors and to my descendents." She points to the comb. "Look at the dragon. The heads do not just look east and west. They also look backward and forward. It is a symbol they do not explain at the museum. You see, in Korea, when we look back, we see all of our ancestors all the way back to the Three Kingdoms to Tan'gun, the father of Korea who lived three-hundred years before Christ. Each of our ancestors has given us a duty that we must fulfill. And, when we look forward, we see the generations of our descendents. We love them like grandparents, but expect them to honor their duty

to us as we have honored our duty to our ancestors. It is a single, unbroken chain. If I gave the comb away, I would have broken that chain and not fulfilled my duty to Korea."

"And you think I have a duty to Korea too? But I'm an American, not a Korean."

Mrs. Hong taps a finger at me. "Do you think because you were raised in America that you are not Korean? Then why did you come here? And why did you come to my apartment to hear my story? Just like me, you were born in the year of the dragon. The spirits of your ancestors are strong inside you. You have a duty to them—a duty to Korea. You must tell my story for Soo-hee, for Jin-mo, for Korea. And for me. As long as you serve Korea, the dragon will protect you."

I run a hand through my hair and stare at the comb. The dragon stares back at me.

"Ja-young," she says, "now that you have heard my story, you must decide what to do. You have to decide before you go back to America."

Back to America. I check my watch. It's 4:30P.M. "Oh, no!" I say, jumping up from the table. "Excuse me, ma'am. The bus has already left for the airport. Mr. Kwan said he'd arrest me if I miss my flight." I grab my purse.

Mrs. Hong's eyes plead with me. "I have sacrificed everything for Korea," she says. "Take the comb. Tell our story."

I shake my head. "I just don't know."

She puts her hand over her chest. "Ja-young... Anna, what does your heart say?"

I try to search my heart but I'm conflicted, unsure and afraid like I've been since Mother died. I look at the comb. It's a Korean comb, made by Korea's most important queen. But I'm an American and have been since I was a baby. I don't know anything else. Yet in the mirror, I see the

Korean woman. There is a yearning in her eyes. Her heart aches for something that I can't explain.

I pick up the comb and hold it in my hand. I think perhaps it speaks to the woman in the mirror. I think she wants me to take it. I nod slowly. "Okay. I'll take it. Maybe you should send it to me."

"I am afraid that is no longer possible. Now that the government knows who I am, they will be watching me. You have to find another way."

"They're watching me, too," I say. "But I have an idea."

She takes the comb from me and gives it one more long look. Then, she ties the brown cloth around it and says, "I told you there were two things I wanted you to do for me. One was to hear my story. There is one more thing, as well."

"Oh yeah. You never said what it was."

"I want you to help me see my *onni* before I die."

Of course. Mrs. Hong never saw Soo-hee after Dongfeng and now that she's given me the comb, the only thing she has left to do is to see her sister again. "I'm not sure I can do that," I say.

She says she believes I can and hands me the comb. I tell her I'll try.

Then, I stand before her with the comb in my hand. Our eyes meet one last time, and I bow low.

*

I run outside and, thank God, my taxi driver is waiting for me. He complains that he waited for an hour and a half. I toss a hundred dollars at him and tell him to take me to the Kosney's store by our hotel. "Hurry," I say.

We speed through the streets of Seoul and when we get to the store, I tell my driver to wait for me. I run in the store and a clerk says something to me in Korean.

"What?" I say.

"I am sorry," she replies in English, "we are closing soon, ma'am."

I tell her I'll just be a minute. I ask where the celadon pots are. She tells me they're on the second floor and points to an escalator. I take the escalator two stairs at a time and find the area with the blue-green pots. I run up to the counter and a clerk greets me in Korean. I tell her I want to buy two pots.

"Two?" she asks in English.

"Yes. A large one and a small one."

She takes my order and information and I pay for the pots with the cash Dad gave me. I grab the box and run back out to the taxi. I tell the cabbie to take me to the Sejong Hotel. When we pull up to the hotel, Dad is waiting for me at the front door with our suitcases.

"Anna, thank God," he says. "Where have you been? The bus left over an hour ago. We won't make our flight!"

"Get in," I say waving him into the taxi. "We might still make it." Dad shoves our suitcases in the back of the cab, and we cram inside the back seat. I put the box with the celadon pot between us. "Inchon Airport," Dad says. "As fast as you can."

The driver throws the car into gear and we race onto the street. Over the top of the box, Dad asks, "You gave the comb back, right?"

"No," I answer.

His brow furrows. "Some government officials came to the hotel looking for it. They searched our room and asked a lot of questions about it. Anna, you'll get in trouble. They might be waiting for us at the airport."

"Don't worry," I say, trying to sound convincing.

Twenty minutes later, we pull up to the airport drop-off zone. The flight leaves in thirty minutes and we were supposed to have checked in over an hour ago. Dad jerks the suitcases from the trunk and pushes a hundred dollars at

the cabbie. I take my celadon pot and we sprint toward the ticket counter. When we get near the counter, I freeze. There, waiting for us, is Mr. Kwan, Bruce Willis and several airport security guards.

FORTY-FOUR

MR. KWAN SEES me before I can turn away. He marches up to us. "We have been waiting for you," he says with his diplomatic smile. He tells us if we had been any later, he would've let the plane go and arrested us. He says they'll hold the plane for us and if everything checks out, he'll let us go back to America. "You should check in first," he says, pointing to the ticket counter.

Other travelers stare at us as two male security agents take our luggage and the box with my celadon pot. Dad and I go to the ticket counter and give our passports and tickets to the agent. Mr. Kwan steps to the counter and says something to an airline official. The official bows to Mr. Kwan and then shoots an angry look at us. He disappears into an office behind the ticket counter.

After the ticket agent hands us our boarding passes, Mr. Kwan tells us to follow him. He walks to a door just off the entrance to the concourse. An airport security guard unlocks the door with a key attached to his belt and Mr. Kwan points us inside.

The lights in the room are bright and hurt my eyes. There's a long metal table, an airport luggage scanner and a people scanner that leads to an outside door. I try not to stare at the security guard who opens the box with the celadon pot. Another guard lifts our suitcases onto the table and zips them open. They begin sifting through the contents, searching the pockets, our shoes, Dad's shaving kit, our toiletries—everywhere we might have hidden the comb. One by one, they pass everything through the scanner while a third guard stares into a monitor. Bruce Willis has his back against the door and watches everything.

As the guards pick through our luggage, Mr. Kwan tells us that they have to frisk us and then we have to go through the people scanner. A guard stands next to him with a metal detecting wand. Mr. Kwan explains that the 'examination,' as he calls it, is necessary to be sure we're not taking the comb out of the country. "I assure you," he says, "if you have it, we will find it."

"This isn't right," Dad complains.

"Of course," Mr. Kwan says, "if one of you has the comb, you can give it to me now and avoid this unpleasantness."

Dad glances at me, but I say nothing. After a few seconds, Mr. Kwan tells Dad to take off his shoes and raise his arms. The security guard runs his wand up and down Dad's body and legs. When he's finished, Mr. Kwan tells Dad to walk through the scanner. Dad does and the light on top turns green. Mr. Kwan points to the door. "Wait for your daughter in the concourse," he says.

Dad looks worried. "It's alright," I say. "I'll be there in a minute." Dad frowns and goes out the door.

Mr. Kwan tells me to take off my shoes. I give them to a guard who runs them through the scanner. The guard with the wand steps up to me and waves the wand over me like he did with Dad, just like they did in Mrs. Hong's apartment.

This time, I'm strangely calm, almost as if this is happening to someone else. I'm not embarrassed or the least bit afraid. I feel like I'm someone else. I stare at Mr. Kwan.

"So, it's true, isn't it?" I say. "The two-headed dragon is a powerful symbol for Korea."

"It is just a valuable artifact," he says as the guard wands my legs.

"No, it's more than that," I hear myself say. "A five-toed dragon with two heads. It's a symbol from Empress Myeongseong."

The security guard finishes frisking me and hands me my shoes. "Is that what your grandmother told you?" Mr. Kwan asks.

"Yeah, it is," I say, pulling on my shoes. "She said the comb has been in our family for generations. She said that I'm a descendent of Empress Myeongseong."

He shakes his head. "I read your adoption papers, Ms. Carlson. Just because she gave you the same name as the Empress does not make you related to her. Many Koreans say they are descendants of royalty."

"Yes," I say, "but she had the comb with a five-toed dragon that you want so badly, didn't she?"

Mr. Kwan nods almost imperceptibly. "Yes, she did."

I stand before the people scanner with my eyes still locked on Mr. Kwan. He raises his chin. "I see you bought a celadon pot," he says.

The corners of my mouth turn up. "I got it at Kosney's," I say. "I heard the quality is much better than the ones on the street."

For the first time since I met him, he gives me a genuine smile. And then he says, "Take care of yourself, Ja-young."

I'm completely at ease as I walk through the scanner and the light turns green.

*

Dad and I sprint to our gate carrying our suitcases and my celadon pot. When we get to the gangway, a luggage handler is waiting for us. He takes our suitcases and we board the plane. As we find our seats, the other passengers glare at us for delaying their flight.

After we settle in, Dad whispers, "What happened? Where were you all day? And what happened to the package?"

"It's safe," I answer. "I'll tell you all about it when we get home." Dad gives me a look but lets it slide.

We have two seats together next to a window over the wing. Dad's on the aisle and I'm at the window. The airplane pulls away from the gate and rumbles down the runway. Soon, we're crossing over the Korean peninsula toward the Sea of Japan. A monitor on the bulkhead shows our progress with a yellow line over a map of the North Pacific. I'm relieved to be going home.

An hour into our flight, we've crossed over the Japanese island of Hokkaido. The monitor says we're cruising at thirty-eight thousand feet heading toward the Aleutian Islands. The airplane hums quietly and there're only a few overhead lights on. Dad is sleeping. Asleep, he finally looks peaceful.

I'm wiped out. I can't even begin to grasp all that's happened on this trip. I know there'll be plenty of time to think it through when we get home, so I set it all aside. I look out the window at a billion stars.

My eyes are heavy, so I turn off the light and pull the blanket to my chin. I curl up in the seat and soon I'm asleep. As we head home, the people and places of my Korean grandmother's life story fill my dreams.

FORTY-FIVE

When I was growing up my family didn't have a big house or fancy cars or a cabin on a lake 'up north'. We didn't spend money on boats or snowmobiles or ATVs like many of our friends did. We didn't buy the latest fashions. But I didn't mind. We travelled instead.

Dad always said that to understand the world, you had to smell it. So by the time I graduated from high school, I'd smelled Europe and Canada three times each, Mexico and the Caribbean twice each, Central America, Kenya, Australia and New Zealand. I'd been in forty-one states (airports don't count) and had my U.S. National Park passport book stamped twenty-nine times.

And now I've smelled Korea, the country where I was born.

When I get home, everything's different. It's all bigger and more alive. Colors are brighter and sounds and smells are more intense. Yet at the same time, it's somehow more manageable. I can't explain it, really. I suppose it's because I have a new context to put everything into—my birth-

grandmother's amazing life and the new knowledge I have of the people I share DNA with. For the first time since Mother died, I'm looking forward to the next chapter in my life.

The day after we get home, I tell Dad that the woman that gave me the comb was my birth-grandmother. I tell him her incredible story and that I promised to try to help her meet her sister someday. I decide not to tell him about me being a descendent of Empress Myeongseong or that Mrs. Hong says I have to serve Korea somehow. I feel guilty about keeping it from him, but honestly, I really don't know what to believe.

Dad listens carefully and asks questions. I answer them as best as I can. Then he asks about the comb. I tell him it's just a family heirloom that Mrs. Hong wants me to have to remind me of my Korean heritage. "Why were those government officials so intent on it?" he asks.

"It's just an heirloom, Dad," I repeat. He raises an eyebrow, but doesn't ask any more questions.

That night I think about going back to college to finish my senior year. When I left, Northwestern said they'd let me come back. Dad says I should do it, but I decide to stay home and enroll at the University of Minnesota instead. I log onto the 'U's website to see what my class options are. I'm still not sure what I should take and the deadline is only a few days away. I bring up my list of pros and cons for medical school versus law school. Medical school and residency would be an expensive, ten-year grind. But in the end, I'd have a prestigious job and a good income. Law school would be a piece of cake compared to medical school. It'd be three years of school and a few years as a law associate. But a career in law isn't exactly a sure thing like medicine is.

Or, I could do something completely different.

My choices on the computer monitor stare at me. I search my heart for the right answer like Mrs. Hong said I should. It's not telling me anything. So I log off. I still have a few days.

It saddens me when Dad falls back into his miserable routine. Each day he leaves for work early and comes home in time to sit in the dark living room before dinner. When he puts on his grilling apron, he makes the same things each week. On Monday, it's Mother's goulash. On Tuesday, it's Mother's baked tilapia. Wednesday, it's her parmesan chicken… and so on. Every week it's the same thing and every recipe is Mother's. When I offer to make something different, he says, "No. I'll do it."

*

One day, I do a search for the Korean embassy and I see there's an office in Minneapolis. It's on Park Avenue where businesses have converted the 1800's mansions into hip offices. I jump in Mom's Corolla and drive there. The office is on the third floor of a three-story stone mansion. I climb two flights of stairs to a reception area with a flag of South Korea in the corner. A Korean woman sits behind a glass desk. She smiles pleasantly through stylish, red-framed glasses. "May I help you?" she asks.

"I want to arrange a meeting with someone in North Korea," I say.

"I see," she says. "You need to talk with Mr. Han."

She points me to a couch and offers to get me coffee, which I decline. Then she disappears into the back while I wait. On the wall are travel posters for South Korea. It's really a beautiful country. Rolling hills, jagged granite peaks, two seacoasts, the exciting capital of Seoul where I was born.

Eventually, a man in a navy blue suit and white shirt comes to the lobby and greets me with a handshake. "I'm

Mr. Han," he says. "I understand you want to connect with someone in the North?" He speaks English with only a slight accent. He's slender and lean. He has an intelligent face. I guess he's in his mid-thirties.

"Yes," I answer. "It's a long story."

"I would be glad to hear it," Mr. Han says. He tells me to follow him to his office. We walk down the hall and inside a large office. Embroidered rugs cover the hardwood floors, the walls are wood paneled, and a dormered window overlooks the street. A window air conditioner hums quietly. I sit on a couch off to the side of his desk. He sits in a chair next to it.

He folds his hands in his lap and asks my name. I give it and tell him I was adopted when I was a baby. He asks me to tell him more about my request. I tell him about my trip to Korea and how I met my Korean grandmother. I give him a summary of her story. I'm careful not to say anything about the comb with the two-headed dragon or that I'm related to Empress Myeongseong. I tell him I agreed to help Mrs. Hong meet her sister.

When I'm done, Mr. Han nods. "Very interesting," he says. "How do you know your grandmother's story is true?"

I think about it for a second. "I guess I don't for sure," I admit.

He smiles. "Well, we will see what we can do."

I push myself to the edge of the couch. "So, do you think you can arrange a meeting?"

Mr. Han shrugs. "There are times when it can be done. But, I am afraid we are not in one of those times, presently."

"Why not?"

He leans forward. He then tells me that the North and South Korea are still officially at war. There was no formal peace treaty signed after the hostilities ended in 1953. He says the two sides only agreed to a cease-fire and that

tensions are very high right now—especially with the North testing nuclear weapons.

"Yeah, I know. But I've read that families sometimes get to meet."

He nods. "It depends on the state of affairs between the two countries. Sometimes these meetings can shut down for years. And when they open up, it has to be done through... unofficial channels."

"What do you mean, 'unofficial channels'?"

"What you call bribes, Ms. Carlson, for both sides. It costs a lot of money."

I ask, "Okay. So how much does it cost?"

He says an amount that's a lot more than my tuition at the 'U' for a year. "I'm not sure I can afford that," I say.

"It doesn't matter if you can," Mr. Han replies. "As I said, the two countries are not allowing any contact right now."

"When do you think they will?"

"It is impossible to say."

I nod. "Well, can you let me know? I made a promise."

"I will be glad to. Give all your information to Ja-Sook at the reception desk. In the meantime, we will see what we can find out about your grandmother's sister. She might not even be alive. But if she is, and when things open up, we can help make the arrangements if you have the fee."

Mr. Han stands, extends his hand, and I shake it. "It was a pleasure meeting you," he says.

I give him a bow and ask for his business card. When he gives it to me, I remember to examine it respectfully. I thank him and I say I hope to hear from him soon.

*

When I get home, I'm relieved to see that the small celadon pot I shipped from Kosney's has arrived via Federal Express.

I open the box and reach inside the pot beneath the packing paper where I slipped the comb with the two-headed dragon when the store clerk wasn't looking. It's still there. Somehow, I knew it would be.

I take the comb to the bank and open a safe deposit box account. The ancient female clerk gives me my key and shows me to a privacy room. Before putting it into the box, I take the comb out of the brown cloth and study it one more time.

It really is amazing, a thing worthy of royalty. And now it has found its way to me. I wonder—and worry—what it will mean for me.

FORTY-SIX

IT'S THURSDAY—pot roast day—and I go home from class in a freezing December wind. It hasn't snowed yet this season, but the ground is frozen and the wind is blowing from the north. The low clouds threaten our first big snow of the season. Weeks earlier, I dug out my winter coat from our basement storage room, and now I wrap it tight around me. I put my shoulder in the wind for the three-block walk to the parking lot.

It's a week before fall finals and it's been the most amazing college semester I've had. I decided to take a class on world history and two on political science. I'm getting all 'A's and I'll graduate near the top of my class. I'm also taking Korean. I'm learning it so fast that my instructor is encouraging me to take two accelerated courses next semester.

I took the law school entrance exam last month. I was nervous about it. I mean, some of these people have been studying for the LSAT for years. So I was shocked when I scored in the upper five percent. I've always been a good

test-taker. But seriously, the upper five percent? I'm already getting letters from top schools across the country inviting me to apply. Naturally, I'm making a 'pros and cons' list. But I'm also trying to listen to my heart.

Before I reach my car, my phone rings. It's Mr. Han from the Korean consulate. He says he has news and wants to meet with me. Over the past several months, I called Mr. Han every month to check in. He always gave the same answer. "We don't know anything yet," he says. "Please be patient. These things take time."

This is the first time he's called me, so I tell him I'll meet with him right away. I jump in my car and go to the mansion on Park Avenue. When I get inside, Ja-sook shows me into Mr. Han's office. After a short wait, he comes in carrying a folder. He apologizes that it's taken so long for him to get back to me. He tells me that over the past several months, it was impossible to reach their contacts in the North because Pyongyang was testing nuclear weapons and the two countries had cut off all contact. Now, however, relations have improved and they've learned that Hong Soo-hee is alive and living in Pyongyang. "I must admit," he says, shaking his head, "when you told me your grandmother's story, I was skeptical. I thought you might be involved in a scam. So, I inquired about your grandmother. I am pleased to tell you, everything she told you is true."

I look out the window. So that's it. My birth-grandmother's story is true. I guess in my heart I knew that it was. "Well, if that's the case," I say, "I want to set up the meeting between Mrs. Hong and her sister as soon as possible."

"Of course. It could still take months. And, there is the issue of the money."

"I think I can get it."

Mr. Han frowns. "I am sorry to tell you there is a change with respect to the cost. You see, it has become more expensive."

"Oh?" I say, sagging into my chair. "How much more?"

"Well, there is a large backlog. Years worth, I'm afraid. And that has caused the cost to double."

"Are you serious?" I reply with a gasp. I do some quick math in my head. "I can't afford that."

"Well, you could wait until there isn't a backlog. But there is no saying how long this window will stay open.

"There is one more thing," Mr. Han says. "You will have to go to Korea personally to sponsor your grandmother. It is all very complicated and it would be difficult for an elderly woman like her to do this on her own."

"Yeah, I understand. That's another expense I suppose. I'll have to let you know."

He smiles politely and extends a hand. I respectfully take his hand with both of mine and bow my head, like I've learned proper Koreans are supposed to do.

On the drive home, I think about Mrs. Hong and her sister and how they haven't seen each other for over sixty years and I'm torn. I think about law school and the cost of tuition, books, and room and board. The only way I can pay Mr. Han's steep fee is to get a job and forgo law school for a couple of years. By then, who knows? Law school might have passed me by.

*

When I walk inside our house, I expect to smell pot roast cooking in the oven and see the table set. But I don't smell anything and there aren't any plates on the table.

I call out to tell Dad I'm home and he shouts a hello from his bedroom. I drop my backpack on the kitchen table

and find him in his room. He's facing the mirror, putting on a clean shirt.

"It's pot roast night," I say. "It's not in the oven. What gives?"

"I was thinking, maybe we could go out," he says, tucking his shirt in.

I almost fall down. "Seriously? On a Thursday night?"

He turns from the mirror. "I feel guilty saying this about your mother's pot roast, but I get tired of it every week. I was thinking we could go to Ho Ban instead. We haven't been there in a long time. What do you say?"

After I pick up my jaw from the floor, I agree that Korean food would be a nice change of pace. I tell him I need a few minutes and run off to my room. As I change my clothes and brush my hair, I wonder what's gotten into my father. He hasn't been sitting in the living room in the dark as much. Twice in the past month, he came home late from work and I had to make dinner. And just last week I was shocked to see he stopped wearing his wedding ring.

We drive to the restaurant in a strip mall in Eagan. The restaurant is the only decent business in the tacky suburban mall. It's nearly full of customers, most of them Korean. They give us a table near the kitchen. I notice they've tried to fix up the place since I was there last. There's a new greeting station at the front door and they've painted a Korean landscape on one wall. It doesn't help. The lighting is bad and the tables and chairs are cheap and too close together. It's no big deal, though. People come here for the food—real Korean food, just like we had in Korea. Hot pots, rice bowls, Korean noodles, *katsu*, *bebimbop*, *bulgogi*, Korean monkfish. A dozen plates of *banchan* appetizers fill each table. And, of course, there's *kimchi*. The smells are amazing, just like I remembered them from Korea. I wonder why it's been so long since I've been here.

We decide what we'll order and when the waiter comes, Dad orders extra saying we can have the leftovers tomorrow instead of our usual Friday night spaghetti. The *banchan* arrives and we dive in. The *kimchi* is spicy and wonderful.

"This reminds me of our trip," Dad says, fumbling with his chopsticks.

"Yeah it does," I say, picking up more *kimchi*.

We make small talk and when our entrees arrive, we attack them. Dad eats like he hasn't eaten for a week. He finishes his dish and then sneaks a few bites off my plate. I notice that he's filled out a bit over the past few months. His cheekbones don't stick out and his color is better. And it makes me happy to see him smile more.

I tell Dad that I met with Mr. Han from the consulate after school. He asks me why. "They discovered that Mrs. Hong's sister is alive and living in Pyongyang," I say. "Apparently tensions between the North and South have let up and they can arrange a meeting now."

"Hmm, I see," Dad says. "And you made that promise."

"I'm not sure I can keep it. The cost has gone way up. It's ridiculous. I'd have to put off law school and get a job."

"No," Dad says shaking his head. "You shouldn't put off school."

"I don't know how I'll do it any other way," I say.

Dad turns quiet as we finish our meal. When we can't eat another bite, the waiter puts all the leftovers into boxes and we head home. Snow is falling as we drive north over the Minnesota River. There's not much traffic and Dad drives slowly. The meal has subdued us.

Halfway home Dad says, "Anna, I want to talk to you about something."

"Oh?" I say. "What about?"

"Tell you what," he says. "Let's take a drive around the lakes. Your Mother and I always went out driving in the first

snow. It scares people off the roads, but I think it's beautiful."

We turn off the freeway and go to the parkway that connects the Minneapolis lakes. The snow is making everything clean and quiet. I ask Dad what he wants to talk about. He tells me that he's looked into my comb and the two-headed dragon.

"I thought I should," he says, apologetically.

"What did you find out?" I ask.

"A two-headed dragon with five toes," he says. "I found out what it means. The dragon protects Korea and those who possess it so they can serve Korea." And then he says, "Five toes on a dragon. It means..."

"Yeah, I know what it means," I say. "It means it belonged to Empress Myeongseong. It means I'm a direct descendent."

"Only if Mrs. Hong's story is true," he says.

"It's true, Dad," I say. "The consulate looked into it. Her story checks out."

Dad doesn't respond to this bit of information. He keeps his eyes on the road as we turn onto the boulevard that circles Lake Harriet. The mansions surrounding the lake have their holiday lights on which sparkle off the new snow. The pointed roofs of the Lake Harriet band shell make it look like it's straight out of a winter fairytale. It feels like Christmas Day and I understand why Mom and Dad liked driving in the snow.

"Sweetheart," Dad says finally, "This whole thing makes me nervous. But I've been doing a lot of thinking lately. I've been thinking about your mother and how she died. It was horrible how that damn cancer killed her. But she didn't let cancer or even death define her. She simply made them a part of her life. And it made me realize that you can die when you're still alive, holed up in your house, in your living room with the lights off." He shoots me a guilty look.

"And I've been thinking about you, too," he continues. "Your mother and I sensed there was something special about you when you were just a kid. You were smart, of course, but there was something in the way you carried yourself. I never figured out what it was, exactly. But now you have that comb with the two-headed dragon. I don't know how you're meant to serve Korea, but I think you need to find out. And I can help. Let me pay Mr. Han's fee."

I start to protest, but Dad cuts me off.

"I'm not just doing it for you," he says. "It won't be easy. But it might keep me out of the dark living room."

"Thank you," I say and Dad smiles.

"There's one condition," he says. "Promise me you'll be careful." I assure him that I will.

"I love you, sweetheart," he says.

"I love you too, Dad," I reply.

I'm finally at peace as we come full circle around the lake and Dad turns off the boulevard to go home. I can feel the two parts of me—Korean and American—coming together. Like Dad, I don't know how I'm supposed to serve Korea, but I'm not afraid anymore. As Mrs. Hong said, the courageous little seed has broken through and someday, a flower will bloom.

FORTY-SEVEN

AFTER DAD CLOSES on a second mortgage on our house, I call Mr. Han and tell him I have the money for his fee. He calls me back two months later and tells me that they can arrange a meeting between the sisters any time. All I need to do is tell him when I can go.

I make the travel arrangements for July, after finals and graduation. I tell Dad he should go with me, but he says no. He tells me he'd love to meet my birth-grandmother, "but this is your thing," he says. "You should go alone." So I buy my plane ticket and, as I always do, I make out a detailed itinerary for while I'm in Korea. On the list is an entire day at Gyeongbok Palace.

Two months before I start my first year at Columbia Law School, I send a letter to Mrs. Hong telling her I'll be in Seoul and that I want to meet her. I don't tell her why. A week later, I get on an airplane for Seoul to fulfill my promise to Mrs. Hong.

After we land at Inchon Airport, I clear customs and catch a cab outside baggage claim. I give the driver the

address where I'll meet the contact who has the details of the meeting. As we drive through Seoul, I look for what I remember about the city. In a strange way, it feels like a second home now. The soaring Seoul Tower on top of Mount Namsan still dominates the city. And all around, apartment buildings still stand like so many soldiers at attention. The city hums with excitement.

I'm thrilled to be back here. I want to see this country again, now that I know more about its history, culture, and people. I won't be a tourist this time, but someone who shares the sorrow of this country's history and its hopes for its future.

Of course, I've thought a lot about the comb and its responsibility. I've decided that my responsibility to Korea is both as a descendant of Empress Myeongseong and as an American. America has helped this country, for sure. But we've been selfish, too. I mean, we're still stuck in this 1950's Cold War mentality. I'm angry that we call North Korea 'evil' as if we have the right to force our values on them. How arrogant. Yet I don't want them to develop nuclear bombs and they need to be good world citizens. Yeah, okay, I get it—it's complicated. Still, I think America can do a lot more to promote peace. And unification, too.

As a Korean, I'm willing to do what I can for the country where I was born. As an American, naturally I want to help keep my country great. I guess what I'm saying is that I want to make both of my countries proud—the one that gave me life and the one that gave me a family—because I'm proud to be a child of both.

As the cab drives through Itaewon, I reach inside my backpack and feel the envelopes that I've been carrying since I left home. Inside one is twenty thousand dollars cash. Inside the other, is ten thousand.

I'm anxious to get to my meeting. In spite of the fourteen-hour flight, I'm not tired. I'm excited to see Mrs.

Hong and tell her that I'm there to keep my promise to her. But I have to admit that all the secrecy about this meeting has me more than a little nervous.

*

The cab pulls up to a glass building. I see the open space for the Han River a few blocks away. I pay the cab driver and roll my suitcase into the lobby. I give the receptionist the name of the man I'm supposed to meet. She tells me to wait. I take a seat in one of the lobby's Le Corbusier chairs. Ten minutes later, a short man in a dark suit with eyes to match, greets me. "I am Mr. Choi," he says with a slight bow. He doesn't extend his hand.

I bow respectfully and in Korean, I introduce myself.

In Korean Mr. Choi says, "Shall we go for a walk?"

I assumed we'd meet in Mr. Choi's office. Then I remember Mr. Han saying that meetings between people from the North and South are done off the record. So I give my suitcase to the receptionist and follow Mr. Choi out to the street. He walks with his hands behind his back as if he's out for a midday stroll. I start to talk, but he quickly cuts me off with a wave.

"Let us walk a little before we talk," he says.

We walk toward the Han River. White clouds roll across the sky. The humidity is low and the temperature is comfortably warm. We reach a small park and sit on a bench facing the river. Mr. Choi folds his hands in front of him and lifts an eyebrow. "This is a generous thing you are doing for Mrs. Hong," he says.

"She's my grandmother. I made a promise to her."

"Yes, we know about Mrs. Hong. She was an *ianfu* for the Japanese, and she was sympathetic to the communists. She even worked for them. She also worked in a *kijichon*

after the Korean War. She has a thick file. She has had—how should I say?—a questionable past."

Excuse me? *Questionable past?* I turn toward Mr. Choi, ready to tell him what my Korean grandmother did for her country. I catch myself before I do. Perhaps he knows. But, like a typical Korean, he's more concerned about his country's honor than the rights of an individual.

I look at the river and nod. "Yes, Mr. Choi, I know all that about Mrs. Hong. She's had a tough life."

"Why, Ms. Carlson? Why would you spend so much of your money to do this thing?"

I meet his eyes. "Because she's my grandmother," I say speaking Korean. "I have a duty to her."

Mr. Choi half smiles. "You speak Korean well. Korean-American adoptees rarely learn our language. So, do you have the money?"

I reach in my pocket and give him the envelope with twenty thousand dollars in it. He thumbs through the bills and is satisfied that it's all there.

"It is arranged for tomorrow," he says, tucking the envelope inside his suit coat. "You will need another ten thousand dollars for the North Koreans."

"I have it," I say. "So what's next?"

He gives me a slip of paper with the address of a bus station in the Shinchon area of Seoul. He tells me I should take Mrs. Hong there tomorrow morning before 8:30AM. He says we have to find the bus to Munsan. It's not an official bus, he says, so I won't need a ticket. There, we'll meet a man named Mr. Ryu who'll collect the fee for the North Koreans. The bus will take us to the American military base outside the Demilitarized Zone. The Americans will do an inspection. Then, they'll take us to Panmunjom where our meeting will take place.

Mr. Choi puts on a serious look. "Ms. Carlson, do exactly as you are told. Panmunjom is not a place to be taken lightly."

"I understand," I say.

Mr. Choi pushes himself off the bench and heads back to the government building as if I'm not there. I walk behind him in silence. When we get there, he goes to his office without saying goodbye. I grab my suitcase, go outside and hail a cab. I give the driver the address for Mrs. Hong's apartment.

*

It's late afternoon when we pull up to the eight-story apartment building. I take my backpack and suitcase and climb out of the cab. As I walk up to Mrs. Hong's building, I'm surprised at how nervous I am.

I press the number 627 on the intercom and wait. There's no answer. I press it again. Finally, a voice comes over the intercom and says something in Korean. I can't tell if it's Mrs. Hong.

"This is Anna Carlson. I'm looking for Mrs. Hong."

There's a pause. Then, "Ja-young. How nice of you to pay a visit. You may come in." The security door buzzes and I walk through. I take the elevator to the sixth floor and go to Mrs. Hong's apartment. I knock and the door opens.

It's only been a year since I saw her last, but she looks several years older. Her hair is grayer and the wrinkles on her face are deeper than they were before. Her head shakes slightly with what looks like the early onset of Parkinson's disease. She doesn't stand as straight as she did, but her eyes are still bright.

"*Anyahasao,*" I say with a proper bow.

"*Anyahasao,* Ja-young," she replies.

"It's very good to see you," I say in Korean.

"Your Korean is very good," she says, keeping the conversation in Korean. "You don't have much of an accent."

"I've been told I have a good ear for languages," I say.

My Korean grandmother smiles and tells me to come in. I take off my shoes and follow her to the low table in front of the window. A fresh *mugunghwa* blossom floats in a bowl on the sill. The frame that holds the photographs of Mrs. Hong's family and my birthmother still sits on the table. And of course, the room smells of *kimchi*. I can't believe I'm back here in Mrs. Hong's apartment. It's surreal.

I take a seat at the table and put my backpack on the floor. Mrs. Hong leans in to the table. "Ja-young, do you have the comb?"

"Yes, ma'am," I answer. "It's safe at home."

"And how do you feel about having it?"

I sigh. "It's a lot of responsibility."

Mrs. Hong sits up straight. "Yes," she says, "I know."

After a moment, I say, "I brought you something." I reach inside my backpack and pull out the photo album that I made a year earlier. "I thought you'd like to have this. I made it for my birthmother. I've added pictures from my senior year in college. I didn't have a chance to tell you much about myself last year."

Mrs. Hong bites her lower lip. "I am honored," she says, taking the album as if it were a treasure. "I want you to tell me everything about each photograph."

Since Mother died and I had to move back home, I haven't had anyone to share my life with. Dad has his own issues and anyway he's my Dad if you know what I mean. All my girlfriends want to talk about is men and sex. And even my adopted friends don't understand how I feel about being Korean. But now I have Mrs. Hong, my Korean grandmother who's been through so much. I know I can talk to her about anything.

So I pull my chair next to her and open the photo album. We go through it together, page by page, like best friends catching up after a long time apart. We talk in both English and Korean. She listens carefully as I tell the story behind each photo. She asks questions and nods thoughtfully at my answers. We laugh a lot.

Two hours later, we close the photo album and I pick up Mrs. Hong's photos from the table and study them. "I'd like a copy of these, if it isn't too much to ask. I want to know more about them. And your grandparents and aunts and uncles, too."

"Of course," Mrs. Hong answers. "They are your family, too. It is important that you know."

"But not tonight," I say, setting the photos down. "I'll be in Seoul for five days. We'll have plenty of time to talk. I need to go to my hotel and rest. You should rest, too. We'll have to get going early tomorrow."

Mrs. Hong raises an eyebrow. "Tomorrow?"

I pick up the bowl with the *mugunghwa* and stare at the purple blossom with the yellow pistil in the center. I say, "Last year, I promised I'd help you meet your sister. I'm here to keep that promise."

Her eyes soften and her mouth opens a bit. "Soo-hee? Do you know something about my *onni*?"

"Yes. She's living in Pyongyang. She never married or had any children. After the Korean War, she became a nurse."

"That sounds like her," Mrs. Hong says. "What else can you tell me?"

I set the *mugunghwa* blossom on the table. "Well ma'am, you can find out for yourself. You and I are going to Panmunjom tomorrow, where you'll meet her. It won't be a long meeting—less than an hour."

She stays silent for a long time and her head shakes a little. I can almost see the images of her sister in her mind as

she takes in what I just said. Her eyes turn watery. She gazes at the photographs and says, ""

She looks from the photos and smiles at me. "Tonight will be a very long night."

FORTY-EIGHT

THE NEXT MORNING I get up before my alarm goes off and take a cab to Mrs. Hong's building. Before I can press 627 on the intercom, the security door buzzes open. I take the elevator to the sixth floor and go to Mrs. Hong's apartment. Her door is open when I get there, and I go in.

She's standing in the middle of the room facing me. She's wearing her yellow *hanbok*, with long, loose sleeves. She has braided her hair and pinned it back with a beautiful ebony *binyeo*. She is stunning.

I greet her with a bow. "Are you ready?" I ask.

"I am," she replies.

I pick up her travel bag and she takes my arm. We walk out to the cab. I help her in and climb in the other side. I give the driver the bus station address. We pull onto the street and make our way across the Han River and into the Shinchon area of Seoul. The streets are steep and all around are green hills, some topped with granite cliffs. The flat spaces between the hills are crammed with apartment buildings. Shinchon is alive with energy. We make our way

through narrow streets and arrive at a bus terminal. I pay the cab driver and then help Mrs. Hong. She holds my arm as we walk through the bus station filled with college students carrying suitcases and backpacks. The students stare at Mrs. Hong in her *hanbok*. She keeps her eyes forward.

We find the bus to Munsan. Before I can help Mrs. Hong aboard, a short man in a black suit comes up to us. "I am Mr. Ryu," he says from underneath twitchy eyebrows. "Who are you?"

I tell him and he checks us off a list. "Do you have the fee?" he asks.

I give him the envelope with ten thousand dollars inside. He does a quick count and lets us on the bus. We take seats near the front. The bus is less than half-full of people waiting silently.

"Are you comfortable?" I ask Mrs. Hong.

Her head shakes a little and I think she's saying 'no'. Instead, she says, "I am a little nervous."

Yeah, I'm nervous too, although for a different reason. I'm not sure if Soo-hee will be in Panmunjom when we get there. It seems like this entire arrangement was a little too easy, a little too dependent on money. I'm worried that I've been scammed.

After a few minutes, an overweight bus driver in a white shirt and black cap climbs aboard and starts the bus. We pull away and Mr. Ryu takes a seat in the front row. The bus grinds through its gears and we head north. Soon, we're out of the city. Rice paddies in amazing geometric patterns cover the hills. The morning sun makes diamonds in the paddy water. Farmers in straw hats bend over rice stalks. A crane stands like a statue at the edge of an irrigation pond.

Mrs. Hong sits straight with her hands in her lap. She looks out the window. Her reflection doesn't show her wrinkles and scars and she looks like a much younger

woman. Her head shakes again, as if she approves of what she sees outside.

The countryside changes from fields to forest. We pass through the city of Munsan and cross the Imjin River. I remember reading in my history class about the battle that took place here in 1592. The Japanese army defeated the Korean cavalry, forcing King Seonjo to seek an alliance with the Chinese. The battle of Imjin created a divided Korea. And now, over 400 years later, it's still divided. How ironic.

A few miles later, we come to a gate and a high fence surrounded by razor wire. The sign over the gate reads 'Camp Bonifas – In Front of Them All.' Behind the fence are green military buildings and a huge tank with its gun facing the gate. An enormous American flag flies atop a tall flagpole. An American soldier holding some kind of assault rifle raises his hand. The bus stops and the soldier stands in front of it with his rifle at his chest. Another soldier walks around the bus with some devise that lets him see underneath.

An American sergeant sporting a crew cut, and a Republic of Korea soldier in a white helmet come through the gate and get on our bus. The American sergeant comes down the aisle asking to see everyone's papers. My heart beats faster when he looks at my passport and says, "You're an American?"

"Yes, sir," I answer. "I'm here with my Korean grandmother. She's meeting her sister." I notice the large, black pistol on his hip.

He points at Mrs. Hong. "Why's she dressed like that?"

I'm flustered and only manage a shrug. The sergeant glares at me over the top of my passport. "I don't like it," he says. "This is the most dangerous place on earth. We don't allow just anyone through here. And I don't like the way she's dressed. Both of you need to go back."

Then, someone inside me takes over and I'm not flustered anymore. I stand to face the sergeant. "Sir," I say, "I'm here to help my grandmother. I won't cause any trouble. She's dressed like this because it's what Korean women wear on special occasions. Surely you and the American government don't want to stop a meeting between two sisters who haven't seen each other in over sixty years. Do you, sergeant?"

I return the sergeant's stare. After a few seconds, he closes my passport and gives it back to me. "Be sure you follow the rules," he orders. He goes back to the front of the bus and I take my seat next to Mrs. Hong. She nods at me.

The ROK soldier steps forward and talks to the passengers in Korean. He tells us the bus will take us to Panmunjom where there will be North Korean soldiers. He tells us to stay together and not make any gestures or even make eye contact with them. He says an ROK soldier will take us inside a building where our meetings will take place.

The ROK soldier and the American sergeant get off the bus. The soldier with the rifle in front of the bus steps aside and we drive on toward Panmunjom. The road goes past open fields and through another high fence with razor wire on top. We pass through a security gate and come to a row of pale blue, one-story barracks. Between each barracks is a ROK soldier at the *taekwondo* ready position. At the other end of the barracks, North Korean soldiers stand holding rifles to their chests. Mr. Ryu tells us to get off the bus and go inside the building in front of us. "Do not say anything until you are inside," he says, firmly.

We let the other passengers go ahead of us and then follow them outside. The sun makes me squint. As a ROK soldier hurries me to the door, I catch a glimpse of a North Korean soldier at the other end of the barracks. He looks at me with hate-filled eyes.

We enter a long, plain room with metal tables and chairs. There are windows all around and a door at the opposite end. I help Mrs. Hong into a chair and sit next to her. As we wait, the North Korean soldier I saw outside peers through a window at us. I turn away before our eyes meet again.

One-by-one, people come in through the door at the far end and North Korean and South Korean loved ones meet again. They bow, hug, cry a little, and settle in to tell each other about their lives.

Mrs. Hong and I wait five minutes, then ten. I'm a basket case. There must have been a mistake—or maybe they've scammed me. I look at Mrs. Hong. She has her hands in her lap, watching the door at the far end of the room. Her head no longer shakes.

We wait another five minutes. I'm about to ask Mr. Ryu where Soo-hee is when the door at the end of the room opens. Sunlight pours through and an old woman steps in. Her back is bent and she leans heavily on a cane. She's wearing cheap gray slacks and a blue sweater over a white blouse. Deep wrinkles line her face and her left eye is white with cataract. She searches the room with her good eye.

Mrs. Hong slowly stands and steps to the middle of the room. In her *hanbok,* she moves with dignity and grace. Soo-hee sees her and comes to her. They stand apart, looking at each other for several seconds. Then, Soo-hee raises her hand and her sister reaches out and tenderly takes it. They clasp each other's fingers making a single fist, and do the same with their other hands. As everyone in the room goes quiet, the sisters step close to each other, holding each other's gaze. Without a word, they turn around each other in a slow dance and nod their approval.

*

I see Ja-hee and Soo-hee sitting in front of their home in the hills outside of Sinuiju playing *yut*. From the kitchen window, their mother looks on with a smile. Their father leans against the front door, arms crossed, watching his girls with obvious pride.

Ja-hee tosses the *yut* sticks in the air and all four land with the flat side down. She has tossed a *mo*, the highest possible score, and has won the game. She giggles with delight. Soo-hee pretends to be upset that she has lost. Ja-hee sidles up to her *onni* and Soo-hee puts an arm around her. "You are lucky at *yut*, little sister," Soo-hee says. "You are lucky in everything. I think, someday, you will be an empress."

And they sit together, side-by-side, under the persimmon tree, and watch the setting sun turn blood red.

AUTHOR'S END NOTE

Saving the Soul of a Nation

"If we don't learn from history, we are doomed to repeat it."
                                        -- George Santayana

EVERY WEDNESDAY AT NOON, a group of elderly women march on the Japanese embassy in Seoul, South Korea. They march in the pouring rain, bitter cold and stifling humidity that only Seoul can dish out. They have not missed a single Wednesday in over twenty-one years. They are the last of an army of comfort women—women the Japanese military raped and tortured as sex slaves during World War II. They are all more than 80 years old now and many are in their 90s. The Koreans call them "grandmothers," a term of honor and respect.

Their ranks are dwindling fast.

The estimated number of women forced into sexual slavery by the Japanese varies depending on who is doing the counting. Some Japanese nationalists say there were fewer than 20,000 and that they were former prostitutes or willing volunteers. But the evidence supports a much higher number. Today most historians agree there were more than 200,000[1]. 200,000 women serving an army of over seven million. That's one woman for every thirty-five soldiers. They were Filipino, Chinese, even Dutch, but the vast majority were Korean. Some were as young as 13.

As the women march, you can still see the pain and humiliation in their faces seventy years later. The Japanese raped these women, these

---

[1] ʌ "An estimated 200,000 to 300,000 women across Asia, predominantly Korean and Chinese, are believed to have been forced to work as sex slaves in Japanese military brothels", BBC 2000-12-08;
"Historians say thousands of women – as many as 200,000 by some accounts – mostly from Korea, China and Japan worked in the Japanese military brothels", Irish Examiner 2007-03-08;
AP 2007-03-07;
CNN 2001-03-29.

grandmothers, up to 40 times per day. They were repeatedly beaten and tortured. They suffered horribly from venereal disease and the Japanese forced them to have crude abortions when they got pregnant. Many were executed. And many committed suicide. The Japanese government has never formally apologized to them. And as the grandmothers march, the blinds on the Japanese embassy remain closed.

The Empire of Japan formally surrendered on September 2, 1945. Since then, it has issued a number of mostly informal apologies for its actions during the war. Many apologies were insincere at best. For example, on September 6, 1984, thirty-nine years after the war ended, a famously disingenuous 'apology' delivered to Korean President Chun Doo Hwan by Emperor Hirohito was stated as follows:

> *"It is indeed regrettable that there was an unfortunate past between us for a period in this century, and I believe that it should not be repeated again."*

In the early 1990's, after a few comfort women finally found the courage to come forward, the Japanese issued a series of informal apologies. But just like the Hirohito apology, many were disingenuous. They often used the word *owabi* for "apology"—a word in Japanese only slightly weightier than "excuse me." But the outrage grew around the globe and finally bowing to the pressure, the Japanese government set up the Asian Women's Fund in 1995. The fund was a quasi-public organization to collect donations from Japanese citizens (there were no government contributions) to distribute compensation to comfort women. Run by volunteers (not the government) the fund collected less than $5 million and distributed it to only 285 of the 200,000 comfort women. The Japanese government closed it in March of 2007.

In 2006 in a special election, the Japanese Diet elected Shinzo Abe as Japan's prime minister. Abe, the first prime minister born after World War II and a right-wing nationalist, is a historical revisionist. On the homepage of his website before he was prime minister, he questioned the extent to which the Japanese used coercion toward comfort women. Then, in March of 2007, Abe publicly stated that there was no evidence that the Japanese government had kept sex slaves. Abe also led the Japanese Society for History Textbook Reform that published the *New*

History Textbook that whitewashes the criminal actions of Japan during World War II. Schools throughout Japan use the textbook today.

Abe served as prime minister for two years, and was forced to resign after several scandals in his administration. But in the 2012 general election, he was reelected prime minister. And it appears that Japan is finally digging out from a two-decade-long economic slump. Under Abe, Japan might again become the leading economic and political global force it once was. But, given that Abe is a historical revisionist, it seems they will not take with them lessons from the past.

So outside the Japanese embassy the grandmothers March. They have simple demands.

1. Admit the drafting of the Japanese military's "comfort women"
2. Apologize officially
3. Reveal truths about the war crimes
4. Erect memorial tablets for the victims
5. Pay restitution to the victims or their families directly from the government
6. Teach the truth in public schools, so the events are never again repeated
7. Punish the war criminals

These seem reasonable. However, it's unlikely Japan will ever meet them, especially with Shinzo Abe sitting in the Prime Minister's office. It's a shame—a tragedy really. Meeting these simple demands before all the grandmothers die could help restore a modicum of the dignity stolen from them seventy years ago.

But just as importantly, it would restore Japan's own honor and save its very soul.

William Andrews

For more information or to donate, go to:
http://www.comfort-women.org

PHOTOS OF COMFORT WOMEN

A young comfort woman liberated in southern China

Comfort Station 1943

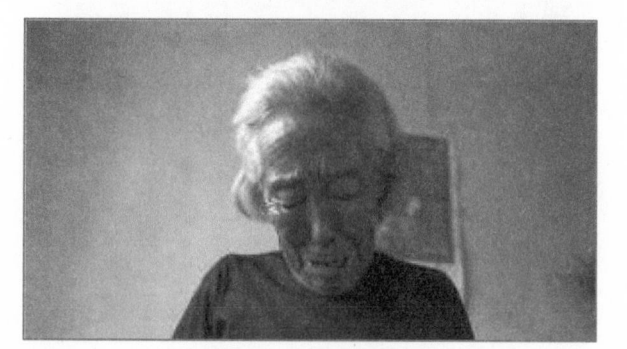

A former comfort woman interviewed in 2009

For more photographs and descriptions, go to www.williamandrewsbooks.com.
Photos used by permission

SELECTED BIBLIOGRAPHY

This book is a work of fiction. Nevertheless, it is based on historical facts. To learn more about comfort women and Korea, see the following books.

On Comfort Women

1. Wallace Edwards. *Comfort Women: A History of Japanese Forced Prostitution During the Second World War*, Amazon Digital Services, 2013

2. George Hicks. *The Comfort Women: Japan's Brutal Regime of Enforced Prostitution in the Second World War*. W. W. Norton & Company, 1997.

3. Dai Sil Kim-Gbson. *Silence Broken: Korean Comfort Women,* Mid-Prairie Books, 1999.

4. Korean Council for Women Drafted for Military Sexual Slavery by Japan. *True Stories of the Korean Comfort Women*, Cassell, 1996.

5. Jan Ruff-O'Henne. *Fifty Years of Silence: The Extraordinary Memoir of a War Rape Survivor*, Random House, 2008.

6. Peipei Qui. *Chinese Comfort Women: Testimonies from Imperial Japan's Sex Slaves*, Oxford University Press, 2014.

7. C. Sarah Soh. *The Comfort Women: Sexual Violence and Postcolonial Memory in Korea and Japan* University of Chicago Press, 2009.

8. Yoshimi Yoshiaki. *Comfort Women*, Columbia University Press, 2002.

9. Yuki Tanaka. *Japan's Comfort Women*, Routledge, 2001.

10. Yuki Tanaka. *Hidden Horrors: Japanese War Crimes In World War II*, Westview Press, 1997.

On Korean History

1. Michael Breen. *The Koreans. Who They Are, What They Want, Where Their Future Lies.* Thomas Dunne Books, 2004.

2. Bruce Cummings. *Korea's Place in the Sun: A Modern History*, W.W. Norton & Company, 2005.

3. Don Oberdorfer. *The Two Koreas: A Contemporary History*, Basic Books, 2001.

4. Keith Pratt. *Everlasting Flower: A History of Korea*, Reaktion Books, 2006.

5. Michael J. Seth. *A Conscise History of Korea*, Rowman & Littlefield, 2006.

ABOUT THE AUTHOR

Photo by: Thoen Photography

WILLIAM ANDREWS is a retired advertising executive living in Minneapolis, Minnesota. His first book, *The Essential Truth* won the Mahaven Book Award.

Visit Bill's website at:

www.williamandrewsbooks.com

AUTHOR Q & A

Q: What inspired you to write this book?

A: Probably the most influential thing is my daughter who was born in Korea. Because of her, I learned about the country and thought it was fascinating. Especially considering what happened in the 20th Century.

Q: Like what?

A: The three regimes that controlled the peninsula. The Japanese, the communists and the Americans. And the comfort women. I'm continually amazed at how few Americans know what happened to these women.

I believe this story needs to be told. And if I may, I'd like to encourage readers who agree and who enjoyed the book, to recommend this book to others and write reviews on retailers' web sites.

Q: There's a lot of history in this book. Is it accurate?

A: First, please know that I'm a storyteller, not a history expert. Still, I tried to make this book as historically accurate as possible. I did a ton of research and got help from several history experts. So I'd have to say yes, it's accurate.

Q: Was it difficult to write some of the more brutal scenes?

A: Very difficult. I tried hard to be respectful of the reader and the comfort women. I did not want to be exploitive. But I felt I had a responsibility to show what actually happened to these women. It has to be brutal because that's what they experienced.

Still, there were things I couldn't write. For example, when Colonel Matsumoto first rapes Ja-hee, I couldn't write that in real time. I had to pull it out of the narrative into the present-day frame. Even then, it was a challenge to write that chapter.

Q: You draw parallels between what the Japanese did in the comfort stations and what the Americans did in the *kijichons*. Were the Americans as bad as the Japanese?

A: Of course not. But, what I wrote about the Americans is true. Until recently, the US military turned a blind eye to some of the illegal and unethical things our troops were doing in the *kijichons*; tricking girls, putting them in situations they could not possibly get out of. It wasn't anything close to what the Japanese did, however. They actually sponsored the comfort stations. But as Ja-hee says to Colonel Crawford, from the girls' perspective, what's the difference?

Q: What about the two-headed dragon with five toes?

A: I invented the two-headed dragon. However, the emperor and empress were the only ones allowed to have dragon artifacts with five toes.

Q: You talk a lot about Empress Myeongseong.

A: Yes, she's a fascinating figure in Korean history. The Koreans worship her. And please forgive a plug, but I'm working on a loose sequel to *Daughters of the Dragon* called *The Korean Queen*. It's the story of Empress Myeongseong. (See the following pages for more information.)

One last thing. I'd like to ask readers to please go to their online retailer and write a review of this book. Or, send me an e-mail at bill@williamandrewsbooks.com. It's the only way I can get feedback from my readers!

Coming in 2016: THE DRAGON QUEEN

By William Andrews

THE DRAGON QUEEN is the remarkable story of Empress Myeongseong, Korea's last empress. A poor country peasant, Ja-young becomes the leader of the Hermit Kingdom through her intelligence and great courage. Called the 'Queen Victoria of Korea' the Empress leads her country into the modern world all the while fighting the Japanese imperialists and her lazy husband's father, Daewongun, Korea's treacherous regent.

Anna Carlson tells the Empress' story to State Department official Nick Blackburn as war between North and South Korea threatens. In the story, Nick see surprising similarities with the current situation in Korea and realizes true leadership requires great courage which is often at odds with the political establishment. He decides to risk his career and along with Anna who he has learned has a surprising heredity, pushes for a controversial, but peaceful solution to the Korean situation.

Watch for THE DRAGON QUEEN by visiting:
www.williamandrewsbooks.com.

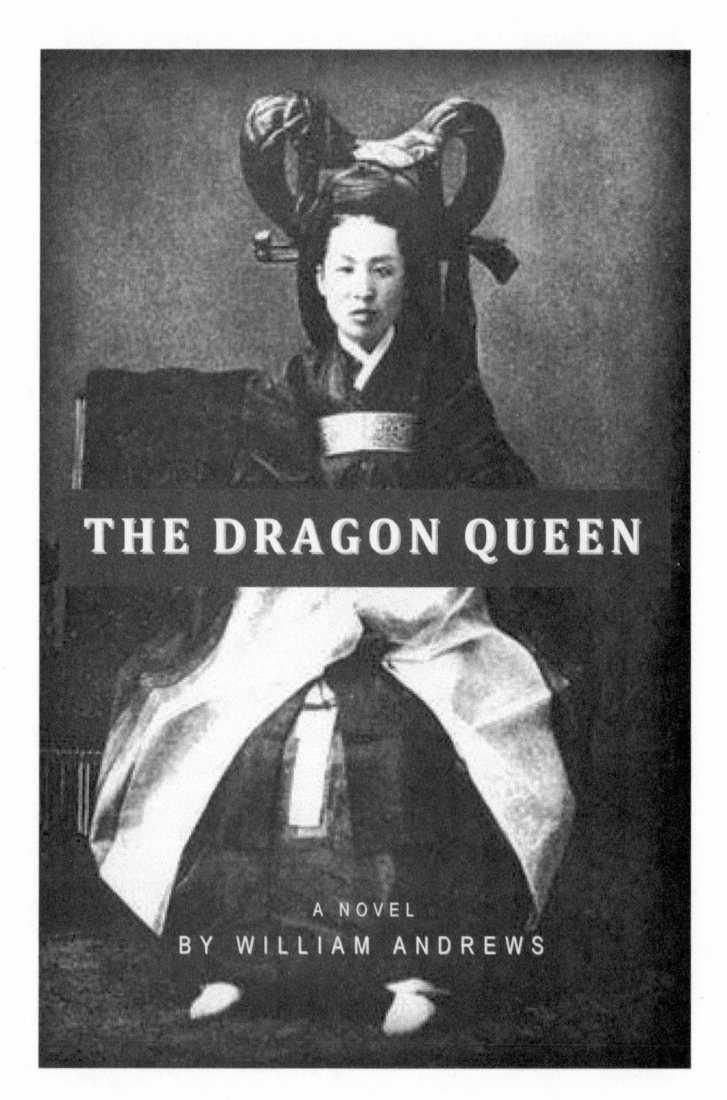

THE DRAGON QUEEN

A NOVEL
BY WILLIAM ANDREWS

THE
ESSENTIAL
TRUTH

a novel by

WILLIAM W. ANDREWS

THE ESSENTIAL TRUTH

A Novel by William Andrews

WHEN THE FOUNDER OF Jacob and Marin Advertising mysteriously dies, Ben Smith must take over the agency just as their largest account comes up for review. He becomes the victim of Watergate-like dirty tricks because his agency does the campaign advertising for Congresswoman Janice Theilen who is running against Senator William Howard for his senate seat. Sheldon Hanrahan, the billionaire head of a rival advertising agency, controls Howard and needs the Senator to win big in the election so he can launch a presidential campaign. If Howard wins the presidency, Sheldon will impose his radical vision on America. To keep the agency afloat, and to keep Howard from winning reelection, Ben must confront not only Sheldon but also demons from his past. And, he must learn to become a leader. The stakes are high, and Sheldon is a powerful and cunning foe, but Ben has secret allies behind the scenes.

The Essential Truth is full of suspense, mystery and action as well as plot twists, a murder investigation and even a chase scene. And, *The Essential Truth* shows the reader the quirky personalities and workings of an advertising agency.

WINNER OF THE MAYHAVEN AWARD FOR FICTION

Available soon through major on-line booksellers. For updates visit:

www.williamandrewsbooks.com

AN EXERCISE IN SACRIFICE

A NOVEL BY WILLIAM W. ANDREWS

AN EXERCISE IN SACRIFICE
A Novel by William Andrews

NAN SMITH, THE STATE campaign manager for Democratic presidential Election Reform hopeful George Bloomfield, discovers a dirty secret about Bloomfield's opponent, Senator William Howard when an old woman tells her, "He murdered my daughter." The revelation thrusts Nan into the center of a massive conspiracy led by Sheldon Hanrahan who will do anything to get his man the presidency. Along the way, Nan learns how poorly regulated U.S. elections are and what candidates are able to get away with. In the end, she finds the smoking gun to expose the conspiracy but powerful forces from all sides threaten her life to prevent it.

An Exercise in Sacrifice is about bravery, commitment and one woman's resolve to do what's right for her country and family.

Available soon through major on-line booksellers. For updates visit:

www.williamandrewsbooks.com